MARKED

After taking his Bachelor's degree and then a PhD,
David Jackson became a full-time academic. He is married,
with two daughters and a menagerie of animals. *Pariah*,
his first novel, was Highly Commended in the Crime
Writers' Association Debut Dagger Awards.

You can find him on Twitter @Author_Dave
Or online at www.davidjacksonbooks.com

By David Jackson

Pariah

The Helper

Marked

MARKED

DAVID JACKSON

PAN BOOKS

First published 2013 by Macmillan

This edition published 2014 by Pan Books
an imprint of Pan Macmillan, a division of Macmillan Publishers Limited
Pan Macmillan, 20 New Wharf Road, London N1 9RR
Basingstoke and Oxford
Associated companies throughout the world
www.panmacmillan.com

ISBN 978-1-4472-0297-4

1 3 5 7 9 8 6 4 2

A CIP catalogue record for this book is available from the British Library.

Typeset by Ellipsis Digital Limited, Glasgow
Printed and bound by CPI Group (UK) Ltd, Croydon, CR0 4YY

Visit **www.panmacmillan.com** to read more about all our books
and to buy them. You will also find features, author interviews and
news of any author events, and you can sign up for e-newsletters
so that you're always first to hear about our new releases.

Acknowledgements

A huge and heartfelt thank-you to Wayne Brookes, my new editor at Pan Macmillan. Changing editors can be an unsettling time for all concerned, but I'm more than happy to be working (and socializing!) with Wayne, who is a larger-than-life character with an unrivalled record of looking after the authors in his charge. Thanks also to the rest of the Pan Mac team for the incredible work they have done yet again, and especially to Louise Buckley for her extensive editorial comments that have improved the novel enormously. A huge shout-out to all my Twitter pals: they are too numerous to mention individually, but I will be eternally grateful for their support and friendship. Finally, it would not be possible for many of us to remain as authors were it not for the love, encouragement and understanding of our partners. My undying gratitude goes to my wife, Lisa, who is with me every step of the way.

This is for Bethany,
although she'd probably prefer a pony

ONE

So yet again she's on the edge of death.

A tumor. A friggin tumor. Why would it be a tumor, for Chrissake? Why can't it be a headache like any normal person would have? A migraine even. He could cope with her saying it was a migraine. People get migraines all the time. They don't immediately assume their brains are about to disintegrate.

It was the same when she had those stomach pains last month. Appendicitis, she said. Or maybe even bowel cancer. He told her what it was. It didn't take no medical expert to work it out. The bananas. Too many friggin bananas. She should be a monkey, the number of those things she eats. A big hairy ape.

He chuckles to himself. I'm married to a gorilla in a dress, he thinks. King Kong in frilly underwear. I better not take her to the Empire State Building anytime soon. Might give her ideas.

Harold Bloor hefts the two large garbage sacks out into the hallway, then closes the door softly behind him. He knows she'll only complain if he makes the slightest noise. 'You slammed it,' she'll say. 'My head is pounding like a drum, and you went and slammed the door, you unfeeling bastard.'

He knows this because he's heard it all before, many times. When she was anemic it was because he'd once talked her into making a blood donation. When she had a stiff neck it was because he'd thoughtlessly opened a window behind her. He's always the one to blame. If she *does* have a friggin tumor – which she doesn't – there'll be an explanation that involves his inconsiderate behavior. Like not insisting they should move farther away from Japan when those nuclear reactors were hit by a tsunami.

He hitches his pants over his ever-expanding gut, picks up the bags again, and heads out of the building. At the top of the front stoop he pauses and watches a group of young men go past, dressed in T-shirts even though it's the middle of October and heavy rain is forecast. He inhales a deep lungful of the city air. He smells exotic spicy food from the restaurant next door, mixed with the usual heady aroma of exhaust fumes. It makes him cough. This city, I should wear a face mask, he thinks. Or I could get one for the wife. A full face mask, completely covering every inch of visible flesh from the neck up and suppressing all noise generated in that vicinity. Purely for health reasons, of course. She shouldn't keep breathing in these nasty city germs.

He chuckles again, then descends the stone steps. When he gets to the sidewalk, he turns and shuffles into the shadows of the stoop. He puts the bags down and removes the lid from the nearest trashcan.

Son of a bitch.

He replaces the lid, then tries the next one. And the next, and the next.

That's it, thinks Harold Bloor.

This means war.

Two blocks away from the flashpoint of World War Three, Geoffrey Landis stares intently at his caramel torte, his arms and legs tightly crossed and his lips pursed in what he believes to be his most indignant pose.

'It won't jump off the plate and into your mouth, you know. You have to make a degree of effort.'

Geoffrey turns his glare on his boyfriend. 'And what effort did it take to put whatever went into your mouth today? That's what I want to know.'

'Oh, puh-lease,' says Stuart. 'Don't tell me we're back on that again. I told you. It was a drink. One drink. He's my boss. How could I say no?'

'You start with an *n*, and then you put an *o* after it. It's not difficult. Just because Antonio is your boss, it doesn't mean you have to mince after him every time he clicks his fingers. There are limits, you know.'

Stuart gets up from the table and picks up his empty plate. 'For God's sake, you can be so childish sometimes. I had a drink with my boss in a public bar. I didn't go down on him in the back of a taxi. Get it in perspective, Geoffrey. Maybe if you had a job of your own, you'd understand it a little bit more.'

He turns then, heads toward the kitchen area.

Geoffrey pushes back his chair and follows him. 'I wondered when that would come up. I *do* work, and you know it. I work on this apartment. I work on doing all your washing and cleaning and ironing. I do all the jobs you hate to do. If it wasn't for me, this place would be the stinking shithole it was before I moved in. So don't you tell me—'

'I'm not denying what you do here, Geoffrey. I'm simply pointing out that you don't have an employer. You've never had an employer. If you did, you would understand that it's sometimes a wise move to keep on your employer's good side. And just because Antonio's a good-looking Mediterranean type—'

'You think he's good-looking?'

'Don't you?'

3

'No. With those teeth, I think he looks like a horse.'

Stuart smiles. 'Well, he has been compared to a horse before, but not because of his teeth.'

Geoffrey crosses his arms again. He does it so abruptly that he punches himself in the bicep and has to pretend it doesn't hurt.

'Oh, so now we're getting to it,' he says. 'The sex angle.'

'Which angle's that, Geoffrey? Do we need a protractor?'

Geoffrey has to resist the impulse to stamp his foot. He has done it before, and it only causes Stuart to laugh at him.

'You know, you're really starting to infuriate me. This is serious. I'd like to have a proper adult conversation about this, please.'

Stuart throws down his dishcloth and rounds on his partner. 'Well, we can have an adult conversation when you stop behaving like a child. Now if you don't mind, I need to clear away all this food you didn't eat while you were sulking. So go away and come back when you're in a more civilized frame of mind.'

Right, thinks Geoffrey as Stuart shows him the back of his head again. Right!

He storms toward the apartment door. Thinking, I'm going out. I'm going to find a bar and get drunk and maybe even pick somebody up and go back to their place. I may never even come back here again.

He opens the door, pauses at the threshold while he takes the deep breath he needs for the commencement of this decisive journey.

'And don't forget Agamemnon,' Stuart calls after him.

Geoffrey lets the air out of his lungs again. The dog. It's time for his walkies.

Not my problem, he thinks. Let Stuart do it for once.

Except that it *is* my problem. Aggie is my dog. He'll miss me, even if nobody else in this place will.

Sullenly, Geoffrey heads back into the apartment, the planned demonstration of his independence on indefinite hold.

They're all smiles when he first walks in. That's because they figure he's just another dumb schmuck they can rip off with their overpriced monosodium glutamate crap.

'You want table?' the girl asks him.

She's pretty, thinks Harold. Even if she is a gook.

'No,' says Harold. 'I want manager.'

The girl looks helplessly behind her, and one of her co-workers scurries over. He's beaming idiotically too.

'You want table?'

'No. I want the manager. Are you the manager?'

'No. No manager.'

'Then get me the manager.'

'No manager. Is family business. No manager.'

Harold sighs. 'Okay, then get your dad.'

'Dad?'

'Your father.'

'He not here. He very busy.'

'Doing what? Putting out the trash?'

The young waiter simply blinks his lack of comprehension. Around them in the restaurant, the customers sense that something untoward is taking place, and the buzz of conversation fades, to be replaced by a few uneasy whispers.

'I'm asking you about the trash,' says Harold. 'The garbage. Who put the garbage out tonight? Was it you?'

'Garbage? No garbage.'

Two more male staff members glide silently toward Harold.

The smiles have all evaporated now, but Harold isn't fazed by the pathetic attempts to look stern. These guys have never encountered Mrs Bloor.

'You don't have garbage? Of course you have garbage. Everybody has garbage.'

One of the men calls over to the man behind the bar. Gives him some instructions in Chinese. The barman picks up a phone.

Says Harold, 'You want to know where your garbage is? In my trashcans, that's where. Your stinking garbage is in my trashcans.'

There is much head-shaking now. A whole row of heads on swivels. 'No garbage.'

'Yes garbage. In my trashcans. And it's not the first time, neither. Every time I go to put out my trash, I can't because the trashcans are full. They're full of your shitty Jap food.'

'Not Jap food. We not Japanese. We Chinese. Is not same.'

'Whatever. It's your garbage. From your restaurant. It stinks. It brings rats. Put your crap in your own friggin trashcans.'

He hopes that that will be an end to it. He hopes they will get the message and say sorry, and he can go home, secure in the knowledge that his waste will never again be adulterated by these people.

But no.

'Maybe . . .' says one of the men. 'Mmm . . . maybe is your people eat Chinese food. Is people in your building trash.'

Harold wonders how these people get by on such piss-poor English. Well, I ain't got all night to teach 'em how to talk good, he thinks.

He wags a finger at them. 'No you don't. I know my tenants.

They haven't changed for the past five years. I know their trash. This is restaurant garbage we're talking about here. *Your* garbage.'

But the waiter is undeterred. 'Yes, I think so. Is your people trash. Not restaurant.'

Harold looks each of them in the eye. He sees no sign of contrition, and every sign that they are going to continue to act dumb when it suits them. This softly-softly approach isn't even scratching the surface.

Time to break out the big guns.

'I'll be back,' he says, thinking they must have heard of Arnie. Everybody's seen the Terminator movies. Even the Japs.

Tell someone you have a dog called Agamemnon, and they'll assume you have a Rottweiler or a bull mastiff or some other nasty-ass monster just looking for the next limb to tear off. Geoffrey Landis's Agamemnon is a tiny West Highland terrier. The only chance it has of killing something is to get it stuck in its throat. He's had it for five years now – two years longer than he's lived with Stuart. Probably have it a lot longer after his relationship with Stuart too, the way things are going.

He is ambling along East Sixth Street, heading in the direction of Tompkins Square Park. Aggie is on one of those extensible leashes that allows him to have a good roam and to investigate all those aromas that assail his doggy senses.

Stuart should be on a leash too. I mean, why does he think it's perfectly okay to entertain other men in bars without even telling me? What if I did the same? What would he say about that?

Ahead, a burly man turns the corner of the block and starts coming toward Geoffrey. Although not as the crow flies. He weaves along the sidewalk as though he's aboard a ship in a storm.

Geoffrey pauses. Winds in the leash a little. Wonders whether to cross the street. The man looks far too inebriated to be capable of putting up much of a fight, but Geoffrey's maxim has always been that discretion is the better part of valor.

The man continues his serpentine meandering, but then lurches to his right and trips over his own feet. He crashes into an array of trashcans outside a drugstore, knocking a couple of them over and causing their contents to spill out onto the sidewalk.

The drunk struggles to his feet again, but then seems confused as to where he was going. Seemingly at random, he selects a bearing and follows it, apparently oblivious to the fact that he's going back the way he came.

When the man has disappeared around the corner, Geoffrey resumes both his walk and his train of thought. He gets to the corner of the block, still seething over Stuart's actions, and tries to decide which way to go next. It doesn't seem sensible to follow the path of the drunk – Geoffrey's other maxim being that it is better to be safe than sorry – so he could either continue along Sixth or take a left onto Second Avenue. Whichever direction he chooses, he thinks he should take his time about it. Give Stuart something to worry about. And if he phones me I'll just ignore it. Maybe then he'll realize just what—

He sees them then. Seated at the table in the window of that nice Italian restaurant across the street.

Antonio.

Or, to be precise, Antonio plus one. The plus one being a male friend. Although 'friend' seems a somewhat weak description, given that he has just twirled something onto his fork and pushed it into the mouth of Antonio.

Geoffrey's evening suddenly seems a whole lot brighter.

It's like disturbing a hornet's nest.

When he walks back in carrying all those garbage sacks, the staff go crazy. All running around like headless chickens, yelling and jabbering.

Harold can't stop a smile of satisfaction creeping into his jowly face. This is what you call an entrance.

When they descend on him, he holds his ground. He notices that they seem to have a leader now, an old guy with wild eyes and wild gray hair that looks to have been cut by its owner.

'What you do?' cries the old man.

'Your garbage,' says Harold, dropping the bags onto the floor. 'I'm bringing it back to you.'

'No. Not our garbage. We tell you before. Not garbage from here. You take back.'

The man picks up one of the sacks and pushes it into the arms of Harold, then bends to retrieve another one.

'Not yours, huh? Okay, let's see.'

Harold digs the fingers of both hands into the bag he's holding. The flimsy plastic gives way easily, and he rips the whole thing open in one movement. As its contents hit the floor, a brown wet sludge splashes onto the old man's shoes, and he jumps back in horror. Harold hears gasps from the customers, and even some laughter. They seem to be enjoying the show. The staff, on the other hand, are yammering furiously again and looking to each other to decide who's going to do something about this refuse-slinging lunatic.

'Well, what do we have here?' says Harold. 'Looks like gook food to me. And if my eyes don't deceive me, I'd say those are napkins just like the ones you got on your tables here. Let's try another one, why don't we?'

He doesn't wait for an answer. Just picks up another bag and tears it wide open, enabling it to disgorge its stinking sodden payload onto the intricately patterned Chinese carpet.

The staff are working themselves up into a frenzy now. They're jostling each other and pointing at Harold and barking commands, but nobody seems to know what to do. It's left to the old man to take action. He grabs at the third bag as Harold lifts it. Tries to yank it away from him. For a few seconds the pair form an absurd sight as they tug back and forth. It's East versus West in a wrestling match for a prize that is literally garbage.

The inevitable occurs when the bag splits, and once again a pile of detritus cascades to the floor.

And that's when time freezes.

This isn't Chinese food, or Japanese food, or any kind of food for that matter.

It's paper, mostly. Newspapers and magazines.

But there's something else too.

It hits the floor hard and rolls across the carpet, stopping when it bumps up against the soiled shoes of the elderly restaurant owner. Everyone looks down at it. Customers seated at the nearest tables get to their feet for a clearer view. The yelling stops. The warring factions are on the same side now, united against whatever may have brought about the incredible apparition that has landed in their midst.

Harold stares at the object in disbelief. Is it really what it looks like?

When the place erupts again – the screams of horror, the yells of fear and confusion, the sounds of people retching and vomiting – Harold knows he is not mistaken. Everybody else has seen the item for what it is.

A human head.

Geoffrey doesn't move for several minutes. He remains on the street corner, a huge smile on his face as he dreams about how he is going to break his news to Stuart.

That boss of yours? Antonio? The one who took you for a drink? The one you think is so good-looking? Wanna know something about him?

And then it hits him. How bitchy his imagined words sound. His smile drops away, to be replaced by immense sadness at his planned cruelty to the most important person in his life.

Because what he realizes then is that Stuart was being honest with him all along. There was nothing to it. A harmless drink with the boss – that's all it was.

I need to make it up to him, he thinks. I should go back there right now and tell him how sorry I am for jumping to conclusions and being spiteful. Yes, that's what I'll do.

He almost wants to run across the street and knock on the restaurant window and blow Antonio a kiss for his unwitting part in all this. But he doesn't. Instead, he turns away, feeling that he is a happier and wiser man.

Agamemnon seems happy too, although maybe not so wise, buried as he is in the trash that the drunk spilled onto the ground. Geoffrey tightens the leash and tries to yank him away, but the dog continues with its burrowing into the mound.

'Aggie, come on! What the hell have you got there?'

Geoffrey takes a few steps closer. He sees that Agamemnon

is concentrating on one particular garbage bag, ripping at it with his front paws and teeth.

'Aggie!'

He heaves on the leash, dragging the dog backwards as its claws scrabble on the sidewalk for purchase. It's only once Aggie is out of the way that Geoffrey gets a good look at the item of interest now exposed to the air.

It looks like . . .

Geoffrey brings a hand to his mouth as he utters a high-pitched giggle.

Well, it looks like . . . An ass. A tush. A pair of buttocks. All by themselves.

It has to be something else. A part of a store mannequin, maybe. Something like that. It can't just be—

But when he steps closer and sees the tattoo of the angel at the base of the spine, its wings unfurled over the wound-ridden globes of flesh, when the aroma hits him and he is instantly transported into a butcher's store, when his dog continues to strain to get back to its feast of raw meat – that's when he knows this is no dummy.

And that's when he scurries to the curb to empty his stomach.

TWO

She hears the voice, but it seems just a faint drone in the distance. She doesn't catch the words.

She stares at the television, but the pictures make no sense. They are just blurs of color.

There's a cup of tea on the table in front of her. It's cold and untouched.

Her senses are almost closed. They will stay that way until things are right again.

Something touches her shoulder. The voice repeats, louder and more insistent this time. The words are forced into her head.

'Nicole. Come to bed. You need to get some sleep.'

Sleep. What is that? Why is that important? Doesn't he know? Doesn't he understand?

She stays where she is. She would sit here for ever if she knew it could make a difference.

Detective Second Grade Callum Doyle is feeling good about this night. Even though he's reaching the end of an October day that has been dismal and gray enough to thump misery and depression into the most optimistic of souls, Doyle has no complaints about it. To Doyle this could be the first day of spring. He could be witness to lambs gamboling and daffodils pushing their heads above the earth and the sun getting its ass into gear with some seriously overdue illumination. Doyle is so full of joy he could sing. And does, in fact. 'Norwegian Wood' by the Beatles, for some reason. It's not exactly tuneful, but he belts it out anyway, ignoring the grimacing of his partner in the car passenger seat.

The reason Doyle is so buoyant tonight is that he has caught a homicide. Which is not to say he relishes the thought of staring death in the face, or of the consequences of death for the innocents who are left to deal with it. Far from it. What's important here is the symbolism. The fact that the Police Department is willing to entrust its lowly detective with solving a crime of such enormity. Which might sound odd, given that's exactly the kind of thing Doyle is paid to do.

It wasn't so many months ago that the relationship between Doyle and his employers was less than amicable. He was being given all the shitty jobs – the cases nobody else wanted to handle. Cases that served to keep him occupied but out of the limelight and out of everybody's hair. It got so bad that Doyle was seriously considering abandoning his police career.

And then he got a break. Second fiddle on the murder of a young girl in a bookstore. He was meant to be doing the menial stuff, freeing up the other detectives to do the real investigatory work. But it turned out to be a whole lot more than a simple homicide. It grew into something gargantuan that threatened to chew Doyle into tiny pieces and spit him out. It could have been the end for Doyle.

But he survived. He came through it, not exactly unaffected by his experience, but in the NYPD's eyes something of a hero. And since that time he has become a cop again. A true detective rather than a helping hand. Back on the cases that matter.

Like this one, for example. A homicide. Handed straight to Doyle as soon as the call came in.

After what he's been through, how tough can a case like this be?

Doyle practically jogs into the Chinese restaurant, he's feeling that good. He doesn't wait for his partner: he's not even aware that the kid is struggling to keep up.

Doyle still doesn't know what to make of LeBlanc. He's probably a perfectly good cop, but he's young and he's inexperienced and he has this aura about him of not knowing what the hell he's doing. He doesn't even dress the part. He goes for trendy instead of functional. Skinny ties and pointy shoes and stupid designer spectacles. When you're in need of an authority figure to follow in a moment of crisis, this kid with his waxed blond hair is almost certainly the last person you'd consider.

Inside the restaurant, Doyle's ebullience subsides a little when the first person he sees there is a guy called Kravitz. It would have been difficult not to spot Kravitz, seeing as how he's nearly six foot seven tall. He's unnaturally thin too, which makes him appear even taller. Or his height emphasizes his lack of musculature. Either way, he's a man of mismatched dimensions. He looks to Doyle like someone who should permanently have a basketball under his arm. 'Ah,' people would say, 'you're a basketball player.' And they would no longer question his freakish frame.

Kravitz is a cop. More specifically, he's a member of the Manhattan South Homicide Task Force – a mouthful that is usually condensed by his fellow cops to the more memorable Homicide South. Doyle bears no grudge against this cue-stick of a man; it's his partner – a more meagerly proportioned individual called Folger – who is the one to watch. Doyle's last run-in with the poison dwarf is still fresh in his mind.

Steeling himself, Doyle moves toward the center of the activity. Kravitz is the first to notice Doyle's arrival, his eyes turning on him from his lofty position like a lighthouse scanning the seas.

'Well, well. Hello again, Detective.'

Doyle looks around him. 'Where's Tom Thumb? I didn't step on him, did I?'

Kravitz smiles. 'You mean Detective Folger? We had a parting of the ways. We didn't see eye to eye.'

'More like eye to crotch, huh? You get sick of him poking his nose in your business?'

Still Kravitz smiles, and Doyle feels he's doing so in apology for what has gone before. He decides he should stop being so hard on the guy. At least for now.

Kravitz gestures to the man standing next to him. 'Meet my new partner. This is Detective Fenster.'

Fenster nods, but doesn't proffer his hand. He seems to be studying Doyle intently. Probably wondering why Doyle is smiling.

The reason Doyle is smiling is not because of anything pertaining to Fenster's physical appearance. Whereas the man's predecessor was massively challenged in a vertical sense, and played an important part in amusing his fellow officers by merely standing next to his cloud-scraping partner, Fenster's own build is unremarkable. In fact, aside from a slight reddish tinge to his hair that only the cruelest of jokesters would refer to as a disability, his looks present negligible entertainment value. No, Doyle is smiling because he knows that Kravitz is often given the nickname Lurch, after the ugly tall butler in *The Addams Family*.

And because Doyle remembers that in that family was also an ugly bald guy called . . .

'Fester?'

So much for not giving the Homicide boys a hard time. Hey, how many opportunities get handed to you on a plate like this?

'Fenster,' says Kravitz sternly, obviously already acutely sensitive to the likelihood of this comparison.

'Not Fester?'

'No.'

'Ah.'

Fenster continues to stare at Doyle. 'Have we met before? You look awful familiar.'

Before Doyle can answer, Kravitz chips in again: 'You've probably seen him over breakfast.'

'Huh?' says Fenster.

'In your newspaper. Or on TV. This here is the famous Detective Callum Doyle of the Eighth Precinct. The Eighth Wonder, as I like to think of him. You remember that serial killer we had a few months back? Only nobody knew we even had a serial killer?'

'Oh,' says Fenster. 'Yeah. Doyle. I remember that one.'

'Of course you do. Doyle solved it all by himself. He was the only cop in the whole city who realized the murders were connected. It was uncanny. I still haven't figured out how he did it.'

Doyle remains silent. It's clear to everyone listening that Kravitz is suggesting that Doyle must have been privy to more information than he ever revealed at the time. And the reason Doyle fails to respond is because he accepts the accusation is true. He knew a lot more. And he still feels the pain every time he thinks back to that case. The guilt over deaths that should never have happened. Deaths he might have been able to prevent if only he'd acted differently. He has tried telling himself that he shouldn't dwell on thoughts involving 'should' or 'ought'. But still it hurts.

He says, 'You're right. It was a little weird. I guess I was just thinking outside the box. I mean, I'm just one cop in one small precinct. It's not like I got a wider picture of things. Not like, say, the boys in Homicide . . .'

Doyle's targets glance at each other, and then Kravitz says to his partner, 'You should know that Doyle here is not a man to be crossed. He's upset a lot of cops in the past, not least my previous partner, with whom he had a little altercation.'

'Is that so?' says Fenster, and again he stares at Doyle.

Kravitz continues, 'But then Doyle knows what it's like to lose a partner. Ain't that right, Detective?'

Same old same old, thinks Doyle. It always gets dredged up. I miss my partners more than anyone, yet still some people insist on trying to taint me with their deaths. How much longer am I going to be haunted by it?

For a few seconds the three men stand in strained silence. Then Kravitz says, 'Speaking of partners, you wanna complete the introductions?'

Doyle suddenly remembers that LeBlanc is standing behind him.

'Uh, this is Tommy LeBlanc. He's gonna be working this with me.'

'Pleasure, Detective,' says LeBlanc, moving in front of Doyle and thrusting his hand out. Doyle rolls his eyes, while Fenster regards the younger man with disdain until he sheepishly drops his outstretched arm.

'You been on a homicide before?' asks Fenster.

LeBlanc shrugs. 'A couple. Nothing like this, though.'

It's only then that the four men turn their collective gaze on the reason they are all here. The head is that of a blond girl. No more than twenty, and probably pretty too. Once. Devoid of blood, of life, of spirit, her wavy hair matted with food, her white skin blotted by injuries – it's difficult to imagine how she appeared in life. Impossible to imagine how she ended up like this.

'You think she's dead?' asks Kravitz.

'Hard to say,' answers Fenster, 'us not being medical experts. I'd hate to make such a pronouncement and then be proved wrong when the ME gets here. What idiots we'd look then.' He glances up at his partner. 'You know about chickens, right?'

'Chickens?'

'Sure. Those bastards can live for some time even without a head. There was this one chicken, lived for months that way. Its owner would put food into its gullet with an eye-dropper.'

'Really? Where'd you learn about such a thing?'

'Ripleys. You know? The Believe-It-Or-Not people? 'Course, what we got here ain't exactly the same. We got the head, and I don't think the chicken's head stayed alive.'

'Maybe not. Although we humans are more highly evolved than poultry. I've yet to see a chicken program a computer or drive a racing car. Hell, those fat feathery fucks can't even fly for shit. Who knows how long we could live without heads if we put our minds to it?'

'We certainly are the master race, all right,' says Fenster as he puts his finger up his nose.

Doyle is grateful when the door opens again and another figure breezes in. The man is Chinese, but he's not here for a meal. He wears spectacles with lenses so thick they magnify his eyes to cartoon proportions. He is wearing an overcoat that looks several sizes too big, and he is carrying a large black bag.

Fenster nudges his partner in the ribs. Doyle recalls that the much tinier Folger used to do similar nudging, only it was much more painful.

'Watch this,' says Fenster.

He steps out in front of the Chinese man. 'Hold on there, fella! Who let you in? This is a crime scene. The restaurant is closed. No more food. Savvy? You speakee English?'

Unfazed, the man blinks his saucer-sized eyes at the detective. 'You're an idiot,' he says in perfect English, which gets a bigger laugh than Fenster's own attempt at humor. 'You're an idiot if you believe your prejudicial – dare I say *racist* – comments were funny, which they weren't, and you're an idiot for calling this a crime scene, which it ain't. Now get outta my way.'

Realizing that his stunt has backfired, a sheepish Fenster steps aside to admit the man, who marches straight past the four detectives and up to the focus of all the activity here. He stops, shakes his head and makes tutting noises.

'What a waste,' he says.

'Yeah,' says Doyle. 'She looks so young.'

'I'm talking about the food. This is so symptomatic of what's wrong with society today, the amount of food we throw away. But yes, the girl too.'

That the girl seems almost an afterthought to this man says a lot about him. It is not that he is incapable of sympathy or sorrow. It is just that death in all its various guises is nothing new to him. He sees it regularly. He lives with it. He has become hardened to it, not out of choice but out of necessity. Norman Chin, MD, has lost count of the number of corpses he has examined over the years, many of them mutilated, decomposing or maggot-ridden. As one of the city's Medical Examiners he views this as just another job, and the cops here understand that.

Chin checks with the crime-scene people that he can proceed, then he snaps on a pair of latex gloves and sets to work. He picks up the head, rolls it around in his hands for a while, then puts it down again.

'Okay,' he says. 'I've seen it. Now I can go back to bed. Get it bagged, tagged and shipped, and I'll get on it as soon as I've caught a few z's.'

'That's it?' says LeBlanc.

Doyle glances sharply at him, but it's too late.

'What do you want from me?' says Chin. 'Like I told your wisecracking bozo friend over there, this ain't a crime scene. She wasn't killed here, and aside from her head, she wasn't even dumped here. That ain't a lot to go on. You want me to do more, you need to find me more. So get out there and do your job before you start criticizing me over how I do mine.'

LeBlanc looks helplessly at Doyle. 'I wasn't criticizing. I was just saying—'

'You know there's another body part, don't you?' says Fenster.

'Yes, I do know that,' Chin snaps. 'Because, unlike you guys, I have already visited the site where the other part was found. And what I also know, with all my years of expensive and intense medical training, is that a head and a pelvis are not the sole components of the human body. There are other pieces out there, gentlemen, and finding them is your job, not mine.'

He starts to move toward the door, pausing only when Doyle says to him, 'Norm? Anything you can give us to go on right now?'

Chin turns to him. 'Now that's more like it. A civilized intelligent question. Okay, a coupla things. There are cuts, abrasions

21

and burn marks on both body parts. Looks like this girl was tortured before she was killed.'

'And the other thing?'

'It may be nothing, but the girl had a tattoo at the base of her spine. Picture of an angel.'

'Lots of girls get tattoos done there,' says Fenster.

'That's true. Like I say, it may mean zilch. But this tattoo looks fresh to me. Like it was done in the past few days.'

He heads toward the door again. 'Happy hunting, guys!'

LeBlanc mutters something, but Doyle doesn't hear it. He's too busy thinking about something Chin just said.

Something that summons up dark memories and an unquenchable thirst for justice.

A second after midnight. It's now my birthday. Happy birthday, Nicole.

She says nothing out loud, and the voice in her head is a dull monotone. She doesn't even smile. Last year, at this exact time, she started bouncing up and down on the bed and singing birthday wishes to herself like an over-excited child, waking Steve so she could demand to know what presents he'd bought for her.

Not this year. This year she remains motionless in the bed. Stares at the illuminated face of the alarm clock and counts the seconds as they eat into what should be a special day.

When the digits blur, she doesn't dab at her eyes. Just lets the tears come. Lets them roll down her cheek and slide over her nose and pat softly onto the pillow.

This is not a day for celebration. Never will be again unless things change. Birthdays, Christmas, Thanksgiving – how will she ever be able to enjoy them in the same way again?

But I should be positive, she thinks. This being my birthday, maybe I'll receive the only gift I really want.

And then I can sleep again.

It becomes a long, dirty night. Long because Doyle was supposed to have gone home when his shift finished at one o'clock in the morning, and now he can't. Dirty because of what he has to spend his sleepless hours doing instead. Which is submerging his arms elbow deep in piles of crap.

He's not the only one, of course. Every available cop in this and the neighboring precincts, uniformed or not, has been called in to help out on the search, and the Department of Sanitation has been told not to do any collections in the area while it proceeds. The cops move from building to building, opening up trashcans and dumpsters, shining their flashlights into them while they sift and root and examine.

It's not something that can be done furtively. An army of cops on the prowl like this attracts attention, and it's too big an area to cordon off. Passers-by stop to ask questions. Vehicles slow to a crawl so that the drivers can lower their windows and yell questions. Residents leave the warmth and safety of their buildings just so that they can put their damn questions. To each and every one of them Doyle and the other cops say the same thing, which is basically nothing.

The task has its lighter moments. One woman asks Doyle to let her know if he manages to locate her missing dentures. Another tells him that she has just thrown away the last of her apple pie, but that he can have it if he finds it. One bedbug warns him that the trashcans are really the pods of alien visitors, and that he should leave well alone. In response, Doyle assures him that his flashlight is equipped with the latest extraterrestrial threat alert systems.

The media are less easy to shrug off. Who would have guessed that lifting the lid from a trashcan would make such a newsworthy photograph? Or that the sight of a patrol officer poking his nightstick into a garbage bag would make for footage so exciting that it would be replayed endlessly on the news channels?

Eight hours later, when daylight returns almost grudgingly, and the streets start to overflow again with people and cars and noise and the hustle and bustle of life, it is time to take stock. Time to assess the results of the exercise. To wit, a bunch of exhausted cops who smell like they haven't bathed in years.

Oh, and one other thing.

A human arm.

THREE

She feels a little better the following morning. A little more hopeful. She even manages to force down a few spoonfuls of breakfast cereal.

And then Steve has to go and spoil it.

He spoils it with a book-sized rectangular package wrapped in bright-pink paper with pictures of balloons and cakes and all kinds of happy words on it. Words such as 'Celebrate!' and 'Hooray!' and 'Yippee!'

'Here,' he says simply, and he accompanies it with a smile. As if that'll work. As if that'll make it all right.

And she puts down her spoon and stares into his face and says what shouldn't need saying.

'Steve, what are you doing? We agreed. No presents. Not yet.'

'I know. It's not from me. It's from Megan. She asked me to get it for you and she wanted you to have it today. You know what she's like. She hates the idea of belated presents.'

Nicole suddenly wants to bring all that cereal back up again. She looks at her husband in disbelief. She can see that he doesn't know what he's doing wrong, but that doesn't make it any more right. He should have thought. He should have known. He can't just pretend that carrying out Megan's wishes puts her back in this room.

'Take it away.'

'Nicole. Please. She wanted you to—'

'Then she can give it to me herself. Take it away. Don't you understand? She needs to give it to me herself. Here, in person. From her hand to mine.'

'Nicole, look, it's just a—'

She picks it up then and throws it across the table at him. *'Take the fucking thing away!'*

'Jesus Christ, Nicole!' He looks at her in silence for a while, then he picks up the gift and leaves the room.

Doyle goes home while others continue the search. He wanted to carry on, but neither his body nor his boss would allow him. He goes home and he takes a fifteen-minute shower, finishing off a bottle of shower gel in a desperate attempt to eliminate any lingering odors. He shampoos his hair three times. The foam blocks his ears and stings his eyes. He wishes he could force it into his head. Brainwashing. A clean mind in a clean body. He needs to wipe it spotless and start all over again. There are too many dark thoughts in there.

The past is whispering to him. Calling to him. Reminding him of things he thought were over and done with. Avenues he believed were closed suddenly seem to be yawning wide open again, beckoning him to enter.

After his shower he lies on the bed and tries to sleep, but his subconscious keeps hurling out sporadic images and sounds that jolt him awake. He sees a girl. Sees what is being done to her. Sees a man. The ace of spades. The skull and crossbones. He hears the girl's screams.

When sleep eventually claims him, it is short-lived and fitful.

He tosses and turns for three hours, and when he drags himself off the bed again he does not feel refreshed.

He needs to get back into work.

He needs to find out whether this is what he thinks it is.

And if it is, he must find closure this time.

While Steve goes out for a jog, she puts on the television. The news channel. It's the only thing on which she can properly focus her attention. She forces herself to watch it. Just in case.

There's a story about a police search in the East Village. Nicole and Steve live in Forest Hills, which is in Queens, which is way over on the other side of the East River. So it can't have anything to do with them.

The reporters conjecture that the police may be hunting for body parts, following the gruesome discovery of a severed head in a restaurant.

But it's in the East Village. Megan wouldn't have gone to the East Village. Not alone. So that's all right, then. No news is good news, as they say.

She is aware of all kinds of synapses firing in her brain, trying to make connections, trying to posit various scenarios. She refuses to let them. This is nothing to do with their life. It's a world away. Their life is a nice big white house in a tree-lined road in a friendly part of Forest Hills, Queens, where the neighbors have time to talk and smile and help each other out. That stuff on the TV is dirt and violence and crime and sadness. Megan would not visit that world.

She shuts the television off. It's annoying her now. Why can't they ever talk about nice things on the news? Good news. Happy news. Why does it always have to be about disaster and death and shock and war? Is that really what people want to hear? What if they created a channel that carried only good news? Surely there would be an audience for that? And surely it would make for a happier, more positive-thinking population?

When I'm president, she thinks. But she doesn't smile.

She goes over to her chair at the front window. The chair never used to be there, but now she won't allow Steve to return it to its four indentations in the rug. She spends a lot of time in that chair.

She sits at the window and she looks out at the leaden sky and she tells herself that it will rain soon. And that means that Megan will come home, because she hates the rain.

Nicole stares at that sky. It is a deep, oppressive gray. It looks bloated with moisture. It has no option but to relieve itself of the pressure it contains. It will unburden itself. And then Megan will come home.

It'll be a phone call, thinks Nicole. She won't just turn up at the door, because she's worried that we'll be angry with her. She'll phone instead. She'll say, 'Mom,' and her voice will be cracking and fearful, and then she will say, 'I want to come home.' That's how it will be. That's how the agony will end. And when they meet up, Megan will appear tired and hungry and not a little frightened by her experience, and there will be hugs and tears and a lot of emotional release, and everyone will say sorry and promise to do better and they will forgive but not forget and they will all be supremely grateful for the happy outcome.

That's what will happen.

When it rains.

Doyle at his desk in the squadroom. On the phone to Norman Chin.

'What can you tell us, Norm?'

'I can tell you many things, oh seeker of wisdom. What I can't tell you is cause of death. Not with just three body parts. She could have had her heart ripped out for all I know, but without a torso . . .'

'Yeah, I know, Norm. We did our best. So far, that's all we got.'

'No problem. With a genius like me on the case, who needs a body, right? So, we're running a tox screen. Results aren't back yet, but I'll let you know.'

'What about time of death?'

'Again, not easy. I got no core temperature readings to work with, not much in the way of body fluids, the parts were tightly sealed in the garbage bags against infestation . . .'

'Best guess?'

'Recent. No more than about twenty hours ago.'

Doyle checks his watch. It's one-thirty in the afternoon now. That puts TOD at somewhere after 5.30 p.m. yesterday.

'Anything else?'

'Yeah. The body was cut up with a serrated blade. There's no finesse about it. No evidence of any surgical expertise. She was basically sawn into pieces, probably just to make her easier to dispose of.'

'What about the other wounds you mentioned, on her face?'

'I was coming to that. They're present on the other parts too. Numerous incisions made by a sharp blade – a razor blade or scalpel, probably. Burn marks. I don't know what caused them, but I don't think it was a cigarette. Then, on the buttocks in particular, there are many long raised welts. It looks as though somebody got their kicks by whipping the hell out of her. Sometimes they've ripped right through the skin.'

Doyle closes his eyes. The images return. A naked girl, terrified and screaming. A man standing over her. The whip he yields lashing at her flesh.

The feeling of déjà vu is nauseating.

'Jesus,' he says.

'Yeah, and that's not the worst of it. There is extensive damage to the anus, rectum and vagina, consistent with the insertion of sharp-edged implements. This poor girl was subject to intense and prolonged torture of the worst kind. This is one sick individual you're looking for here, Doyle.'

Doyle finds himself nodding. His lips curl in disgust and fury at what this bastard did. He badly wants to get his hands on the twisted fuck.

'Tell me about the tattoo,' he says.

'Sure. You ever had one?'

'No.'

'What, not even a little one somewhere? One that only your darling wife knows about?'

'Not even that. Get on with it, Norm.'

'All right. What you should know about tattoos is that they tend to fade over time. When they're new, the colors are vivid. The colors on this girl's tattoo are really bright. The other thing you need to know is that a tattoo isn't like a painting. It's an open wound to the skin. That means it has to heal. Because of that, fresh tattoos often scab over until the healing process is complete.'

'And this one had scabs, right?'

'Correct. It's a very recent tattoo. Put there in the last few days.'

That's all Doyle needed to hear. He didn't need the explanation of the deductive process. He's heard it all before. He knows a lot more about tattoos than he's willing to reveal right now.

'You said it's a picture of an angel.'

'Yeah. It's good work. Very artistic. This is no backstreet hack job. Should make it easier to narrow down the list of people who could have put it there.'

Doyle already has a list in mind. If it were any narrower it would be squeezing the fuck out of the one person it contains. Something he would be perfectly content to watch.

'How old was she?'

He waits for the evasive answer. Another rough estimate. Still, it could be helpful.

'Sixteen. She'd have been seventeen on the third of next month.'

Doyle feels the surprise, takes a mental step back to determine what he would have been thinking if it hadn't been a surprise.

'You know who she is,' he says.

'Like I said, who needs a whole corpse when you got me on the team? I cross-checked with the Missing Persons records. Found a girl who disappeared last Saturday.'

Yesterday was Tuesday, thinks Doyle. That's a lot of time she spent in the company of her torturer before he finished her off. Jesus.

'You sure it's her?'

'Positive. Photographs match. Dental records match. Fingerprints match. I even found an old fracture to her thumb, done when she was nine. I've ordered a DNA test, which we'll have to wait for, but I'm certain we have the right girl.'

'Okay, Norm. Thanks. That's great work. So who is she?'

'Name's Hamlyn. Megan Hamlyn.'

*

Nicole Hamlyn sits in her house in Forest Hills, which is light years away from the East Village, and stares out of her window again. The clouds are black now, and appear to be hovering just feet above the houses. She imagines a black balloon being filled with water, stretching and straining as it fills, becoming more pendulous every second, threatening to burst at any moment. The expectation, the tension, as she waits for the explosion.

And then it happens. One huge deep rumble of thunder. A roar of relief as the heavens relent and release their unbearable load.

The rain comes not in droplets but in globules. Massive spheres that crash into the ground and throw up huge splashes. Rain that looks as though it could hurt.

She pictures her Megan. Frightened. Running for cover. Pulling her coat over her head as she hurries through the downpour, looking for somewhere, anywhere, that will afford her protection from this onslaught. She pictures her huddled under an awning or in a doorway, shivering and wet.

But, above all, she imagines her wishing for her home. Her family. Warmth and dryness and love.

And then Nicole sees the car.

It's a sedan. It cruises like a shark through the waters. It is long and sleek and dark. Too dark. This is not a bringer of happiness. It glides like a predator, and as it nears her house she wishes for it not to notice her, not to see this house or the woman watching from its window. She prays that it will continue on its deadly prowl, that it will seek out some other unfortunate victim.

But then it slows, and she feels the terror start to build inside. Wishes that this house was not so stark and white, that it could blend into the shadows and the grayness. Wishes that her outline was not so clear in the window. Wishes that she could run and hide and cover her ears and wait for the outsiders to go away again.

But she finds herself transfixed. She cannot move from that chair she has spent so many hours in lately. It is as if it has taken hold of her and is forcing her to play this out, this most dreaded of outcomes.

The car stops, and it is directly in front of her house. Not even slightly to one side, so that she might imagine they are going to see one of her neighbors. No, it is here, lined up with her front door. They are coming to see her. Even in this rain, they are coming.

She sees the car doors open. One either side. Driver and passenger. They always come in twos. She sees them glance up at the sky, as if they too cannot believe what a backdrop nature has created for them on this fateful day. She sees them turn up their collars and make a dash toward the house. Her house. The house where she is sitting and watching and waiting for Megan to come home. Because that is who is supposed to be coming up her path now. Megan.

And, in a way, she knows that that is what is happening. She knows that Megan is here, in the form of these two men. It is the story of the Monkey's Paw. She has wished for the return of a loved one and that wish has been granted, but in a way that is more horrific than anything she could have imagined.

When the doorbell rings, and its usually joyful notes sound like the solemn doleful tolling of a church bell, she cannot move. She stays glued to her chair at the window and pretends it's not happening, even though she can feel the tears already starting to build.

She hears a noise behind her, and she looks. Steve is moving to answer the door. He glances at her, and there are questions on his face because he knows she has seen the people who have come to darken their lives, and all she can do is shake her head slightly, even though it is not enough to stop him, not enough to prevent this happening.

She hears the door being opened. Hears the voices. Officious male voices. Voices dripping with the promise of unbearable sadness, which Steve doesn't seem to notice because he is allowing them in. He doesn't know what he is doing. He is letting them in and actually closing the door behind them.

And now they are all trapped here together.

Now it is too late.

FOUR

Doyle hates this. Hates being the bearer of the worst news possible. He particularly hates it when the recipient of his devastating message is a woman, and a breakable-looking one at that. What he dreads most is that they will go to pieces in front of him, because he never knows what to do. He's relieved that, in this case, the husband is here too – someone to step in when the emotional waves get rough. It doesn't always play out that way, of course. Sometimes it's the man who falls apart and the woman who provides the comfort. For some reason he has yet to analyze, Doyle can cope better with that. Men he understands, women he doesn't. That's all there is to it, he thinks. Sue me.

The house is beautiful. Quiet. There is a peacefulness here. He imagines it to be one of those houses that would never be on the market for very long. You would walk into it and it would feel right and you would instantly want to buy it.

The decor and furniture are modern and tasteful. No dark colors anywhere. Doyle feels a little embarrassed at the rivulets of rainwater that are dripping from his leather jacket and onto the oatmeal carpet. A distance of only a few yards from the car to the house, and he feels like he's just climbed out of a swimming pool.

There's one thing out of place here. So out of place it hits you as soon as you walk in. It's the chair by the window. Doesn't belong there at all. But Doyle understands the reason.

He nods toward the occupant of that chair. Doesn't smile. This is not a time for smiling. Wouldn't want to send out the wrong message. What you have to do in these situations is be officious. It may sound cruel, but the message has to be clear and unambiguous. You can't tell someone their daughter is dead with a stupid grin on your face.

The woman looks to be just shy of forty. She is good-looking, and is probably stunning when she tries. Today she hasn't tried. Her long blond hair is tied loosely at the back. She wears no makeup. She is dressed in a baggy sweatshirt and blue leggings. Today is a 'throw it on and leave it be' day.

Her husband is of a similar age, but of a different disposition. He is clean-cut, has precisely preened hair and smells of aftershave. He wears a Diesel T-shirt and well-pressed jeans. He appears to Doyle like someone who is obsessed with looking after himself. Hitting the gym, eating all the right foods, not smoking or drinking – all that annoying healthy stuff.

'Come in,' says Mr Hamlyn. 'Please.' He turns to his wife. 'Hon, these guys are from the Police Department. The Eighth Precinct?' He looks to Doyle for confirmation of this, and Doyle nods.

Doyle hears the shakiness in the man's voice. Sees the uncertainty in the woman's eyes.

Doyle looks down at his clothes. 'We got kinda wet out there. I wouldn't want to ruin your furniture . . .'

'No, it's okay. Please. Take a seat. Would you like some coffee? Tea?'

Doyle sees LeBlanc's eyes light up, and quickly interjects. 'No. Nothing. Thank you.' He looks across the room. 'Mrs

Hamlyn? Perhaps if you came over here, next to your husband? We need to speak with both of you.'

Nicole Hamlyn gets up from her chair like it's a supreme effort. She stares warily at her visitors as she approaches. Steve takes her arm and helps her to lower herself to the sofa, as though she's an elderly grandmother.

Doyle starts walking to the vacated chair. 'You mind if I bring this across?'

Mr Hamlyn shakes his head, and Doyle restores the chair to its rightful place for what must be the first time in days. As he does so, he sees that Mrs Hamlyn is watching him. He hopes that she doesn't regard the moving of her chair as some kind of disrespectful act.

The two detectives take their seats opposite the Hamlyns.

'Mrs Hamlyn, as I was just telling your husband, my name is Detective Callum Doyle, and this is Detective Tommy LeBlanc.'

'Are you from Missing Persons?' she asks. Her voice is quiet but clear.

'No. No, we're not from Missing Persons.'

'Because all the detectives we've met so far have been from Missing Persons. And so I thought maybe you were from there too. I thought maybe you were more senior detectives from there. Because, well, it's been a while now, and so the case should be given more urgency, don't you think? Something more needs to be done.'

'Mrs Hamlyn, we're not from Missing Persons. We're precinct detectives. From the Eighth Precinct, which covers the East Village and the Lower East Side.'

She flinches. Something has hit home. She crosses her arms, then lifts a hand and tugs at a strand of her hair.

'I . . . I don't understand. The East Village? Why would you be involved in this? Why would you—'

'Mrs Hamlyn, there's no easy way to tell you this. We believe we've found your daughter, and I'm afraid to say she's not alive.'

There's a silence then. Doyle rides it out, gives the words time to sink in and percolate into their consciousness. Lets the fact of what he has just said become established in their minds.

Steve Hamlyn rubs his hand up and down his thigh. Up and down, up and down. He starts to shake and his eyes glisten. To his left, Nicole's face contorts into a mask of intense anguish.

Mr Hamlyn finds some words. 'You're saying our daughter is dead? Megan is dead?'

'Yes. I am. I'm sorry.'

Nicole emits a high-pitched keening noise that is barely recognizable as a long, drawn-out 'Noooo.' Her husband puts his hand on hers, but he still stares with incredulity at the police officers who have dared to invade his house and present him with this story.

'You're sure?' he asks. 'I mean, could there be a mistake?'

'There's no mistake. The Medical Examiner ran tests. We're as sure as we can be that it's your daughter.'

'As sure as you can be? But not a hundred percent, right? Maybe if I could . . . The body you've found. If I could . . .'

'Steve, no.'

This from Nicole. She grasps her husband's hand tightly and utters the words in a small quiet breath through her tears. And in that instant Doyle knows that she has skipped a chapter beyond the text he has given them so far.

'But what if they're wrong, Nicole? Don't you think we should at least—'

'Stop it!'

'Hon—'

'NO! Please. Stop it. She's dead, Steve. Can't you hear what they're saying to you?'

She turns to Doyle then, and the look in her eyes is one of heartbreaking comprehension. 'The news. This morning. The East Village. It was her, wasn't it?'

Doyle says nothing, because he doesn't need to and because he can't. It would be a slap to the face.

She stands up then, and her courteous announcement seems almost surreal: 'Excuse me, gentlemen. I'm going to be sick.'

She runs out of the room, her hand to her mouth. From somewhere else in the house come retching noises followed by the sound of running water.

Steve stands up, unsure whether to go to her or to stay and satisfy his burning need to understand what's happening to his family.

'The news? What's she talking about? What news?'

'Mr Hamlyn,' says Doyle, 'could you sit down, please?' He waits for the man to sit, then says, 'The police undertook a large-scale search of the East Village last night—'

And that's all he has to say. Because now Steve gets it too. His brain finally allows the connection it has probably been vetoing all along.

'Oh God, no! Not that. Not to Megan. Please tell me that wasn't her.'

'I'm sorry,' says Doyle.

The roar of anguish that the man lets out then is primeval. It chills Doyle to the bone and he feels the goosebumps break out on his skin. He experiences a sense of loss himself that seems profound but is mere fallout. How more unbearable must that feeling be at its source?

An age passes while the detectives allow the man his release. Doyle can almost feel the discomfort radiating from LeBlanc.

When Hamlyn speaks again, his words seem as misplaced as those of his wife. 'Thank you,' he says, his words coming out as a squeak through the emotion.

Doyle says nothing in return. Out of the corner of his eye he sees LeBlanc looking at him, willing him to take him the hell out of here. Doyle waits, because he must.

Hamlyn clears his throat to bring his voice down an octave, then continues: 'For being straight with us. For being honest. I want you to know we appreciate it.'

'Mr Hamlyn,' says Doyle, 'I don't want to take up any more of your time, especially at this moment. But there's one thing I need to ask you about.'

Hamlyn wipes his eyes and sniffs deeply. 'What is it?'

'Megan's body . . .' He uses the word body, even though there wasn't much of one. '. . . It had a tattoo.'

He sees the puzzlement on Hamlyn's face then, and he rushes out his next words before bafflement becomes doubt becomes hope.

'It was done recently. In the past few days.'

'A tattoo? What kind of tattoo?'

'A picture of an angel. At the base of her spine.'

Hamlyn bows his head and pushes his hand through his hair. 'Aw, Jeez.'

'Does it mean something to you?'

He raises his head again. 'Yeah. Kind of. She wanted a tattoo. For years she's wanted one. We told her she couldn't have one. She was sixteen, for Chrissake. I don't think it's even legal at sixteen, is it? But even if it was, I didn't want her to have it. I wouldn't want her to have it even if she was twenty.

I told her: Those things don't come off. You're stuck with them for ever. But still she kept banging on about getting a damned tattoo.'

'Far as you know, though, she didn't have it done before she disappeared?'

Hamlyn strains against his helplessness. 'No. I don't think so. At that age . . . I mean she was practically a woman, you know? I wouldn't see . . .' He pauses as a thought strikes him. 'Wait. She went swimming with Nicole. On Friday. The day before she went missing. They always get changed together. There's no way she could have hidden it.' He pursues his own chain of thought, then looks hard at Doyle. 'You think, whoever gave her that tattoo, maybe he . . .'

'I don't know. It's too early. But it's something for us to look into.'

Hamlyn starts rubbing his hands together. His leg shakes. The crying is on its way again.

Doyle stands up. Motions LeBlanc to do the same. He is only too eager to comply.

'We'll leave you alone now, Mr Hamlyn. We may need to come back and ask you some more questions, but right now I think you and your wife need some time together.'

Hamlyn gets up. 'Sure,' he says, but he finds it difficult to turn his tear-stained face to the cops. It's a man thing, not wanting to appear weak. Doyle knows that when they've gone, he will bawl like a baby. And that's okay.

Then, at the door, Hamlyn grabs Doyle by the arm. This time he looks Doyle straight in the eye, because this time it's about what he regards as the appropriate male response.

'Promise me,' he says. 'Promise me that you'll get this bastard.'

Doyle nods. 'We'll get him.'

'And . . . if there's any chance . . . I mean, if I can be there when you do . . .'

The sentence is left unfinished, but the message is up there in neon. Doyle doesn't know what to say. He'd like nothing more than to grab up this sicko and hand him straight over to Hamlyn and anyone he wants to invite to a revenge party. But he knows it's not going to happen. All he can do is give a hint of a nod, meaning nothing more than the request has been noted.

And then the detectives leave. On the way out, Doyle hears sobbing coming from upstairs. When the door closes behind them, LeBlanc makes a dash through the rain. Doyle takes his time. He ambles down the driveway, through the tidy front yard with its manicured patch of lawn, out onto the street with its perfect line of trees. And all the way there, while the rain batters down on him, he thinks about his promise to Hamlyn.

He will not allow the killer of this young girl to walk free. Not this time.

FIVE

See, it's the preconceptions that bother Doyle.

Not so much the clothes. Or the spectacles. Or even the inexperience. No, thinking about it, what it all boils down to is the preconceptions.

LeBlanc has been a detective for only about a year. He joined the Eighth not long before Doyle had all those problems with everyone around him being whacked just for knowing Doyle. What a joyful Christmas that was. *Hi, my name's Doyle. And you are? Oh, now you're dead. Sorry about that.*

Since that time, Doyle has never been partnered with LeBlanc. LeBlanc has worked with several of the other detectives since his arrival, but has spent most of his time with one in particular. A man named Schneider.

And the thing about Schneider is that he hates Doyle's guts.

It all dates back to a time in prehistory when Doyle was in a different precinct uptown and working with a woman called Laura Marino who had a thing for him and was not very discreet about it and then ended up being killed by a shotgun-bearing skell in a Harlem apartment. Which was tragic enough in itself, except for the fact that some people started suggesting that Doyle himself may have had something to do with her demise –

43

suggesting it so forcefully, in fact, that Internal Affairs became involved and Doyle nearly lost his job, his freedom and his marriage. That episode was the trigger for Doyle to transfer to the Eighth with the hope of making a clean start.

Only things are never as simple as that, are they? Police precincts do not operate in isolation, oblivious to the events in other precincts. Believe it or not, they talk to each other – an aspect of modern policing that is actively encouraged. Occasionally, friendships are struck up between members of different precincts, or existing friendships endure even after one of the friends transfers out.

One of Schneider's close friends is Danny Marino – widower of the aforementioned Laura Marino. And being such a good buddy, he has always done his damnedest to ensure that everyone in the Eighth remains aware of what a checkered past Doyle has.

All of which brings us full circle to LeBlanc. Because – though Doyle has no evidence to support this – Schneider will have been relentless in pouring his poison into his protégé's ear over the past year. He will have been unable to prevent himself. It's what he does. And the young impressionable LeBlanc, looking up to his older and more experienced mentor, will have soaked all this up as the gospel truth and established preconceptions that Doyle is now powerless to eradicate.

And that's the real reason why Doyle feels uneasy about LeBlanc.

He figures this out while he's driving, and feels that he's done a pretty fine job of self-analysis, even though head-shrinking is a practice he usually avoids at all costs. In fact, he wonders now why he bothered. What's wrong with disliking LeBlanc for his style choices? Who says I'm not allowed to be superficial?

'That was tough,' says LeBlanc.

He's in the passenger seat. Doyle has the wheel, because only he knows where they're going.

'For them or for us?'

'For everyone. I, uh, I liked the way you handled it, by the way.'

'Why?' says Doyle. He knows he shouldn't act so snippy. With anyone else he would take the compliment and shine back his gratitude. But not with LeBlanc. Not with the preconceptions he's got.

'What?' says LeBlanc.

'Why did you like the way I handled it? What was so special about the way I did it?'

'I . . . well, I don't know why. I just thought you were . . . professional about it. You showed compassion back there.'

'Uh-huh. And why does that surprise you?'

'Surprise me? I didn't say it surprises me. It's just that . . . well . . .'

'Go on.'

'Well, we've never worked a case together, you and me. So I don't know anything about you, and—'

'What would you like to know?'

'What?'

'You wanna know stuff about me? Shoot.'

'Well, I . . . It's not like I've got questions or anything. I just thought I could learn a lot from someone like you.'

'Someone like me meaning . . .'

LeBlanc shrugs. 'Meaning an experienced detective who seems to know what he's doing. That's all.'

'Uh-huh,' says Doyle, and even that carries an undercurrent of coldness to it.

They lapse into silence then. It lasts while they get across the

Williamsburg Bridge and plunge into the thick Manhattan traffic. Doyle stares intently ahead, trying to see where he's going through the vertical rods of rain. The car's wipers swat wildly, but the rain just keeps on coming. It creates a moving, shimmering film of water across the windshield, and just beyond, countless plumes of spray as the drops explode on the hood of the car.

It's not until the car sails across East Seventh Street that LeBlanc gathers up the courage to speak again. 'Where you going, Cal? You missed the turning for the House.'

'We're not going to the House,' says Doyle. 'I got someone to see first.'

He doesn't bother to tell LeBlanc where they're going, and he doesn't bother to say who they're about to visit.

It's the preconceptions, you see.

That, and the stupid dress sense.

LeBlanc thinks they've got him all wrong.

He's heard a lot of bad things about Doyle. That he's a maverick. That he's ruthless. That he's a dirty cop. That he has no great love for his fellow officers. That he will even stoop to murder when it suits him.

He tries not to believe it. At the very least, he tries to keep an open mind. It's how he was raised. *Treat people as you find them*, his parents used to say. *Give folks the benefit of the doubt until they prove otherwise.*

He smiles as he casts his mind back to those times. Simpler times, in a simpler life. It was easier to follow advice like that in a tiny God-fearing community in Iowa.

Not so easy in a place like New York City. Especially when you're a cop. The niceness gets squeezed out of you. Cynicism gets hammered in. You can't give the benefit of the doubt to a junkie who may or may not be holding onto an AIDS-infected hypodermic needle in that pocket of his, or to a hooker who may or may not be about to whip a six-inch blade out of that purse. Shit like that happens, and you have to assume that it will happen unless you take precautions to prevent it. Otherwise you don't last long as a cop.

But as for Doyle . . .

He's also a cop. A brother. A fellow Member of Service. And no matter what people say, LeBlanc has seen nothing to confirm that he's bad.

Look at the way he handled the Hamlyns. That was impressive. He was in control, but he was sympathetic with it. He knew exactly what to say.

No doubt about it, thinks LeBlanc, he's an interesting guy. Hidden depths. There are some people who don't like such a closed book. They'd like him to be a little easier to read. Well, maybe he'll open up to me. I think I could learn a lot from him if he'll let me. The impression I get is that he's a stand-up guy. He just wants to do things in his own way. Nothing wrong with that.

It's a hard shell he wears, though. Gonna be difficult to break through that one.

But give me time . . .

He feels a jolt as Doyle suddenly yanks the wheel and pulls the car into a parking space. LeBlanc looks through all the windows, trying to figure out what they're doing here. They're at the uptown end of Avenue B, parked outside a TV-repair place. Straight ahead, on the other side of Fourteenth Street, loom the drab brown boxes that are the Stuyvesant projects, while here on this block are just a variety of small stores fronting low-rise tenements criss-crossed by fire escapes.

'We here?'

'This is it,' says Doyle.

'This is what, exactly?'

Doyle doesn't answer. He just opens his door and steps out of the car.

'Just asking,' LeBlanc mutters. He climbs out of the car and circles it to join Doyle, who is preparing to dodge through the dense traffic. As if deciding that anyone foolhardy enough to challenge its ferocity without so much as a hat is in need of a good dousing, the rain seems to choose at that moment to step up its intensity a notch or two. By the time the two cops have fought their way to the other side of the street, they are already drenched.

'Damn this rain,' says LeBlanc. It's been his experience that the weather is often a good way to start a conversation. Doesn't work with Doyle. The man just picks up the pace. When LeBlanc does the same to keep up, he ends up stepping in a puddle so deep it comes over the top of his shoes.

'Shit!'

When Doyle stops suddenly, LeBlanc almost crashes into him. He turns to see what has attracted Doyle's attention.

He sees dragons. He sees tigers. He sees naked women and snakes and movie stars and sharks and hearts and flowers and crosses. All here on display in the window. And above them all, in dark Gothic lettering, the name of the place: Skinterest.

Doyle doesn't budge for what seems like ages. Doesn't seem to notice that the rain isn't willing to wait with him. We're standing here like idiots, thinks LeBlanc, just getting wetter and wetter.

And then Doyle moves. He opens the door to the shop and steps inside. LeBlanc hurries in after him, even though his haste seems pointless now. He closes the door firmly behind him and savors the instant warmth. He'd like to get a good look at the interior, but his glasses have fogged up. He has to dig into his pocket for a tissue to dry them off. The tissue comes out somewhat moist, but it's all he's got.

The place is eerily quiet after the white noise of the rain outside. LeBlanc puts his glasses back on and looks around. He sees a small waiting area with a black sofa and a glass coffee table holding a stack of magazines. Farther ahead is an adjustable chair of the type one might find in a dentist's, complete with an attached overhead spotlight. Next to that is a typist's chair on casters. Black curtains on rails allow that area to be screened off for when the tattooist is working on more private areas of the body. On the walls are mirrors and framed close-up photographs of tattooed body parts. The air is thick with chemical smells. Disinfectant and ink.

Beyond a counter at the far end of the room, a door opens and a man steps out. 'Hey, guys,' he calls, then steps around the counter and comes closer. When he gets as far as the dentist's chair he stops. His welcoming attitude suddenly withers and his smile droops. He lowers his hands to his sides and says no more.

The man is tall and scrawny. Late twenties, probably. His dark hair is shorn at the sides but long on top, and he has a small goatee. Large black studs in both ears. He wears a blood-red T-shirt that carries a picture of some kind of screaming demon with pointed teeth and vertical slits for eyes.

LeBlanc waits to take his cue from Doyle, since he doesn't even know what they're doing here. But Doyle just stands where he is and stays mute. All that can be heard is the steady dripping of water from the clothes of the detectives onto the tiled floor. It's like the prelude to a gunfight in an old cowboy movie.

'Hello, Stan,' Doyle says finally.

'Detective Doyle,' says the man, and it is clear to LeBlanc that there is no joy in that recognition.

LeBlanc shuffles up next to Doyle. Just in case he's forgotten he has company.

'You two know each other?'

Doyle nods. 'We know each other. This here is Stanley Proust, tattoo artist extraordinaire. Ain't that right, Stan?'

Proust doesn't answer. He just blinks, as if in fear.

Doyle takes a few steps toward Proust, and LeBlanc trails after him. His shoes squelch as he walks. Proust backs away, putting the chair between himself and Doyle.

'How's business, Stan? A lot of pain happening here lately?'

Proust's mouth twitches, as if he is trying to smile but can't quite manage it.

'I do okay.'

Doyle inclines his head toward LeBlanc, but keeps his eyes fixed on Proust.

'This guy's good, ya know? A real artist. You ever feel the need to get a tat done, Stan here's your guy. Stan the man. No hatchet jobs here. Huh, Stan? I'm saying you don't do hatchet jobs. You don't hack away at someone like they're a piece of meat. You're careful. You know how to do things right. Sure, there's pain. But what's a little pain? It's the end result that counts, am I right?'

Proust gives a minimal shrug. 'I guess.' His voice is only just above a whisper.

'Show him,' says Doyle. 'Go ahead, show him your work.'

Proust looks at the detectives with uncertainty. Doesn't move.

'Go on,' urges Doyle. 'Show him.'

Proust turns slightly and reaches a tentative hand out to the counter behind him. 'Well, I got some books here . . .'

'No, no,' says Doyle. 'Not the books. Photos don't do it justice. We need the real thing. In the flesh. Show him yours. You know . . .' Doyle taps himself on the chest.

Proust looks at Doyle, then to LeBlanc, then back to Doyle. He shakes his head, and again the movement is infinitesimal. Like he's trying to conserve energy.

'No, man, I don't—'

'Come on. Don't be shy. Show him.'

Doyle starts to move around the chair. Proust puts his palms up in front of him.

'Please. I . . . I don't want to . . .'

Doyle's voice hardens. 'Show him, Stan. My partner would like to see how good you are at your job.'

'No, I—'

'Show him!' Doyle grabs hold of Proust by his shirt. He starts to pull at it. 'Come on, Stan. You should be proud. Your work is great. It's a masterpiece.'

'Please,' says Stan. A pathetic whimper.

LeBlanc has no idea what's going down here. If this is scripted, then a heads-up before they entered the place would have been nice. But it doesn't look like it's being done for show. It looks like Doyle has lost his senses.

'Cal,' says LeBlanc. 'It's okay.'

'No,' Doyle snaps. 'It's not okay. He needs to show you.'

And then LeBlanc can't believe what he sees. Because Doyle is ripping at the man's T-shirt. Tearing it apart at the seams while Proust cowers and whines.

This isn't right, thinks LeBlanc. He's terrorizing the guy.

He calls out: 'Cal!'

But Doyle doesn't stop. Proust bounces around while Doyle puts all of his strength into ripping that shirt right down the middle. And when he is done, his face looks to be burning with the effort and the heat of his anger.

'There,' says Doyle, gesturing toward the man he has just attacked. 'What do you think of that? Pretty cool, huh?'

Proust himself is a sad spectacle. His frame is slumped in defeat and humiliation. His shirt is in tatters, with a hoop of material remaining like a slack noose around his sinewy neck. His panting chest is hairless and concave, and his ribs are clearly visible beneath the thin skin.

But that's not what LeBlanc focuses on. It's not what anyone would focus on right now.

Not when there's an image like that to look at.

It makes it look as though Proust's chest has been torn open. A pair of hands pulls aside the ragged flesh, and a head pushes out through the bloody opening. It has Proust's own face, but it is contorted in pain. Its mouth is open in a scream, and the eyes have rolled back into their sockets. And it's all so lifelike. It looks three-dimensional, like there really is a copy of Proust desperately trying to escape from inside his own body.

For a moment, LeBlanc forgets what events have just caused that picture to be put on display.

'Jesus,' he says. 'That's . . . that's awesome.'

'Told you,' says Doyle. 'This man is a genius. He did this all by himself. Can you believe it? He can tattoo anything you like, wherever you want it. So tell me, Stan. What other examples of artistic brilliance could you share with us? What are you most proud of out of the stuff you did recently? Why don't you show me? Are they in these books of yours?'

He reaches out and grips the back of Proust's neck, then forces his head down to look at the books on the counter.

'Show me, Stanley. Tell me what's good in these books.'

Doyle opens a book at random, flicks through its pages of photographs.

'What about this? Do you like this one?'

He tosses the book aside. It slides off the counter and crashes to the floor. He pulls another book across.

'How about this book? Would you say these are better than the other ones? I'd say so. Look at that picture of Marilyn Monroe there. That's terrific, it really is. And this one of a Corvette. That's a peach. But you know what I don't see here, Stan? I don't see any angels. Where are the angels? Are they in one of these other books here? Could you show me, please, Stan? Because I like angels. They're my favorite. And I'm sure you could do a real good angel if you tried. What do you say, Stan?'

Proust suddenly slaps Doyle's arm away and takes several steps backward, out of arm's reach. Doyle closes the gap again.

'Get off me, man! Leave me alone! I don't know what you're talking about. Why are you here?'

'You know why I'm here, Stan. I'm here about an angel. The one you did recently.'

'What angel? I haven't done an angel for months. What is this?'

'You did one a few days ago. On a girl. And now she's dead.'

Proust shows his palms again. 'Now wait a minute, Detective. Don't do this to me again, man. I know you don't like me, and I don't know why. But I'm not a killer. I'm an artist. I do tattoos. That's all, man.'

'Oh, I like you, Stan. I like you for the murder of Megan Hamlyn. Sixteen. That's how old she was. Just sixteen years old.'

Proust looks across to LeBlanc, as if hoping for a more receptive ear.

'Ah, well, there you go. She couldn't have been a client of

mine. You have to be eighteen to get a tattoo in this state, and I always insist on ID. No way would I have—'

The slap he receives from Doyle resounds around the room. Proust brings his hand to his cheek. Tears well in his eyes.

'Don't fuck with me, Stan,' says Doyle.

LeBlanc feels he has to cut in. He says, 'Cal, don't you think—'

And then suddenly he's the target of a finger aimed in his direction, behind which is the face of a man who looks like he could pull the trigger if it were a real gun.

'Stay out of this, Tommy,' says Doyle. He turns back to Proust. 'Where were you last night, Stan?'

'Last night? I was here, man. I'm always here. I live back there, behind the shop. I don't go out much.'

'What about Saturday night?'

'Saturday? Here. I'm always here.'

'Can you prove it? Anyone who can vouch for you?'

'N–no. I live alone.'

'Tell me what you did last night.'

'I . . . I watched TV.'

'What did you watch?'

'Well, actually it was a DVD. The *Transformers* movie.'

'*Transformers*? Exactly how old are you, Stan?'

'Twenty-eight.'

'Uh-huh,' says Doyle, as though that makes his point. LeBlanc feels faintly embarrassed. He enjoyed the *Transformers* movie himself. What's so wrong with that?

'You didn't go out at all?' Doyle asks.

'No, man. I told you.'

'So if we ask around, nobody would've seen you out on the streets last night?'

'No. How could they?'

'What about the rest of the time between Saturday and now? Did you go anywhere?'

'I guess.'

'You guess what? You did or you didn't?'

'I went out. Sunday night. I got a pizza at Oscar's on the next block, and then I called in at the liquor store.'

'And that's it? You didn't go anywhere else in that time? Not even for your lunch?'

'No. I make my lunch here. A sandwich and fruit. Every day.'

'So we're not gonna find anyone else who says different? Nobody who saw you in the subway or taking a cab, or in a different part of town? Is that what you're telling me?'

'Yeah, man. Like I said.'

'Jesus, you're a real hermit, aren't you, Stan? You don't go out. You don't see anyone . . .'

Proust shrugs. 'It's how I am. I'm not good with people.'

'What about girls? Are you good with them?'

Proust hesitates before he answers. 'I don't know what you mean.'

'Sure you do. A young guy like yourself. You got all these girls coming in here, getting undressed, asking you to put pretty pictures on parts of their bodies they wouldn't let any other stranger see. Must be pretty tempting, Stan. Must be quite a turn-on.'

'It's my job. It's like being a doctor. I don't look at them in that way. All's I see is a canvas for my art.'

Doyle nods without conviction. 'You got a girlfriend, Stan?'

'No. Not at the moment.'

'Had any girlfriends since the last time we met?'

'I . . . I don't have the time.'

'So that would be a no. Any particular reason for that? I mean, where's your outlet? All that sexual tension building up in you over these young semi-naked girls, and you don't have an outlet? Christ, that must be really frustrating.'

'I told you, man, it's not like that.' He turns to LeBlanc again. 'Can he do this? Can he ask me these personal questions? I haven't done anything. I swear. Please.'

LeBlanc finds himself wanting to come to this guy's aid. He wants to say something in his favor. It's not that he's never seen a cop come down heavy on a perp or a skell before. He's often had to get in people's faces himself. The worst thing you can do in the street is show weakness, because one thing the scum out there excel at is spotting the vulnerable and pouncing on them without mercy.

But this is different. This is a one-on-one in the guy's own place of business. Actually, it doesn't even feel like a one-on-one, given the differences in size, strength and ability. It seems more like an army-on-one. And even that can be okay in the right circumstances. For some perps, it's the only approach that gets through to them.

All that LeBlanc can do now is trust his partner. But he tells himself that Doyle better have a damn good explanation for this. The train of thought better be a lot more convincing than 'Victim has tattoo; I know a tattoo artist.'

For now, discomforting though it is, all he does is give Proust a helpless look.

Says Doyle, 'Don't ask *him*, Stan. This is between us. And I want you to know that this is just the beginning. You know what you did, and I know it too. So I'm coming back. I'm gonna come back again and again until you admit what you did. From now on, you're mine, Stan. Every spare minute I have is gonna be spent watching you. You're mine. Do you understand that?'

'Man, that's not right. I'm clean. I didn't do nothing. I just do tattoos.'

Doyle grabs him by what's left of his shirt and shakes him. LeBlanc finds himself taking a step forward.

'*I said, Do you understand, you piece of shit?*'

Proust's mouth curls down as if he's about to cry. 'Okay. Yeah. I understand.'

Doyle pushes him away. 'I'm coming back, Stan. While I'm gone, I want you to write down everything you did since Saturday morning. I want places and times, to the exact minute. That includes details of any customers you had here. Because, believe me, I am gonna check them out. And if I find one anomaly, just one . . . well, you know what would happen then, don't you, Stanley?'

Doyle doesn't wait for an answer. He just turns on his heel and heads for the door. When he brushes past LeBlanc, it's as if he doesn't see him. His face is a perfect match for the thunderous weather outside.

LeBlanc takes a last look at the pathetic figure of Proust, busy trying to pull the fragments of shirt together around his skinny frame as if it's somehow possible to reassemble it. Again he feels he should say something, but doesn't. Instead, he leaves the shop and runs to catch up with Doyle.

In the car, LeBlanc puts the obvious question. The one that will clear all this up and put his mind at rest. The one that will lend logic to Doyle's actions and attitude.

'You want to fill me in? Tell me what all that was about?'

Doyle's answer is in his scowl and in the way he puts his whole body into twisting the ignition key and in how he slams forward the transmission lever. Words are hardly necessary, but he supplies one anyway.

'No.'

And that's it. That's the best LeBlanc's going to get. A single syllable infused with venom. And as Doyle whips the car out into the traffic and pounds his horn at the first driver who dares to object, LeBlanc starts to wonder whether the stories are true after all. He starts to imagine that this big guy in the leather jacket and with the bent nose could easily fit into the role of a criminal. Maybe even a killer.

Sitting next to this man about whom he really knows nothing, LeBlanc feels incredibly uneasy.

If not a little afraid.

SIX

She is no longer sure what to do with her time.

When there was hope, she could stare for hours out of the window and picture Megan walking back to the house. She could tell herself that it was an episode with an end. One of those crazy things that hormone-filled teenagers go through in attempting to understand themselves and their place in the world. Megan would return.

Now that has gone. The window holds no interest for Nicole. The world beyond this house holds no interest. It is dark and it is filled with evil and it destroys. The chair remains where the detective put it, back in its rightful place. A tiny attempt to restore order in a home where normality has been ripped to shreds.

The crying won't stop. Whenever she thinks all her reserves of tears have been squeezed out of her, her body seems to manufacture more, and five minutes later the valves are open again. Her head is pulsating with pain at the effort of dealing with the grief.

She is tired, so tired. But she cannot sleep. Not yet. Not until she collapses with exhaustion.

She doesn't want to see anyone or talk to anyone. When her mother phoned, she had to tell her the dreadful news. There was little conversation: it was mostly mutual wailing and silent sobbing. Her mother wanted to come over; Nicole ordered her not to.

Steve has his own ways of dealing with this. Or not dealing with it. She can hear him upstairs now. Loud animal grunts as he lifts his weights. Before that he went on a five-mile run. He hasn't trained this hard for years.

She remembers little of the hours that have passed since the visit from the detectives. That time is a hole in her life, devoid of content. Her anguished mind pushed everything else away. She saw nothing, heard nothing, was not even conscious of time. She could have been dead.

Now, she tries to find things to do. Little jobs to occupy her mind. But Megan is there. She will always be there. Nicole will wash the dishes and see Megan take them from her to dry them. She will switch the kettle on and hear the tiny clinks of crockery as Megan fetches down the mugs. She will tidy the bathroom and smell Megan's body spray.

Her head is so filled with Megan. Her life is so empty without Megan.

Outside, it continues to rain. Lord, how it rains.

She hears a steady thud, thud, thud. Steve coming downstairs. Much more heavy-footed than usual. There is anger in those footsteps.

He comes into the kitchen and opens the refrigerator and takes out a carton of orange juice and drinks straight from the carton. A manly dismissal of social niceties. She would rebuke him for it, normally.

She watches him drink. The bobbing of his Adam's apple. The fluttering pulse in his neck. The sheen of perspiration on his face and pumped-up arms. She can smell the sweat. She can feel his pain.

'You should take a shower,' she says, because she doesn't know what else to say.

He drains the carton and tosses it into the flip-top trashcan.

'I'm not going to let this rest, Nicole.'

She folds her arms and leans back against the counter. 'What do you mean?'

'The police. I'm going to call them later. I'm going to call them every couple of hours if I have to. I'm going to stay on their case until they catch this sonofabitch.'

'Steve, you don't have to—'

'You know what I've been thinking? A private eye. We should get a private eye on this. I don't care how much it costs. We've got to find the bastard.'

She keeps her voice soft and low. Soothe the savage breast, and all that.

'We don't need a private detective. Let the police do their job.'

'Boy. I tell ya. If I could just get my hands on that . . .'

He doesn't finish his sentence. Just puts his hands out and tightens them around an imaginary neck. She can see his tendons flex. She can sense the power in that grip and the satisfaction he is getting from his envisioned deed of vengeance.

Like many men she has met, Steve does not deal well with emotion. He was brought up by a very competitive sports-man of a father. Crying is weakness. Forgiveness is weakness. Surrender is weakness. The stereotypical view of manliness was one of the things that attracted her to Steve in the first place, and there has been many a time she has been grateful for the reassurance and feeling of security it has brought her.

Not now, though. She heard him crying earlier, but it wasn't enough. He didn't purge himself. He kept too much inside, where it will fester. Where it will gnaw away at him. And when he does release it, it will be at the wrong time, in the wrong place, and for the wrong reason. Watching him now as he chokes the life from his invisible victim, she feels not a little afraid.

She walks across the room and puts a hand on his arm. It's like oak. Hard and unyielding. He needs to yield. He needs to give a little. Otherwise he'll break.

'Steve,' she says. Calm. A whisper. 'That's not the answer. It won't change anything.'

He looks at her, but seems blind to what he sees. It's as if he doesn't recognize her. She wills the tension to leave his body, the coldness to leave his eyes. She needs him, and she longs for him to need her in return. Because what are they without that?

'I need a shower,' he says, and he walks away, and she stays in the kitchen and stares at the space where he stood and she wonders why everything she holds dear in her world is being taken away from her.

LeBlanc sits at his desk, staring at Doyle, who is pouring himself a coffee on the other side of the squadroom. He's still not sure what happened at the tattoo shop. What got into the man? Why was he behaving like that?

Or maybe that was the true Doyle. Maybe that's the way he is with people.

'How'd it go this afternoon?'

The voice is low. Conspiratorial. LeBlanc turns to find Schneider watching him. Schneider is a bull of a man. Stocky and menacing. His steel-gray hair is cut close to his skull, giving his head the look of a bullet. He chews his gum behind a smile that doesn't ask you to be his friend.

'How'd what go?'

Schneider chin-points toward Doyle. 'Working with Irish. You two get along?'

LeBlanc looks at Doyle again. He would like to say yes to Schneider's question. He would like to say that, contrary to all expectations, Doyle is beyond reproach. An upstanding cop of the highest caliber. A true team player who sticks to the rules.

But he finds that the words catch in his throat. They linger there so long that Schneider makes up his own answer, and his smile broadens into something that could stop a heart.

'A piece of work, ain't he? You want my advice, you should ask for another partner on this case. Doyle is no good. He's a bad cop. Working with him is like walking through a minefield. Just make sure he doesn't make you go first.'

Schneider sidles away then, but he leaves his thoughts behind. They trickle into LeBlanc's head and begin to simmer.

Doyle opens the first of the files on his desk. It's the autopsy report. Pages of medical jargon, plus some photographs. The parts of the report that Doyle is able to decipher tell him nothing new. The photographs, on the other hand, mesmerize him.

He starts with the head. Placing his hand over the area beneath Megan Hamlyn's chin, he tries to imagine her whole. Tries to picture her as the young pretty girl that she was just a few days ago. It's difficult. The face in front of him is a mess. God knows the pain she went through.

He flips through the other photographs, then pulls out one which gives a close-up of the tattoo. It's superb work, all right.

You can see the serenity in the angel's face. The wings have a soft, fluffy quality to them that makes them look like they're made from real feathers. The angel's robes have pleats and folds that make them seem as though they could really move. Whoever did this worked for a long time on it. They spent ages staring at this young girl's flesh. Touching it. Talking to her. Getting to know her.

But this *whoever* has a name, doesn't he?

Stanley Proust.

Oh yeah, a name to remember. A name seared into Doyle's brain. A name that causes Doyle to clench his fists and grind his teeth every time he thinks of it. He's like Pavlov's dog with that name. The mere mention of it causes him to salivate at the thought of eating Proust alive.

He lost it in that tattoo shop. In the cold light of hindsight he accepts that the way he acted there was unprofessional. God knows what LeBlanc must have thought.

In fact, he realizes, it's probably a good thing that LeBlanc *was* there. I don't know what I might have done to Proust if I'd gone there alone. It wouldn't have been pretty and it wouldn't have been right. But damn it if that man doesn't deserve a little harsh treatment. If LeBlanc knew what I know . . .

'Doyle. LeBlanc. In my office.'

Doyle raises his head to see Lieutenant Cesario looking straight at him. Set against his permanently tanned features, Cesario's teeth light up the room with their whiteness. But this is no welcome smile, no invitation to a coffee morning. It's more the rictus of the big bad wolf inviting two little piggies into his den.

Doyle closes the file, sighs and gets up from his chair. He sees the questioning looks from LeBlanc as he joins him.

Doyle says, 'What have you done this time? Don't be looking to me to save your ass.'

They get into Cesario's office, and the lieutenant motions LeBlanc to close the door. Cesario is as smartly turned out as he usually is. Not an unintentional crease anywhere. Doyle would be willing to bet he irons his socks. His undershorts too.

Cesario is a recent addition to the precinct, and Doyle still finds it difficult to take him seriously. Not that the guy's done anything wrong – after all, he's the one who gave Doyle the opportunity to work on the homicide of the bookstore girl – but something about him doesn't sit right. He's a little too perfect, too glossy. His hair doesn't move. His eyebrows look drawn on. It's like he's an actor playing the part of a cop in one of those ridiculously glitzy TV shows.

Doyle snaps a glance at LeBlanc, who is also impeccably attired, then drops his gaze to his own garb. Okay, he thinks, maybe I'm the odd one out here. Maybe if I dressed like these guys I wouldn't attract so much flak.

His sartorial musings are interrupted by Cesario: 'I just had a very long phone conversation. A conversation I'da preferred not to have. You wanna guess who it was with?'

Doyle can guess. He decides it's wise not to admit it.

'I'll tell you,' says Cesario. 'It was from a man called Stanley Proust. A man I'd never heard of before today. But I think you know him, don't you, Cal?'

'We've, uhm, crossed paths.'

'Uh-huh. Care to tell me why you went to see him today?'

'He's a suspect. On the Megan Hamlyn case.'

'I see. And why is he a suspect?'

Doyle sees the files in front of Cesario. He reckons the

lieutenant already knows the answer to his question. Doyle figures he's got nothing to lose.

'Because he's a murdering scumbag. Because he puts tattoos on young girls and then he abducts them and rapes them and tortures them and kills them. That's why.'

'Hold on. Rewind this for me, would you? You know all this how?'

'I know it because I've investigated him before.'

'Yeah, that's all on your record, Cal. Remind me how that went again. You must have got the goods on Proust that time. I mean, for you to be so sure about him on this occasion. How long did he go down for?'

Doyle shifts uncomfortably. 'He didn't go down for it.'

'Oh? And why was that? A technicality in the court case, maybe?'

Doyle says nothing.

'There *was* a court hearing, wasn't there, Cal?'

'Not exactly.'

'Not exactly. You mean no. In fact, Proust was never even formally booked, was he, Cal? And the reason he was never booked was because you couldn't produce any evidence he did something wrong.'

'It was him,' says Doyle. 'He did it last time, and he did it this time. I know it.'

'Nobody else knows it, Cal.' He turns to LeBlanc. 'Do you know it, Tommy? You were there today. Did you come to the same conclusions as your partner regarding the guilt of Mr Proust?'

LeBlanc clears his throat. 'I, uh . . . this is all new to me, Lieutenant. I don't have the same background knowledge of Proust that Cal has.'

'Oh, really? You mean your own partner hasn't even brought you up to speed? He hasn't made you privy to all the important information on someone he regards as a key suspect in this case?'

Doyle sees LeBlanc redden a little. With embarrassment, probably, plus at least a soupçon of anger at his partner.

But Cesario hasn't finished hammering a wedge between them. 'Didn't Cal tell you what happened last time? About his obsession with Proust? About being officially warned to lay off the guy? About him then ignoring that directive and finding himself being taken off the case? Hasn't he told you any of this?'

The answer, of course, is no. But LeBlanc can't admit to that without also admitting that his partnership with Doyle isn't all that it's supposed to be. So he claims the Fifth.

Cesario aims his weapons at Doyle again. 'Jesus, Cal. I don't know if I'll ever understand you. I get given this squad hearing all kinds of negative things about you, and most of the time you prove to me they're unfounded. Then you go and do something stupid like this, and all my doubts come jumping back again. When are you going to start thinking about the consequences of your actions?'

'I'll bear it in mind, Lou,' says Doyle. He gets up from his seat.

Big mistake.

'*Sit down, Detective! I am not done with you.*'

Doyle sits again. Thinks, This is not going well.

There is a moment's silence while they wait for the echoes of Cesario's roar to die away. Doyle realizes they must have heard it out in the squadroom. Schneider is probably having the time of his life.

Says Cesario, 'Tell me what happened when you went to see Proust this afternoon.'

Doyle shrugs. 'I asked him some questions. He answered them. We left.'

'That's all? No pressure tactics? No need to twist his arm a little to refresh his memory?'

'Why? What does Proust say?'

'He says you frightened the living daylights out of him. He says he doesn't want to go into detail or put a complaint on record, but you came on real strong with him. Any truth in that? You think maybe you overstepped the mark?'

Before Doyle can answer, LeBlanc pipes up. 'Proust got a little overexcited, Lou. His behavior became threatening. At one point we had to restrain him physically. My opinion, we used minimum force.'

Cesario looks at LeBlanc in surprise. Doyle feels a little surprised too, given the ankle-high rating he must now have in LeBlanc's eyes.

Cesario addresses Doyle again. 'You got a good partner there, Cal. Treat him like one. Show him what a good cop you can be when you want to.'

To Doyle it sounds like the sermon is over, but after what happened last time he thinks he should check.

'We done here?'

The way Cesario looks at him makes Doyle realize his response was perhaps a little curt. Maybe a more deferential 'Yes, sir' would have been better. Never ask me to be a diplomat, he thinks.

'Not quite,' says Cesario, as though feeling the need to punish Doyle for his impudence. 'I want to make things clear before you go. From now on, Proust is off-limits, understand?'

'What? That's crazy. He's a suspect, Lou. No, scratch that.

He is *the* suspect. How am I supposed to work this case if you tie my hands like this?'

'You bring me something concrete to implicate him in all this, then maybe I'll change my mind. Until then, you back off. If we need to talk to this guy, then fine, Tommy does it. Without you present. I'm not giving this guy a chance to sue my ass for ignoring his complaint. And if you hassle him again, I'll take you off the case and glue you to a desk for the rest of your days. Do you get what I'm saying to you, Cal?'

Doyle doesn't answer. He can't say no, and he doesn't want to give Cesario the satisfaction of hearing him acquiesce.

Cesario says, 'Now get out of my sight, the pair of you. Run this like you would run any other case, preferably without letting prejudice cloud your judgment.'

Doyle stands up and heads for the door. LeBlanc is right behind him. As soon as they get back into the squadroom, LeBlanc starts up.

'Cal, you got a few minutes for me? We need to talk.'

Doyle doesn't want to talk. After the verbal assassination he's just been through in Cesario's office, talking is the last thing on his agenda. He heads toward where his coat is hanging on a rack, still drying off.

'Cal, are you listening to me? I said we need to discuss this.'

Doyle glances at Schneider, who has tipped his chair back on two legs. His arms are behind his head and there's a stupid smirk on his ugly mug. Doyle wishes like hell for those chair legs to snap.

He grabs his coat and starts to put it on as he heads out the door.

LeBlanc calls after him. 'Where the hell are you going? Why are you doing this, man?'

And then Doyle stops listening. He doesn't want to debate and he doesn't want to listen.

He just wants to act.

Proust is at work when Doyle gets there. A shirtless guy is having a mermaid tattooed on his upper arm. He's big, but it's mostly flab. Doyle walks across the room and casts his shadow over Proust.

'We need to talk. In private.'

The bare-chested client nudges Doyle's arm with the back of his hand.

'Hey, asshole. We're busy. Come back another time.'

Doyle gives the man his best look of disdain, then turns again to Proust.

'Let's go out back.'

Another nudge, harder this time. 'You deaf or just stupid? I said come back later.'

Doyle looks at the man again. 'You touch me one more time and I'll break every finger on your hand. And then I'm gonna take that tattoo gun and write "Nil by Mouth" across your forehead. Might help you shift some of that ugly fat you're carrying.'

'Right, that's it! You fucking piece of shit.'

Incensed, the man starts to shift his bulk. His pallid flesh quivers as he struggles to raise himself from the reclined chair.

Doyle puts his left hand around the man's throat and forces him back into the chair. His right hand whips out his detective shield and suspends it two inches in front of the man's nose.

'Don't get yourself so worked up, fatso. You'll give yourself a heart attack. At the very least you'll get your ass kicked before I throw you in the slammer.'

'You didn't say you was a cop.'

'Yeah, well, think of it as a test of your social skills. You got a failing grade, by the way. Now do you wanna stay and appeal the decision, or do you wanna go get a coffee for ten minutes while I talk to Michelangelo here?'

'I, uhm, I could do with a beer.'

'Sure you could. There's a good bar on the corner of this block. They don't even have an anti-obesity policy. Take your time.'

Doyle releases his grip, then helps the man out of the chair. He waits until the man has dressed and left the building before he turns his burning gaze on Proust.

Proust backs away a little, cowering just as he did on their previous encounter.

'Cut the act, Stanley. There's nobody else here to see it.'

'What act? I'm not acting, man. You're here to scare me. You wanna hurt me.'

'I'm not here to hurt you. Not this time. I'm here to warn you.'

'W–warn me about what?'

'It's not gonna work, Stan. Calling up my boss. Putting in complaints about me. All you've done is made me mad. It ain't gonna stop me coming after you. In fact, you've just started a whole new ball game. From now on, I only come here alone. No partner to see what I might do to you. And that way, I can deny I was ever here. You haven't made yourself safe, Stan. You've made it a hundred times worse for yourself. Think about that before you try to jam me up again.'

Proust shrinks back against the counter. 'I don't understand. Why are you doing this to me? I didn't touch those girls. I never even met them. You've got it all wrong about me.'

Doyle steps forward. Gets right in Proust's face. So close he can smell the onions he must have had on his sandwich.

'It's just you and me now, Stanley. Nobody can save you. Start being afraid.'

Doyle stands there for a while. Allowing time for this moment, this threat, this promise, to burn itself into Proust's consciousness.

When he finally turns and leaves, he feels himself trembling. He runs through the rain and gets into the car. He looks at his hands. They're shaking, and he has to grip the steering wheel tightly to stop them.

He wonders what he's becoming.

SEVEN

Why won't they listen?

He's right. About Proust. But nobody will listen. Just as nobody listened last time either. Jesus, what is wrong with these people?

The first forty-eight hours after a killing are crucial to the solving of the case. If you get nowhere in that time, chances are you'll get nowhere period. Over half of that time has already elapsed. Try as he might to stay calm and allow the wheels of the investigation to grind on, Doyle can't suppress the feeling that the Department is giving Proust space to slip out of the net. Ordering Doyle to back off is the exact opposite of what they should be doing, and it frustrates him that he doesn't know a way to make them reconsider.

In his uptight state, he pulls into the parking space too quickly. Has to slam on the brakes to stop the vehicle from jumping the curb and mangling a street lamp. He feels his blood boiling in his veins as he gets out of the car. When the rain hits his skin he expects it to sizzle and burn off as steam.

And that's another thing: this damned rain. When will it ease off? Maybe if it could give these other cops a chance to think in peace and quiet, they'd realize he needs to be listened to.

He ducks his head and jogs into the station house, sick of

being constantly wet. He gets a nod from a uniform. He ignores it. The desk sergeant mutters something to him. He ignores that too. If it's something trivial, then he doesn't need to know; if it's something important, he doesn't want to be troubled by it. He's got enough on his plate already.

He pounds up the stairs, heading for the squadroom. He's not sure what he'll do when he gets there. He is supposed to work the Megan Hamlyn case. That's his top priority. Except he can't work it the way he wants to work it, because nobody in this place wants to open their fucking ears and listen to what he has to say.

On the stairs he bumps into LeBlanc coming the other way. LeBlanc puts an arm out, gesturing for him to hold up.

'Hey, Cal. Where'd you get to?'

Doyle keeps moving. 'Not now, Tommy.'

LeBlanc puts a hand on Doyle's arm, not knowing that another man has just been threatened with having his fingers broken for doing a similar thing.

'Cal, we need to talk about this.'

'No. We don't.'

He pulls away from LeBlanc's grasp and continues up the stairs.

'Damn it,' says LeBlanc. 'I saved your ass with the boss today. I coulda told him what you did to Proust, but I didn't. You know why? Because you're my partner. Like it or not, we're partners on this case. So how about you start treating me like one?'

Doyle pauses on the stairs, his back to LeBlanc. Thinking about the preconceptions. LeBlanc's, but maybe his own too.

Slowly, he turns. 'You wanna know what it's about? I'll show you.'

He continues up to the second floor, LeBlanc almost scraping his heels. He looks into an office normally occupied by one of the PAAs – the Police Administrative Aides – and finds it empty.

'In there,' he says to LeBlanc. 'I'll be right back.'

While the bemused LeBlanc enters the office, Doyle continues down the hall and into the squadroom. Ignoring the stares from Schneider, he goes to his desk, grabs one of the folders from its surface, then retraces his steps to join LeBlanc. In the office, he closes the door behind him.

LeBlanc says, 'What's with all the cloak-and-dagger stuff?'

Doyle doesn't respond. He sits at the PAA's desk, opens up the folder, and takes out a DVD. He presses a button on the computer in front of him. A tongue of black plastic slides out, and Doyle feeds it the disk and watches it swallow.

LeBlanc leans forward to get a better look at the screen. 'What is this, Cal?'

Doyle mouse-clicks the play button. 'Watch.'

The movie starts up. There are no opening credits. We go straight into the action, and boy, does it grab you by the throat. This is one to make you pause with the handful of popcorn on its way to your mouth.

Opening scene – what looks like a basement. Sparsely furnished. Plaster peeling off the walls. No carpet on the floor. In the center of the room, a crude platform fashioned from two wooden doors set atop a number of plastic crates. On the platform, a naked girl, face down. She is anchored to this dais with ropes on her wrists and ankles. There is no sound to this movie, but it is clear that the girl is crying, that she is in agony. Her body carries marks all over it. It's hard to tell what they are or what caused them. Here and there, rivulets of blood trickle down her skin.

A man steps into view. He is visible only from the waist down, and it seems that he is wearing only tight leather shorts, which would be comical if the subject matter were not so serious. His legs are stout and hairy. And he is carrying a bullwhip.

And it is only seconds later that he is raising his arm out of view and bringing that whip down again. Slicing it through the air. Firing its tip at supersonic speed into the flesh of the young woman. There is no eroticism here. No soft spanking with a leather thong. This is sheer sadism, acted out on an unwilling participant. A victim, no less. When the tip of this whip strikes, it does so with ferocity. It opens up her flesh. It gouges out chunks. Her face pleads for mercy. She receives none.

Fade to black. No end credits. See you at the Oscars.

Except that this isn't acting. This ain't Tinseltown. Doyle knows it, and he can tell that LeBlanc knows it too.

'Jesus,' says LeBlanc. 'What the fuck was that?'

'A home movie. Or at least part of one. It was found on the hard drive of a scumbag who got arrested on porn charges. He said he found it on the Internet.'

'Okaaay,' says LeBlanc. 'And this is relevant how?'

Doyle grabs the mouse and manipulates a slider on the screen to rewind the video a few frames. He's not good with computers, but this he can manage. He's done it enough times. He must have studied every frame of this clip.

'Tell me what you see.'

LeBlanc leans forward again and pushes his spectacles up his nose.

'A guy. A girl. The guy is torturing the girl. That's it. Cecil B. DeMille it ain't.'

'Closer. The detail.'

A pause while Doyle waits for LeBlanc to get it. And then he gets it.

'Tattoos. On the girl and the man. Is that it? The tattoos?'

On the frozen image, a blotch of color is just visible on the girl's shoulder. It's almost lost amongst the wounds there. The man's tattoo, on the back of his lower leg, is more obvious. For one thing, it's darker, but on this grainy picture it's still just a blob.

LeBlanc says, 'I don't get it. That's not Megan Hamlyn, and that's not Proust. They're just two people with tattoos. What are you telling me here, Cal?'

Doyle swivels the chair to face LeBlanc. 'Six months before I came to the Eighth, I caught a homicide. A floater in the Hudson.'

He opens up the folder, extracts a large photograph and passes it to LeBlanc. The photo shows the body of a young woman. She is naked. Her body is bloated and mottled, but the numerous injuries it carries are still evident. And, on her shoulder, what looks like a tattoo.

LeBlanc studies the picture, then switches his gaze back and forth between it and the computer screen.

'Looks like her.'

'It *is* her,' says Doyle. 'The wounds and the position of the tattoo match up exactly. And before you ask, that's not just my opinion. It's also the opinion of a Medical Examiner and an expert in image-comparison techniques.'

'Okay, so it's the same girl. Who is she?'

'Name's Alyssa Palmer. She disappeared just over a week before she turned up in the river. She was seventeen. Her friends told me she was obsessed with the idea of getting a tattoo, but that her parents wouldn't let her have one until she was old enough. The day before she went missing she told her best pal that she thought she'd found someone who would do the tattoo for her.'

LeBlanc looks up. 'And she named Proust?'

Doyle doesn't answer, because his answer isn't the one he wishes he could give.

He slides another photograph from the folder and hands it over. 'This is a close-up of the tattoo.'

LeBlanc studies it. It's a red-winged butterfly, hovering over a flower. Delicate curling fronds from the plant intertwine above the insect.

'Nice,' says LeBlanc. 'You trace it to Proust?'

Again, another negative that Doyle doesn't want to voice. 'We talked to every tattoo artist in the city. A couple of them said it looked like it could be Proust's work.'

LeBlanc nods. Says, 'Uh-huh.' Makes it pretty damn obvious that he doesn't think it's a lot to go on. Which, Doyle has to admit, it isn't.

'And the other tattoo? The one on the guy's leg?'

Doyle gives him the next photograph in the sequence. 'Best we could get.'

It's a magnified view of the guy's calf. Unlike blow-ups you see done in TV programs, which magically supply absent detail, this one is highly pixelated. The tattoo consists of a black symbol containing a blurred white smudge at its center.

'That's the ace of spades,' says LeBlanc. He taps the photograph. 'What's this in the middle?'

'We think it could be a skull and crossbones,' says Doyle, using a plural rather than the more accurate singular pronoun. He watches as LeBlanc squints at the image and makes no attempt to confirm that he sees the piratical symbol too. Doyle wants to snatch the picture back from him and tell him to forget it if that's going to be his attitude.

Then LeBlanc compounds his error. 'What makes you think that?'

'Because . . .' Doyle begins in a louder than necessary voice. He softens it again. Tries to find some patience for the inexperienced young cop. 'Because Proust has done a number of tattoos of the ace of spades with a skull and crossbones in the middle. They're in his books. Okay?'

He glares at LeBlanc, daring him to make further challenges. Keeping suppressed deep within him his knowledge that there is a lot to challenge.

Heedless of the danger, LeBlanc presses on. 'Hold up. What am I missing here? You have one tattoo that a coupla people say *could* have been put there by Proust. And you have this other tattoo that might possibly be similar to some others that Proust has done. And this is why you like Proust for two murders?'

And now Doyle does snatch the photograph back. He grabs it back so fast he hopes he gives LeBlanc a paper cut.

'No. Did you hear me say this was everything?'

'So, then, what? You pin some forensic evidence on him? Maybe locate the basement in the video?'

None of the above, thinks Doyle. Oh, what he would give for something as concrete as that. And oh, how lame it sounds when his answer leaves his lips:

'I talked to the guy.'

LeBlanc moves quickly on to his next question, but Doyle sees the irritating flash of disbelief on his face before he does.

'Proust? What did he say?'

'He denied everything.'

Thinks Doyle, You just go ahead and say, 'Okaaay,' in that long, doubting way again.

'Ah,' says LeBlanc. Which is almost as bad. 'But you caught him out on something. Right?'

Now he's being patronizing, thinks Doyle. Throwing me a line like that.

'I told you. I talked to him. I spent hours with that son-ofabitch. He did it. I could smell it on him. He killed Alyssa Palmer. And now he's killed Megan Hamlyn.'

Which, to Doyle, should be an end to it. LeBlanc should shut up now and bow to the wisdom of his older, more experienced partner, and leave it at that.

But he doesn't.

'What exactly did Proust do or say? How do you know all this about him?'

Doyle stuffs the photographs back into his folder, then presses the eject button to retrieve his DVD. He gets the computer's tongue again, the disk still sitting there like a pill it refuses to take.

'He didn't *exactly* do or say anything. It's a feeling, Tommy. I know this guy. I know what he is. I know what he did.'

LeBlanc thinks about this for a moment. 'We can't work on hunches, Cal. We need something more.'

Doyle stands up. 'For fuck's sake, do you think I don't know that? I'm sick of everyone in this damn squad telling me how to work this case. You do what you want, Tommy. I'm going after Proust.'

LeBlanc gets up. 'Cal, I didn't mean—'

But Doyle is already out the door. LeBlanc wanted an explanation, and now he's got it. If he doesn't like it, he can shove it.

Doyle is getting used to working alone. Even when he has a partner.

EIGHT

This should be an oasis of calm. Here, at home. With his wife. In their beautiful apartment in the Upper West Side.

But it isn't. He knows how tense he is. Everything he says or does seems loaded with pent-up energy. Earlier, when he tripped on the corner of a rug, he felt compelled to kick the damn thing across the room. And when he went to sit at the table and found that the leg of his chair was caught up in one of the other chairs, he almost turned the whole set of furniture upside down in an effort to get himself seated.

He wonders if he's going through a mid-life crisis. If he is, then he's going to have a short life. It should be way too early for one of those.

Maybe he's hormonal. A problem with his thyroid or whatever. It's playing havoc with his system. Yeah, that's it. He's ill. He can't be blamed for the way he's been acting lately. People need to be more understanding.

He's not ill.

He's obsessed. Which, he realizes, could also be classed as a form of illness. Except that he's obsessed for the right reasons. His obsession is justifiable. He's not some kind of irrational stalker. He just wants to put a killer behind bars. Is that so weird?

Rachel comes out of the kitchen, carrying his meal in an oven mitt. Note to self, he thinks: don't touch the plate.

She sets it down in front of him. Some kind of pink fish. He has a love-hate relationship with fish. He loves the taste, but hates picking out the bones. He can't bear to have even those flimsy little bones in his mouth. Rachel never seems to notice them. She just swallows them. Doyle doesn't understand how she can do that.

He turns the plate.

'Shit!'

'It's hot,' says Rachel. She holds up the oven mitt for emphasis.

So much for my fucking mental notepad, he thinks. When was that – all of five seconds ago? The fish on this plate probably had a better memory than mine.

He picks up his knife and fork. It's supposed to be a fillet. Maybe it won't have bones.

Rachel removes the mitt and sits at the table. She tucks some wisps of her dark hair behind her ears, then puts her chin on her hand and waits for him to start eating.

He cuts into the fish. Pulls a piece away. Sees the bones spring into view like the prickles of an agitated hedgehog.

He wants to sigh.

'How's the case going?' asks Rachel.

He's told her about it. On the phone this afternoon. He let her know he would be home late, and he let her know the reason. Didn't give her all the details, though. Nothing about Proust, for example.

'Okay,' he says. Which is giving her nothing. It's a shitty response. He knows it, and yet he can't help it.

He leaves the fish alone and takes up a forkful of potato instead.

'Did you identify the girl?'

He nods while he chews. 'Yeah. Her name was Megan Hamlyn. She lived out in Queens. She was only sixteen.'

He thinks, There, see? You *can* do it. You *can* have a proper conversation.

'Oh, God,' says Rachel. 'Sixteen. That's so young.'

She lapses into silence for a while as she contemplates this. Then: 'You got anything to go on?'

'A few things. We'll get him.'

She waits for more. Doesn't get it.

'Is that just you giving yourself a pep talk, or do you actually have something concrete?'

He ventures another assault on the fish. Tries teasing out those menacing white barbs. He just knows he's not going to get them all. One of the little bastards always manages to bury itself deep. It'll lurk, just waiting for its chance to jump out and impale itself in his cheek or, even worse, lodge in his throat. Why do fish need so many damn bones anyway?

'We're close,' he says.

'Well, how close? You know who did this? You know where they are? What?'

The answers are in the affirmative. Yes, he knows who did this, and yes, he knows where he is. But if he tells Rachel what he knows, then she'll go all negative on him. She'll tell him to back off. She'll remind him of how it went last time. And he can do without that right now.

'Rachel, can we change the subject, please?'

He waits for her to snap at him, which she has every right to do. But she doesn't snap. She sits there, more calmly and patiently than he deserves.

'How's the fish?' she asks, which is certainly a change of

subject. Makes him feel guilty, though. He knows she really wants to talk about big, weighty matters, but he has diluted her conversation to the point of dealing with trivia.

'Bony,' he says, and then wonders if he has a death wish. He should have said the fish was fine, even though it isn't. Instead, he has to go and mix it up. That's the sort of self-destructive mood he's in today.

Rachel leans across and peers at his dinner. 'They're not bones.'

He jabs at his food with his fork. 'Look.'

'What, those puny little things? You make it sound like the dinosaur exhibit in the Natural History Museum. You won't even notice them.'

He begs to differ. He already *has* noticed them. And if he allows them into his mouth he will notice them even more. But for once he makes the right decision and keeps his objections to himself. Time for another change of topic. Who'd have thought a fish dinner could be the cause of such friction? Bones of contention, if you will.

'How's Amy?'

'Oh, she's all right.'

Even in his distracted state of mind, Rachel's tone is not lost on him. It's a tone that says, *Well, actually, she's not so great.*

'Something happen today?'

'Yeah. I yelled at her.'

Her voice is tinged with regret, and Doyle blinks in surprise. Rachel almost never loses her temper with Amy.

'You yelled at her? Why?'

'She had some things. In her schoolbag. Things that don't belong to her.'

'What kind of things?'

'Pens, erasers, rulers – that kind of thing. I think they belong to the school.'

'Did you ask her about them?'

'Of course I did. I sat her down and I asked her. I gave her every opportunity to explain how they got there.'

'And what did she say?'

'She said she didn't know they were even in her bag. Said she'd never seen them before.'

'Okay, so maybe somebody else put them there.'

Rachel shakes her head. 'No. She wasn't telling the truth, Cal. Amy's a terrible liar.'

Doyle puts down his fork. 'Rachel, have you heard yourself? You're calling our daughter a liar and a thief. How can you say such—'

'I didn't say she was a thief. I said she knows more about this than she's saying. And I'd like you to back me up on this, please.'

'Back you up how?'

'By talking to her. By asking her how she got hold of that stuff.'

'She's seven years old, Rachel. She's not a criminal master-mind. She doesn't need me giving her the third degree over some little mistake she's made.'

'She's old enough to know right from wrong, Cal. And when she gets confused over that, it's up to us to set her straight.'

'Okay, tell you what – why don't I haul her into the station house and take her fingerprints and stick her in the cells? You think that'll teach her?'

Rachel slumps back in her chair, her mouth working like she doesn't know what sounds to make with it next.

'Why are you being like this? I'm asking you to have a quiet word with her. Father to daughter. It doesn't have to be a confrontation. I just want you to—'

'There's no evidence, Rachel. She says she's done nothing wrong, so I think we should believe her. I can't go accusing her just because—'

He stops then. Stops because he realizes things are getting all jumbled up in his head. He's talking to Rachel about Amy, but in his mind he's working on the murder case. He's saying things that Rachel would probably say to him if he told her how he was going after Proust. That's how much of a hold Proust has on him. He knows things won't be normal again until he nails that sonofabitch.

He pushes his chair back and stands up. 'I gotta go out.'

Rachel stares at him. 'What do you mean? Why do you need to go out all of a sudden?'

'I just do. Something I forgot to do on the case.'

'And now it comes to you? Right in the middle of your dinner? Right when we're having a conversation about something important like this?'

'I won't be long,' he says.

He starts to head out of the room. Behind him he hears Rachel muttering something about how he should eat more fish because it might do his stupid brain some good.

The rain has subsided to a light drizzle. Doyle is glad, because it will make it easier to see. To make doubly sure, he winds down the window of his car. Then he kills the engine. Then he waits.

It's not the same, he tells himself. Proust and Amy. Two totally different kettles of fish – there we go with the fish again. Amy has made an innocent mistake of some kind. No big deal. It'll be cleared up in no time.

Proust, on the other hand . . .

See, you had to be there. You had to be the one who spent hours talking to Proust. Getting into his head. Getting to know how his mind works. Getting to understand how an apparently normal guy could commit such a heinous act. Explaining this to other people doesn't cut it. You can tell people what you believe as many times as you like, but they're never going to be convinced. Not without further proof.

And, if he's to be honest, why should they accept his word? Would he act any differently if it were another cop laying down conclusions like this?

But they weren't there. They didn't see.

They didn't see the bloated naked body of Alyssa Palmer, draped over the river-washed rocks below the Henry Hudson Parkway. They didn't see the heart-splitting expressions on the faces of Alyssa's parents when he had to inform them that their daughter had been found. Dead. Tortured. Raped. And they didn't see the coldness in Proust's eyes when confronted with these facts, these images. When Proust looked down at the photo of Alyssa, there was no recoil – not even a grimace or an out-breath of sorrow. Doyle knew then that this was his man.

But how do you explain all that to someone? How do you tell them it was all there, in the man's eyes, his body language, his lack of emotion? How do you convince them without more concrete evidence?

They looked for it. Of course they looked. They must have talked to every tattoo artist in the city. Only one of them felt right, and that was Stanley Proust. An artist extraordinaire, all right. But no matter how hard they looked, they found nothing to prove Alyssa had ever visited Proust. They found nothing to suggest that Proust was into the S&M scene. They found nothing to substantiate Doyle's opinion that this seemingly mild-mannered individual was in fact a deranged homicidal maniac.

The most disturbing and yet exhilarating piece of evidence that landed in their laps was the Internet video. But even that fizzled into nothing. Other than the presence of some blurry tattoos, it provided no connection to Proust. They never even located the basement in which it was filmed.

But it did play a more unexpected role.

Doyle remembers it vividly. He'd pushed and pushed at Proust, but had gotten nowhere. Despite being warned by his superiors to cool it with Proust, he continued to hammer on the man's consciousness.

'Take a look, Stan. Look at the photos. Look at what you did.'

'I didn't do nothing. That wasn't me. I didn't make that video.'

And then the pause. The long pause while Doyle and Proust stared at each other, the truth suspended between them.

'Who said anything about a video, Stan? And who suggested you were the one who made it?'

He tried to backtrack then, of course.

'You did. You said these were stills taken from a video.'

'No, Stan. I never said that. Why would you think it was a video?'

'Well, somebody said it. One of the other cops, maybe.'

'No, Stan. That came from you. You just put yourself behind the camera too.'

'No, I . . . you're putting words in my mouth. You're twisting things. I never meant . . .'

'You were there, weren't you, Stan? You did things to this girl. Maybe not all of it, but some of it. Tell me, Stan.'

'No. NO!'

That was the closest he got. Proust's biggest slip. Doyle

pursued it, of course. As doggedly as he could. But Proust got a lot more tight-lipped after that. Stuck to his story that somebody must have mentioned a video to him.

And he walked. To Doyle's fury, Proust walked away a free man.

He wonders now why he didn't mention this episode to LeBlanc, but doesn't have to wait long for the answer to come to him.

He was frightened.

He was scared that LeBlanc, cynical young pup that he is, would have ripped any meaningful content of that conversation to shreds. He would have refused to interpret it as the undeniable proof of Proust's guilt that it so obviously is.

Because it *is* proof, thinks Doyle. You don't understand, Tommy, because you weren't there. None of you understands.

The Alyssa Palmer case would have continued to haunt Doyle anyway, but fate decided to lend her ghost a helping hand. Following the fireworks surrounding the death in service of his female partner, Doyle transferred to the Eighth Precinct. For which the station house is situated just a few blocks from Proust's place. Doyle has driven or walked past it countless times since then, and every time the sight of it has taunted him. Each time, it reminds him of how he failed the Palmers.

And now the gods have decided to ratchet up Doyle's torment further by making him relive the nightmare all over again. The circumstances of Megan Hamlyn's case are almost identical to those in the Palmer case. The young dead teenage girl. The grief-stricken parents. The untouchable Mr Proust.

Identical except for one thing, thinks Doyle. This time the outcome will be different. This time, Stanley, you pay for what you did.

He looks out of the half-open car window. Cool rain spits into his face as his eyes read and re-read the sign.

Skinterest.

An interest in skin. An interest in flesh. You got that all right, Stan. Young, innocent skin that you put your mark on. A permanent mark. You mark them for life. You mark them for death.

Movement catches his eye. From inside the shop. A huge shadow, gradually shrinking as its owner gets closer to the door. And Doyle is parked right in front of that door.

The shadow is replaced by solidity. The scrawny frame of Stanley Proust, standing behind the glass panel.

Doyle hears a key being inserted and turned, then the sound of bolts being drawn.

That's when Doyle switches on the interior light of his car.

Proust stops moving for a second. Then Doyle sees him press his nose against the rain-spotted panel as he peers out.

Doyle doesn't do a thing. Just sits there and stares back. Lets Proust know that this is how it's going to be from now on. Lets him know that this is what he's prepared to do, for as long as it takes. He will stay on Proust's back until the man can take the weight no more and he buckles. He will break him. He will do this for Alyssa Palmer and for Megan Hamlyn and for their families. He promises all this in the intense stare that he sends Proust's way.

Slowly, with trepidation, Proust reaches up and lowers the roller blind into position.

NINE

'I wasn't trying to give you grief, Cal. Okay? I want you to know that.'

Doyle has only just sat down at his desk. Hasn't even touched his first coffee of the day yet, and already LeBlanc is jabbering in his ear. Which would be okay if it was something valuable, like letting Doyle know he's just managed to nail Proust with a murder rap. This touchy-feely stuff he can do without right now.

'Forget it, Tommy.'

LeBlanc looks around the squadroom, as if checking for eavesdroppers, even though nobody else on their shift has arrived yet.

'I don't want to forget it. I want this to work between us. If you think Proust has something to do with this, then that's good enough for me.'

Doyle puts down his coffee mug. 'Meaning what?'

'Meaning that . . . I'll talk to him.'

'You'll talk to Proust?'

'Yeah. Sure. If you think he's involved. But even if he isn't, maybe he can give me something useful on the tattoos. Like maybe suggest some other artists I could talk to.'

Doyle wants to tell LeBlanc he's wasting his time. He will

get nothing from Proust. In fact, Proust will have LeBlanc eating out of his hand, he's that clever.

Well, let him find out for himself.

'Yeah, maybe. You do that, Tommy.'

LeBlanc nods, but still lingers at Doyle's shoulder.

''Course, I can't take you with me. Much as I'd like to. You heard what the boss said.'

'I heard him. Don't worry about me. You go ahead. Knock yourself out.'

Tommy nods some more, and seems to Doyle to be relieved at having cleared the air like this.

'What about you? What are you going to do this morning?'

'Me? I thought I'd drive over to Queens and talk to the Hamlyns again.'

Yet more nodding. LeBlanc no doubt even more relieved that Doyle is not planning to get into trouble. Seemingly satisfied, LeBlanc sidles back to his own desk.

A half-hour later, Doyle leaves the station house and gets into his car. As he said to LeBlanc, he's off to see the Hamlyns.

Via a quick stop-off at Proust's place.

He starts the car up and pulls his sedan out into the traffic of East Seventh Street.

He doesn't see the black Dodge SUV as it also pulls out and starts to follow him.

'Hi, Stan.'

Proust continues with the job of cleaning his counter. He sprays some fluid onto it, then wipes it down with a cloth.

'What's the matter, Stan?' says Doyle. 'Not speaking to me today?'

Proust says nothing. He just carries on with his task. Spray and wipe, spray and wipe.

Doyle moves away from the door and crosses the room. He wipes a finger along the counter and looks at it.

'Seems pretty clean to me. Don't you think?'

Proust maintains his silence. He sprays the area of the counter that Doyle has just touched, then rubs it vigorously with the cloth.

Doyle cups a hand behind his ear. 'What was that, Stan? I don't think I heard you.'

Proust doesn't look up, but he does find his voice. 'Hygiene is important in my work. Everything has to be ultra-clean.'

'Ultra-clean, huh? I see. Ultra-clean. No fingermarks. No bodily fluids. No DNA of any kind. You musta got pretty good at that over time.'

'I don't know what you mean.'

'Yeah, you do. I'm talking about contamination, Stan. Making sure you don't leave anything behind. Like you were never there.'

Proust goes quiet again, so Doyle picks up where he left off.

'Except that's not totally true, is it, Stan? You do leave a mark. A permanent mark. A piece of yourself that will never disappear.'

Doyle takes a photograph from his inside pocket and slides it under Proust's nose. It's a picture of Megan Hamlyn's detached pelvic section.

'Oh, Jesus Christ,' says Proust. He drops the cloth and puts his hand to his mouth.

'Yeah, yeah. Get the amateur dramatics outta the way, Stan. It's not like this is news to you. You've seen it before.'

Proust turns his head and closes his eyes. 'Take it away, man. Please. I think I'm gonna be sick.'

'Shut up, Stan, and look at the picture.'

Proust shakes his head, his hand still clamped over his mouth.

Doyle reaches out and grabs hold of Proust's hair. Ignoring the yells, he twists Proust's head and forces it back down to the photograph.

'What do you see?'

'Part of a body. Please, Detective, stop.'

'What else? On the body?'

'A . . . a tattoo.'

With his free hand, Doyle reaches into his pocket again and takes out another photograph. He drops it on top of the first. It shows the blow-up of the tattoo.

'Yeah. This tattoo. Recognize it, Stan?'

'N–no. I didn't do that. It's not my work.'

'It's a damn good angel, Stan. I bet there aren't many artists in this city can do angels as good as that. You could, though, couldn't you?'

'It's not my work.'

'That's what you said about the butterfly on Alyssa Palmer. Other people disagreed. They said it looked very much like your work.'

'They were wrong. Look through my books. There's nothing like either of those in there.'

''Course not. You're not stupid. Why would you do a tattoo that's exactly like any you did before? I bet you even changed your style a little, just so nobody could say it was definitely yours. But we know, don't we, Stan? You and me, we know what really happened.'

'Please, you're hurting me.'

Doyle realizes just how tight his grip has become. When he

removes his hand and opens his fingers, he sees it contains a number of Proust's hairs.

Proust straightens up. He touches a hand to the top of his head.

'You didn't have to do that. I told you. I don't know how many times I have to tell you before you'll believe me. I didn't hurt either of those girls. It wasn't me.'

'Say it as many times as you like. Don't make it true. You want me to start believing you, then start telling me what really happened with those girls. I want answers. The girls' families want answers. You wanna talk to them? You wanna tell them how you don't know anything? Maybe I should arrange that. You wouldn't believe how badly Megan's father would like to have a private little chat with you about his daughter.'

'You can't do that. You can't endanger me like that.'

'Answers, Stan. Until I get them, I stay in your life. See you later. I ain't sure what time yet. Don't wait up. It could be late the next time I show up here.'

When Doyle leaves, he slams the door shut behind him. The rain has started up again, and it's getting heavier.

'Shit!' he says, and steps onto the street.

Despite what he said to Proust, he's not sure how long he can keep this up. The anger and the frustration are eating him up inside. It's a question of who will break first, and he's not sure it will be Proust.

He thinks about this as he hurries along the block to where his car is parked.

It keeps him distracted from the man who comes up behind him and presses the muzzle of a gun into his spine.

★

'Don't make a scene. I haven't shot a cop in a while. I could do with the practice.'

The voice is deep and gruff and menacing. Doyle knows that any sudden move could carry the danger that his spine gets blasted in two, leaving him permanently paralyzed from the waist down. It would be a stupid, insane thing to do.

So he does it, knowing that it will be the last thing the man behind him will expect.

He whirls around, simultaneously chopping his arm into the gun hand of the man. The huge semi-automatic flies out of the man's grasp, while Doyle completes his maneuver with one of the most powerful punches it has ever been his satisfaction to deliver. The man pulls his head back just in time to avoid having it removed from his neck, but the blow still lands on his chin, sending him reeling backward across the sidewalk.

In that instant, Doyle is back in the boxing ring of his youth. Not long after he was dragged all the way from Ireland to the Bronx and started getting into scrapes with those who saw this pasty-faced kid with an impenetrable accent as an obvious target, his mother decided that the best substitute for his absent father to advise him how to deal with such matters was a boxing coach. Turned out Doyle was a natural. He got stronger, he got faster, and he learned technique. But most of all he learned not to fear his adversary, no matter how big or ferocious he might be.

He puts all that training to good use now. He doesn't know who this prick is. He just knows he wants to pound the crap out of him.

And so he goes after him. Doesn't pause to give the man a chance to recover. Doesn't even waste time trying to pull his own gun. That can wait until this piece of shit hits the ground.

He lands another punch. A good solid strike that bursts open the man's lip. He pulls back his left for an uppercut that should finish this . . .

Which is when something hard and heavy smacks into the side of Doyle's head.

He turns, sees another burly figure in front of him. It comes as something of a surprise. You don't normally have more than one opponent in the ring. Queensberry Rules and all that.

Doyle raises his defenses. Ignores the pain in his skull. Ignores the fact that he's now outnumbered by two to one.

Another blow, this time to the back of his head.

Make that three to one.

Doyle topples forward. He puts his arms out before he hits the ground, then remains there on his knees, trying to shake the dark swirling shapes out of his brain as the rain rolls over his back and down his arms.

He feels strong hands grip him and yank him to his feet. The two new attackers drag him back across the sidewalk and slam him against the side of his own car. They stay on either side of him, pinning him in position with his arms wide like a scarecrow. Doyle blinks. He sees the first guy come staggering toward him with murderous intent in his eyes. There's not much Doyle can do to prevent the beating he's about to receive.

Other than to kick the man in the nuts, that is.

He drives his foot with unerring accuracy into the man's groin. The force of the impact is magnified by the man's own forward momentum. He comes to an abrupt halt as though he has just run into a brick wall – which would probably be less painful – then clutches at his privates as he drops heavily to the ground. Doyle sees tears well in the man's eyes before he bows to touch his forehead to the wet sidewalk like a praying monk.

One down, two to go, thinks Doyle. Although he starts to

acknowledge that's a little ambitious when the other two gorillas start smashing their fists into his midriff. He hears his own breath being forced out of him as the men pummel his ribcage and pulverize his abdominal wall. And when they've run out of steam and they allow their captive to sink to his knees, Doyle notices that the first attacker is back on his feet. He approaches warily and shakily, and Doyle prepares himself for the coup de grâce.

Raising his face, Doyle looks at the man, who is still clutching at his groin and baring his bloodstained teeth in agony.

'That's a terrible Michael Jackson impression,' says Doyle.

Instead of a laugh, he gets a kick to the face. Doyle's head flies back and bangs into his car door. The dark shapes flood into his consciousness again. They try to merge together to form total blackness, and Doyle has to fight to keep them separated.

He feels himself being dragged again, his feet scraping the ground. He hears a car door being opened. The hands frisk him and take away his gun. Then he feels himself being lifted from the ground and tossed into a vehicle. More doors open. The three goons climb in. Doors slam shut.

Doyle does his best to raise himself into an upright position in his seat. As the car takes off, he looks through the rain-washed window. The streets are mostly empty. Everyone has fled from the rain. The ones who are still out there stare back at him from beneath their umbrellas. One person points. Doyle knows that it's unlikely they will report the incident.

Fighting the nausea that is starting to creep into his system, he starts to turn toward the man in the seat next to him. Stops turning when his temple touches the gun barrel leveled at him.

'Gimme an excuse, dickwad,' says the man.

'Where are we going?' Doyle asks. 'Did Proust hire you?'

'Who's Proust?' the man answers, and Doyle can tell he really doesn't know. It was a long shot anyhow. Why would Proust risk organizing something like this, right outside his own premises?

No, somebody far more dangerous than Proust is behind this.

TEN

The conversation isn't exactly sparkling during the journey. Doyle puts several questions, gets several stony glares in return. Oh, except that one time when one of the men tells him to shut the fuck up.

The guy sitting next to Doyle – the one who started all this with his offer of a free lumbar puncture – has white hair that contrasts starkly with the blood still dribbling from his lip. Not old-person white. Just white. And he's not an albino either. Doyle wonders whether to ask him if he's had an accident with bleach recently, but thinks better of it.

The other two bozos sitting up front are big and ugly and stupid. All muscle and no brain. It's a wonder either of them has enough intelligence and coordination to drive.

But somehow they manage to transport Doyle across town without incident. He keeps an eye on the changing streets as he tries to work out where they're taking him. The buildings around him become large brick-built warehouses, now mostly converted for use as bars and restaurants. Directly ahead, he sees the horizontal slash of the High Line – the elevated park that was once a section of the rail system. His stomach begins to churn.

His fears are confirmed when the SUV makes a sudden turn into a narrow alleyway. That's when the sun comes out, if only figuratively. In reality, the rain clouds continue to piss on everyone. But at least Doyle now knows exactly where he is. Knows exactly whom he has been brought to see. Knows exactly why he's here. Shoulda guessed, he thinks.

This is the meatpacking district – a tiny quadrilateral that once somehow managed to contain over two hundred slaughterhouses and packing plants. The smell of death is rarer here now.

But not always entirely absent.

Doyle has been here before. Last Christmas, to be precise. It wasn't fun then, and it won't be any more hilarious now.

When the men drag him out of the car and he stands on the slick cobblestones, looking up at the dark-brick building, it all comes flooding back. He remembers every detail of that night. He has never told anyone else about it. Not the police, not his wife.

He has never told them about how he shot and killed a man in this alley.

The man with the whiter-than-white hair steps up to a side door in the building, pulls out a bunch of keys, and opens up. His two associates take Doyle by the arms and lead him inside.

They move through a dim utility room, then through another door that opens into a vast empty chamber. Doyle has never seen it like this before. The last time he was here, the place was heaving with gyrating, sweaty bodies. The air was filled with a rhythmic pounding that shook his bones. Everyone stoned and happy and oblivious.

Now, though, the nightclub is as forlorn as an abandoned ship. The dance floor is deserted and marked with scuffs and numerous unidentifiable stains. The bar is unmanned, and black steel shutters have been lowered to keep out intruders. The walls are of bare brick – harsh and unwelcoming.

The footfalls of the men echo around the converted warehouse as Doyle is led over to an iron staircase. They start to climb, and the metallic clatter reverberates. They arrive at a walkway that runs the length of one wall. Doyle can still picture the half-naked female dancers that were positioned here on his last visit.

They don't stop here, but continue up another staircase to the next level. Doyle is guided along the walkway to a door at its center. Whitey knocks three times and waits.

'Maybe he's in the shower,' says Doyle. 'Or busy jerking off.'

The man to Doyle's left gives him a smack on the side of the head.

When the door is finally opened, another man-mountain comes into view. He's even bigger and uglier than the three who were sent to collect Doyle. The kind of guy who should be holding a peeled banana in one hand while picking his nose with the other.

'Would you like to buy some of our cookies?' Doyle asks him. 'Or chocolate brownies? You look like a chocolate brownie kind of guy.'

The man furrows his eyebrows slightly, like he's smelled something unpleasant in his cave. Then he looks at Whitey, and a spark of recognition fires in the recesses of his brain. He pulls the door wide open and steps aside.

The men hustle Doyle into the room, and he feels his breathing become faster. It's a large office. Wood floor and oak paneling on the walls. A massive oak desk in the center of the room. The air is cool – the building designed to prevent its carcasses from rotting when it was used to house animal corpses.

That time was way before Doyle's last visit here, but even in his own memory this is a place of violence and bloodshed. He will never forget what happened here in front of his eyes.

There are two things vying for Doyle's attention here. One is an object covered by a gray tarpaulin. It stands over to Doyle's left, like a life-size sculpture waiting to be unveiled. Doyle isn't sure what's under that tarpaulin, but he can make some guesses.

Then there's the man seated at the desk. He wears a dark suit, no tie, shirt open at the collar. He is broad of shoulder, broad of head, and carries a broad smile. His name is Lucas Bartok. Despite his smile, he is not a pleasant man. In fact, as Doyle knows only too well, Lucas Bartok is the stuff of nightmares.

'Doyle! Glad you decided to accept my invitation.'

Doyle shrugs, then jerks a thumb toward Whitey. 'How could I refuse, with your boy here asking so nice? For a while I thought he was gonna get down on one knee and propose.'

'Yeah, Sven's a charmer, all right.'

Doyle turns to the man with the snowy hair. 'Sven, huh? And what part of Ireland are you from? Maybe I know your folks.'

Sven just glares back at him, possibly because he's not sure if Doyle's question is serious or not. Possibly because he doesn't give a shit and just wants to tear Doyle's limbs off.

Bartok says, 'Looks like you didn't fall for him right away, though, Doyle. That's some whack you took to the cheek there.'

'I'll take your word for it. I can't look at it without a mirror. Makes my eyes go funny.'

Doyle waits for everyone to tense, and he gets it. He gets it because he just broke the cardinal rule. The one which says: Don't make fun of Lucas Bartok's eyes.

Lucas Bartok is cross-eyed. And we're not just talking a mild squint here. Not a slight drifting of a pupil. No, Bartok's eyes are so misaligned he can have staring competitions with himself.

Everyone in this room is aware of Bartok's condition, but none of the other men here will have dared mention it. Not ever. Otherwise they wouldn't be in this room. They'd be somewhere nobody would ever find them. Decomposing.

Doyle says it because he needs to show these people that he's not afraid. The jokes too. Humor to hide the fact that he's actually scared shitless. To hide the fact that, although he may seem unruffled on the surface, inside he's trembling. Because if there's one thing he knows not to do right now, it's to show weakness. Weakness could get him killed. But then again, so could pushing Bartok too far, because Bartok is certifiable. Doyle found that out last Christmas. He witnessed first-hand what this man is capable of when roused.

'Get him a chair,' Bartok orders, the amusement gone from his face now.

'I don't mind standing,' says Doyle. 'I don't plan to stay all that long.'

One of the men brings a heavy oak chair over, places it behind Doyle, then pushes down on his shoulders to make him sit.

'Long time no see,' says Bartok.

It seems to Doyle that it's a statement just crying out for a personal insult, but he decides it's prudent to hold back this time.

'Yeah, we should get together more often. Say, what are you doing next Thursday? I got tickets for Springsteen.'

'Yeah? I'm tempted. Let's wait and see if you're still alive then, huh, Doyle?'

'Why? What's my doctor been saying to you?'

'You got a clean bill of health. For now. Which is good news for me, because I got a job for you.'

'No thanks. I already got a job. I got a long list of scumbags to lock up.' Doyle selects one of Bartok's eyes at random and focuses on it. Letting him know that he's high on that list.

'Yeah, well you'll just have to fit this into your busy schedule. You don't get to say no to this one.'

'And if I say no anyway?'

Bartok glowers at him. At least, Doyle thinks it's aimed at him. Then Bartok slides open a drawer in his desk and takes something out of it. He holds it up and studies it, allowing Doyle to do the same.

It's an icepick.

It could be worse. It could be a meat hook, that being Lucas Bartok's implement of choice when he really wants to go to work on someone. But an icepick can be lethal enough. Go ask Trotsky.

'What does this say to you, Doyle?'

'You're expecting another ice age?'

Bartok's sigh is more of a snort. He gets up from his chair, still brandishing the pick. Doyle's eyes dart around the room as he tries to decide his best move. He's got a psychopathic killer in front of him, and a wall of muscle behind him. And they're armed too. The odds don't seem in his favor.

He relaxes only slightly when Bartok walks across the room, away from Doyle and over to the tarpaulin-covered object.

'You know what's under here?' says Bartok.

Doyle doesn't answer. He doesn't want to see what he's about to be shown, because he knows what it is.

When Bartok whips away the tarpaulin, Doyle's fears are confirmed. It's a man, sitting on a chair. To be precise, it's a man who is very naked and very dead. And, also to be precise, he's not exactly sitting; he's more kind of perched there. He's scrunched up into a ball, his knees pushed up to his abdomen and his arms folded across his chest. His fingers are stiffened into claws and his eyes are open. He stares accusingly at Doyle. As well he might.

The sight of this figure is disturbing enough, but there's something else that makes it all the more horrific.

The man is frozen solid.

Doyle can see the vapor tumbling down the frost-whitened flesh. He tells himself it doesn't matter to the victim. He's beyond feeling the cold. But still it doesn't sit right with Doyle. You freeze turkeys. You freeze fish – even those with bones in. You don't freeze humans. Even in the mortuary, bodies are usually stored a couple of degrees above freezing.

'What are you thinking, Doyle?'

Doyle can't tear his eyes away from that grotesque solidified corpse. Can't shake the feeling that it in turn is looking right into Doyle's soul. The icy glare chills him, and he wants to shiver.

'Pretty good, Lucas. Can you carve swans too? I prefer swans.'

Another quip. Bravado. Trying to prove how unmoved he is. But it lacks conviction. It sounds hollow, even to himself.

Bartok leans closer to the frozen head of the man. He seems morbidly fascinated, like a kid observing a bug after he's pulled the legs off it. Slowly he raises the icepick, then with the tip of it he gently taps one eyeball. The harsh clicking sound sets Doyle's teeth on edge.

'Now that's what I call a stiff. You remember this guy?'

Doyle swallows hard. Do I remember? Of course I remember. Sonny Rocca. He worked for the Bartok brothers, back when there were two of them. I killed him. I had no choice.

Even though Rocca was a career criminal – a failed Mafia

applicant who saw the Bartoks as the next best thing – Doyle kind of liked him. In life Rocca was good-looking and had a disarming smile, and Doyle almost felt sorry for him because of the treatment he received from the Bartoks. He never desired to see Rocca dead. But fate put the two of them in the alley outside, guns drawn, and it was clear only one of them was going to walk out of there alive. Doyle decided it had better be him.

All of which might have been fine had Doyle been here on official police business, fighting the good fight against the forces of evil. But he wasn't. He came here because he'd struck a deal with Lucas's brother, Kurt. A deal that effectively involved Doyle signing his soul over to that man, putting him forever in his service. Luckily for Doyle, but not so luckily for the Bartoks, Kurt wound up dead shortly before Rocca did. That put an end to the deal, but it didn't make Doyle's actions any more forgivable. He couldn't tell anyone that he'd consorted with known violent criminals, and he certainly couldn't reveal that he'd killed one of them.

He watches now as Bartok traces the point of the icepick down the face of Rocca. Onto his neck. Then down his torso. Doyle listens to the scraping sound it makes.

'See here?' says Bartok. 'Four holes, though not the best grouping in the world, Doyle. The slugs are still in there. Your bullets. From your gun. The cops would know that, wouldn't they? I mean, if I was to give them Rocca's body here and they took a look inside, they'd be able to figure out who did it, wouldn't they?'

Doyle has always dreaded this day. Last Christmas, Bartok told him he had Rocca's body. Told him, too, that one day he would come back to Doyle for a favor. As the months came and went, Doyle started to believe it was a bluff. He almost convinced himself that Bartok had dumped the corpse.

But no. Here it is. Bartok kept it. Put it on ice, literally. And now he's found a reason for using it as his bargaining chip. Doyle is no expert on ballistics, but he knows that discharged bullets bear rifling marks unique to the weapon that fired them. If the tech guys get to the bullets inside Rocca, it won't be long before Doyle is fingered as the owner of the gun involved. Especially if someone like Bartok helpfully points them in that direction.

'What do you want, Lucas?'

Bartok smiles again, and his grin seems even more malevolent below those unruly pupils of his.

'Anton Ruger.'

'Who's Anton Ruger?'

'Piece of shit used to work for me.'

'Used to?'

'Yeah. We didn't see eye to eye.'

Another cue for a wisecrack. Doyle is starting to think Bartok is acting the straight man on purpose, just to test him. He lets it ride. He's decided he wants to get out of here alive.

'What's your beef with him?'

'He's got something belongs to me.'

Bartok steps back to his desk. He flips open a folder that's lying there, then takes out a large photograph and hands it to Doyle. The photograph shows Lucas Bartok and his brother, Kurt, posed at a desk. Kurt is smiling into the camera. It's hard to tell what Lucas is looking at. He could be checking his watch for all Doyle knows.

'Ruger's got your brother?'

'You know, Doyle, that's some fucking mouth you got on

you. Cut the clown act before I shove this icepick up your ass, you get me?'

Doyle returns his gaze to the picture. 'All right, so what am I looking at?'

'Our hands, dick-brain. Look at our fucking hands.'

Doyle looks. The siblings are sporting matching rings. They're garishly huge, and shaped into a letter B. At the center of each curve of the letter is a large sparkling gem.

'Solid platinum,' says Bartok. 'And those rocks? Diamonds. We bought them for each other.'

Doyle can almost swear he hears Bartok's voice catch as he says this. Very touching, he thinks. Or at least it would be for normal brothers. With Bartok, this uncharacteristic display of sentimentality makes him seem even more deranged.

'Very nice. I'm lucky if I get socks.'

'That's because you're a nobody, Doyle.'

'Thanks for the confidence booster. And what do you want this nobody to do?'

'When Ruger left my employ, he didn't go empty-handed.'

'He took your ring?

'You catch on fast for a dumb mick cop.'

'You should put in an official police complaint. We take that kinda thing very seriously.'

'This here is my police complaint. And I know you're gonna take it deadly serious.'

'Meaning what? What is it you're asking me, Lucas?'

Bartok leans forward. He has the icepick out in front of him, its tip pointed directly at Doyle.

'What I'm *telling* you, Doyle, is that you're gonna kill this fucking piece of crap.'

Doyle stares at Bartok for several seconds.

'Okay,' he says.

Bartok flinches. 'Okay?'

'Sure. When do you want it done?'

Bartok's eyes rove even more uncontrollably than usual. His lip twitches. 'Are you fucking with me, Doyle?'

''Course I'm fucking with you, Lucas. I ain't killing nobody. Now are we done here? Because I got places to be.'

He sees the look of sheer evil on Bartok's face. The icepick is still aimed between Doyle's eyes. He braces himself. Waits for the onslaught. Tries to figure out how he's going to defend himself.

But Bartok smiles. Not the most comforting of expressions when it's worn on a man like this, but surprising nonetheless. Bartok steps away from Doyle. His smile develops into a low chuckle, then a deep-throated laugh. He looks across to his men, and they join in with the merriment. Nervously, it seems to Doyle.

Bartok continues walking away. He steps past the rigid contorted figure of Sonny Rocca.

And then he spins back to face Doyle. And as he turns, he raises his arm, the one carrying the icepick, and he lets out a huge angry roar and he brings that arm down again. Brings that icepick down. Sinks it handle-deep into Sonny Rocca's skull. Doyle hears the crunch of bone. He winces. The laughter stops. Somebody sucks air through their teeth. Bartok releases his grip, leaving the icepick still embedded in the top of Rocca's head. He's dead, Doyle tells himself. It doesn't matter. But still it hits Doyle as a shocking, senseless act of violence.

And then Bartok is advancing on Doyle again. Coming straight at him, charging at him, fists bunched, teeth bared. And Doyle cannot read his intent. Cannot work out what those crazy eyes are looking at . . .

And then Bartok stops. He stops and he points at Doyle. He laughs again. He holds a hand against his paunch as he laughs, like this is the funniest thing ever. And again the men join in, but still it is not genuine amusement: it is a release of tension. Because everybody in this office except one knows that they are in the presence of insanity.

'You should see your face,' says Bartok to Doyle. 'What a picture.'

Doyle is the only one who isn't laughing. He doesn't find this the least bit funny. He finds the whole situation unsettling and scary in its unpredictability.

Says Bartok, 'I know you wouldn't kill this hump. Don't matter what goods I got on you, you wouldn't whack somebody for me. I know that.'

'So what *do* you want?'

'My ring. I want my ring back.'

'You want me to get your ring back for you?'

'That's what I want.'

Doyle considers asking one more time whether he's heard correctly. It seems such a mundane request, unrepresentative of Bartok's fearsome reputation.

Says Doyle, 'What about Ruger?'

'Ruger is nothing. He's less than nothing. One day our paths will cross again and I'll waste him. Until then, all I want is what belongs to me.'

'Why don't you waste him now? Get your ring back yourself?'

'Because I don't know where he is, dumbass. That's why you're here. You're a detective. I want you to do some detecting. Find this cocksucker and get my property back. If it helps, think of it as returning stolen goods to their rightful owner.'

'You really think Ruger's still got it? I'm no expert, but I'd say a ring like that has to be worth a lot of money.'

Bartok shakes his head. 'Nah, he's still got it. For one thing, I put the word out that I'm looking for it. Everybody who Ruger could possibly sell it to knows who it belongs to. Ruger tries to sell it, I find him. That's the last thing he wants, believe me. Besides, what I'm hearing is that Ruger likes to wear it himself. His story is that it's my brother's ring, and that he whacked him to get it. It's his way of trying to build up some respect. Anyone who would dare to cap one of the Bartok brothers has to be a real bad-ass, right?'

Doyle mulls it over. Considers his options. Decides he doesn't have any.

'And that's all you want me to do? Get the ring?'

'Don't make it sound like a walk in the park, Doyle. Ruger, he don't wanna be found. And if he hears you're looking for him, he's gonna try stopping you. He may be an asshole, but he's an asshole with teeth.'

Doyle thinks some more. Okay, so maybe it's not such an innocent request after all. Maybe I'm underestimating the amount of danger involved in this operation.

'If I do this? What then?'

Bartok strolls back toward the gruesome seated corpse. 'You scratch my back, I scratch yours. I get my ring, you get the wop. You want, you can dig the slugs out yourself. I'll make sure he's nice and defrosted for you. You got till eight o'clock on Sunday morning. Drop it in on your way to church.'

'Sunday? It's already Thursday. No dice, Lucas. I need longer.'

'Sunday morning. After that, I get rid of the body before it starts to smell. I'll tie a ribbon around it and leave it outside police headquarters, somewhere like that, and you can start looking forward to your jail time.'

Doyle looks at the sad spectacle of Sonny Rocca. Sitting there, all hunched up, with four bullets in his chest, a length of steel in his brain, and every cell in his body turned to ice. Could the guy be any more dead?

Doyle sighs. 'How do I get in touch?'

'Sven will give you a number. You don't call, then he comes looking for you. Don't make him have to do that, Doyle.'

Doyle stands. 'You better keep your side of this, Lucas.'

Bartok returns to the chair at his desk. 'I told you. You scratch my back, I scratch yours. Just make sure Ruger don't scratch you first.'

The four meatheads escort Doyle out of there then. It's a relief to be away from Bartok, but he could do without this new mission.

As he clatters back down the iron staircase he thinks, Don't I have enough on my plate already? Now I have to go on a quest for a damn ring.

Now I'm Bilbo fucking Baggins.

ELEVEN

Stanley Francis Proust sits at his table and stares at the man opposite.

He doesn't like bringing people back here, into his living quarters. The shop, fine. He can keep things professional out there. He can be in charge. But here, the presence of others always makes him feel defensive.

He wonders what the man thinks of his home. There is nothing expensive here – Proust doesn't make a lot of money and hey, we're talking Manhattan rental here. The furniture is old and battered. The wallpaper is peeling in several places. The paintwork is faded and scratched. Proust has done his best to liven things up with some pictures and photographs and arty curios from charity stores, but he always feels that visitors can see through to the cheapness and nastiness that lurks beneath.

The man's name is Ed Gowerson. Other people may call him Eddie or Edward, but Proust will stick with the name that was given in the introduction. He doesn't want to risk causing offense.

Gowerson is one of those men who shave their head completely to hide their premature baldness. Proust guesses he can't be much older than thirty. He is wearing a black sports jacket and a blue striped shirt, open at the collar to reveal a silver chain around his neck. He has incredibly square teeth, like a row of Chiclets. Unlike his head, his lower jaw is darkened by a pall of stubble that threatens to erupt from his face at any moment. If Proust were to make a tattoo of Gowerson, or even just a sketch, he would focus on that darkness and make a feature of it. He would echo it in the blackness of the man's eyes. That is how he sees this man: a figure of intense shadow.

Proust clears his throat, then wishes he hadn't because it makes him sound nervous. Which he is.

'You, uh, you want a coffee or something?'

Gowerson shakes his head. 'No, I'm good.'

'A soda, maybe?'

Gowerson leans forward and places his arms on the scarred wooden table. His shoulders strain against the fabric of his jacket. He is not a large man, but Proust guesses that there is a mass of muscle tissue rippling beneath that jacket. Proust glances at Gowerson's hands, now lightly clasped together. There are no rings on his fingers, but his wrist bears a huge watch with lots of dials on it. Like one of those diver's watches. Proust can imagine this guy at the bottom of the sea, pounding the shit out of a Great White.

'Mr Proust, why did you call me?'

Mr Proust. So formal. It seems anomalous in the circum-stances.

He clears his throat again. How to put this? How to be clear in such an unusual request?

'You . . . I mean, I heard you were good at this kind of thing.'

'What kind of thing would that be?'

'Hurting people.'

There, thinks Proust. It's out there. In the open. We both know what we're talking about here.

Gowerson stares for a while. 'Yes. Yes, I am good at hurting people. But what I often find is that those who employ me don't truly understand the nature of my work.'

Proust wants to say, *You beat the crap out of people. What is there to understand? It ain't exactly splitting the atom.* But he doesn't.

'I . . . I'm not sure I get you.'

'What I'm trying to say to you is that it's not like on TV or the movies. You've seen those fights they have, where they go back and forth, back and forth, smacking each other hundreds of times until one falls unconscious and then the other one walks away with no more than a cut lip and a bruise? Well, it's not like that. What I do is brutal and messy and it hurts. And sometimes people never get up again after I'm finished with them.'

'I'm not asking you to kill anyone. Jesus, why are you saying all this? This isn't what we discussed on the—'

Gowerson holds up the palm of his hand. 'All I'm trying to do is make sure you know what you're getting into, okay? There's nothing that pisses me off more than when a client starts bleating afterwards about how they didn't know what they were buying from me. I will do exactly what we agreed. I won't go beyond the boundaries you mentioned. Occasionally, however, things don't always go as planned. A guy might have a weak heart or something wrong with his brain. It's like there's a bomb in there, and all it takes to make it go boom is something as small as a light tap to the chin.'

'You're saying there are risks involved.'

Gowerson nods. 'Is what I'm saying. You need to be aware of those risks. You also need to be aware that there will be blood and there will be pain. Now, are you still certain you want me to go through with this?'

Proust wishes he hadn't been asked this. He doesn't want to

be confronted with all this doubt and uncertainty. He doesn't want to think about risks and ramifications. He thought he would just meet the guy, pay him, and the job would get done. Clean and simple.

And so the upshot now is that he's having second thoughts. Does he really want this to happen? Does he really want to unleash this Rottweiler of a man?

And yet what choice has Doyle left him? Doyle will never let up. He has made that crystal clear. The man is obsessed. He needs to be taught that he can't keep harassing people like that.

'I'm certain,' says Proust.

Gowerson watches him for what seems like an age. Proust can feel himself withering under the man's gaze.

'All right,' says Gowerson. 'Then there's just the little matter of payment for my services.'

Proust gets up from the table, glad to be moving away from this man, if only for a few seconds. He goes over to a low book-case and pulls out an envelope that he previously secreted between two science fiction novels. When he turns around again, he sees that Gowerson is on his feet. He is not tall, but he is imposing, and Proust suddenly wishes he could pass the envelope across on the end of a long fishing rod. His steps toward Gowerson are tentative, and his arm has a discernible tremble to it when he presents the envelope.

'Once I take the money,' says Gowerson, 'that's it. Our agreement is binding. There's no going back, no calling me off. Think of me as a cruise missile. Once you launch me, you can't pull me back in. You cool with that?'

It's the point of no return. Proust considers pulling his hand back. Forget it, he'll say. I made a mistake. I don't really want to do this . . .

But he doesn't do or say any of this. He can't back out now.

He takes a step closer to Gowerson. Puts the envelope right under Gowerson's nose.

Gowerson reaches up a hand and takes the envelope. He doesn't open it. Just slips it into his inside jacket pocket.

'It's all there,' says Proust. 'You can count it if—'

The blow comes from nowhere. One second Proust is talking, the next a fist is crashing into his jaw with the force of a sledgehammer. He feels something explode in his mouth and he reels backwards. He blinks furiously to clear his vision and sees Gowerson coming toward him, his fists clenched. Proust puts his hands up to protect his face, but then another blow smashes into his ribcage. He swears he hears his ribs shatter into a thousand pieces as the air is forced out of his lungs, and as his arms drop again another cannonball lands on his cheek. His head snaps back and forth like a punchbag in the gym, and now he wants to tell his attacker to stop. He wants to say he's had enough, but he knows it will be fruitless. This is just the beginning. He knows this. He has signed up for this. He has handed over good money for this. And so the beating continues, and he continues to endure it. He absorbs blow after crushing blow, wondering when he will die or fall unconscious or simply fragment. He sees blood on his hands and on his clothes, and then he loses the ability to see because of the blood in his eyes – at least he hopes that is what it is and that he hasn't been made blind. And when he loses the will to do anything but be a target he drops to the floor and curls into a ball and puts his hands over his head and listens to the thud, thud, thud as feet and fists pummel his body into mush. And while he does this he reaches a curious state of detachment. It feels to him as though he leaves his body, rising above it to watch as it is mercilessly battered. Pain leaves him. Fear leaves him. The experience becomes almost . . . exquisite.

It takes him some time to realize when it is over. The thudding stops. The pain floods back in. He realizes he is not dead, and that it is not necessarily a good thing. He craves the relief that unconsciousness would bring.

He unfurls his arms slowly, surprised that he can still move them. He raises his head, sees nothing. He brings a hand to his eyes and wipes them. He feels warm wetness on his fingers – his blood, presumably – and his cheeks seem grossly swollen and tender. He blinks. Dark fuzzy shapes come into view. Gradually they sharpen. He sees the figure of Gowerson standing a few feet in front of him. He prays that he is not merely taking a rest, and that the ordeal has truly ended.

He manages to twist himself into a sitting position. The pain will permit him to do no more than that. He is seized by a sudden need to cough. As he does so, it is as though a razor-sharp spear is thrust into his chest. Blood sprays from his mouth, then dribbles down his chin. He explores with his tongue. Finds a loose tooth. He pushes against it with the tip of his tongue and it comes away. He spits it out. More scarlet dribble. Another agonizing cough. He looks again at Gowerson. It takes an effort, but he manages to push out two words that seem so absurd they are almost comical.

'Thank you.'

TWELVE

He frightens her, this man Doyle.

It is not just his physical presence, although he is a big man. He is tall and broad and carries himself with an air of confidence that suggests he is afraid of no one.

Nor is it the fact that he is no stranger to violence. The slight bend to his nose from an old break attests to that, and the massive swelling on his left cheek suggests that he still doesn't go out of his way to avoid it.

Nor is it merely his eyes. Those startling emerald-green eyes that are the first things everyone must notice about him. You cannot help but be drawn to them, and they in turn seem to penetrate beyond mere flesh and bone, and drill deep into your very thoughts.

No, what it is about Doyle that disturbs Nicole Hamlyn so much is that she gets the unshakeable feeling that he is an iceberg. What she sees in front of her now is merely the tip. There is much more that is hidden, that will probably remain hidden. Things he has seen. Things he has done. Things he can never talk about. She does not know quite why she senses this about him, but she knows she is right. She would bet on it.

And yet . . .

And yet, despite the aura of danger and dark, unimaginable

happenings, she feels that this is a man you want on your side. This is a man who will never give up. He will always uncover the truth, whatever the cost to himself.

She wants – needs – that to be so about Doyle. And as she realizes that, she starts to wonder whether her needs are distorting her reality. Maybe Doyle is nothing special, after all. Just another regular cop.

But she doesn't think so.

She allows him into their home again. He comes alone this time, and he is wet again, but not as soaked as last time.

She touches her fingers to her own cheek. 'What happened?'

He looks puzzled at first, and then he understands.

'Oh. This. Occupational hazard.'

And that's it. That's how lightly he dismisses the violence that left this imprint on his face. Nicole has met many men who would have been severely traumatized by such an act. And others who would be seething with anger and a self-destructive need to exact dreadful revenge. Steve falls into the latter group. He would neither forgive nor forget. He would seek retribution.

She wishes that Steve could be more like Doyle. She wishes he could allow himself to process the grief in whatever way he needs so that they can prepare to move on.

'Please,' she says. 'Take a seat. I'll fetch Steve. Can I get you tea or coffee?'

'No,' says Doyle. 'Thank you.'

She walks through to the kitchen and then to the door that opens into the garage. She can hear clattering and banging on the other side. It's been like this all morning.

She opens the door and steps into the garage. Steve is bent over a cardboard box, hauling things out of it and tossing them onto the concrete floor. The whole of the floorspace is covered in items that were previously tidied away in crates.

'Steve,' she says, and when he doesn't hear her, she shouts, 'STEVE!'

He pauses and looks across at her. 'Why did we keep all this junk? What the hell were we thinking?' He grabs an object from the box. 'Look at this. A clock with no hands on it. Why the fuck did we keep a clock with no hands? What possible use could it be?'

He hurls it away from him. It hits the wall and shatters. Pieces ricochet across the garage.

It occurs to her to remind him that the clock was a family heirloom passed down to her by her mother. The missing hands were taped inside the casing. Steve had put them there with the intention of restoring it one day. All of this occurs to Nicole, but she says nothing. She just stares down at what is left of the clock, now damaged beyond repair. Perhaps like their marriage, if they do nothing to stop it fragmenting.

'The police are here,' she says, fighting to disguise her sadness. 'Detective Doyle. I thought you should know.'

'What does he want? Have they caught the guy yet?'

'No. I don't think so. I think he just wants to ask us some more questions.'

'Then you don't need me. I got nothing more to say.'

She thinks, Nothing to say? Your daughter has been murdered and you have nothing to say?

He turns away from her and starts rummaging in the box again.

'Steve?' No answer. '*Steve, please!*'

He stops again. Looks at her with more than a hint of annoyance. Stands up.

'Five minutes,' he says. 'I'll give him five minutes.'

Thanks, she thinks. For your precious time.

She lets Steve push past her without a word, then follows him into the living room. Doyle is looking at her. He knows something is up, she thinks. She gives him a smile that is meant to say, *No problem. We're all pulling together here.* But she knows he's not deceived.

They all sit down. Nicole takes the sofa. Doyle takes the chair opposite – the same one he sat in last time. She hopes that Steve will come and sit next to her, but he doesn't. He perches himself on the arm of another chair. A clear signal that he doesn't intend to hang around.

'First of all,' says Doyle, 'I just want you to know that we're working flat out on this case. It's our top priority.'

'I should think so,' says Steve. 'A young girl hacked to pieces like that, why wouldn't you pull out all the stops?'

Nicole glances at Steve, but he seems not to notice. She wonders if she did the right thing, bringing him into this room.

She shifts her gaze back to Doyle. Searches his face for signs of irritation. She is relieved to find that he seems unperturbed.

Don't ruin this, Steve. We need this man.

'You're absolutely right,' says Doyle. 'It's a natural assumption. Why wouldn't we want to catch this lunatic? But I also know that most families of victims don't want to be left alone to assume things. Sometimes they like to hear us put it into words.'

There, Steve. See? They're doing their best. Don't give him a hard time.

'We don't want words,' says Steve. 'We want action. We want you to get the bastard.'

Shut up, Steve. Shut up! You're not helping.

'Of course you do,' says Doyle. 'I understand.'

'Do you? Then you'll understand if I don't want to answer any more questions. I already told the cops everything I know. It's all in your files. Go read them, catch the guy, then you can come back.'

Steve pushes himself up from the chair's arm. Nicole thinks he's about to escort Doyle to the door, but he doesn't. He disappears into the kitchen again. She hears the slam of the door to the garage.

She looks at Doyle. 'I'm sorry. He's . . . he's not dealing with this very well.'

Still Doyle does not appear concerned. 'It's okay. You've both been through the worst kind of ordeal. Different people react in different ways. Give him time.'

She blinks. Give him time? The advice surprises her, but maybe he's right. Megan's body has only just been discovered. Steve needs time to come to terms with that.

'Do you . . . do you have any news? On the investigation?'

'Nothing significant yet. We're looking into all the possibilities. The reason I came here, I want to be sure I got all the facts right.'

'Okay. Sure. What can I tell you?'

'According to the Missing Persons report, Megan told you she was going out with some friends of hers last Saturday. Is that right?'

'Yes. Three of her girlfriends from school. She said they were going to see a movie.'

'But the girls never saw her on that day?'

'No. They didn't even know about any arrangements to meet up.'

'You spoke with them?'

'Yes. I met with each of them, and their parents.'

'And did you believe them? You don't think they were trying to cover anything up?'

She blinks. The thought has never occurred to her. She has met the girls countless times. They seem like good girls. What would they be covering up?

'No. Why do you ask? Do you think they might be?'

'I don't think anything, Mrs Hamlyn. I'm just filling in all the gaps. We'll talk to the girls ourselves. I just want to know what your thoughts are.'

She wonders then about the nature of Doyle's job. He's a cynic, because he wouldn't be doing his job if he wasn't. He's trained to be suspicious of everyone, to question everything. It must be hard to live like that – in constant distrust.

'I don't think the girls were lying.'

'Did Megan often lie to you?'

She wants to take offense at this. She opens her mouth, ready to ask him what the hell he means by making such an accusation. She stops when she sees on Doyle's face that there is no spitefulness in the question. He's calling it as he sees it. Megan said she was going to the movie theater, and she didn't. It was a lie. No other word for it.

'Do you have any children, Detective Doyle?'

'Yes. A daughter.'

'How old?'

'Only seven.'

'Does she ever tell lies to you?'

She sees a small smile of recognition tug at the corner of Doyle's mouth. 'Sometimes. She's not very good at it, though.'

'She'll get better with practice. Kids always lie to their parents. Or they simply withhold information. It's part of growing up.

It's their way of rebelling, of gaining independence. Didn't you lie to your parents?'

She gets another smile, and presses on: 'Of course you did. We all do. We mean no harm by it, and usually no harm is done. But sometimes, just sometimes, there are consequences that go way beyond what we can imagine.'

'Tell me about the tattoo,' says Doyle. 'Did you argue about it?'

'We had some conversations about it. Occasionally it got a little heated. Megan had wanted a tattoo ever since she was thirteen. We told her she was too young, and that if she wanted one she would have to wait until she was eighteen.'

'How'd she take it?'

'Not well, but we thought she'd accepted it. We thought she'd wait.'

She watches Doyle as he thinks about her answer.

'You keep coming back to the tattoo,' she says. 'Why?'

'It was done during her disappearance. Whoever did it saw her after you did and before the killer did. There could be something important there.'

'But you don't know who made the tattoo?'

'Not yet, but we're looking.'

There's something in the way he says those words that don't quite ring right to Nicole. There's something there he's not telling her.

'Do you have any suspects yet?'

He shakes his head. 'Not yet. But it's early days.'

Again, something in his voice. She can't put her finger on it, but it's there, and its presence irritates her. Makes her question the faith she has placed in this man.

Or is it because he is so committed to this case and this

family that he is unable to keep his suspicions buried as well as he should? Maybe that's it. He desperately wants to tell her something, but his job doesn't allow it. Maybe she's not wrong about him at all.

Before she can pursue it, Doyle changes the subject: 'Was Megan in the habit of going to the East Village on her own?'

'No. I don't know that she ever went there before.'

'What about Manhattan generally?'

'Not on her own. With friends or with us, sure.'

'But once she was there, did you ever let her off the leash? Give her some space to do her own thing?'

'Well . . .'

'Go on.'

'Steve, he's an accountant. He's based here in Queens, but sometimes he goes to meetings at the head office in the city. Now and again, Megan would go with him. She would go shopping, then they would get together after his meeting and he would bring her back.'

'Okay.'

'I . . . It was shopping. For a couple of hours. That's all.'

'It's all right. I'm not judging you, okay? I'm just trying to work out how she ended up where she did. Maybe she went there, maybe someone took her there. Maybe she had no intention of even going to Manhattan when she left here. If I can figure that out, then maybe I can get a handle on how she met the tattooist.'

Nicole nods. She understands now. She can start to see how Doyle's thought processes are working. He really isn't here to pass judgment. He simply wants answers. And it seems to her that all his questions are the right ones to be asking right now. She trusts this man.

'How will you know? I mean, how will you be able to figure out where she went and who she met?'

'From talking to people. From studying camera footage at the subway stations and so forth. It'll take time, but we'll do what we have to do.'

She nods again. 'Thank you.' She pauses for a long time, then says, 'Did . . . Did they find any more? Of Megan, I mean.'

'No. We're still looking, and not just in the East Village. A bulletin went out to all precincts. We're checking the rivers, construction sites, derelict buildings – any place we can think of. We're even going through the garbage in the landfill sites. But, well . . . a place like New York, you can't freeze it for long while you search it.'

'I understand,' she says. And she does. New York isn't a huge area, but it's tightly crammed and intensely busy. Constantly shifting and changing. It's amazing they found what they did. But three pieces. It's nothing. Somewhere out there is more of Megan. Undiscovered, unclaimed. She deserves better. She deserves to be brought home.

Nicole feels herself filling up again – when will this crying ever stop? – and says, 'It's just that . . . The burial. You understand? We'd like to be able to bury Megan. I mean . . . all of her.'

She sees Doyle's discomfort, and realizes she is putting him in an impossible situation. How can she expect him to answer that? He's doing what he can for us. Let that be enough.

And yet . . . If he really wants to help . . .

'There's something else,' she says. 'Maybe you can't answer it, but I'd like to know.'

Doyle studies her for a while, then nods. 'Go ahead.'

'Was Megan . . . Was she . . . I mean, did the killer . . . did he interfere with her?'

There. A tough question to get out, but she did it. And now it's out there, hanging around for a response, she's not sure she's done the right thing. She's tempted to reel it back in.

Doyle looks at her again, long and hard. He chews on his lip, as though he's debating what to do with this big fat question mark being dangled in front of him.

Finally, he says, 'There is evidence of sexual assault, yes.'

She knew this. Not definitively, but in her heart. She tried to prepare herself for the confirmation when it came, but still it seems to slice deep into her gut. The tears that had welled up in her get squeezed out with the pain. As they roll down her cheeks, she keeps her gaze fixed on Doyle. And as he stares right back, she senses something from him. Defiance. Not of her, but of whatever constraining forces are being applied to him. Screw the rulebook, he seems to be saying.

'You weren't supposed to tell me that, were you?'

Doyle shrugs. 'I do a lot of things I'm not supposed to do.'

She nods her gratitude. Any other cop would have refused to answer. Would perhaps even have lied. Doyle won't lie.

She says, 'Whoever did this, he's a monster. He's evil. Megan was a child. She was my baby. How could anyone hurt a child?'

'I don't know. And I can't imagine your pain. Just thinking of this happening to my daughter makes me sick to my stomach.'

She blinks in surprise. Should policemen say such things? Aren't they supposed to remain detached and objective? He's full of surprises, this one.

She finds herself relaxing in his presence a little. He has that effect. A calming influence. She feels as though she could talk to him about anything, no matter how personal. She gets another jolt when her next thoughts of Megan do not involve death and agony, but instead are fond memories stretching back in time. Of Megan as a child, a toddler, a baby.

'Megan could be hard work, you know.'

There is a slight smile on her face as she says this, and Doyle reflects one back at her.

'Mine too.'

'Right from birth she was determined to be a troublemaker. Ripped me to pieces so badly I can't have any more kids.'

'Yeah?' says Doyle. 'That happened to my wife too. At one point I thought I was gonna lose both of them.'

She narrows her eyes at him. What is this? Whatever happened to *Just the facts, Ma'am*? Where's his little notebook, into which he jots down times, places, names? The uniformed cops weren't like this. The Missing Persons cops weren't like this either. How is it possible for this man to let his humanity through like this when he has to deal with murderers, rapists and other scum? How can he shoot the breeze about his wife's pregnancy while contemplating how he's going to catch a man who has just raped a teenage girl and cut her into little pieces?

Her voice becomes bolder, less mired in intense sadness. Like it's the first normal conversation she's had in days. 'You should have heard me in the hospital. I thought I was going to be all calm and collected. The model mother-to-be. You know what I do for a living?'

'No, I don't think I saw that in the files.'

'I'm a midwife. I've lost count of the number of babies I've delivered. I've seen every complication there is. The only thing that worried me about giving birth to my own child was that I would try to tell the other staff how to do their jobs. But boy, once I got my feet in those stirrups it was a totally different story. I lost it. I forgot everything there was to know about midwifery. I just lay there and screamed.'

She sees that Doyle's smile has broadened, and realizes that hers has too. And it feels okay. It doesn't feel disrespectful, because it's about Megan. It's about celebrating who she was and how she did things. And that's fine. She's allowed to do that. In fact, she believes that the only way she's going to get through this is by holding on to the happy moments, even though she knows it won't always be possible.

'That's what I don't get,' she says.

'What is?'

'I bring life into the world. It's what I wanted to do ever since I was a kid. I get a huge kick out of it. New life – there's nothing more sacred than that. But this man, whoever he is – this murderer – he enjoys raping and torturing and killing and dismembering. How do such opposites get to exist in the world? How is it possible for a person to enjoy such things?'

And now Doyle's smile has gone, and she regrets the fact that she has soured the atmosphere again.

'Because he's not really a part of this world,' says Doyle. 'He's sick, and I don't think he can be cured. That's why he needs to be removed from it.'

She listens to his words, and it seems to her that Doyle could be talking about a specific person rather than some unknown killer he has never met.

'Can I ask you something else, Detective?'

'Sure.'

'Could you remove this man from our world? Permanently, I mean. Not prison.'

When Doyle says nothing for a couple of seconds she adds, 'I'm sorry. Maybe I shouldn't be asking—'

'If it were up to me?' says Doyle. 'In a heartbeat. No doubt about it. If I was sure I knew who had done this to your daughter, and the law allowed me to do it, I would put a bullet in this scumbag's brain without hesitation.'

'And if the law said no, but you thought nobody would ever find out?'

She sees the muscles twitch in Doyle's jaw. It's a tough ethical question, but she genuinely wants to hear his response.

'I'm a cop,' he says finally. 'I have to uphold the law. Otherwise what am I doing in this job?'

The right answer, she thinks. But the expected answer. She's not certain that it accurately reflects his position. She knows what Steve would do. Steve would hunt this man down and make him endure as much pain as possible before killing him as slowly as possible – that's what Steve would do.

And I bring forth life, she thinks. That's what I do. That's what is right.

'Mrs Hamlyn, I should go now,' says Doyle.

'Please,' she says. 'Call me Nicole.'

He nods, then stands up. 'There's a lot of work to be done.'

She shows him to the door. When she opens it, the noise of the rain suddenly intrudes. They both look out at it.

'You think it's ever gonna quit?' Doyle asks.

'Yes,' she says. 'In time.'

Then Doyle steps into it and is gone.

He drives just far enough to be out of her view, then pulls the car over.

Damn!

Why did I even come here? For all I've learned in this meeting, wouldn't a phone call have been just as good?

And why did I let her get to me? Why do I always have to get so fucking involved?

Telling her about how we can't have any more kids. Letting her know that I'd happily cap the sonofabitch killer of her daughter. What the fuck was that about?

And, to top it all, the lies. Telling her there were still no suspects, when the one and only suspect is sitting at home in his crappy apartment, laughing his ass off at the failure of the police to nail him.

Doyle sits there for a full five minutes, working through his anger, berating himself for his stupidity.

But he knows why he came to the Hamlyns' house. He came because he cares. He cares about the Hamlyns and he cares about their daughter and he cares about finding her killer. He cares far too much, in his opinion. It's a fault which always tears him apart, and he doesn't know what he can do about it.

It'll be the death of me, he thinks.

Stanley Proust stands naked in front of his bedroom mirror. His shoulders are slumped slightly because he cannot straighten up. It hurts too much.

He has managed to staunch the flow of blood from his various cuts, but he still looks as though he has been hit by a train. There are marks and swellings all over his body. His face looks like that of the Elephant Man. One eye is so puffed up it's difficult to see out of it. His ribs in particular feel like a hot poker is being inserted between them when he breathes. He has taken some strong painkillers, but they don't seem to be making much difference.

He puts his tongue in the gap where his tooth used to be,

and pushes gently on the cap of congealed blood. Shame to lose a tooth, but he can always get a false one put in.

But what an experience!

He has never been through anything like that before. The last time he was punched was in a fist fight in middle school that lasted barely five seconds. He didn't even get a bloody nose on that occasion. Since then he has often wondered whether it would toughen him up to get involved in a proper no-holds-barred brawl – to find out what it's really like to absorb a barrage of stinging blows. But he has always been too scared. He has always backed down from any confrontation that has threatened to become physical.

Well, now he knows. He understands. The pain is nothing. He can transcend the pain.

And he could go through it again. Now that he has done it once, he could do it again and again. Whatever Doyle throws at him, he can take. And that means Doyle can never win.

Proust drops his eyes to the tattoo on his chest, still clearly visible behind the bruises. He looks at the image of himself, clawing its way through his flesh.

That's me now, he thinks. That's what I've been waiting for.

I am reborn.

THIRTEEN

LeBlanc knows something is wrong as soon as Doyle walks into
the squadroom.

Actually, he suspected Doyle was up to something when he
disappeared for the whole morning. Showing up now with that
shiner under his eye merely confirms it.

This is not good, he thinks. This is definitely not going to
be something I want to hear.

He accosts Doyle before he even has a chance to sit down.
Before he has even had a chance to remove his jacket.

'Cal, can we talk? In private?'

'What, again?' says Doyle. 'This is how rumors start, ya know,
Tommy?'

'You mind?'

Doyle looks around. Only Schneider is staring back at him.
'All right. Come on.'

They leave the squadroom and move down the hallway, where
Doyle opens the door to an interview room. That is, it's officially an interview room. Unofficially it's a dumping ground for
anything that can't be squeezed in anywhere more appropriate.
File cabinets in particular seem to end up here. There is hardly
an inch of lower wall space that doesn't have a file cabinet in
front of it.

'What is it?' asks Doyle, and it seems to LeBlanc that there is already a hint of irritation there.

'You mind if I ask where you been all morning?'

'You mind if I ask why you're asking?'

'Because I'm your partner. I thought you were gonna talk to the Hamlyns.'

'Then you just answered your own question.'

'It took you all morning to do that?'

'I'm nothing if not thorough.'

'Go anywhere else?'

'Hey, Tommy, cut it out, okay? I know we're in the interview room, but that doesn't mean you have to get in character. You wanna get some practice in on your Q and A technique, go drag in some skells.'

LeBlanc breathes out. A long slow breath. This isn't how he wanted it to go.

'Look, I'm sorry. I'm finding it difficult to get used to the way you do things.'

'The way I do things?'

'Yeah. You know, the way you just disappear. The way you don't always tell me what you've been doing or what you're about to do.'

He realizes he's starting to sound a little like an abandoned wife. But he also knows just how close partners can get. They need to rely on each other. They need to trust each other. Each needs to understand precisely how the other one ticks. LeBlanc doesn't know whether he will ever manage to reach that depth of familiarity with Doyle. Maybe this partnership wasn't such a good idea. But he's not going to be the one to give up on it.

'You know what?' says Doyle. 'You're right. I haven't been telling you everything. Just don't take it personal. I had some things I needed to do this morning. Stuff that doesn't concern you, okay? From now on, I'll try to bring you in whenever I can.'

'Is that how you got the mouse? From these other activities you can't talk to me about?'

Doyle touches a hand to his cheek. For a moment it seems to LeBlanc that Doyle's expression is that of someone who has just been caught in a lie and is frantically trying to manufacture a way out of it. And when Doyle smiles, it seems to come far too late.

'Yeah. Nothing to do with the Hamlyn case. Now can I go, please, Officer? I'm beginning to feel like I should ask for a lawyer.'

LeBlanc answers with a smile of his own. But it wilts as soon as Doyle leaves the room.

Fuck!

He wants to believe Doyle. He wants to trust him. But why does the man insist on making it so damned difficult? Why can't he at least talk about this, for Chrissake? What's he got to hide?

When he leaves the interview room, he doesn't follow Doyle back into the squadroom. He heads the other way, out of the building.

Skinterest looks to be all closed up. The blinds are drawn and the lights are off. LeBlanc stands in the rain for a while, telling himself that it's nothing. The man's decided to close for the day, is all. Nothing to worry about.

He thumbs the buzzer anyway.

He hears nothing, so he buzzes again, then hammers on the door with his fist.

A light comes on. A shadow appears behind the blinds. LeBlanc hears a fumbling of chains, the drawing back of bolts, the turning of keys. As he pulls open the door, Proust shuffles backwards, maintaining the door as a shield between him and LeBlanc. Only a fraction of Proust's face is visible, and even that is cast into silhouette by the light behind it.

'Mr Proust? You mind if I come in for a moment?'

'Is Doyle with you?'

Proust's voice is faint, croaky and filled with fear. LeBlanc swallows. It worries him that Proust's first question should be about Doyle. He seems terrified of the man.

'No. No, he's not. It's just me. Is that okay?'

'I . . . it's not really a good, unh, time.'

LeBlanc hears the slight grunt. Like Proust is in pain. Jesus, could he . . .

'Mr Proust, I promise this won't take long. And I'm not here to give you any trouble. A couple of questions and I'm gone.'

Proust says nothing. Just stands there. Then the door swings open a little wider.

LeBlanc steps inside. Takes a quick look around. Nothing amiss that he can see. Everything in order. He turns back to Proust, who is closing the door. From the back he seems strangely bent and stiff, like an old man.

And then Proust faces him.

LeBlanc gasps. 'Jesus Christ! What happened? What the hell happened to you?'

The man is a wreck. He looks as though he has just tumbled from the top of a mountain to the bottom. How is he not on a slab in the morgue?

'I'm okay,' says Proust.

'Okay? You're not okay. Have you seen yourself? How did you get like this?'

Proust limps past LeBlanc. 'I was, uhm, I was mugged.'

As soon as LeBlanc hears the explanation he knows it is not true. And then he starts to feel sick with the realization of what the truth might be.

'You were mugged? When were you mugged? Where?'

'Here. Two guys came in this morning. They wanted my money. I told them I didn't have any. So they beat the shit out of me.'

LeBlanc says nothing for a while. He doesn't know what to say. Proust's story is a crock, but he's not certain he wants to drag the real one out of him. He watches as Proust sits himself down on a stool, wincing as he does so.

'Have you reported this to the police?' LeBlanc asks.

LeBlanc snorts a laugh, then follows it up with a cry of pain. 'The police? Are you kidding me, man? After the way you guys treated me yesterday? Something tells me I wouldn't get a whole load of sympathy from you people.'

LeBlanc looks him up and down. Jesus! This was no ordinary beating. Somebody wanted to give him a message. They probably didn't even care if he lived or died.

'These men. What did they look like?'

'I don't remember. They were big and they were mean. That's all I know.'

'They use fists or weapons?'

Proust shrugs. Winces again.

LeBlanc chews his lip. Break through the lies, or leave it be? This is a fellow cop we're talking about here, Tommy. Do you want to know? Do you really, really want to know?

'Did Detective Doyle come here again this morning?'

Slowly, Proust raises his head. Turns his battered, misshapen face full into the light. Through half-closed lids, his eyes twinkle as they stare at LeBlanc.

'Detective Doyle?'

'Yes. Was he here this morning?'

A long pause. Then: 'No.'

Except that it's a no which means yes. It's a no which says, *You're a cop too and I don't trust you and so I'm playing it safe, because all you cop bastards stick together and anything I say against one of you is said against all of you.*

All of that in one word. That's what LeBlanc hears. That's what shakes him to the core.

And now he's not sure what to do. A part of him wants to pursue this. A part of him wants to put the badge away and talk to Proust as another man, another human being. He wants to tell him that he will listen, and that whatever Proust says to him will be treated in the strictest confidence. He thinks that might work. He thinks that Proust might open up to him.

And then he takes a mental step back. He thinks, I am a cop and Doyle is a cop, and Proust is still a suspect. Despite the apparent fuck-up that Doyle seems to be making of this case and his own life, our roles haven't changed.

It is not without some shame that he opts not to side with this man against one of his own, and so he offers to do what he can: 'Get up,' he says.

Again there is fear and suspicion in Proust's eyes. 'Why?'

'I'm taking you to the hospital.'

'I don't need no hospital, man. I'm okay.'

'You might have broken bones. Internal damage. You need to be checked out. Come on, I'll take you in my car.'

Proust stares at LeBlanc's beckoning hand for some time

before making a decision. As he gets off his chair, he grimaces. If he wasn't in so much obvious discomfort, it could almost be mistaken for a smile.

Doyle sees the glance from the man with the backpack. He knows the guy has seen him. Can tell by the way the man speeds up his rhythmic lope that he's trying to put as many yards as he can between him and Doyle without it seeming too obvious.

Doyle pushes himself away from the window of the bodega and takes up pursuit. The man speeds up. Doyle speeds up. The man risks a quick look behind him and increases his pace a little more. Doyle decides he's not in the mood for burning calories.

'Freeze!' he calls.

Coming from a cop, that would usually mean only one thing. It would mean, *I have a gun trained on you right now, mother-fucker, and if you so much as blink too fast then I'm gonna blow your sad ass off of this planet.*

Or words to that effect.

On this occasion, however, it doesn't mean that. The man Doyle is chasing is called Edwin Jones, but nobody other than his mother ever calls him Edwin. They know him as Freezeframe Jones, or Freeze for short. And the reason they call him that is because one of the ways he chooses to scrape a living is by selling pirated DVDs. Doyle knows he's built up a thriving business over the years. Freezeframe prides himself on always being able to get hold of the latest movies, sometimes even before they hit the theaters. His boast is that he had the first Harry Potter movie before J. K. Rowling had finished writing the book.

Freezeframe stops and turns, then affects a grin of recognition. He is as tall as Doyle, but gangly with it. He has an angular face, with prominent cheekbones. His arms seem too long for his body, and he has a habit of waving them around with abandon, threatening bodily harm to those who get too close.

'Yo, D! S'up, man?'

'Hey, Freeze. For a minute there I thought you were avoiding me.'

'Who, me? Nah. Just didn't recognize you, is all. Can't blame a cat for tryin' to stay safe and shit, you know what I'm sayin'?'

'Got something worth protecting?'

'Only my *life*, yo. Worth sumthin' to me, even if no other motherfucker give a damn.'

'My heart bleeds for you. I was talking about the movie business. You made director yet? Producer? Or is sales and marketing still your thing?'

Freezeframe feigns puzzlement. 'You lost me, D. I don't know nothin' about no movie business.'

'Uh-huh. I bet the bodega owner does. What's his thing? The new Tom Cruise? Or is he more your alien invasion kinda guy?'

'Only thing I know is he sells gum.' Freezeframe digs a pack of chewing gum from the pocket of his hooded top and shows it to Doyle. 'You want a stick?'

Doyle shakes his head. 'What's in the backpack?'

Freezeframe looks over his shoulder as though he's just been told there's a bug crawling there.

'This? I don't know.'

'You don't know what's in your own backpack? The one you think is important enough to be carrying around in the rain like this?'

'I found it, D. Planning to hand it in to the po-lice at the next opportunity.'

'But you didn't bother to look what was in it?'

'Nah, D. None of my business, you know what I'm sayin'?'

Doyle sighs and looks up at the rain clouds. It seems to him that they don't plan on dispersing anytime soon. Seems more like they're waiting for reinforcements.

'Step over here,' says Doyle, moving under the awning of a hardware store. Reluctantly, Freezeframe joins him.

'I tole you, D. I don't know shit about no DVDs. This ain't—'

'Forget the DVDs. I want some information.'

Freezeframe pulls his neck back in surprise, his head disappearing turtle-like into the shadows of his hood before it slowly emerges again. Then he suddenly breaks into raucous high-pitched laughter as he slaps his thighs with those elongated arms of his.

'You fucking with me, right?'

Doyle keeps his face straight. 'No, I'm serious.'

Freezeframe stops laughing. 'I ain't no snitch, D. And if I *was* a snitch, which I ain't, I would not be *your* snitch, because I heard 'bout what happens to your snitches. Motherfuckers be ending up dead.'

'This ain't an offer of permanent employment, Freeze. It's a one-time deal.'

'I still ain't interested. I got a reputation, yo. Folks get to hear I been talking to the man, they be smokin' my ass.'

Doyle pulls out his wallet, opens it up and strips out a few bills.

'Tell you what. I can open up your backpack there and then I can run you in and we can talk about this down at the station house, or you can make yourself a little green for one small piece of information and then walk away. What's it to be?'

Freezeframe looks out into the rain as if for guidance, then back at Doyle.

'Shit, that ain't no kinda *choice*. That's you putting a nine to my head, is what that is.'

'What's it gonna be?'

Freezeframe looks around again, this time appearing a little more nervous. Which tells Doyle that he's on the verge of accepting his offer.

'Suppose I ain't got this particular piece of information?'

'Do your best, Freeze. Ain't nobody else I know mixes with the criminal fraternity like you do.'

As Doyle suspected he would, Freezeframe takes this as a compliment, and his face brightens.

'I do got a lot of contacts, that's true. Aiight, what you wanna know?'

'I'm looking for someone. Man called Anton Ruger.'

Wide eyes now. Astonished eyes.

'Uh-uh, D. You don't wanna be messing with that shit. That cat is *nasty*. Word is he offed one of the Bartok brothers. Anyone even insults the Bartok brothers got to be either insane or havin' balls of steel.'

'I wanna know where he is.'

'I don't know where he's at. Nobody does.'

'Somebody does. Somebody must have mentioned his name to you, at least.'

Freezeframe pauses. 'You didn't hear this from me.'

'No problem.'

'Aiight. There's a white boy I know. Likes to talk big. Says he did some work for Ruger.'

'What's his name?'

'Likes to go by Cubo. Thass all I know.'

'Where can I find him?'

'He cribs at his girl's place. Skinny-ass ho called Tasha Wilmot. She live at 309 Stanton. Top floor. Apartment 5D.'

'That's pretty damned specific, Freeze. How'd you know all this?'

'Boy likes to watch movies, when he's not getting it on with his girl.'

Doyle nods. He scans the street himself, then palms off the wad of bills to Freezeframe.

'You made the right decision.'

Freezeframe slips the money into his pocket. 'Yeah, and you be making the wrong one. Don't say I didn't warn you.'

LeBlanc tries every which way he can to justify it to himself.

I'm young, he thinks. Relatively inexperienced. Still got a helluva lot to learn. Older, wiser cops are still capable of surprising me. Sometimes I need to hold back before I interfere. Give them a chance to—

Scratch that. It's bullshit.

This is Wrong, with a capital W.

LeBlanc has seen many things that have made him feel uncomfortable. Cops who have accepted one too many 'free-bies'. Cops who have been a little bit too free and easy with their fists during their interrogation of suspects. Cops who have suggested that LeBlanc look the other way while they have a 'private conversation' with a perp. He has witnessed all these things. He is not naive. He knows how the world turns.

But this . . .

He can't let this go.

When he enters the squadroom he is ready for a fight. Not a physical fight – he knows that Doyle would put him on his ass in a second – but a squaring off while some serious truth-seeking takes place. He doesn't care if anyone else is there to listen. He needs to hear what Doyle has to say for himself. Doyle owes him that much, and he will demand that Doyle gives it up.

Except that there is no sign of Doyle in the squadroom. His desk is unoccupied. His jacket isn't on his chair or the rack. LeBlanc came in here with adrenalin pumping through his system, and now he has no way of putting it to use.

'What's the matter, kid?'

This from Schneider, who has watched LeBlanc thunder into the squadroom like he's about to tear it apart.

LeBlanc rounds on him. 'I'm looking for Doyle. You seen him?'

'Me? No. But then he's not a guy I make it my business to find very often. Ain't he supposed to be your partner?'

LeBlanc knows what Schneider's doing. He's saying: *Doyle is your partner. He should be keeping you up to speed. You shouldn't have to ask where he's gone.* And he's doing this to turn LeBlanc against Doyle, because every day that Schneider can create another enemy of Doyle's is a successful day in Schneider's book. LeBlanc knows this; he's not stupid. But right at this moment he's willing to overlook the obviousness of this ruse. Right now he's pretty amenable to being asked to play for the opposing team.

'That's what I thought too,' he snarls. 'But hey, what do I know?'

Schneider raises his eyebrows in obvious surprise at the vehemence of LeBlanc's reply.

'I told you. Doyle doesn't do partners. You get put with him, you still have to watch your own back. Remember that. Look after number one, kid, because you can be sure that's what Doyle's doing.'

LeBlanc doesn't know what to do. This is unfamiliar territory. The last thing he wants is to jam up a fellow cop, especially his own partner. But Schneider is right. In his own blunt, opinionated way he is uttering wise words. LeBlanc needs to make sure he doesn't end up getting accused of covering up for Doyle through his failure to speak out. He needs guidance. An older, wiser head to whom he can turn for help.

'You wanna talk about it?' says Schneider.

And there it is. The offer of assistance. Right here, right now.

'You got a few minutes?' LeBlanc asks.

The marks are already darkening into savage bruises. Purples, blues and greens stain almost his entire body, making it look as though it bears one huge abstract tattoo.

Proust is impressed by the workmanship.

One missing tooth, another broken in half, and a hairline fracture of one rib.

That's pretty damned good. To be carrying all those marks and to have only those underlying injuries – well, that's the sign of a true craftsman. Gowerson performed exactly as advertised. Proust has always admired those who not only have great skill, but who also go to great pains to make things just so.

Speaking of pains . . .

The rib hurts like crazy. A red-hot dagger into the chest every time he breathes or moves, both of which he tends to do frequently. Who would have guessed that such a tiny crack could make its presence felt so emphatically?

The hospital staff told him there was nothing more they could do for the rib. Rest and strong painkillers is what they prescribed. They told him he was lucky to come through an assault like that with nothing more serious. Said he was, in fact, fortunate to be alive.

He wanted to laugh when they told him that. He does it now instead. Naked in front of the mirror, he lets out a long, loud burst of laughter, stopping only when the tears running down his cheeks are those not of amusement but of indescribable agony.

He hasn't taken the painkillers. He wants to experience this pain. He is so used to others enduring pain at his hands in the tattoo shop, and yet he has suffered very little in his lifetime. He has never broken a bone before or had toothache or even a severe headache. Pain has always been something to avoid, to fear. He feels that he is somehow conquering that fear. He is becoming stronger. He can cope much more easily with what life may throw at him.

Bring it on, Doyle, you miserable, puny fuck. Bring it on.

FOURTEEN

'You need to talk with her.'

This from Rachel, across the dinner table. It's spaghetti bolognese tonight. Not fish. There shouldn't be bones. If there are bones, then his wife has planted them there to teach him a lesson.

'Tomorrow,' he says, even though he knows it's pointless.

'No, not tomorrow. I know what it's like when you're working a homicide. We hardly ever see you. You'll be out before Amy is up for breakfast, and you'll be home after she's gone to bed. I'm not complaining about that. That's just how it is. To be honest, I'm a little surprised you're home right now. But since you are, you should take the opportunity to talk to Amy. It can't wait, Cal.'

The reason Doyle is home right now is that it's probably his only chance today to see his family and have a decent meal. He hasn't told Rachel yet, but he's got a busy night planned, and it doesn't involve dancing or drinking. It doesn't involve solving the murder of Megan Hamlyn either. As far as Doyle is concerned, he's already nailed that one. All he needs to do now is find a way to prove it. And it's precisely because of what he intends to do tonight that he is determined the couple of hours he can spend at home now will be friction-free.

'All right,' he says. 'Gimme five minutes, okay?'

She smiles at him. Doyle finishes his meal. Doesn't find a single bone.

'What's for dessert?' he asks.

'Chocolate mousse,' says Rachel. 'It'll be your reward for counseling Amy.'

Doyle frowns at her. 'You do know that attempting to bribe a police officer is a felony, don't you?'

'It's also an offense for an officer to accept a bribe. Let's see what you do when the chocolate mousse is on the table in front of you.'

Doyle gets up from his chair and starts to head out of the living room.

'This mousse better not be something you made up just to get your own way,' he says.

He finds Amy in her bedroom. She's lying on her bed, wrapped in a fluffy white towel, her head buried in a book.

He's had a lot of conversations with Amy in this room. For some reason, it has become a place of opening up, of voicing fears and innermost thoughts and wishes for the future. And not only by Amy. Doyle has often found himself putting his own opinions and worries under the spotlight during these brief one-on-ones with his only daughter. She has that effect on him. Her innocence and complete trust never fail to make him lower his shield.

'Hey, sugar,' he says. 'What's the book?'

She looks up at him, beams a cheeky smile. 'Hi, Daddy. It's about stromony.'

'Stromony, huh? What's that?'

She looks wide-eyed at him. 'You don't know what stromony is?'

'Nope. Is it about dinosaurs?'

'No, silly.'

'Ponies?'

'Uh-uh.'

'Fairies?'

'No, Daddy,' she says in despair. 'It's about stars and planets and space.'

'Ah. And little green moon goblins?'

'No. No moon goblins. Don't you know anything?'

'Not a lot, I guess.'

He tries to dredge up a fascinating astronomical fact, and fails miserably. All that comes to mind is a limerick that begins, 'There was a young space-girl from Venus,' but he decides it's best not to share it.

He says, 'Tell me something about stromony.'

'Well . . .' says Amy. 'You know all the stars?'

'You mean the movie stars?'

'No, silly. The stars in the sky. The twinkly ones.'

'Oh, those stars. What about them?'

'Well, they're really suns.'

Doyle allows his jaw to go slack. 'No. Suns? Tiny little suns?'

'No, they're not tiny. They're big, like our sun. But they're really far away.'

'How far? You mean, like, from here to Ellie's apartment?'

'More than that.'

'How about here to New Jersey?'

'More.'

'To the North Pole?'

Amy has to think about this one. 'Can we see the North Pole from here?'

'No.'

'Then maybe not that far.'

'But still a long way,' Doyle says.

'Yes.'

'Wow!'

'Yes, it's amazable, isn't it?'

'It certainly is amazable. Are you doing this stuff at school too?'

He thinks, Subtle switch, you sly dog.

'Sometimes. Not all the time.'

'No. You have to do lots of other work too, don't you?'

'Yes. Hundreds.'

'Sure. And I bet you get through lots of pencils and erasers and things, don't you?'

Amy goes quiet then, and drops her gaze. Even at seven she can see Doyle's ploy for what it is. She knows exactly where this is headed.

'Honey, you listening to me?'

She nods. Says nothing for a while. Then: 'Are you mad at me?'

'No. Why would I be mad at you?'

'I don't know. Mommy's mad at me.'

'No she isn't. She just wants to understand.'

Amy picks at a stray thread on the edge of her towel.

'Pumpkin?' says Doyle. 'Is there something going on at school? Something you don't want to talk about?'

Amy shakes her head.

'You sure?'

'Yes. I told Mommy. I don't know how those things got in my backpack.'

'You didn't put them there?'

'No.'

'You weren't looking after them for a friend?'

'No.'

Her head is bowed really low now. So low that Doyle cannot see her expression. But it seems to him that she is on the edge of tears. He feels his own heart cracking.

And then a sequence of images starts to play in his head. He is back in Proust's tattoo parlor. Ripping the guy's shirt off. Threatening him. Letting him know that there is no doubt in Doyle's mind about his guilt.

So why the difference?

Why the heavy-handed approach with Proust and the soft touch with Amy? Why believe one and not the other?

And what if he's wrong? What if Proust is actually innocent and his own daughter has become a thief? Is that possible? Could Doyle's own judgment be so impaired?

No, he tells himself. I'm right, on both counts. Even if nobody else trusts me on this, I'm right.

'All right, Amy,' he says. And when she doesn't reply, he touches a curled finger to her chin and raises her face to look at him. 'I believe you. No big deal, okay?'

He spends a few more minutes with her, changing the subject and doing his best to blot the earlier conversation out of her mind. But when he leaves her bedroom he cannot shake off the profoundly sad feeling that a little something has died between the two of them tonight, and with it, a little of his belief in himself.

Lorenze Wheaton ain't afraid of no man. Not tonight. Not any night.

That's what he tells himself. That's what he believes. He doesn't see what's underneath. He's blind to the young man in constant fear for his life. That version of Wheaton is a pussy.

This here is the real Wheaton, walking tall and slow, not afraid of meeting the gaze of any motherfucker who might feel the need to stare him out.

His bravery is supported by the six-pack of beer he just shared at Tito's place. The blunts they fired up there didn't hurt neither. That was some seriously good shit Tito had there.

And then of course there's the nine. The biggest confidence booster of them all.

He reaches behind, taps himself on the back, just over the right kidney. Feels through his jacket the reassuring hardness of the Beretta 92 tucked into his waistband.

Go ahead, Mojo, he thinks. Make your play. This nigger's strapped, motherfucker, and don't that change everything?

He's strolling back from the projects on the other side of Avenue D, heading along East Seventh Street. It's after midnight and it's raining hard and the slick street is quiet. He doesn't mind the rain. In fact he likes it. It calms him. He thinks he could just stop and stand here for hours, his face upturned to the sky, feeling the heavy raindrops beating softly on his face.

But he doesn't stop walking. Something is dragging him home. Not fear. He ain't afraid.

He knows Mojo wants to down him. Mojo has been putting the word out on this for weeks, and for no good reason. Not unless getting it on with Mojo's huge-titted girlfriend counts as a reason.

Wheaton chuckles to himself. She was a fine piece of ass, all right. He'd loved to have seen Mojo's face when he found out.

He hears the deep-throated roar of a car as it accelerates behind him. He turns, and is dazzled by the headlights. He halts and puts his hand behind him. The car goes straight past, the passenger, a blond white woman, giving him a cursory glance.

Wheaton blows air. Ain't nothin'. Not Mojo's boys and not Five-O. Besides, he can handle either one of them. If it's Mojo's crew, he pulls his nine and starts downing those bitches. If it's the police, he books. He's got it all figured out. Soon as a cop shows interest, he takes off like Road Runner, *meep-meep*. Maybe they catch him, maybe they don't. What matters is that it gives him time to toss the strap. And if they find it, he can deny all knowledge. He always wears gloves when he takes the Beretta out with him. He's not taking chances. If he's caught carrying a concealed weapon it would mean serious jail time.

It's but a short walk to his mom's place. She won't be there. She's hardly ever there. She'll be out with that new boyfriend of hers. She'll turn up some time tomorrow. Lunchtime probably. Looking like shit. Then she'll go straight to bed.

Wheaton doesn't care. He likes having the crib to himself. When he gets in he'll be able to play his music as loud as he wants while he has another beer and smokes some more weed.

Another car approaches. Wheaton tells himself to ignore it. He's already at his apartment building. Seconds from safety. Not that he's scared or nothing.

He doesn't even bother to look as the car flashes past and he hears the spray of rainwater churned up from the wheels. No gunfire, no yelling at him to freeze. Nothing to get worked up about. He smiles as he permits himself a moment of feeling bulletproof before he abandons the street.

He looks up at his building. One light shines out from the top floor. The rest is in blackness. On the other side of the tall stoop he can make out bags of garbage stacked high on the trash cans. He kicks open the iron gate and starts down the steps to the basement apartment. The front door is set into the side of the stoop. He pats his pockets as he tries to get his fogged brain to remember where he put his damned keys. He hears a small metallic sound somewhere in his jacket. He reaches into one of his inside pockets, finds the key. He inserts it into the keyhole and turns. Pushes the door open.

The shape is on him in an instant.

It floats down from the street level. Barely seems to touch the steps. The slightest of sounds is all it makes. Wheaton has time to turn only a fraction before the dark shape is level with him. And although it seems to Wheaton that this must be some terrible ethereal demon to be able to travel so quickly and silently, when it strikes he discovers just how solid it actually is. Something – a fist, a weapon, he doesn't know – connects with the side of his head with force enough to make everything go temporarily black, and when he next can see again, it's the tiles of his floor he's staring at.

He feels hands sliding over his back. At least he presumes they are hands. Right now he's not even sure his attacker is human. What if these are some kind of feelers or claws running over him?

He hears a whimper, and realizes it's himself.

He feels his jacket being yanked up and the Beretta snatched from under his belt. Now he's utterly defenseless. Something grabs him at shoulder level. It lifts him from the ground slightly. Starts to drag him along the floor and into the interior of the apartment. There are no lights on in here. He cannot see anything. He feels like he's being dragged into the lair of a giant insect of some kind, to be trussed up and eaten at its leisure.

Another whimper. Then he remembers he has a voice. 'Hey! HEY! What is this? Who are—'

He gets hit again. Another blow to the right side of his head. He grunts, then starts to feel the burning pain in his ear.

His arms are grabbed and pulled behind his back. Something is tied tightly around his wrists, binding them together.

He raises his head from the floor. 'Please, man . . . Whoever you are . . . Please . . .'

He knows he's making no sense, but he has no idea what is going on here. He doesn't know what he should say, what he can do to stop this.

Something presses to his face. It forces his head back onto the cold floor. It's a hand – a human hand. He's sure of this now. *'Course it's a human hand, Lorenze, you dumb fuck. What the fuck else would it be?*

The hand is gloved. He can smell the leather as he struggles to draw air into his lungs.

And then his ear burns some more, but this time because hot breath is being blown onto it. Breath that carries three simple words that explain all this.

'Mojo says hello.'

So this is it. The moment he has been preparing for but which, deep in his heart, he never really thought would come. He thought it was all bluster on Mojo's part. Trying to sound big. Trying to maintain control through fear. All part of the game. The game that Wheaton has been playing too. Carrying that piece to show that he is also a warrior, ready to do battle at any time, even though he believed he would never have to pull the trigger.

And now that time has actually come, and he has already lost. He is about to die. Here in his mother's place, where he ought to be safe. And tomorrow she will come home and find her only son with a bullet-hole in his skull, and his blood and brain matter spilled across her cold tiled floor.

'I got money,' he says. 'I can get it for you. Just don't—'

But his words are lost when the sack comes over his head and is fastened tight around his neck. He hears only his own breath now, coming fast and shallow, and his pulse, booming in his head. He closes his eyes. Even though he can see nothing anyway, he screws his eyes up tight and clenches his teeth and waits for the gunshot.

But it's not going to be so quick and easy. His mental torture is not yet over.

'Sing,' the voice hisses against the cloth. At least that's what it sounds like to Wheaton.

'Wh–What?'

'I want you to sing.'

'Sing? You want me to fuckin' sing? S–sing what?'

'Whatever. You choose.'

Wheaton's mind races. He can't focus on songs right now. For his hesitation he receives a slap through the hood.

'I said, "Sing!"'

'I–I can't think. The words won't come. I can't—'

'All right, then. *I'll* choose. Sing "White Christmas".'

'What? You fucking with me, right? You want this nigger to sing 'bout a *white* Christmas?'

'Just do it.'

'I . . . I can't. I only know the first line. Bill Cosby ain't exactly my thing, yo.'

'All right, then. "Jingle Bells". The chorus, okay? Everybody knows the chorus to "Jingle Bells".'

'But . . . but it ain't even Christmas. Why the fuck do you—'

Another slap. 'Do it! Now!'

'Aiight! I'm doing it, I'm doing it . . . Jingle bells, jingle bells, jingle all the way . . ."'

'Louder!'

'. . . Oh what fun, di-dah-di-dah, on a sumthin' sumthin' sleigh, hey!'

'Again, Lorenze. Even louder. Keep repeating it. Stop and you're dead, hear?'

Wheaton knows he's dead anyway. He doesn't know why he's singing, but he does it. In truth, he's glad of it. It takes his mind away from what's about to happen. He doesn't want to hear a round being chambered or a safety being flicked off or a hammer being cocked. So he sings. Louder and louder. Sings like he's trying to fill Carnegie Hall with his tuneless voice. Sings like he really does want this to be Christmas, and he's standing in the cold air of Washington Square Park, belting out his festive chorus for all to hear, for all to know just how wonderful he feels at this happy, happy time of peace and generosity and good will to all men. Sings like he knows it will—

Where the fuck is that bullet?

He stops singing. Strains to listen through the thick cloth. Hears nothing.

'Yo,' he says quietly. He tenses, still expecting the gunshot. When it doesn't come, he risks raising his voice. 'Yo, you still there?'

Still nothing.

He dares to move. Lifts his head from the floor first of all. Rotates it in all directions while he tries to detect the slightest sound. Any indication that he is not alone.

Silence.

He rolls onto his side, brings his knees up and manages to push himself up into a sitting position.

'Hey!' he calls. 'Whatchoo doin'? Where you at?'

It takes Wheaton a while to convince himself that his attacker is not still here, playing some kind of cruel joke for which the punchline is a bullet to Wheaton's brain. And when he eventually does manage to believe it, he still can't understand what this was all about. Why is he still alive? Was this simply some kind of warning? A message to let him know that he's not untouchable and can be taken out at any time?

He sits cross-legged in the darkness of his mother's apartment. The hood still on his head. His hands still bound behind his back.

'Fuck!' he says. 'Fuck you, motherfucker!'

His outburst is fueled by anger, but also by self-loathing. He wishes he had fought back more. He wishes he had been more of a man in the face of death. Above all, he wishes it had been the truth when he told himself he was not afraid.

He was very afraid. He knows it now, and it stings.

He could try denying it again. Try acting the hard man he wants everyone else to see.

But his lie would be betrayed by the tears on his cheeks.

Those, and the large wet patch on his pants.

Doyle pulls the car over. He strips off the leather gloves and drops them onto the black ski mask he has already tossed onto the passenger seat.

It doesn't rattle him that he's just terrorized another human being. Lorenze Wheaton hardly enters into that category anyhow. Lorenze Wheaton is a punk. A lowlife. He sells drugs to schoolkids. Rumor has it that he also raped a girl of fifteen, but the cops never managed to make that one stick. So what if he's just had a taste of the misery he doles out to others?

But of course that's not the real reason Doyle paid him that little visit. He's not in the business of setting up as a vigilante. No, something else drew him to Wheaton's place tonight.

He'd heard on the streets about Wheaton's feud with Mojo. Heard too that Wheaton had taken to carrying a semi-automatic pistol around with him for protection.

Doyle reaches into his pocket and pulls out the Beretta 92. Wheaton's gun.

He doesn't know how dangerous this mission he's on for Bartok is likely to get. What he does know is that if he needs to shoot someone, this time he's going to make damn sure he doesn't use a weapon that can be traced back to him.

Not that it will come to that. Doyle doesn't plan to shoot anyone.

And don't his plans always work out?

FIFTEEN

It's after two o'clock in the morning when he kicks in the door.

He hopes this will be straightforward. He hopes that Cubo and his girl will be tucked up in bed. Fast asleep. Not expecting any interruptions to their sweet dreams. Doyle will present his most fearsome aspect, wave his gun around, offer up a few simple questions and then get out of there. That's how it will go.

Sure.

The first thing he sees is Tasha Wilmot. Which is a surprise in itself because he wasn't expecting to be able to see a damned thing. But he can see Tasha because there is a lamp on in the room. Not only that, but there is some R&B playing quietly in the background. And Tasha is stark naked on the sofa. Welcome home, sugar.

And yet Tasha does not scream. Despite the fact that she is unclothed and is looking at a burly man in a ski mask who has just barged uninvited into her apartment and is now pointing a cannon at her face, she does not yell. Doesn't even attempt to conceal her assets behind a cushion or two. And the reason for this apparent devil-may-care attitude of hers is not bravery or indignation; it is that she is stoned out of her skull. Doyle sees immediately that she can hardly focus on him, and that the only response he's likely to get from her is some random eye-rolling accompanied by a little drooling.

He wastes no time in racing across to the bedroom, his heart now thumping warnings against his ribcage. If Tasha is awake, then there is every possibility that Cubo is also awake. And if he's only a little more compos mentis than his girlfriend, he could well be reaching for a weapon of some kind right now.

Doyle shoulders the door open. Flies into the room. Scans the area with gun outstretched in a two-handed combat stance that would be a dead giveaway to any observer that this intruder is probably a cop, ski mask notwithstanding.

But there are no observers here. Except for perhaps those of the six-legged variety. There is a lamp on in this fleapit of a room, but no Cubo. Which leaves only . . .

He hears the noise before he gets there. The bathroom. He launches himself at the door with his leg raised. Drives his foot into the area just over the handle. The door practically comes off its hinges as it crashes open. Doyle's momentum carries him into the room, and for a terrifying moment he wonders whether an entrance like this is the wisest of moves.

He's found Cubo.

Luckily his quarry doesn't pose a threat. In fact, he's probably the least threatening quarry imaginable. For one thing, he's naked. He also makes size-zero models look obese: every bone in his body is visible through his thin pallid flesh. And his response to Doyle's invasion is not to come at him with a knife or a gun, but to contemplate jumping out of the window he has just opened. He sits straddling the windowsill, one leg outside, one in, his gaze oscillating between Doyle and the blackness on the other side of that wall.

'You don't wanna do that,' yells Doyle. 'You're five floors up and you're not over the fire escape. You jump and you're dead. And if you don't die, where you gonna go with no clothes on?'

Cubo turns his head to the night air again. A gust of wind blows rain into his face. He turns back to Doyle.

'I just wanna talk,' says Doyle. 'Don't risk it, man.' He pushes his Beretta into his waistband, then steps closer to Cubo. He sees that Cubo seems to relax a little, as though he is resolving his dilemma. As though he is on the verge of accepting that an encounter with a masked gunman, however undesirable that might be, beats a fall to certain death.

Doyle makes the most of the opportunity. He covers the remaining distance between himself and Cubo in one sudden bound. He reaches out his hand . . .

. . . and pushes Cubo out of the window.

Sometimes Doyle thinks he can be a little too impulsive for his own good. Can be a little too *reckless*.

Take now, for example. Dangling a naked guy out of a window by his ankles has to be one of the more outrageous acts he has perpetrated in his career. He would slap his own wrist if it didn't mean letting go of this lowlife.

'Quit the yelling!' he calls down to Cubo. 'You want the neighbors to hear? You want them to step into the backyard and see you like this?'

'Bring me up!' yells Cubo. 'Get me the fuck inside, will ya!'

'The sooner you quit yapping, the sooner I haul you back up. I ain't exactly enjoying the view I got from up here, if you know what I mean.'

'Okay,' Cubo says, his voice unnaturally high-pitched. 'Okay. I'm shutting up. Now bring me in. I ain't good with heights.'

'Then what the hell were you doing opening the window, dumbass? Don't answer that. I got a more interesting question.'

'What? What question?'

'Anton Ruger. Where can I find him?'

'Who? Who?'

'Don't prolong this, Cubo. My hands are getting pretty slippery in this rain. Anton Ruger. Where is he?'

'I don't know what you're talking about, man. I ain't never heard of no Anton Ruger.'

Doyle allows Cubo's ankles to slip through his grasp by about an inch. It's enough to cause Cubo to let out another ultrasonic yelp.

'Don't fuck with me, Cubo. I know you been mouthing off about how you've been running with Ruger. Now where can I find him?'

'All right, man. It's true. I did say that. But it was just talk. I ain't never met the guy.'

Doyle jerks his arms enough to shake the coins from Cubo's pants, if he were wearing any. He gets another girlish scream.

'Then why say it? Of all the scumbags you could claim to fraternize with, why pick Ruger? How come you know so much about him?'

'All right, listen. There's this other dude I know. He's copped from me once or twice. When he was high, he told me about Ruger. About how he works for him. That's all I know, man. It's all hearsay. Now, please, let me up.'

Doyle doesn't relent. Not yet.

'Who is this guy?'

'Calls hisself Ramone. I ain't got no last name.'

'What's he look like?'

'He's a spic. Smart dresser. Likes the ladies. Has a gold earring.'

'Where can I find him?'

'I don't know. Please. I ain't got his address.'

Another shake. Another cry.

'Then where'd you meet him?'

'A strip joint in Brooklyn. The Arabesque. You know it? Close to the river.'

'He go there every night?'

'No. Saturdays. He goes there Saturdays.'

'Every Saturday?'

'Yeah. Every fucking Saturday. Now will you bring me up, please?'

Shit, thinks Doyle. This is turning into a wild-fucking-goose chase. How many more of these assholes do I have to lean on before I get to Ruger himself?

What makes it worse is that this Ramone guy is Doyle's only lead to Ruger, and Saturday night is only hours before the deadline for getting the ring back to Bartok. There's a big time period between now and then in which Doyle could be just sitting on his hands as far as locating Ruger is concerned.

He decides that this is the most he's going to get out of Cubo, and hauls him back into the bathroom.

Sitting on the hard floor, dripping and shivering and rubbing his ankles, Cubo looks up at his masked attacker. 'You didn't have to go and do that.'

Doyle pulls his gun and aims it at Cubo's head. 'This never happened. All right, Cubo? I hear you talked to anyone about this, then I'm coming back. And next time it won't be your ankles I'll use to dangle you, if you catch my drift.' To make his point clear, he lowers his aim. Cubo hastily places his hands over his shriveled genitals.

'I won't say nothing. I swear.'

Doyle nods. He believes what he's just heard. Cubo is too terrified to risk another encounter like this one.

He leaves the bathroom. On his way out of the apartment he sees that Tasha hasn't moved from her position on the sofa. Still hasn't bothered to cover herself up.

Seemingly oblivious to the events that have just taken place in her bathroom, she gives Doyle an idle wave and a spaced-out smile. 'Bye,' she says. 'Have a nice day.'

Cubo sits on that bathroom floor for a long time. Sits there shivering until he can't take the cold anymore.

He drags himself up and closes the window. A last glimpse of the darkness out there makes his head swim. That guy was gonna drop him. From five floors above the ground! Jesus! He would have done it, too. It was in his voice. That dude was serious.

Cubo pulls open the bathroom door. He half expects to see the intruder still there. Maybe balling Tasha or drinking his beers or stealing his stash. And it shames him that, even if the motherfucker is doing any of those things, Cubo will smile and say nothing and wait while the guy has his fun.

But the man is not there. Just Tasha, waving her arms and yelling occasional words she remembers in the song being played, the dumb bitch.

Cubo crosses the living area and goes into the bedroom. He picks up a sweatshirt and jeans from the floor and puts them on. Then he goes back into the living room and paces up and down.

The guy said he would come back if Cubo told anyone about this, and Cubo believes it. Busting down his door, dangling him out of his own window, pointing a nine at his junk – that is one scary-ass motherfucker, man.

But, scary as he is, he is only one man. And, scary as he is, he is not scarier than Ramone, and the men who work for Ramone. When the guy goes after Ramone, and Ramone wastes him, as he surely will, then Ramone will want to know how the stranger found him. He will make inquiries – persistent and forceful inquiries that will undoubtedly lead him back to Cubo. And then hovering five floors above the ground will seem like a carnival ride in comparison to what Ramone will do to him.

And if, perchance, the man in the ski mask defeats Ramone – which he won't – then he has to go up against Anton Ruger. And then all bets are off. Ruger is the baddest of the bad. Ruger will eat this guy for breakfast. And he too will want to know which rat squealed the information that led to him.

So weigh it up, man. Who frightens you more? A guy who is too chicken-shit even to show his face to you, or an army of killers led by a man who would slice up his own mother just to avoid boredom? Which of those is likely to triumph here, hmm? Which of those would it be sensible to stay on the right side of?

Making his decision, Cubo yells at Tasha to turn the music down, then picks up the phone.

SIXTEEN

Doyle hasn't had a lot of sleep. Which means he's irritable on this Friday morning. Which means that LeBlanc is not choosing the best moment to get in his face.

'You went to see Proust yesterday,' says LeBlanc.

Doyle thought he would be the first one in this morning, but LeBlanc has beaten him to it. In fact, Doyle gets the impression that LeBlanc has been sitting here for some time, just itching to get something off his chest.

Doyle looks down at LeBlanc behind his desk. The seriousness in the kid's eyes seems intensified by the stark frames of his spectacles.

'You put the coffee on?' Doyle asks. 'I could really do with a coffee right now.'

'Was it worth it?' says LeBlanc, refusing to be distracted from his agenda.

'It's gotta be strong, though. Plenty of caffeine. What about you, Tommy? You want some coffee?'

He starts to move away, but LeBlanc leaps from his chair and grabs him by the arm.

'For fuck's sake, Cal. I'm trying to talk to you, here.'

Doyle lowers his gaze to his imprisoned arm, then yanks it

out of LeBlanc's grasp. 'Seems lately you always want to talk to me, Tommy. What the fuck is your problem?'

'You went to see Proust.'

'Yes. All right. I went to see Proust. Now will you get over it and move on?'

'Move on? You act like it's nothing. Like it's an everyday occurrence for you. What kind of cop are you, Cal? I thought you were better than this.'

Doyle stares at him. 'Tommy, why are you getting so bent out of shape about it? Okay, so I didn't tell you where I was going yesterday. What's the big deal?'

LeBlanc releases a mirthless laugh. 'You don't even know, do you? You don't know what you did wrong. Have you seen what you did to Proust? Have you actually given him any thought this morning?'

'Not since I ate my Fruit Loops, no. Tommy, what's this about?'

LeBlanc pauses. Gathers his thoughts. 'I went to see Proust too. A few hours after you did.'

Doyle shrugs. 'So?'

'Cal, he was really bad. So bad I had to take him to the hospital.'

Doyle stares again. Realizes he's not on the same page as LeBlanc at all. Not even in the same book.

'Bad? In what way?'

'Bad in the way that people get when they've had the crap beaten out of them.'

'What? He . . . what?'

'I've seen tune-ups before, Cal, but this goes way beyond that. I don't know what you were thinking, but—'

'Wait. Hold up, Tommy. You're telling me that Proust has been assaulted? And you think I did it?'

'Are you denying it?'

'Of course I'm denying it. Does Proust say different?'

'Not in so many words. He made up some lame story about being mugged by a gang, but it's bullshit.'

'So he didn't say it was me. But you still think it was?'

'What am I supposed to think, Cal? You go to see him without telling me, even though you're not supposed to. You come back with a bruise under your eye that you won't explain. And when I go to see Proust, he looks ready for a body bag. How else am I supposed to read that?'

'Not in the way you're doing. I don't know what happened to Proust, and I can't say I feel sorry for the guy, but it wasn't me. I didn't hit him. Not even once.'

Doyle can tell from the look on LeBlanc's face that he's not convinced. And he can't really blame him. Doyle has already let LeBlanc see his lack of regard for Proust. Yes, maybe he did go too far when he ripped the scumbag's shirt off him. And yes, maybe the secrets he has kept from his partner have done nothing to promote his integrity in LeBlanc's eyes. But that doesn't mean he would beat Proust to within an inch of his life, even though there are times when he pictures himself doing a lot more than that.

He turns away then, and starts heading out of the squad-room. LeBlanc runs past him and blocks his way.

'Where you going, Cal?'

'To sort this out with Proust. To get the truth from him.'

'Uh-uh. Can't let you do that.'

Doyle almost laughs in surprise. This kid has balls.

'You can't let me do it? What, are you gonna arrest me?'

LeBlanc chews on his lip for a moment. Doyle can see how nervous he is, and in a way he both admires him and feels sorry for him.

'The lieutenant has already given strict instructions for you not to go anywhere near Proust. You disobey that now, and I'll have to talk to the boss.'

'You'd do that? Why? You think I'm gonna take another pop at Proust?'

'No. Because somebody needs to protect you from yourself.'

'Nice of you to care, Tommy, but I don't need no protection. Get out of my way.'

Doyle takes a step forward, but LeBlanc doesn't budge.

'Okay, then, if you won't listen to me for your own sake, then do it for the case.'

'What are you talking about?'

'Proust is your number-one suspect, Cal. You got a real hard-on for this guy as the perp. And maybe you're right. Maybe he did do it. But you going at him like this won't prove anything. In fact, it could jeopardize the whole case. Let's take it slow and easy. We'll follow the leads and we'll find the evidence. But you need to keep him at arm's length while we do that. Okay?'

Doyle thinks about it. He wants to shoulder LeBlanc aside and storm out of here. Go straight over to Proust's place and squeeze the truth out of him. And it's not LeBlanc's words of wisdom that are stopping him. If anything, the kid's patronizing tone is irritating him to the point of making Doyle want to pull off his partner's spectacles and stomp on them. No, what's holding him back is LeBlanc's earlier threat. Doyle believes it. The kid will go straight to Cesario as soon as Doyle leaves the building. And that will be it. He will be off the case.

He can't risk that.

'I haven't had that coffee yet,' he tells LeBlanc. Then he turns around and heads back into the squadroom.

'Go ahead, Mom. Get your ass up there.'

Nicole turns. Megan is standing just a few feet away, grinning, showing her dimples. Her blond curls are tucked up under her swimming cap. She is wearing her favorite swimsuit – the black Speedo with the cut-outs. God, she's so shapely now. Going to be a real heartbreaker.

Nicole tilts her head back and gazes up that staircase that seems high enough to take her to the moon, then looks across at Megan again. Megan urges her on with a wave.

'Go on. You can do it.'

Nicole gives her the subtlest of nods. A nod which says, *I'm doing what you say but I'm not convinced in the least.* Biting her lip, she starts up the steps of the tower. When she gets to the first platform, she pauses and looks down.

'Uh-uh, Mother,' calls Megan. 'All the way up.'

Nicole continues her ascent. She feels the fluttering starting in her stomach. Her teeth begin to chatter, more from nerves than the cold. She thinks she may vomit. She goes up and up and up until the roof of the building seems close enough to touch.

On the top platform she grabs the handrails and looks directly ahead. She doesn't want to look down, because her thoughts are already starting to swirl with the knowledge that there's a vast space beneath her, just waiting to swallow her up.

But Megan is yelling for her attention: 'Mom! Mom!'

Nicole grips the handrails tighter and risks a quick glance downward. Tries to focus on the tiny figure of her daughter rather than the fact that she's a million miles straight down.

Okay, so not a million miles. But ten meters is still pretty damned high. That's thirty-three feet. It would be like falling off the roof of a house.

Megan is gesticulating wildly, urging her mother to move along the platform.

Nicole gives another tentative nod, more for her own benefit than for Megan's. She faces forward again, starts to step gingerly along the board. Keeps forcing herself onward until the handrails disappear and there is only a narrow rectangle of solidity preventing her from plunging into the depths below.

Somehow – she's not sure how – she makes it to the end of the platform. Even manages to curl her toes over its front edge. She's breathing hard, but not through exertion. Her pulse is pounding in her head. She tries to focus. She knows exactly what to do, what the technique is. She has seen Megan do this a thousand times. Has even acted as her daughter's sternest judge and critic of her efforts.

Megan is good, though. Superb. Nicole can picture her now. Launching herself into space, her arms out, her spine arched. Sailing through the air for what seems like an age. Then, at the last possible moment, bringing her palms together in the flat-hand position, her arms tight against her ears. A perfect 'rip' entry into the water with barely a splash. And throughout this, her mother watching from the benches, unable to breathe through both admiration and fear.

Nicole ventures a snap glance into the dive well. Jesus, it's high up here.

She can't back out now. She has driven twenty miles to get here. She's at the Nassau County Aquatic Center in East Meadow. It's only eight-forty. The place isn't even open to the public yet. But that's okay. The staff here know her well. The countless hours she spent here with Megan while she trained and competed.

'Go, Mom! Nothing fancy. A simple dive, just like all the others.'

Simple. Easy for you to say. I'm crapping myself just standing here.

Focus, Nicole tells herself. She has limbered up with twenty lengths in the main pool. She has done several practice dives from the three-meter springboard. She has worked her way up the tower to the 7.5-meter platform. What's this but just a little extra height?

She purses her lips and exhales hard, trying to control her breathing. She flicks water from her fingers at her sides. Curls her toes over the platform edge again. I'm ready, she thinks.

'Stop thinking about it. Just do it.'

Nicole looks down. This time, she thinks. I can do this.

And then she turns around and almost runs back to the safety of the handrails.

'Jeez, Mom! What are you doing?'

But Megan isn't annoyed. She's laughing. And Nicole is laughing too. They are both laughing because it's the same every time. Nicole goes up, Nicole comes down. But it's always via the stairs. It's become a running joke between mother and daughter. Something Nicole will never forget.

As she clambers her way down the steps, she can hear Megan practically screaming with laughter. And Nicole cannot help but join in. They will laugh together until the tears run down their faces, and Megan will refuse to let it lie. She will tease her parent all the way home. Tell her that she cannot believe how her own mother cannot even—

The laughter stops.

It stops because Nicole cannot see Megan anywhere on the poolside. She is not here.

She was never here.

And now Nicole knows why she came all the way to the Aquatic Center in East Meadow. When she got up this morning she told herself she needed to get out of the house. She needed some exercise. Something to take her mind away from the horrors of reality.

Swimming, she decided. She has always been a good swimmer.

But now she knows it was her mind playing tricks on itself. She didn't really have to settle on swimming as a distraction. And even if that was all she could come up with, she could have visited a pool closer to home.

No, she came here not to forget but to remember. To make a connection. This is Megan's place. This is where she spent a huge portion of her free time outside school hours. Not hanging around on street corners. Not going off to places like the East Village. Why would she? This sport was her life.

And now Nicole knows why she didn't execute her dive. It wasn't just her fear. It was the fact that it wasn't right. It wasn't what was expected. By either of them. If Nicole had dived, there would have been no laughter, no ribbing. It would have been the end. It would have closed a door.

'Nic? Are you okay?'

Phil. One of the pool guards.

'I . . . I heard about Megan,' he says. 'I'm real sorry.'

'It's okay,' she replies. But then she hurries away. Back to the changing rooms. She doesn't want to lament; she wants to celebrate. She wants to keep the laughter of Megan ringing in her ears for ever.

★

A crap.

That's all he'd gone for. A quick dump.

It's always the same when he drinks strong coffee. It pushes everything else out of his system. He couldn't contain himself any longer.

Besides, he's not a nursemaid. He's not paid to sit here minding Doyle all day.

But he can guess where Doyle has gone. His choice of the very moment that LeBlanc slips out of the squadroom to do his own disappearing act is no coincidence.

Of that LeBlanc is certain.

He is angry, but his anger is tempered by a sense of sadness. He feels he has given Doyle every opportunity to do things in the right way and, every time, Doyle has insisted on shrugging off his partner's helping hand.

I can't stop Doyle's march of destruction, thinks LeBlanc.

All I can do is make sure the only one destroyed by Doyle is himself.

SEVENTEEN

'Jesus, Stan! What the hell happened to you?'

He's not concerned, thinks Proust. Curious, yes. But Doyle doesn't care about my welfare. Wouldn't matter to him if I was dead.

'I got on the wrong side of someone.'

There, Doyle. Make of that what you will. You wanna play games, let's do it, you sonofabitch.

'Who would that be, Stan?'

'Why? You think they should be arrested? Think they should be locked up for doing this to me?'

He sees the confusion in Doyle's eyes. The uncertainty. He's on unfamiliar ground now, and he doesn't like it. Well, fuck him. He started this.

'What's going on, Stan? You looking to jam me up for what happened to you? You really think you could pull that off?'

Doyle advances as he says this. He cuts a threatening figure, and although Proust has the counter between him and Doyle, he still feels nervous. He can feel himself starting to tremble.

No, he tells himself. You can do this. Stand up to him. He's a bully, and there's nothing a bully likes better than a willing victim. Show him what you're made of. What's the worst he can do? Inflict pain? Ha! I can do pain now, you bastard. Try me. Go ahead, you big fucking nobody, try me.

'I'm not looking to do anything, Detective. Why would I? What would be the purpose? I'm just a plain ordinary citizen, wanting to get on with his plain ordinary life. There something wrong with that?'

When Doyle slams his palm down on the countertop, the bang echoes around the room and Proust flinches visibly.

Stay calm, he tells himself. Anyone would have jumped at that. Doesn't mean you're scared. Don't let him get to you.

Doyle raises his voice. 'No, Stan. You're not a plain ordinary citizen. Ordinary citizens don't torture and kill other citizens. You're special in that way, Stan. That's why you get my special attention.'

Proust can feel his eye twitching. Shit! He gets it sometimes. A nervous tic. He rubs his eye, trying to massage it back into its normal behavior. He doesn't want Doyle thinking he's intimidated by him, because he's not. Damn straight, he's not.

'I ain't nothing special. I just do tattoos. And you need to stop making all these accusations about me.'

Doyle leans forward over the counter, his expression menacing. 'Or what, Stan? What will you do?'

Proust wants to maintain eye contact. He wants to look this bastard right back in his pupils and tell him what a sad, pathetic clown he is. He wants to punch him. Right in the mouth. Knock a few teeth out.

But he can't do any of that. Can't even endure the staring match. He has to look away. And it shames him to do so. Reminds him of all the times he backed down from the bullies at school. It makes him sick to the stomach, and he feels the self-loathing start to rise in his gullet.

And then, as if to make amends for all the times he has been put through situations like this, fate offers him a helping hand. If he hadn't averted his gaze just when he did, he might never have detected the opportunity being presented to him.

In one of the wall mirrors he sees a movement on the street outside. A man, getting out of his car. It's Doyle's partner. The blond cop. LeBlanc, or whatever his name is. He's looking at another car parked behind his own. Doyle's car. And now he's throwing his hands up in despair and shaking his head.

'Are you listening to me, Stan? I asked you what you were going to do about it.'

Proust runs his hand through his hair. Pretends he's considering Doyle's question. Acts as though he's about to collapse under this onslaught, which is exactly what Doyle wants him to do.

He sees LeBlanc move to the curb, a look of grim determination on his face. He's getting ready to cross the street. Getting ready to barge straight in here.

He doesn't know where it comes from, but that's when Proust gets his idea. The muse strikes. Oh, yes, that beautiful muse grabs him right by the crotch and whispers sweetly in his ear.

'I ain't doing this no more,' he says to Doyle, and then he's gone.

It takes Doyle by surprise, Proust walking off like that. It's as if the man was suddenly seized by an impulse to get away. As if he knows that a bomb is about to go off in here.

Doyle knows he can't leave it at that. He can't just go back to his car. He has to find out what the hell is going on. Why is Proust acting so peculiarly? Why the sudden need to go into his living area? Has he finally snapped? Is he going to fetch a weapon of some kind, or to call the cops?

Doyle steps around the counter. He pushes open the door through which Proust has just exited. It leads to a small, narrow room. Windowless, it is illuminated by only a single naked bulb of feeble wattage. The walls are mostly lined with dark wooden shelves holding tattoo equipment and books on art and design. At the far end of the claustrophobic space, in the left-hand wall, another door creaks as it slowly closes. Proust has just left through that door.

Doyle picks up his pace as he traverses the storage room. He doesn't want to give Proust time to set a trap or locate a weapon. He gets there before the door can finish closing, and puts a hand out to stop it. The door consists almost entirely of a panel of translucent glass, enclosed in a narrow painted frame. The glass is an ugly pale yellow, like paper aged by sunlight, and through it Doyle can just make out the shape of Proust in the room beyond. He pushes the door open and steps inside.

The place hasn't changed much since Doyle was last in here, all that time ago when he was looking into the Alyssa Palmer case. To Doyle's right is a counter, beyond which is a kitchen area so small you could fetch food from the fridge, wash it, slice it and cook it without your feet even shifting position. Next to the kitchen is a tiny living area containing a lumpy sofa and chair huddled in front of a television. The TV sits on top of a hi-fi unit that leans to the left because one of its front wheels is missing. In stark contrast to the clinical cleanliness and modernity of the tattooing room they have just left, everything here seems shabby and faded and threadbare.

Directly in front of Doyle, Proust is standing with his back to an old dining table. There is an odd expression on his face.

Doyle isn't sure what to make of it. Terror? No, not that. What then? Expectation?

Behind Doyle, the door swings back and clicks home, the glass rattling slightly in its frame.

'Stan? Is there something you need to tell me?'

'N–no.' Proust's eyes dart from side to side. He rubs his palms up and down his pants. It's about the most nervous Doyle has ever seen him. Why is that? What does he think I'm about to do to him?

Suddenly this all seems so wrong to Doyle. He can't put his finger on it, but there's something happening here of which he's not aware.

A trap? Is this a trap of some kind? Would this little shit dare to attempt such a thing?

Doyle finds himself scanning the cramped living quarters. Can there be somebody else here?

'Stan? What the hell is eating you?'

The buzzing noise startles them both. Proust in particular almost leaps up onto his dining table. On the wall to Doyle's left, a red light starts flashing.

Says Doyle, 'You got a customer?'

'I don't know.'

Doyle furrows his brow. 'You don't know? What do you mean, you don't—'

'I don't know, I tell you. I DON'T KNOW!'

Doyle's eyes widen. Proust's reaction is totally disproportionate. Why is he shouting like this?

'All right, Stan. Take it easy. I was just—'

And then Stan is moving away from his table. Sidling around Doyle. There is a crazed, hunted look in his eyes.

'I DON'T KNOW ANYTHING! PLEASE! STOP THIS!'

There is deep pleading in his voice. He could almost be begging for his life. Doyle feels the situation has suddenly spun out of control. Any logic that was here before has abandoned ship. A crash is about to take place and he doesn't know what he can do to stop it.

He starts to reach for his gun.

'Stan! Stay where you are!'

'PLEASE! NO! STOP!'

'STAN!'

And then it happens. It happens so fast that all Doyle can do is stand there and watch. He watches as Proust starts running. Watches him run straight at the door. The door with the glass panel running all the way down it. Watches as Proust raises his arms and crashes right through it, the glass exploding into thousands of shards. Watches as he falls through into the storeroom on the other side and hits the floor, the fragments of glass still raining down on him.

'Jesus!'

Doyle moves across to what remains of the door. Stares through it at the motionless figure of Proust lying on his bed of glinting needles. His mind struggles to make sense of what he has just witnessed. What the hell is going on here?

'Stan! You okay?'

He steps through the hole in the door. Feels and hears the glass being crunched beneath his heel. He starts to bend toward Proust.

'Jesus fucking Christ, Cal! What have you done?'

Doyle looks to his right. Sees the silhouette of the figure standing in the other doorway, the one leading into the shop.

And then he understands. It all clicks into place.

The clever bastard. The clever, manipulative, devious, conniving bastard.

Doyle reaches down, slaps his palms onto Proust's shoulders. Grabs hold of his shirt and flips him over.

'Oh you fucking sonofabitch!' he yells. 'You twisted fuck!'

'Cal!' LeBlanc shouts.

Proust's eyes are closed. His face is streaming with blood. He lets out a low moan.

Doyle drops to his knees, arrows of pain shooting into them as the glass penetrates. He grasps hold of Proust's shirt collar and begins to shake him violently.

'It won't work, Stan. You think you can get away with this? Well, think again. It ain't gonna work. I am gonna nail you, you sick bastard.'

'Cal, get the fuck off him, man. What the fuck are you doing?'

Doyle feels the arm snake around his neck. When he doesn't let go of Proust, the pressure increases and starts to choke him. Doyle allows himself to be dragged upward, away from Proust. When he gets his feet under him again, he launches himself backwards, propelling LeBlanc into the shelves behind him. LeBlanc grunts but doesn't relax his grip, so Doyle drives his right elbow hard into LeBlanc's solar plexus. Doyle feels an explosion of breath on his neck, and when LeBlanc drops his arms, Doyle spins around and grabs him by the throat. He draws back his free hand, ready to drive it into LeBlanc's face.

'Cal!' LeBlanc squawks. 'Cal! Look at yourself. Look at what you're doing.'

Doyle freezes. He is glad there are no mirrors in here. He can imagine what he must look like. He can picture the crazed fury written on his face and in his eyes. He can feel the tautness in the muscles and tendons of the arm that is about to pulverize his own partner's features.

Christ, he thinks. He's right. What am I doing? Can this really be me?

He relaxes the fingers wrapped around LeBlanc's throat. Starts to lower his clenched fist. LeBlanc slaps Doyle's arm aside and pushes himself away from the shelving. He moves toward Proust, still lying on the floor, groaning.

'He jumped,' Doyle says.

LeBlanc whirls on him.

'What? What did you say?'

'He jumped through the door.'

LeBlanc's laugh is without humor. 'What, not even a trip? A stumble? A fainting spell? Come on, Cal. Even you can do better than that.'

Doyle feels his anger building again, and he has to fight to push it back inside. 'He jumped, Tommy. It's a set-up. He's trying to put me in a jam to save his own ass.'

LeBlanc just shakes his head and kneels down to examine Proust.

'What,' says Doyle, 'you don't believe me? You think I'd make up something as ridiculous as that?'

LeBlanc glares at him. 'I don't know what to believe. All I know is what I heard and what I saw. What do you think a jury would make of that, Cal? Especially given your history with this guy?'

LeBlanc stands again. He reaches into his pocket and pulls out a cellphone.

'You giving me up, Tommy?'

'You must know, I'm calling in EMS.'

'He doesn't need an ambulance.'

'Oh, so you're now a medical expert too, Cal? The man has just gone through a sheet of glass. Maybe there's a piece of glass in an artery and he's bleeding to death here. Maybe he's fractured his skull. Maybe he's broken his freaking neck.'

'He doesn't need an ambulance,' Doyle repeats. Then, to Proust, he says, 'Get the fuck up, Stan. Cut the act.'

LeBlanc suddenly forgets about his phone call. He steps toward Doyle. Reaches under his jacket. Whips out his Glock.

Doyle's pulse races. What the hell has gotten into LeBlanc?

'Here,' says LeBlanc. He offers his gun to Doyle. 'Go ahead, take it. You wanna finish this, go ahead. Put a bullet in his brain. You really hate this guy so much, then take him out.'

Doyle stares at the younger man. He wonders how things got to be so twisted around. How it is that he, Doyle, is acting like a rookie who doesn't know what the hell he's doing, while LeBlanc is being the true professional. How did that happen? When did the world get turned upside down?

He has no answers. And he has no words for LeBlanc. Instead, he starts walking away. He's done here. He doesn't care anymore, and maybe that's because he cared too much. Let LeBlanc make his call. Let him report Doyle to the bosses. Let them take him off the case, off the squad, off the job.

Who gives a fuck?

EIGHTEEN

The noise is driving her crazy.

The hammering, the drilling, the sawing – she can't hear herself think. It was going on most of yesterday, and it was going on when she had breakfast this morning, and now it's lunchtime and it's still going on. What the hell is he doing in there?

Nicole pours the remainder of her still-steaming coffee down the drain and places her cup in the sink. She walks across to the door leading into the garage, then pauses.

It's gone quiet. Eerily so. She puts her ear to the door. Nothing. Not even the shuffling of Steve's feet. She presses her head harder against the wood. Holds her breath . . .

Whirrrrr.

She leaps back, afraid that a drill bit is about to come straight through the door and into her skull. Angrily, she flings the door open and steps inside. Ready to confront him.

Only she can't speak.

She can't talk because of what she sees here. This is not the garage she was expecting. All of its contents have been pushed to one end. In the center of the space, Steve has set up his work-bench. A length of wood lies across it, and on top of that is a saw and a retractable tape measure.

But what really grabs Nicole's attention here is the shelving.

Miles of it. Or at least there will be when Steve has finished. Almost every square inch of wall space now has brackets running up it, and some are already supporting wooden shelves.

Steve is standing at the wall separating the garage from the kitchen. He is holding a cordless drill. There is masonry dust and wood shavings all down the front of his coverall and on his face. He looks blankly at his wife as if to say, *What's the problem?*

'Steve,' she says. 'What are you doing?'

'The place is a mess. It needs organizing. I want it neat and tidy.'

She stares at him, incredulous. 'You want . . . What about what *I* want? Were you planning to consult me on this major change to our property?'

'Nicole, don't wig out over a few shelves. You never come in here anyway. Anytime you want something you send me in here to find it. Takes me hours sometimes, going through all that stuff.' He gestures behind him at the boxes and crates and bicycles and gardening equipment. 'This way we'll be able to find things instantly.'

Nicole moves into the center of the garage and looks again at Steve's handiwork. She's not convinced that all these shelves are necessary. Not at all sure that they have enough items in here to fill them.

She turns to look at the possessions they keep in the garage, and notices that Steve seems to have divided them into two piles, one larger than the other. She steps closer to the smaller pile. Opens up one of the boxes. It's full of old auto magazines.

'Steve, what are the boxes on this side of the garage?'

He turns to face her, the drill still in his hand. 'Things we can throw out. We don't need them anymore.'

She nods, but something tugs at her. Whispering to her that

something isn't right here. It's in Steve's body language. It's in his voice. Awkwardness. Anxiety.

She opens another box. Peers inside. Her heart stops. She faces Steve again, sees the guilt on his face.

'Steve. Please tell me you've made a mistake.'

'What?' he says, but she can tell that he understands her exactly.

'Some of Megan's things are in this box. In this pile that you say is garbage.'

'I didn't say they were garbage. That's not the word I used.'

'You want to throw them out. What the hell else do you call stuff you're throwing out?'

'I . . . It's all really old stuff, Nicole. Stuff we never look at anymore. Stuff you probably don't even remember keeping. When's the last time you asked me to dig out any of those things, huh?'

She glares at him. Her eyes blur. She wipes away the tears.

'I don't believe you,' she says. 'Megan has been dead for what seems like five minutes, and already you're throwing away her stuff. How could you do that? How could that idea even occur to you?'

He shifts his gaze away from her then, and she can tell that he's lost the argument. He knows that what he did is wrong. Probably knew it when he set up the two piles. But he did it anyway. What she can't comprehend is why.

She hopes he will explain. She hopes he will apologize and say that he didn't know what he was thinking, and then he will cry and they will talk and they will start to come to terms with their grief.

But instead, when he looks back at her there is anger in his eyes. 'Nicole, we have to move on. The only way we're going to survive this is if we move on. Megan is dead, and we have to accept that.'

She takes a step toward him. 'No, Steve. *You* have to accept it.'

'What do you mean?'

She waves her arms to indicate the space around them. 'All this! The way you're keeping so busy. The way you won't come near me. The way you won't talk. The way you're pushing Megan's things away from you. You're in denial, Steve. Can't you see that?'

He shakes his head, and his lips twist into a sneer. 'That's crap.'

'No. No, it isn't. Take a look at yourself. Tell me this is normal. Tell me you're acting exactly the same way you did before Megan was taken from us.'

'Of course I'm not the same. Nothing is the same. I'm just trying to cope, Nicole. You do it your way and I'll do it mine. Is that okay with you?'

She goes back to the box and takes out one of the items. A swimming trophy. A shiny shield set upon a polished wooden plinth. One of the first things Megan ever won. She carries it over to Steve and holds it up to his face.

'This is Megan, Steve. It's not just a memory. It's what she was. And it's all we have left of her. If you think you're coping, then fine. But don't you dare, don't you *dare*, throw anything of Megan's away. Not a trophy, not a photograph, not a school report, not even a drawing she made when she was two. Because if you do, if I find that a single possession of hers has gone missing, then I'm going missing too. I'm taking Megan's things and I'm walking out of this house and I'm never coming back. Do you understand me?'

He looks at her for some time, and she tries to work out

what's going through his head. Is he ashamed? Or is he steeling himself for round two?

'I hear ya,' is all he says. Which tells her only that he doesn't want to continue this conversation. It's a nothing answer. A cop-out. She feels her own anger growing. She wants to slap this man, to bring him out of this semi-conscious state he has imposed on himself.

But then suddenly her rage is elbowed out by pity. This is her husband. Megan's father. He wasn't responsible for her death. He didn't ask for this. And he can't deal with it. That's not his fault either. He is strong in so many ways but he can't handle this. What is so wrong with that? What is so weak about a man who cannot accept the loss of his only child, his beautiful daughter?

She takes a step closer. She wants to hug him. Wants him to hug her. She reaches out a hand and touches it to his arm.

'You're hurting,' she says. 'We're both hurting. We need to help each other. Nobody else can do it for us.'

He takes a deep breath and exhales slowly. She hopes that a whole lot more will follow that breath. Some tears. Some release. Some emotions other than hate.

'I should finish these shelves,' he says.

She nods. She closes her eyes and then opens them again, and a tear falls.

She walks over to the shelving. Puts Megan's trophy on one of them. Turns it slightly so that it is square on. She steps back and lets the metal reflect the light into her eyes.

'It looks good there,' she says. 'Don't you think?'

He doesn't answer, and she steps out of the garage and closes the door softly behind her. She waits for a while, then puts her ear to the door. She remains poised there, her fingers on the handle, praying for a cry of anguish or at least a rhythmic gentle sobbing.

Hearing nothing, she walks away.

He's crazy.

Has to be.

Nobody throws themselves through a panel of glass like that. That only happens in the movies, where they use fake glass. The real stuff is dangerous, man. It can cut you to ribbons. It can slice through your jugular or another artery, or it can take part of your face off, leaving you permanently disfigured. Nobody in their right mind would risk that.

Which is kinda the point, really. Because Proust isn't in his right mind, is he? Anyone who could do what he did to those girls has to be certifiable.

Or desperate.

What? No, surely not. Nobody could be that desperate. Sure, Proust is afraid of me, but not as shit-scared as he pretends to be. That's for show. That's for the likes of LeBlanc and anyone else who's willing to act as an audience. Proust is clever. He knows what he's doing. He's devious and manipulative and crazy. And that makes him dangerous as fuck.

And let's not forget guilty. Let's keep that on the list. Because he is. This act of his is all a smokescreen, designed to hide the real story here. Which is that Stanley Proust murdered those two girls. That's what I need to hang on to. That's what I need to make others see too.

'Cal!'

It's Tommy LeBlanc who interrupts his thoughts. He's just come into the squadroom, and he's standing there with his legs apart and his hands twitching at his sides like he's a gunslinger calling out his sworn enemy.

'Lemme guess,' says Doyle. 'You wanna talk.'

'Yes, I want to talk. That okay with you?'

Doyle starts to rise from his chair. 'Lead on, Macduff.'

He follows LeBlanc out of the squadroom and into the interview room along the hallway. LeBlanc closes the door. He marches across to the window, then back again. Then back to the window, all the while refusing to look Doyle in the face.

'This an exercise class?' Doyle asks. 'I forgot to bring my gym shorts.'

LeBlanc halts and turns angrily on Doyle. 'This is no joke, Cal. What the hell were you thinking? You promised me you would keep away from Proust.'

'Uh, no I didn't. *You* said I should keep away. I never agreed to that.'

'Didn't you even think to keep me in the loop?'

'You weren't here when I decided to go see him.'

'Jesus Christ. I went to the washroom. I was gone for all of five minutes.'

Doyle shrugs. 'What can I say? I make snap decisions.'

LeBlanc shakes his head. Paces up and down a little more. Says Doyle, 'How is he?'

'Proust, you mean? You really wanna know? He's dead, Cal. He didn't make it.'

Doyle tenses. He stares in disbelief at LeBlanc. Proust dead? No. He can't be. It can't end like this.

'What? No. He can't be dead.'

'No, he's not fucking dead, Cal. But isn't that what you wanted to hear? Don't you want him taken out? Wouldn't you love to see him lying on a cold slab in the morgue?'

Doyle feels a stab of irritation. 'All right, Tommy, that's enough. I don't like being told what my thoughts are, and I don't like little pranks like the one you just pulled on me. You got this all wrong.'

'Have I? Have I, Cal? Tell me how I should see this. Tell me what I should think when I see you attack Proust, ripping his shirt off like that. Tell me what conclusions I should reach when you come back from seeing Proust with a huge shiner under your eye, and he ends up with broken ribs and missing teeth. Tell me what I should imagine happened when Proust comes flying through a glass door and you're the only other guy in the room, and then you continue to assault him. What kind of picture should I be seeing here, Cal?'

'Not the obvious one. I know how it looks, but it's phony. Proust jumped through that door. He must have seen you outside and then he ran into his apartment so that I would follow. When he heard you come through the front door he started yelling and then he dived through the glass.'

'Uh-huh. And the bruises? The fractured rib?'

'I don't know. He threw himself down some stairs. He picked a fight in a bar. I have no idea. But I didn't do it. That I do know.'

'Then how come it looks so much like you did?'

'Because that's what he wants you to think. He wants you seeing him as the victim instead of the perp. He wants your sympathy. He wants me off his back.'

'Pretty extreme way of doing it, don't you think?'

'Absolutely. But we're not talking normal here, Tommy. Proust is a man who gets his kicks from torturing young girls. That makes him not right in the head. But he's also a fucking genius. You remember that tattoo on his chest?'

'Yeah. What's that got to do with it?'

'Looked pretty real, didn't it? Proust coming out of his own chest. That's what he's good at. Making pictures that look real but aren't. He makes people see what he wants them to see. You see a helpless victim, in fear of the cops. I see a murdering son-ofabitch. Same guy, though, Tommy. Same guy.'

LeBlanc rubs his chin while he considers this. 'I don't know, Cal. I want to believe you, I really do. But you're not making this easy for me.' He pauses. 'I heard a lot of things about you when I came to this precinct, Cal.'

'That'll be Schneider singing my praises again, huh? That guy loves me.'

'Him, but others too. They said a lot of bad things. They said you were a dirty cop. They said—'

'Yeah, well, Schneider and his buddies can go fuck themselves. They can—'

'See, now that's what I mean.'

'What? What do you mean?'

'That's why I can't understand you, Cal. All of this stuff with Proust, it suggests they're right, you know? It says to me, Hey, maybe this guy really is a dirty cop after all. And if you're not dirty, Cal, then you have to be one of the stupidest cops I've ever known.'

'If you're giving me a choice, I'll settle for stupid.'

'I'm serious. It's like you have a self-destruct button you have to keep pushing. Take your relationship with Schneider, for example. Did you ever try taking him and his pals for a pizza and a beer and just explaining things to them? You haven't, have you? They say something negative and you react instantaneously. You blow them off, without a thought for the consequences, without even considering that you'll have to work with these guys for years to come. And then there's how you are with me, your partner. All this sneaking around behind my back, again not even caring about how it affects me or the case. You're not a one-man band, Cal. You have a partner. You're part of a squad. Why do you insist on forgetting that?'

'You're beginning to sound like my mother.'

'Well, maybe you should listen to your mother a little more often. I may be younger than you. I may be a less experienced detective than you. But Christ do I seem to be a whole lot more aware of what's going on than you are right now.'

The two detectives lapse into silence for a while. LeBlanc paces some more. Says, 'Jesus!' to vent a little steam.

'What are you going to do?' Doyle asks. 'You taking this to the lieutenant?'

'Would you blame me if I did?'

'Actually, no. You should do what you think is right.'

'Well, that's the fucking thing. 'Cause I don't know what's right anymore. You've got my head so screwed up, I don't know what I should be doing.' He pauses again. 'You do know, don't you, that all it will take is one word from Proust to drop you in the biggest pile of crap you ever saw?'

'Did he say it was me, after I left?'

'No, he didn't. But if he does, I won't be able to contain this, Cal. I'll have to tell the boss what I saw and what I heard.'

'Proust won't say anything.'

'What, are you going to make sure of that? Is that what you're telling me, after all we've just discussed?'

Doyle sighs. 'No, that's not what I'm saying. Proust won't accuse me because he knows it's not true. He's not sure he can get away with saying it was me. And he also doesn't want cops looking too closely at him, not with him being a murderer.'

'You're sure about that?'

'About me not hurting him, or him being a murderer, or him not putting in a complaint? Doesn't matter – the answer's the same to all of 'em.'

LeBlanc studies Doyle for a while, narrowing his eyes at him. 'Tell me, Cal. How do you know all this? With such certainty, I mean. So far we've got nothing on Proust. Not one shred of evidence that says he's bad. How can you be so damn sure you're not wrong about him?'

Doyle thinks about this. 'I know Proust. I've spent a lot more time with him than you have. I've looked into his eyes. I've looked into his soul. These homicides are his work, Tommy. I'd stake everything I have on that being true.'

'Yeah, well, you may have already done that,' says LeBlanc. He turns away from Doyle and heads for the door.

'What happens now?' asks Doyle.

LeBlanc halts and faces Doyle again. 'We prove you're right about Proust. We work the case. But by the numbers, Cal. I can't work the way we've been working anymore. You want to carry on treating me like I don't matter, then fine. But I won't take it lying down.'

He reaches for the door, but again Doyle stops him.

'Do you believe me? About me not being involved in what happened to Proust?'

Now it's LeBlanc's turn to sigh. 'Like I said, I want to believe it. Crazy as the story sounds, I think I could probably make myself believe it. But you know what? There's one thing getting in the way.'

'What's that?'

'What you said a minute ago about looking into Proust's eyes? Well, I looked into your eyes, Cal. When you had your hand around my throat in Proust's place? I saw things in your eyes that terrified me. At that moment there was no doubt in my mind that you were capable of doing some god-awful things.'

And, with that, he leaves the room.

He's naked in front of the bedroom mirror again.

Mirror, mirror, on the wall, who is the fairest of them all?

Ha! Fairest! Look at you! Look at that wreck of a man staring back at you. It's Halloween in a coupla weeks. You don't even need a costume.

He has pulled off some of the Band-Aids. Too soon. Blood is trickling down his face. Coursing over the purple-blue flesh. There were healthier-looking specimens in the Michael Jackson *Thriller* video.

He tilts his head to the left, then the right, studying his features. He likes this look. He has undergone a metamorphosis. He is not what he was.

He has some more stitches, but most of the cuts were superficial. That cop – LeBlanc – took him to a different hospital this time. He knows why. LeBlanc was trying to protect his friend and colleague.

'Doyle.'

He says the name out loud. And smiles.

It was painful, going through that door. He doesn't deny that he felt the pain. Mostly in his cracked rib rather than because of the cuts. The cuts are nothing.

The pain, too, is nothing. He has mastered pain. He feels it, but he can choose to ignore it. That is the power he has discovered.

'Do you believe me, Doyle? Do you believe you can't hurt me?'

Proust slaps his own face. Hard. So hard it stings. He slaps it again, and again. A wound on his cheek opens up and more blood flows. It drips onto his chest.

He looks to his side. There is a dresser there. And on the dresser, a small pair of nail scissors. He picks up the scissors with his right hand, puts his left hand on the dresser.

Without hesitation he plunges the point of the scissors into the back of his hand. He yanks the scissors out, stabs it again into his flesh. And yet again. A cry escapes his lips and pink-stained froth bubbles out of his mouth.

He brings his damaged hand to his face and examines it. It trembles, and blood gushes from its wounds. He makes animal-istic keening noises as he watches his hot blood run down his arm. His eyes blur with tears, and then he is laughing or crying or both.

'You see, Doyle?' he says to his mirror image. 'You cannot hurt me. You cannot win.'

He is stronger than Doyle now. In fact, he feels almost invin-cible. He can survive a severe beating. He can jump through glass without serious injury. What's next? How much stronger can he possibly get?

And there are other forces within him that are yet to be released. Doyle doesn't suspect this. He doesn't know what he has unleashed. Well, he will find out soon enough.

Doyle started this.

Stanley Francis Proust will finish it.

NINETEEN

What if Doyle is right?

LeBlanc considers this as he sits in his car. He pulses the windshield wipers, batting away the rainwater for a brief instant to afford him a glimpse of Proust's place.

What went on in there? What really happened?

The most plausible scenario is the obvious one. Doyle beat the crap out of Proust, not once but twice. That account fits all the facts, without the requirement for much imagination or twisted reasoning. When faced with multiple possible explanations, always go with the simplest. Occam's razor, and all that.

But would even Doyle go that far? Would he resort to beating a perp to within an inch of his life? Even if he got a confession, what could he do with it? It would be obvious to the DA and everybody else that it had been obtained through violence and intimidation. Why would Doyle put his job on the line like that?

So then there's the alternative. Doyle is telling the truth. Proust is an evil genius who killed two girls and is now trying to discredit the only cop who believes he did it. And the way he does that is by practically killing himself.

How likely is that? Is Proust capable of such a thing?

He seems the genuine article to LeBlanc. Since the first moment he met Proust, he has felt that this is a man who is truly terrified of Doyle. An innocent man who has been wrongly accused and is being continually harassed and bullied by his accuser. Could that all be an act? Is Proust that good?

'Shit,' says LeBlanc.

He doesn't know what to make of this, whom to believe. The problem is he doesn't know either party well enough. Not even his own partner. Doyle is not the sharing type. Maybe he's got issues. If we were to get all psychological about this, maybe the shit he went through when his partners were killed has turned him into a man who feels he cannot trust anyone but himself. Who the hell knows?

Can I even be sure that he hasn't gone totally off the rails? And as for Proust . . .

Well, maybe I need to get to know him a little better too.

It's almost as if Proust has been waiting for him to arrive.

He is standing behind his counter at the far end of his shop, staring straight at LeBlanc as he comes through the door.

Pangs of pity instantly stab at LeBlanc.

Jesus. Just look at the guy. He can't even stand up straight. If he were an animal he'd be put down.

'Hey,' he says. 'How's it going?'

'Detective LeBlanc,' says Proust, and it seems to LeBlanc that he has difficulty just getting those two words out. 'Are you . . . alone?'

Meaning, *Is Doyle with you?*

LeBlanc catches Proust's fearful glance through the window behind him.

'I'm alone,' he says. 'Thought I'd check up on you. See how you are.'

'I think . . . I think it looks worse than it is.' He attempts a smile, but then winces with his pain.

Putting a brave face on it, thinks LeBlanc. Would he do that if he were faking?

'You got time to talk?'

'Sure. It's pretty quiet right now. You wanna come back for a coffee?'

LeBlanc nods, then walks around the counter to join Proust. He follows him through the first door into the small storeroom. It looks as though most of the glass has been cleared up, but as they get closer to the other door there is still a crunching noise underfoot.

'I made a start,' says Proust apologetically. 'I'll try to get the rest later.'

LeBlanc glances at the spot where Doyle had him pinned against the wall. The image of Doyle's face is still vivid, his expression that of a man who was about to rip LeBlanc's head off.

They step through the now useless door, and into the tiny living area.

'You want coffee? Or do you prefer tea?'

'Tea. If that's okay.'

He watches as Proust shuffles over to the electric kettle, grunting as he picks it up.

'Here,' says LeBlanc. 'Let me do it.'

He takes the kettle from Proust, then tells him to go sit down while he prepares the tea. For the next few minutes, the only conversation is about where the teabags, cups and so on are kept.

When the tea is made, LeBlanc joins Proust at the table. He starts off with some chit-chat. Some meaningless preamble to put the guy at his ease.

'How's business?'

'Two customers today. The first one was a woman. Took one look at me and walked straight out again. Then a guy came in for a neck tat. He asked what happened. I told him I forgot my wife's birthday.'

LeBlanc smiles, putting on a show for Proust's benefit. 'You expecting any more today?'

'I doubt it. Nothing booked in. And this weather, not many people passing by either. You ever consider it yourself?'

'Me? A tattoo? Nah, not my thing.'

'You should. You worried about the pain?'

'Should I be?'

'Not at all. It's like a . . . like a hot scratch.'

'A scratch, huh?'

'Yeah. And you don't need to worry about hygiene neither. All of my equipment is guaranteed bug-free. I use an autoclave. You know what that is?'

LeBlanc shakes his head.

'It's kinda like a pressure cooker, you know what I mean? It makes this super-hot steam which—'

'Stan, what happened here today?'

Proust was happy talking about his work. LeBlanc can see the enthusiasm drain from his face.

'What?'

'What happened? When Doyle came to see you.'

LeBlanc watches as Proust's eyes widen and the knuckles whiten on the fingers of his hand holding the cup.

'We were talking. He wanted to ask me some questions.'

'About what?'

'About the girl who was killed. He thinks I had something to do with it.'

'And did you?'

Proust's stare is one of disbelief at the bluntness of the question. 'No, man. I told Doyle and I'm telling you. I never met that girl. I wouldn't put a tat on someone that young, and I wouldn't hurt a girl like that. I wouldn't hurt anyone. You gotta believe me.'

'Why doesn't Doyle believe you?'

'I . . . I dunno, man. I really don't.'

LeBlanc hears something else in those words. He's not quite sure what it is. Something Proust wants to say but which he's holding back.

'Okay, so he's asking you questions. When I came into your shop, it wasn't just a conversation, Stan. It was getting kinda heated back here.'

'Yeah, I know. He wouldn't let it go. I kept telling him I didn't do this terrible thing, but he wouldn't listen. He kept calling me a murderer. Saying how I enjoyed doing disgusting things to young girls. Sexual things. And then . . . torturing them. Detective, I couldn't even torture an ant. I respect life. He's trying to make me out to be some kind of monster. I couldn't do those things. Please. You have to believe me.'

Proust grimaces and brings a hand to his ribs. He's really suffering, thinks LeBlanc.

'What I heard, it wasn't just an argument. You were pleading, Stan. You sounded like you were being attacked. You were begging Doyle to stop. Stop what, Stan?'

Proust drops his gaze. Stares into his tea. 'The questions. The accusations. I'd heard them a thousand times. So many times I was starting to believe them myself. I needed for them to stop. I felt like he was driving me crazy.'

It's a lie, thinks LeBlanc. Everything in Proust's body language tells me it's a lie. He can't look at me. His words have no emotion. The question is, is he lying because he's afraid of what Doyle might do if he tells me what really happened here? Or is he lying so badly on purpose because it's all part of this elaborate plan to set Doyle up?

'Okay, so then what? What happened after the shouting?'

'I just needed to get away. I ran to the door.' He gestures to the remains of the door behind LeBlanc. 'I wanted to get out of here. Maybe out of the building, if that's what it took. And then . . . I just tripped.'

'You tripped?'

'Yeah. I musta been in too much of a hurry. My foot caught on the rug or something. That's all I remember.'

He's looking down at his tea again. Lies, lies, lies.

'Look at me, Stan.'

Proust raises his head slightly, but not his gaze. His eyelids flutter as though he's struggling to lift them.

'Stan, look at me.'

It's an effort, but Proust finally gets there. They lock eyes.

'Doyle says you didn't trip. He says you jumped through that door.'

'What? No. No. Why would I do that? That's crazy. Why would I jump through a glass door?'

Good question, thinks LeBlanc. Why the hell would anyone do such a thing?

'Maybe you were trying to make it look like Doyle was assaulting you?'

Proust's mouth drops. 'W–what? Trying to make it look . . .? That's ridiculous. He really said that? Do you know how ridiculous that suggestion is? I coulda been killed going through that door. Why would I . . . That's fucking ludicrous, man.'

LeBlanc keeps his eyes fixed on Proust. Christ, he's good. If this is an act, then this guy should get an Oscar. And he's right, of course. Said out loud like this, the suggestion sounds absurd. LeBlanc feels faintly embarrassed that he even dared to voice it.

'There's another possibility,' he says.

Proust says nothing for a while. He picks up his cup. Takes a sip. 'What's that?'

LeBlanc isn't sure he wants to ask this. Proust has told him what happened. Isn't that enough? Is there any need to give him the idea he might want to change that story?

'You sure Doyle didn't throw you through that door?'

Proust's mouth twitches. 'What? What did you say?'

'You heard me, Stan. Answer the question.'

He doesn't really want Proust to answer the question. Or if he does answer it, he doesn't want it to convey the message that, yes, Doyle was responsible for the state Proust is now in.

Suddenly, LeBlanc's heart is thudding. He can hear the blood rushing in his ears. He wants it to grow louder so as to drown out Proust's words.

Proust lowers his head again, mumbles something.

'What was that, Stan?'

His eyes flicker upward once more. 'I tripped. It was like I said. I tripped.'

Right answer. The expected answer. But bullshit all the same. LeBlanc is no closer to knowing the truth.

He slurps some of his own tea, then says, 'I don't get it, Stan.'

'Get what?'

'The whole thing with Detective Doyle. Your relationship.'

Proust gives the subtlest of shrugs. 'He hates me.'

'Yeah. But why? Why does he hate you?'

'He thinks I murdered those two girls, and he can't prove it. And the reason he can't prove it is because I didn't do it.'

'Yeah, but it still seems weird to me. Maybe you are a killer—'

'I'm not.'

'Okay, but suppose I thought you were. I wouldn't waste my time and energy hating you. I would go out and find the evidence. I'd prove it was you.'

'You're not Doyle. That guy is obsessed. He would do anything to see me punished. Even for something I didn't do.'

'See, that's where I get confused. I just don't get why he would be that way. What buttons of his could you have pushed?'

He expects a shrug. Maybe a 'dunno'. He expects Proust to say he is clueless about Doyle's personal crusade. He expects him to say he is not aware of any reason aside from the one that Doyle is convinced he's a cold-blooded killer. Which, LeBlanc reminds himself, could still be the truth here.

And yet . . .

Proust seems to be toying with something. Tossing something around in his mind while he stares at his tea again. Appears to be wondering just how much he should reveal to this cop sitting at his table, drinking with him, acting like he's on his side.

'What?' LeBlanc urges.

'I, uhm . . . The girl. Maybe the girl.'

'You mean the victim? Yeah, but aside from—'

'No, not her. I mean the one I saw Doyle with.'

Something crawls over LeBlanc's skin. 'What girl? Who are you talking about, Stan?'

'The cop. Doyle's partner. Look, maybe I shouldn't be saying—'

'His partner? When was this?'

'When the first girl was killed. The one they found in the Hudson. Doyle came to see me with his partner.'

'You remember her name?'

'I think so. Marino. Something like that.'

'Laura Marino?'

'I don't know her first name.'

'Okay, so what about her?'

'They pulled up in the car one day. I saw them through the window. They were . . . they were necking.'

'They were kissing?'

'Yeah. For about two minutes. Then Doyle got out of the car and came inside.'

'He came in alone?'

'Yeah. She was fixing her makeup in the car. When Doyle came in, I didn't even know he was a cop. I made a joke about what he was getting up to out there.'

'What did he do?'

'He, uhm . . . Let's just say he didn't like what I said. He made that very clear.'

'He accuse you of killing the Palmer girl?'

'Yeah. That time, and every other time too.'

'The other times he came back, was he with his partner?'

'No, I never saw her again. Doyle was alone. One time I made the mistake of mentioning the necking incident again. He went ape-shit, man.'

'Did he assault you?'

'I . . . I don't wanna answer that question.'

LeBlanc's mind races. He doesn't want to believe this. This is information he's not sure he can handle. And yet there is a ring of truth here. A pretty solid ring at that. It ties in with a lot of things he's been told about Doyle, much of which he has always dismissed as fable. Until now.

'If you never spoke with the female cop, how come you know her name?'

There is no hesitation before Proust replies. 'Doyle told me. He said that if I mentioned Detective Marino one more time, either to him or anybody else, he would . . . well, I don't wanna say.'

LeBlanc collapses back in his chair. Shit! Proust can't be making this up. How could he know any of this if it wasn't true?

Laura Marino. The female cop who was killed when an apartment bust went bad up in Harlem. The cop whose death many blamed on Doyle. They said he sent her the wrong way, when he knew there was a killer just waiting to blast her with a shotgun. And why would he do that? Because they were having an affair that he wanted to end and she didn't. She threatened to go public and he couldn't allow that to happen.

That's what many said. It's what some, including Schneider, still believe. But there was never any proof. Nothing to say that Doyle and Marino were actually anything more than just partners. It was all just rumor and hearsay.

But this . . . This changes everything.

LeBlanc asked for a reason why Doyle might hate Proust, and now he's got what he asked for.

He feels like he's just been handed a grenade with its pin pulled out.

TWENTY

Doyle actually feels grateful to LeBlanc.

He has spent most of the afternoon away from his desk, trying to track down leads. Talking to Megan Hamlyn's girl-friends. Trying to find people who may have seen her on the subway, or in the East Village. Questioning the owners of security cameras that may have picked up her image during the final moments of her short life.

More particularly, though, he has stayed away from Proust. And he feels better for it. Proust has an irritating habit of raising Doyle's blood pressure. Of making him think he's about to blow an artery. The man's a health hazard. Which is quite an under-statement for a murdering, torturing piece of shit like Proust.

Calm down, Doyle.

And then there are these stupid games Proust is playing. Making himself out to be the victim. Trying to give the illusion, without actually making the blatant accusation, that Doyle is violently attacking him at every opportunity. What the hell is that about? Does he really think that'll work? What the fuck does that crazy, fucked-up, psychopathic—

Chill, dude. Relax.

He lets out a long, slow breath. He switches on the car radio.

Hears Adele. Nice. Soothing. Sing along, man. You'll be home soon. Away from all that shit.

Because it's driving him out of his skull. He knows this. He knows he is not acting normally. Not with his family, not with LeBlanc, not with anyone.

Poor Tommy. He doesn't know what to make of any of this. Doesn't know what to believe about his own partner.

And yes, it's my fault, thinks Doyle. I'm not playing fair with Tommy. I'm keeping him in the dark.

And yes, I did feel out of control when I had my hand around his throat. The poor kid was scared shitless. That's what Proust does to me. He makes me crazy. But it's not an excuse. What I did back there was unforgivable.

So maybe Tommy is right after all. Maybe this is the way to nail Proust. Play it by the numbers. Proust isn't perfect. He will have made mistakes. With enough time and effort I can find out what those mistakes were. And, by God, I won't stop until I do. I owe it to those two young girls, and to their families.

As he turns onto West 87th Street, he is still thinking about LeBlanc. Thinking he is actually starting to like him. He was never sure before. Didn't know what views LeBlanc had of him, especially with LeBlanc working so closely with Schneider. And because he was uncertain, he tended to shun him. LeBlanc was right about that, too. Doyle is too quick to dismiss people. Sometimes he should give others more of a chance.

Hell, he thinks, maybe I should start going to LeBlanc for psychotherapy.

He also admires the way LeBlanc stood up to him. That took balls. And he didn't jam him up with the bosses when he could have. That took loyalty.

Christ. I'm starting to sound like I'm falling in love with the guy.

Smiling, Doyle squeezes his car into a space several buildings down from his own. He wishes he could get closer, seeing as how there's still no let-up in this damned rain. He clambers out. Locks up the car. Makes a dash along the street. Draws level with his front stoop.

'Hey, Doyle.'

The call is as brief as that, but Doyle recognizes the voice immediately, and it stops him in his tracks. His smile vanishes. His day has grown somewhat darker.

Oh yes, he knows this voice.

It's a reminder of a part of his past he would rather forget.

'Get in,' says the voice through the open window of the gray Chevy Impala.

Doyle doesn't move.

'Come on. You're getting soaked out there. And I'm getting wet with this window open.'

Doyle looks up at the front door of his apartment building. He is just steps away from warmth, dryness, friendly faces. The last thing he needs right now is a conversation of the type he's being invited to have.

But he knows this guy won't go away. He knows how this man operates.

Doyle steps around the car, opens the door and climbs in. The man behind the wheel closes his window and then turns to face Doyle.

It's like being confronted by one of the undead. The man's pale skin glows white in the dim interior of the car. His cheeks are hollow, his lips thin. Lank black hair furls across his forehead like a raven's wing. He wears a dark suit, dark overcoat and dark tie.

'Hello, Doyle,' he says.

'Hello, Paulson,' says Doyle. 'Little early for trick or treat, ain't it?'

They are not, and probably never will be, on first-name terms, these two. Although they go back some way, it has not always been the most affable of relationships.

After Laura Marino died in that apartment on that fateful night, and all the rumors of Doyle's possible role in it began to surface like dead fish, Sergeant Paulson here was assigned the task of investigating his fellow officer. Except that 'fellow officer' is a term that most cops would choke on when trying to describe Paulson and his ilk.

Sergeant Paulson is a member of the Internal Affairs Bureau, that section of the NYPD charged with unearthing corruption in the force. It was at one time known as the Internal Affairs Division, but it got promoted, such was the thirst for its activities amongst the bosses and the politicians, who were determined to demonstrate how seriously they took the integrity of the city's law enforcers. Whatever its name, its job is to police the police. And it is not known for wearing kid gloves when it carries out its mission.

Doyle found that out for himself when seated across a table from Paulson. He found out just what a bastard this man was. He found out what it's like to be the suspect rather than the one doing the suspecting. And he found out what it was like to hate another man with an intensity that brought him close to committing murder.

Paulson was relentless and he was without mercy. He hounded Doyle. His questions were devoid of both subtlety and sympathy.

He seemed determined to destroy Doyle, to the extent of making threats to do precisely that. And despite official assurances that the investigation was confidential, it became apparent that everyone and his dog were aware of what was taking place here. Rumors became fact, whispers became confident voices, blunt opinions became sharpened spears of distrust and dislike. These were carried on the wind, reaching the ears of Doyle's wife and his loved ones. He almost lost them. He almost lost everything.

And all because of this man seated not two feet away from him.

Says Paulson, 'Crappy night, huh?'

'I think it just got worse,' says Doyle.

Paulson adopts a pained expression. 'Now why'd you have to go and say that? Didn't we part on good terms last time we met? You brought me donuts, as I recall. You wished me a merry Christmas.'

'I think your medication must have been too strong. You were imagining things. I don't remember any of that.'

'My medication? Oh, you mean for that bullet I took. The one that had your name on it.'

And there's the thing. That's what makes this relationship so complicated. Doyle wants to hate Paulson with a passion. He feels he's entitled to that. But the best Christmas present he got last year was the one from Paulson. It was the gift of his life. How do you hate someone who does that for you? Why did Paulson have to go and mash up something that was so patently black and white into a muddy gray mess?

'Look, Paulson, I owe you one. I admit it. You saved my life. There. Happy now?'

'It helps. Your recognition of my gallant self-sacrifice certainly goes some way to assuaging my indignation here.' He

214

pauses. 'But, of course, it fails to recognize what else I did for you.'

'Which was?'

'Where shall we start? Well, there was that confidential information I gave you at the time. Information which I think was crucial in getting you out of that jam you were in. Without that you'd probably still be afraid to enjoy the freedom of coming home to your lovely family here. And then there was the fact that I overlooked some distinctly dubious practices of yours while you were endeavoring to extract yourself from said jam. So, taking all of the above into consideration, I'd say I deserve a little leeway here. Wouldn't you agree?'

'You've got your leeway. It's why I'm sitting in the car with you. Think yourself lucky I'm not jumping up and down on the hood right now. Look, Paulson, what you did for me, it's much appreciated. Really. I'll try to return the favor someday. But I can't forget what came before that, and I'm sure it's still fresh in your memory too. You came after me with all guns blazing, and you nearly succeeded in ruining my life. My wife sees me sitting out here with you, she'll be down here choking you with your own tie. That's the kind of love she has for you, Paulson. Think about that.'

'You don't think what happened last Christmas wipes any of that away?'

'I think it complicates things, is what I think. What I would like to do is forget about the past and move on with my life. But certain people won't let me do that. You included. What are you doing here at my home anyhow?'

'Maybe I just thought I'd see how you are. Catch up on things.'

Doyle wags a finger at him. 'Uh-uh. You're here on business.

You're here as an IAB man. Don't try pretending you're not. At least have the decency to be honest about it.'

'What, you think it's always a question of one or the other? Is that how it is for you, Doyle? Do you stop being a cop when you take off your shield and your gun? Is it that easy for you?'

'I'm saying that you have your shield with you now, Paulson. Even though it's in your pocket, your IAB shield is the only thing I can see in front of me right now. I'd like to know why.'

Paulson pats his pockets, and for a second Doyle thinks he's about to pull out his badge.

'You got any cigarettes?' says Paulson. 'I think I ran out.'

'I don't smoke,' says Doyle. 'And if you light up in here, I'm getting out of the car.'

Paulson nods, goes quiet for a few seconds, then says, 'I heard some things.'

'Things? What kind of things?'

'Things concerning you. You and a guy who runs a tattoo place.'

And now Doyle is interested. Also a little concerned. He was always of the conviction that Proust would not put in a complaint. Could he have gotten that so wrong?

'Stanley Proust.'

'Yeah, that's him.'

'What's he say about me?'

'He ain't said nothing yet. Leastways, not to me. Other voices are whispering your name.'

'I don't suppose you wanna say who?'

'Don't matter. The point is, you're making waves again. Disrupting the cosmic karma.'

'So they summoned you to restore order to the universe?'

Paulson smiles. 'Actually, no. I asked for this gig. I kinda feel fate has fashioned an unbreakable bond between us. We're forever joined by elemental forces beyond our feeble understanding.'

'That's a disturbing thought, Paulson.'

Paulson shrugs. 'Who are we to question the actions of the gods?'

Doyle pulls his what-the-fuck-are-you-talking-about face. 'Those cigarettes of yours, they're just tobacco, right? You mind coming back down to earth now?'

'I'm trying to put you in the picture, Doyle. The bigger picture which you never seem to appreciate. You're causing ructions, and there are some who don't like ructions. They are severely ruction averse.'

'I'm doing my job. Proust is a murderer. I'm gonna nail him for it. It's as simple as that.'

Paulson emits a laugh which could cause small children to burst into tears. 'It's never simple, Doyle. You of all people should have learned that by now. Life is complex. It's got hidden corners and trapdoors. The unwary need to be careful. Step on the wrong floorboard, and down you go.'

'Yeah, right. Thanks for the warning. If it's all the same to you, I'd like to go home now.'

Doyle reaches for the door handle, but Paulson puts a restraining hand on his arm.

'Jesus Christ, Doyle. Do you have to be so obtuse? I'm trying to help you here.'

'Help me or threaten me?'

'You're fucking paranoid, do you know that?'

'Like the joke goes, just because I'm paranoid, it doesn't mean they're not out to get me. Plus, my experience is that there are definitely people out there who would love to see me taken down.'

'Maybe. And maybe you're handing them the ammunition. Proust is a time bomb, Doyle. And you're the guy who's started him ticking. When he goes off, he will shake the fabric of the space–time continuum. Time will be reversed. You and me, we'll be back to square one. It will be as if last Christmas never happened. It will be just you and me in a tiny room somewhere, with only a tape recorder for company. I don't want to see that happen. I don't want to relive that.'

'You been watching too much *Star Trek*. And that still sounds like a threat to me.'

Paulson sighs. Rolls his eyes. 'Like I said, the problem with you is that you only ever see what you want to see. You got tunnel vision. You see IAB sitting next to you. The rat squad, right? The bureau whose only purpose in life is to make you miserable. What you don't see is me. Paulson. The guy who saved your sorry ass. And when you look at Proust, you see a stone killer, right? You fail to see the man who holds your liberty in his fingers. And your ears ain't so good, neither. Remember me saying how I asked for this assignment? You know why? Because if I hadn't taken it, somebody else would have. And this other IAB detective would've marched straight into your squadroom. He would've talked to your lieutenant about what we already know, and then he would've marched you into an interview room to squeeze what else he could out of you. And all this happening while your colleagues are watching and thinking and making up their own version of events. That's what I've protected you from by coming here tonight. You can thank me when you're ready.'

Doyle considers this. It's all true. But what he can't work out is why. A part of him wants to believe that Paulson really is a changed man. Another part wants to know what the catch is.

'Okay, Paulson. Thank you. That what you want to hear?'

'Yeah,' says Paulson, nodding. 'Yeah. That's nice. I'm touched.'

There's something in Paulson's voice that tells Doyle he really means it. But it also feels to Doyle like he's about to be beheaded and he's forgiving his executioner. Handing him a bag of silver before the ax descends.

'Until we meet again,' says Doyle.

He says it jokingly, but Paulson appears to take it seriously. He looks almost . . . sad.

'Sure,' says Paulson.

Doyle opens the door and steps out into the rain. As he walks around the car he hears the engine being fired up. But it's followed by the soft hum of the driver's window being lowered.

Says Paulson, 'Everything's connected, you know. The past, the present, the future. They're all parts of the same river. Nothing exists in isolation. Sometimes we're not even aware of it. But when that truth hits you, it can hit you hard. Take it easy, Doyle.'

Doyle stands there for a while. Watches as Paulson's car pulls away. Tries to figure out what the hell he was getting at.

When he notices that the rain is trickling down the back of his neck, he shivers.

Home sweet home.

He walks in with the expectation that, finally, he can leave all his troubles out there in the rain. He can get out of these wet clothes, have a steaming-hot shower, a nice meal that isn't fish, and then he can spend some quality time with his loving wife and doting daughter.

But those expectations are dashed when he sees the expression on the face of said loving wife. Because it's not so loving at the moment. In fact, it's downright livid.

'What's up?' he asks.

'What's up?' she echoes. 'Your daughter is what's up.'

It doesn't escape his notice that this has suddenly become a one-parent family.

'What's she done this time?'

'She did it again, Cal. She put some stuff from the stationery closet in her bag. Only this time she was seen doing it by another child, and he told the teacher about it.'

'Wait a minute. Are you sure about this? Maybe there's been a mistake.'

'How can there be a mistake? She was seen. Caught red-handed. It's the kind of open-and-shut case police officers can only dream of.'

Doyle feels something inside himself sinking. He doesn't want to believe this. Not of his own daughter.

'What happened? When the teacher found out?'

'I got called in, Cal. I spent an hour in the principal's office this afternoon, desperately trying to defend our family name. Trying to assure them there was no great domestic upheaval taking place in our home. No divorce or terminal illness – that kind of thing. It was humiliating, Cal. And I still don't know what to do about it. What the hell has gotten into that child?'

And now Doyle's mind is racing again. Searching for explanations. Looking for reasons. Wondering what mistakes they may have made in the upbringing of their daughter. He can feel his stress levels building again.

He hasn't even taken his coat off yet, he's still dripping rain-water onto the floor, and already he's wishing for this night to be over.

Home sweet home.

*

Too easy.

That young detective. LeBlanc. Thinking he can play me. Asking those dumb questions about my business just to put me at my ease. Acting like he's my BFF so he can get me to talk.

Well, he got me to talk, all right. Not what he was expecting to hear, though, was it?

He fell for it, the sucker. All those grunts and expressions of pain – he was totally taken in. Well, let me tell you, Detective The Blank, about how I don't feel pain. About how the only one around here who's gonna know pain is your pal Doyle.

Or *is* he your pal? That was a damn straight question you asked about whether Doyle tossed me through that door. A big gamble of yours. Supposing I'd said yes, Doyle did do that? What would you have done then? Taken me seriously or tried to shut me up? Whose side were you on, Detective?

More importantly, whose side are you on now?

Now that your head can't shake out the picture of Doyle sitting in his car with that Marino woman, his hands and his lips all over her, what do you think of your partner? You still believe in him? You really think that anything he says can be trusted? You think he wouldn't resort to beating me up, when it's possible he's done things a lot worse than that?

Stick around, oh blank one, while I finish creating my master-piece. Because I haven't finished with Doyle.

I've got a lot more work to do yet.

TWENTY-ONE

Steve Hamlyn tries to remember what sleep is like.

Proper sleep. The kind where you leave the physical world behind while you explore the surreal, your brain experimenting with new connections that give rise to all kinds of previously unimagined happenings – often absurd, sometimes even comical. The kind where you wake reinvigorated, ready to face all that life can throw at you.

Not this. Not the kind of sleep where you feel like you're lying a mere fraction of an inch below wakefulness. Where the slightest sound – the rustle of a sheet, the heavy breath of your partner, the patter of rain, the rush of your own pulse – is enough to jolt you back into the room, drenched in sweat. Where the dreams, when you can reach them, are of the darkest kind imaginable, filled with violence and fear and gut-wrenching images. And where you know that, even when you escape the nightmares, your reality is little better. It is no longer something you welcome. You wake up crying silently, the tears streaming down your face. You feel the pressure in the center of your chest, as though your heart is ready to burst. And sometimes you wish it *would* burst, because sometimes you would gladly accept death as a way of ending this torment.

Steve turns to look at Nicole lying next to him. He can see

only the back of her head, but her slow breathing suggests that she, at least, has found some peace. He doesn't want to disturb her. He owes her that much. He owes her so much more, in fact. He has not been there for her. Not provided the shoulder she needs. At this very moment he can see that, but such moments of clarity have been rare lately, and this one will also quickly fade and die. His mind gets too crowded with other thoughts, other emotions. But he will make it up to her. Later. When things have been resolved. When Megan's killer has been caught.

He wishes he could do something – *anything* – to help bring this to an end. He wishes he knew people. The kind of people who would undertake any job, no matter how illegal. If he knew people like that, who could guarantee that they would find Megan's killer, then he would give them everything he owns. He would sell his house, his car, everything. He would even sell his soul. And he wouldn't want them to administer any justice. He would do that himself.

Just find the sick fuck. I'll take it from there.

But he doesn't know people like that. All he has is the police, and he's not convinced he can rely on them. They don't seem to be getting anywhere with this. He calls them every day, several times on some days, and they tell him nothing. They're following leads. Making inquiries. The usual bullshit. It all amounts to a heap of nothing. The killer is still out there, and they're not going to catch him.

A tremor passes through Steve as he thinks this. What if they never catch him? What will I do then? How will I ever get my life back?

Anger wells up again. His chest tightens. His breathing accelerates. He wants to let out a roar of frustration. He feels so powerless. So fucking useless. His feelings toward Nicole change in a heartbeat. She transforms from someone he has wronged into someone who is too weak, too understanding and too accepting of this whole fucking mess their life has become. Where is her rage, her thirst for vengeance? How can she not be filled with fury at every waking moment? How can she even sleep?

He tosses back the covers and swings his feet onto the floor. He sits there for a minute, his face in his hands. Wondering how he can care so much while Nicole seems to care so little.

When he stands up and fetches his robe, he catches a glimpse of himself in the mirror. He sees an ugliness in his expression he has not seen before. It's the face of a man who has had enough. A man who feels he has nothing left to lose. A man who could kill.

He goes downstairs. His fists are clenched, his muscles taut. He craves coffee, even though he knows it's probably the worst thing he can take right now. A run. He needs to go for a run. Then a workout. Then . . .

He sees it. There is no way he couldn't. It practically jumps up and screams at him. It begs for him to approach and examine it.

A stark white rectangle. An envelope. There, on the floor. Just in front of the main door. As though it has been pushed underneath.

Steve glances at the wall clock. It's only five in the morning. Somebody has visited them during the night and delivered this message. Somebody has sneaked here under cover of darkness to let the Hamlyns into a secret.

Steve feels his heart begin to pound. He doesn't yet know what the note says, but he is certain it's something of immense importance. Something about Megan that will turn everything upside down.

He steps closer to the front door. When his bare toes are just inches away from the letter, he stares down. It seems to stare back at him, daring him to touch it. Whispering to him that this is the answer to his prayers.

He bends down and picks up the envelope. Straightens up again as he stares at the printed words on the front:

CONFIDENTIAL
For Mr Steve Hamlyn

The letter seems feather light. It cannot contain more than a single sheet of paper. He hopes this isn't some kind of cruel prank. Some twisted bastard's idea of a joke.

He turns the envelope over. Carefully eases open the flap. Slides out the folded note. It holds just a few lines of laser-printed text:

Mr Hamlyn,

I shouldn't be telling you this, but I want to help you. The man you need to speak to is called Stanley Proust. You can find him at a tattoo parlor called Skinterest on Avenue B in the East Village.

Good luck.

Steve re-reads the message again and again. He looks on the reverse of the sheet, then inside the envelope. There is nothing else. No clues as to who sent this. Just the words.

He slips the note back into the envelope, then pushes it into the pocket of his robe.

He knows what he has to do.

As frames of mind go, Doyle has had better. Last night was bad enough. The unexpected encounter with Paulson. Then his abortive attempts to discuss what was going on with Amy. She denied everything. Claimed she had no idea how those things got into her schoolbag, even though she had been seen putting them in there. A thief and now a liar? Is that the kind of daughter they've raised? How did it all go so wrong?

And now there's this. LeBlanc. Shooting daggers at Doyle even though *he's* the one who's being the asshole. Where does he get the right to act so sanctimonious, after what he's done? What were all those little discussions about, if not to clear the air?

'You got something you wanna say to me, Tommy?' he asks.

LeBlanc glares at him across the squadroom. 'With us being so open with each other, you mean? Telling each other everything? That's a good one, Cal.'

Doyle has only just taken off his jacket. This is barely the start of his working day, and he's already wondering if it could possibly be any crappier.

'You just stole the words from my mouth. I thought we straightened things out yesterday.'

'So did I, Cal. So did I. Shows how wrong I was.'

Doyle is mystified. He feels like he's skipped a day. Did LeBlanc reconsider his views and decide he'd been too conciliatory? Why is he suddenly on the offensive?

'Tommy, I think we need to have one those little discussions you're so fond of.'

When LeBlanc gets up from his chair, Doyle rises too. But then he notices that LeBlanc is pulling on his coat.

'No, Cal. We're done talking. I'm sick of finding out that the words coming out of your mouth don't match up with your actions. You feel the need to talk, go see a priest. Someone who might actually convince you to unload the truth.'

Doyle feels his anger building, but it's overwhelmed by his astonishment. Isn't he the injured party here? Isn't he the one who should be letting rip at LeBlanc? How the hell does LeBlanc feel so justified in turning the whole story on its head?

Before he can put his brain in enough order to formulate a sensible reply, he notices that LeBlanc is already on his way out of the squadroom.

'Where the hell are you going?'

LeBlanc pauses. 'I got a case, Cal. A homicide. Remember that? Remember why we were partnered up in the first place? I got people to talk to.'

'Okay, then . . . I'll come with you.'

LeBlanc shows him an open palm. 'No, Cal. I don't think so. We're through. You do your thing and I'll do mine. That's what you seem to prefer anyhow.'

And then he's gone. Doyle takes a step forward, on the verge of following, but then changes his mind. Standing there in the middle of the squadroom, he feels a little foolish. Around him, the other detectives return to their reading and typing and phone calls, pretending they didn't notice a thing. All except Schneider, of course, who is wearing his biggest Cheshire cat smile. If Doyle needed to explain the word 'schadenfreude' to anyone right now, all he would have to do is point at Schneider.

Says Schneider, 'Nice moves, Doyle. I've always admired the

way you mesh so smoothly with your partners. You're a lesson to us all on how to be a team player.'

Doyle wants to tell Schneider to go fuck himself, but finds he is unable to respond. He had thought he occupied higher ground, but LeBlanc's unfathomable behavior has left him no longer certain of his altitude.

TWENTY-TWO

She has been here. He's not sure how he knows this, but he does. Megan was here. This is where she had her tattoo done.

He looks around, searching for something to add substance to his tenuous assumption. He sees how clean and sterile the place seems. Megan would have felt comfortable here. She was obsessive about hygiene. For something as invasive as a tattoo, she wouldn't have gone somewhere that looked even slightly dubious with regard to its harboring of germs. She was the same when she had her ears pierced. Yes, she would happily have signed up to getting a tattoo done here. In that chair.

He stares at the chair, and his thoughts grow dark. He can picture her there. The chair is fully reclined and she's lying on her front, her shirt raised and her jeans pushed down to expose the base of her spine while the artist goes to work. The artist who could also be her killer.

He imagines her biting her lip, trying to stifle her cries at the pain of the work being done on her flawless flesh. He can hear her soft whimpers. Tiny foreshadowings of the cries that are to come later. He wants to reach out a hand and touch hers. Tell her it will be all right. Tell her he has come to take her home.

But he's too late. He knows that. He wasn't there for her

when she needed him. She couldn't trust him enough to let him know what she planned to do. And because he failed her as a parent, he was penalized. She was taken away from him. She was put through hell.

He cannot forgive or forget that. Someone has to pay.

'Hey. Can I help you?'

A man has appeared from the back room. Steve has to blink several times while he works out what he is looking at. The man is covered in bruises and healing cuts. He wears several Band-Aids, and he walks with one shoulder dropped, as though to straighten up would cause him pain.

And what this tells Steve is that there is something going on here. People don't usually look like this. There is a story here. A story involving violence and hurt. This man has something important to reveal. Steve's gut churns as he realizes he is definitely on the right track. The note he received earlier was no prank. This is the real deal. This is not just a man, but a presence.

The man puts down a plate on the counter. The plate holds a piece of toast and a knife smeared with butter.

'Sorry,' says the man. 'I was just getting some breakfast.'

'Uh-huh,' says Steve. Because he's not interested in this guy's eating habits. His domestic life is of no concern. The only thing that matters here is what he knows about Megan. 'You the owner?'

'That's me. Stanley. Stanley Proust. Good to meet you.'

He smiles and reaches a hand across the counter. All bright and breezy, like there's nothing out of the ordinary about this situation. Steve takes the hand. It feels clammy. He pumps his arm only gently, but sees a tremor of pain move across Proust's face.

'I'm Steve.' For now, he withholds his surname. He releases his grip and gestures toward Proust's head. 'What happened?'

Proust starts to raise a hand to his face, but stops halfway. 'Traffic accident. My car was totaled. I'm lucky to be alive.'

Lucky, thinks Steve. Sure, lucky. Not like my Megan. Her luck ran out when she walked in here. And a car crash? Bullshit. You're lying to me, man. Why are you lying?

He watches Proust. Studies his face and senses his discomfort.

Says Proust, 'You thinking of getting a tattoo?'

'No,' says Steve. 'Actually, I'm here about my daughter.'

'Yeah? Okay. How old is she?'

'Sixteen.'

'Sixteen? Sorry, dude, she's not old enough. You could bring her in when she's eighteen, though.'

'You couldn't make an exception? She's nearly seventeen. What's a year or so?'

'No way, man. Sorry. It's against the law.'

'Really? Because I heard you're a discreet kinda guy. You don't say and we don't say, you know what I mean? I'd make it worth your while.'

Proust shakes his head. 'Like I said, no can do. You'll have to try someplace else. But if they're reputable, they'll tell you the same thing.'

Steve nods, like he's accepting this. Except that he still believes Megan was here. Proust is hiding something. It's in there somewhere. All Steve has to do is scratch away at the surface to uncover it. Just a little bit of scratching . . .

'Okay, you're right. I wouldn't want to get you in any kind of trouble. So let's say I bring her back. Maybe for an eighteenth-birthday present, something like that. What could she have done?'

'Whatever she wants. A lot of girls, they go for butterflies, flowers, that kind of thing. I can do whatever. Here, take a look at this. It might give you some ideas.'

He slides a large binder across the counter and flips it open. An array of colorful images jumps out at Steve. He takes hold of the binder and makes a show of looking behind him for a seat.

'You mind if I sit down?'

'Sure, go ahead.'

Steve doesn't go all the way back to the sofa near the door. Instead, he pulls out a nearby stool and sits on that, the book open on his lap. He flips through a few pages, not really looking at the contents. Out of the corner of his eye he sees Proust cut through his toast and then take a bite.

'What about this one?' says Steve.

'Lemme take a look,' says Proust. But Steve stays where he is. Waits for Proust to come to him.

Proust licks butter from his thumb and comes around the counter. That's it, thinks Steve. Come on out. I don't know what you got back there. A baseball bat? A gun? Come over here where I can get at you, you sonofabitch.

Proust stands next to Steve, looking down. 'The rose? Sure, that's a popular one. I did one like that recently, but it had, like, bigger thorns, and they were dripping with blood, you know? Gave it kind of an edge.'

An edge. Blood. Pain. Is that how Proust sees everything?

'No. No blood. I want her to have something gentle. Something beautiful. Like maybe . . . an angel or something. Can you do that? Can you do an angel for my girl?'

As he says this, he lifts his gaze to lock it onto that of the man standing over him. It is a chance for Proust to demonstrate his innocence, to say without hesitation that, yes, of course he can do angels, and would you like to see some examples? To prove once and for all that he is just a man who creates tattoos, and there is nothing sinister in his world.

But Proust fails the test. The delay in his answer is as revealing as the look in his eyes. Together they attest to his undeniable guilt.

'I, uhm, angels? Sure . . . I mean, that wouldn't be, uhm . . .'

'I was thinking just a small one, but with huge wings. Wings that are spread out, you know? And I think my daughter would like this angel on her back. Low down on her spine. You think that would be okay? You think you could do something like that for me? For her, I mean? You ever do anything like that before?'

Proust is saying nothing now. His jaw muscles are twitching like they're trying to work his mouth, but nothing is happening. No sounds are being let out. He's just staring. And the reason he's staring, Steve knows, is because he realizes what this is all about. He knows who I am now. He knows what I'm here for.

Steve stands up, leaving the book of artwork on the stool. His face becomes level with Proust's. His eyes remain fixed on the man.

'Maybe if you saw her,' he says. 'Maybe that would help to give you some ideas. Do you think that would help? If you saw my daughter? If you knew exactly what she looked like?'

'I, uh, I don't—'

'Here,' says Steve, reaching into his pocket. He plucks out a recent photograph of Megan. 'Take a look. Pretty, don't you think? Beautiful, huh? Don't you think so?'

'I . . . Sure. She's a . . . a good-looking girl, all right.'

'Just good-looking?'

'Well, no. More than that. Stunning, I'd say.'

'Stunning? Well, I'm not sure that's the appropriate word. I think that's what you might call overkill. Don't you think? Overkill's a weird word, I know, but I think that's what you did there. Over-*kill*. See, I think you might say a *woman* was stunning. An adult female, I mean. You might use that word if you would love to go to bed with that female, you get what I'm saying? Like, for example, you might say Beyoncé is stunning, right? I wouldn't disagree with you on that one. But in this case, far as my daughter goes . . . well, what you have to remember is that she's only sixteen. Just a kid, really. Not even old enough for a tattoo, let alone anything else, if you know what I mean. You do know what I'm referring to, don't you?'

'I . . . I think so.'

'Yeah, sure you do. Because she looks older than sixteen, especially in the flesh. If she was standing here, right next to you, right where I'm standing, in fact, right here in your tattoo shop, you'd swear she was older than sixteen. Not that she'll ever be older than sixteen. She will always be that age. You know why I'm saying that, don't you, Stan? I can call you that, can't I? Stan, I mean. It's okay to call you Stan, isn't it? You know why I'm saying that my girl will always be sixteen, don't you, Stan?'

He is standing almost toe to toe with Proust now, still holding up the photograph. His hand is trembling and his voice is trembling and he can feel a terrible build-up of emotion inside of him. An awful swell of feeling that threatens to burst out of him at any moment, and he knows he can't prevent it. He knows that any second now he will explode, unleashing all that pent-up energy on this man in front of him.

Proust makes a vague gesture toward the back of the room.

He says, 'You don't mind, I got some things to do.' He starts to turn away, saying, 'If you want, you can—'

Steve takes hold of Proust's sleeve. 'Where you going, Stan? I haven't finished speaking with you about my girl.'

'Well, I . . .' Proust tries to pull away. Steve lets go of the man's shirt and grabs hold of his arm instead. He grasps it so tightly he sees Proust wince, and he's glad of it, glad that he is inflicting pain.

'Her name is Megan. *Was* Megan. She's dead now. But you know that, don't you, Stanley? You know that my beautiful Megan is dead.'

Proust tries to twist his arm out of Steve's grip, but Steve increases the pressure. He is stronger than Proust. Much stronger. He could take Proust to pieces if he so desired, using just his bare hands.

'I . . . yes. Yes. I know she's dead.'

'How? How do you know that, Stan?'

'The police. They told me. Look, man, I don't know what this is about, but you need to let go of my arm. This is—'

'The police? Why? Why did the police talk to you about Megan?'

'I don't know. She had a tattoo done. Before she was killed. They talked to a whole bunch of tattoo artists.'

'They say you killed her?'

'What? No. They were asking about the tattoo, is all. Asking if I knew who might have done the work.'

'What did you tell 'em?'

'I said I had no idea. It didn't look familiar to me. I couldn't help them. Now let go of my fucking arm, man.'

He wrenches himself away then, and it is clear from his expression that the effort causes a bolt of agony to fire through his body. Steve watches as he shuffles back toward the safety of his counter. Back to whatever defenses he has there. Steve senses that he is losing command of the situation. If he allows Proust to get away now, it's all over. He will never find out what this man knows. Never find Megan's killer.

Without thinking, he bounds across the floor. Interposes himself between Proust and his bolt-hole. He sees Proust recoil in shock and fear.

Steve puts his hands up. 'I don't want to hurt you. That's not why I'm here. All I want is some information, okay? I'm trying to find out who killed my daughter. Is that too much to ask? Do you think that's such an unusual wish?'

Proust backs away, one small step at a time. 'I don't know nothing about your daughter. She was never here. I never met the girl. That's exactly what I told the police, and it's what I'm telling you too. Please . . .'

'See, here's the thing, Stan. I'm not sure I believe you. Something about you ain't right. It's like . . . it's like you're holding out on me, you get what I'm saying?'

'No. I wouldn't lie to you. I understand what you're going through, man. But I can't help you. I wish I could.'

'You *can* help me, Stan. All you have to do is give me the truth. For example, tell me how you first met Megan.'

'I told you. I never met her. I—'

'BULLSHIT!'

The ferocity of the yell surprises even Steve himself. He notices how Proust jumps. The room lapses into a deathly silence, as though signaling that the encounter is about to move into more serious, more dangerous territory.

The men stare at each other for several seconds. Steve wonders what is going through Proust's head. He wonders about himself too. How he is going to pursue this. How far he is willing to allow himself to go.

He gets his answer when Proust makes a sudden dash in an attempt to get past him. It's a pathetic maneuver. Steve grabs hold of him, spins him around, and throws him back in the direction he came from. Proust crashes into the wall, causing a mirror to fall and smash at his feet. He doubles over in apparent agony, his arms folded across his torso.

'Please, man. I'm sick. You're hurting me.'

Steve feels no pity. He has gone beyond the point of no return. He wants answers. He will get answers. And he will use whatever it takes.

He reaches into the inside pocket of his jacket. Takes out the hammer he brought with him. He told himself back in the house that it was for insurance purposes only. He wouldn't need it. Wouldn't use it unless absolutely necessary.

Well, now it's necessary.

He advances on Proust, hefting the hammer in his hand. His eyes rove across Proust's bent figure, trying to decide where to strike first. He ignores the look of abject terror on Proust's face. He doesn't deserve mercy. He's asked for this. He has brought this on himself.

'One last chance,' says Steve. 'My daughter. Megan. How did you meet her?'

'I . . . I didn't meet her.'

Thwack!

Into Proust's shoulder. Proust lets out a high-pitched scream. He scuttles away from the wall, still bent over. Steve follows him, the hammer raised.

'You put the tattoo on her, didn't you? It was you, wasn't it?'

'No.'

Thwack!

The ribcage this time. Another shriek.

'Please! Stop it!'

Steve closes his ears to the pleading. He realizes now that he will kill Proust. He doesn't care about the consequences. He will beat Proust to a pulp, because he knows what Proust did. But he wants him to admit it first. As soon as the words of confession leave Proust's lips, Steve will hammer the life out of him.

'You killed her.' *Thwack!* 'You raped and tortured and killed my Megan.' *Thwack!* 'And then you cut her up. You carved her into pieces, didn't you? DIDN'T YOU?' *Thwack!*

Proust collapses onto the counter. Steve stands behind him. His chest heaves, and he can hear only his own breathing and the pounding in his ears. He can feel sweat trickling down the fingers of the hand that is clutching the hammer.

'Look at me,' he says. 'Look at me, you sonofabitch.'

Slowly, Proust lifts his face from the counter and turns it toward Steve.

'Now tell me that you didn't kill Megan. Make me believe it.'

But the expression that Proust shows him is not what he expected or hoped for. There is no admission of guilt written there. No regret. Not even fear. It takes Steve a few seconds to realize what it is. And then he gets it.

Contempt.

Proust is practically laughing at him.

Steve's grip on the hammer tightens. He decides he wants to mangle that face of Proust's. He wants to crush all the bones it contains, to splash that nose across his cheek, to knock every single tooth out of his head.

And so he advances.

He moves toward the pitiful figure slouched over the counter, staring back at him, daring him to put an end to this without hearing what Proust knows of his daughter.

Because that's what it has come to. Steve will learn no more from this man, but he knows beyond all doubt what part he played.

It is time to bring it to an end.

The roar surprises him. A last-ditch deep-throated bellow that stops him in his tracks. He watches, stunned into immobility, as the half-dead creature leaps at him and starts throwing punches. Weak, ineffectual punches that simply rebound off Steve's chest. One, two, three.

And when Proust steps back, Steve wants to laugh at the puniness and the futility of the assault. What the fuck did he think he was doing? What was he hoping to achieve?

He raises the hammer, takes another step forward.

And then the pain.

Why am I feeling pain?

He looks down at his chest. There is blood. Lots of blood. It's soaking his shirt. There shouldn't be all that blood.

He looks again at Proust. Narrows his eyes at him. And then he sees it. In Proust's hand. The knife he used to cut his toast. It had been there on the plate. On the counter.

He understands.

He moves forward again, knowing that it's a mistake even as he does it. Proust lets out another cry and drives the knife in once more, between Steve's ribs, deep into his chest. When

Proust's hand comes away this time, it is no longer holding the knife.

Steve stares at the length of metal protruding from his chest. He feels suddenly giddy and unable to function. His mind has stopped working. He's not sure what to do. What do you do when there's a knife in your heart? What do you do when you're about to die?

He is dimly aware of something thudding to the floor. The hammer he has just dropped. He raises his hand and touches the hilt of the knife. It shines brightly. Stainless steel. It's pretty well stuck in there, all right.

He turns and starts to head for the door. He's not sure why, or where he's going. He just knows it's time to leave now. This little meeting is over. Time to go.

It hurts, though. To walk, I mean. Just to take a step really hurts. Here, in my chest. It really . . .

He collapses then. Drops onto the tiled floor as though his legs have just disappeared from beneath him.

He lies there, staring up at the bright ceiling light. It's ever so bright. So bright it hurts.

He's grateful when a cloud obscures the sun. No, not the sun. Not a cloud either. A face. Proust's face. Staring down at him.

Steve thinks everything is going to be all right now.

Because the face is smiling at him.

TWENTY-THREE

Doyle is in the washroom, drying his hands on a paper towel, when LeBlanc walks in. LeBlanc takes one look at Doyle, then turns to walk out again.

'What?' says Doyle. 'Your bladder suddenly empty again? You don't need to go no more?'

'I don't need to have an argument with you, is what I don't need. My bladder can wait till you're done.'

Doyle is not letting him off that easy. He tosses the paper towel into the trashcan and follows LeBlanc out into the hallway. 'So, is this how it's gonna be from now on? Every time I come into a room, you walk out? That's real mature.'

LeBlanc stops and turns. 'I'm not a kid, Cal, even though you treat me like one. I can be adult about this. But right now I can't be in the same room as you. I can't be anywhere in your vicinity.'

'Okay, fine. Be mad at me. Yell at me. Take a pop at me if you want. Whatever you do, at least have the balls to do it in person. Don't go crawling to others to do your dirty work for you.'

'I didn't go crawling to anyone. I'm not afraid of you, Cal. I just don't wanna work with you.'

'Then how come you felt the need to bring in the rat squad? You prefer to work with them over me? Is that it?'

'What?'

'IAB. Somebody got their little whiskers twitching, and they paid me a little visit yesterday.'

LeBlanc is silent for a while, and there's a look of surprise and dismay on his face. 'It wasn't me. I didn't call IAB.'

'Oh, really? Well, somebody did. And you know what they were interested in? Me and Proust, that's what. Putting that together with the people who are mighty upset with me right now doesn't leave a whole lot of suspects, Tommy.'

LeBlanc rubs his forehead. 'Shit. Look, it wasn't me, okay? I didn't talk to IAB.'

'So who did you talk to?'

'I . . . I might've talked to one or two of the guys here.'

Doyle throws up his hands. 'Great. So now you're bringing the rest of the squad into this. Wonderful. You've been here long enough to learn the background, Tommy. You know there are people here just itching for a chance to burn me. Some of 'em have probably got IAB on speed-dial for moments like this.'

LeBlanc flares up again. 'Yeah, well, maybe if you didn't go around handing out ammunition like you do, you wouldn't be such a walking target. Maybe it's about time you learned a lesson the hard way. You know what, maybe IAB *should* take another look at you.'

He turns and storms off again. Doyle chases him along the hallway.

'What? Where is this coming from? I thought we straightened all this out yesterday. What the fuck is eating you?'

But LeBlanc just keeps on walking. At the entrance to the squadroom, Doyle grabs LeBlanc's arm. LeBlanc whirls on him.

'Stay away from me, Cal. I'm sick of the way you operate. I'm sick of your lies.'

'What lies? What are you talking about?'

'I know, Cal. I know about you and Proust. About why you hate him so much. I know what happened with you and your partner.'

'My partner? Which partner?'

'Do I have to spell it out? You really want to air this in front of everybody else here?'

Doyle is suddenly aware that every eye and every ear in the squadroom is tuned in to this argument. He's not sure that he wants LeBlanc to answer his own question, but he can do nothing to stop him now.

'Laura Marino,' says LeBlanc. 'There. I said it. You happy now?'

Somebody in the room draws a loud breath. A recognition of the force that their ex-colleague's name is still capable of exerting.

'Laura Marino? What about her?'

But LeBlanc is already walking away again. Heading back to his desk.

'Hey!' says Doyle. 'Hey! What about Laura Marino? You don't just toss her name in like that and run off. What the fuck—'

'ENOUGH!'

The single word explodes into the room, and after it there is only deathly silence, as though a teacher has just announced his arrival in a classroom of unruly pupils. All heads turn to locate the source – the dark, solemn figure of Lieutenant Cesario.

He says, 'I don't know what this squabbling is about, and frankly I'm not interested. I've got more important things on my mind, and so should you. Like the Megan Hamlyn case, for example. Because maybe if you were on top of things like you're supposed to be, you would know what's going on out there. You would know that while you're fighting your pathetic little battle here, there's a much bigger war taking place between some of the other people tied up in this case.'

He pauses to let his words sink in, then continues. 'Stanley Proust, the tattoo guy, has just been attacked at his place of work. The man who assaulted him is Steve Hamlyn, the murdered girl's father, but Hamlyn came off worst. He's in hospital, situation critical. I have no idea how these two managed to hook up – I think I've got some serious butt-kicking to do on that score – but right now I want this mess cleared up. So get out there and do your jobs.'

Doyle stares at his boss while he tries to absorb what he's just been told. Proust attacked by Hamlyn? How the hell did that happen? And how did a puny streak of piss like Proust manage to whup Hamlyn's ass?

Behind him he hears LeBlanc getting up from his chair and moving toward the door. Doyle turns to follow him, and it's as if Cesario has been waiting for him to do so.

'LeBlanc, take Schneider with you to see Proust. Doyle, get yourself to the ER at Bellevue.'

Doyle looks round at the lieutenant. 'Lou . . .' he begins, but what he sees on Cesario's face warns him not to continue with his objection. There is something in Cesario's features that tells Doyle his boss has heard things. About him and about Proust. Which isn't that surprising. Tell one guy something in this squad and you tell everyone, the boss included.

Biting his lip, Doyle collects his jacket and heads for the door.

*

Nicole is there already. Alone in a small waiting room off one of the corridors. They use this room for close family of trauma patients. Sometimes they use it to relate the worst news possible. It's a little quieter here, away from the scary chaos of the main waiting area. But it's not quite an oasis of calm. Even as Doyle heads for the open doorway, a man is wheeled past him on a gurney, screaming that his feet have disappeared, and then laughing maniacally.

In the room, Nicole is staring at the floor. A wad of tissues is balled tightly in her clasped hands. When Doyle approaches, she looks up. Her eyeballs are bloodshot, the lids pink and raw.

'Detective,' she says.

He takes a seat next to her. 'How is he?'

She looks into Doyle's eyes. 'I don't know. Alive, but . . . I don't know. I don't think it's good. He was stabbed several times in the chest. He's lost a lot of blood.'

'Do you know how it happened?'

A slight shake of the head. 'He went out early this morning. He didn't even tell me he was going, or where. But later the police called me and told me he'd been in a fight. They asked me what he might be doing in a tattoo parlor on Avenue B. They asked me what I knew about a man called Stanley Proust.'

She starts crying again. She dabs at her face with the damp tissues. Doyle waits.

She says, 'I can't go through this again, Detective. Not again.'

'I'm sure the doctors are doing all they can,' he answers. He knows it's just one of those pat phrases, that it means nothing, but he feels he has to offer some kind of response.

Nicole raises her watery eyes, and they are filled with questions. 'This man Proust. Is he the one? Is he the one who put the tattoo on Megan? Could he be the one who . . . who killed her?'

Yes, Doyle wants to say. He tattooed her. He invaded her. He tortured her. He murdered her. He cut her up into little pieces. Yes to all the above.

'We got no reason to think it was Proust,' Doyle says, and he almost chokes as the words leave him. 'Maybe . . . maybe Steve just decided to do a little investigating of his own and he got a little too . . . well . . .'

She's nodding at this. 'I had a feeling he would do something stupid. I tried to tell him he shouldn't get involved, he should leave it to the cops. But I knew he had to do something. It was eating him up inside. He couldn't just hang around, knowing Megan's killer was out there somewhere. He needed to feel he was doing something useful.'

'I understand,' says Doyle. And he does. He understands completely. He's not sure he would have acted any differently.

'He's not a bad man, Detective. I know he didn't give you a very warm reception that last time at our house. And things between me and him . . . well, they haven't been so good either. But it's only because his head is all messed up. You should have met him before all this happened. Before Megan disappeared. You would have liked him. He's a guy you might have wanted to have a drink with, you know? Just a regular guy, with a good sense of humor. He hasn't laughed for a while now. Maybe he never will again.'

She starts sobbing again, and buries her face in her wad of tissues. Doyle sighs and closes his eyes. There was a time, long ago, when he might have prayed in a situation like this. Now he just lets the pain and hopelessness wash over him. What will be will be, and there's nothing he can do to make it otherwise.

'Would you wait?' she asks.

'Excuse me?'

'I mean, would you mind waiting here with me? Just for a while. I don't want to be alone right now.'

'Sure,' he says. 'I'll stay as long as you want.'

He means it too. A part of him is desperate to get back out there and put every ounce of his energy into nailing Proust for the devastation he has wrought on this family. And that will come. He will do that for the Hamlyns and because it's right. But right now it's not what Mrs Hamlyn wants. What she wants is for someone to be here for her. Doyle can spare some time for that.

And so he settles back in his chair, clasps his hands in his lap, and watches the human traffic go by.

Proust can wait a while.

But his time is coming.

TWENTY-FOUR

Doyle gets to the second floor of the precinct station house just as two uniforms come out of one of the interview rooms. Shuffling between them is Stanley Proust.

'Look who it is,' says Doyle. 'I thought I could smell something bad up here. What, Stanley, the daughter wasn't enough for you? You had to get the father too? You working your way through the whole fucking family?'

Proust tries to hide behind the unis. 'You're crazy. I didn't do nothing. He attacked me. I was just defending myself.'

'Uh-huh? Well, how about you showing me some of those wonderful self-defense skills you got there? How about it, Stan? How about I make a move, and you show me what you got?'

'Cal,' says one of the uniforms.

'What do you say, Stan? One on one. Just you and me, putting on a little show for the guys here.'

'Cal!'

Doyle looks at the officer. Sees the man's eyeballs flick to the right, signaling something of interest along the hallway. Doyle turns his head in that direction. What he sees there is the figure of Lieutenant Cesario, his arms crossed, his expression as rigid as his stance.

'My office,' says Cesario, and then he vanishes.

Doyle gets the impression that Cesario wasn't merely announcing his destination in case Doyle should happen to be interested, nor that any follow-up action on Doyle's part should be taken at his leisure. But he makes the time to turn a final withering stare on Proust.

'Later, Stan. You better get practicing on those prison tats. You know, swastikas and shit. Those Aryan cons like that kind of thing.'

He winks at Proust, and then goes to see what's biting Cesario.

The first thing Cesario says when Doyle enters is 'Close the door.' Which in Doyle's experience is not the best start to any conversation with your boss.

He moves toward Cesario's desk, noticing how uncluttered and impersonal it is. No photos, no memorabilia, no personal shit of any kind. The man's an enigma. The only items in this whole office that are in any way reflective of personal taste are the two huge cactus plants standing guard behind him, and even they were put there by the man's predecessor.

As Doyle pulls out a chair, he points his thumb toward the door and says, 'They taking him to Central Booking already?'

There's a touch of impatience in Cesario's voice, as though he's the only one who deserves to be posing questions. 'Who, Proust? No. No, they're not. They're taking him to the hospital. And after that they're taking him home. It's probably the least we can do.'

Doyle practically collapses onto the chair in surprise. 'The least we can do? The hospital? Why the hell are we—'

Cesario interjects with a force that makes his irritation even more plain. 'The man has just been attacked with a hammer. He needs to be checked out. But then he must be used to that by now. There's a chair in that hospital that must be still warm

249

from the last time he was in there. What the hell have you been doing?'

'Me? What do you mean? I had nothing to do with this.'

'Really?'

'Yes, really. What kind of question is that? What exactly are you accusing me of here?'

Cesario throws his hands up. 'I don't know. I have no idea what the hell is going on anymore. I'm only the squad commander. Why should I get to hear? Maybe it's my fault. Maybe I don't ask enough questions. So while you were out I decided it might be a good idea to start asking a few. Especially after I saw the state of Proust when they brought him in. How did he get to be like that? Can you explain that to me?'

'Would it do any good, now that you've heard everybody else's opinion on the matter? I can bet good old Schneider wasn't shy about putting his two cents in.'

'Schneider isn't the only one with your name on his lips right now. In fact, you've become a bit of a talking point. So think of this as being a chance to put your side of the story.'

Doyle hesitates. He knows how ridiculous this is going to sound.

'Proust is crazy, okay? I mean, out of his skull. He's got this wacko idea that if he can make it look like the police are persecuting him, we'll back off.'

'The police in general, or you?'

'Me in particular.'

'I see. And why would he think like that? Why is he so afraid of you "in particular"?'

'Because I seem to be the only one around here who thinks he's guilty of murder. And he knows I'm not going to give up until I prove it.'

'Is that the only reason?'

Another accusation wrapped up in a question. Doyle resents it, but after what's happened he's not surprised it's being hurled at him.

'Yes.'

'So explain to me how Proust ended up looking like he's been used as a football.'

'I don't know. Maybe he falls out of his bed a lot. Maybe he forgets to check there's water in the swimming pool before he jumps in. Maybe—'

'Maybe he jumps through glass doors.'

'Yes. That too.'

'He really jumped through a glass door?'

'Yes. As insane as it sounds, that's exactly what he did.'

'Why?'

'Because he saw Tommy coming into his place. He wanted to make it look like I was kicking the crap out of him.'

'So he jumped through a door?'

'Yes. Jesus. It don't matter how many times you ask me, Lou, the answer's the same. Proust does not see the world the way we do. Maybe that's why he's such a good artist. His brain doesn't work like ours. How could it, if he can get his kicks from cutting up young women?'

'Assuming you're right about that.'

'Which I am.'

Cesario picks up a pencil and stares at the writing on it for an inordinately long period before tossing it back onto his desk.

'You can see how this looks? On your own admission, you've been to see Proust against my express orders. You kept it so quiet that even your own partner didn't know. After one of these visits,

Proust is black and blue. On another occasion, he comes flying through a glass door.'

'Yeah, I know how it looks. But—'

'And now there's this latest episode. With Hamlyn.'

This throws Doyle. He doesn't understand why it's been tacked on as if it's part of a sequence involving him.

'Yeah, about that. How come he's not a collar for that? You really believe whatever cockamamie story he came up with?'

'That Hamlyn came at him with a hammer? Sure. Does that sound so unbelievable to you?'

'Lou, everything Proust says is unbelievable. He's a lying scumbag. He'd say anything to save his own neck.'

'Yeah? And what if he's telling the truth? What if he's really the innocent party in this?'

'Proust doesn't know what innocent means. He's been guilty since he was born. It's in his blood. People like that don't change. Whatever he told you about what went down with Hamlyn is a lie.'

Cesario sighs. A weighty sigh that tells Doyle he's just dug himself into some kind of hole. What worries him is that he doesn't know how deep it is.

Says Cesario, 'We've seen the recordings.'

Doyle is thrown again. Cesario keeps tossing out comments that seem to bear no relation to the discussion in hand.

'Uhm . . . What?'

'The recordings. From the security cameras in Proust's tattoo parlor.'

'Security cameras? Proust doesn't have security cameras.'

'Yes, he does. And they picked up every second of what happened in there this morning. It's just like he says. Hamlyn came at him like a bull. Accusing him, yelling at him. Then he pulls out a hammer. Starts hitting Proust with it. Proust did the only thing he could. He picked up a knife and fought back. And after it was over, the first thing he did was pick up the phone and dial 911. It's all there, Cal. Every move he made was the move of an innocent victim.'

Doyle is only half listening. His mind is still wrestling with this new information about the cameras. They definitely weren't there the last time Doyle went to see Proust. That means he had them installed just for this. Jesus! The whole thing was a set-up!

Cesario ups his volume: 'Doyle, did you hear what I just said? Proust didn't put a foot wrong. You still want to call him a liar?'

'I want to call him a whole bunch of things.'

'Call him what you want, but the recordings don't lie. And if he was telling the truth about this, then maybe he's been telling the truth all along. Maybe somebody is out to get him.'

'Well, he's not wrong about that. Because I *am* out to get him. But I'll do it legally. Those marks on Proust never came from me.'

'And the Hamlyn thing?'

There he goes again, thinks Doyle.

'What about the Hamlyn thing? What does that have to do with me?'

'You tell me. What did you tell Hamlyn about Proust?'

'Nothing. I never even mentioned Proust's name.'

'You sure about that?'

'Absolutely.'

Cesario opens his desk drawer and pulls out a transparent plastic folder holding a single sheet of paper.

'The uniforms who responded to the initial call found this on Hamlyn when they were checking for ID.'

He hands the document across. Doyle notices a spot of dried blood in the top-left corner. The text reads:

Mr Hamlyn,

I shouldn't be telling you this, but I want to help you. The man you need to speak to is called Stanley Proust. You can find him at a tattoo parlor called Skinterest on Avenue B in the East Village.

Good luck.

So that's how he did it, thinks Doyle. That's how he brought Hamlyn to his door.

'You saying I sent this?'

'Did you?'

'I can't believe you're even asking me that.' He tosses the note back with disdain. 'Proust sent this. He was setting Hamlyn up. He knew Hamlyn wouldn't ignore a message like this, and he knew how to push Hamlyn's buttons when he came to see him. He wanted it to get physical. That's why he had the cameras put in. He was making a movie, Lou. The whole thing was scripted from start to finish.'

Another sigh from Cesario. The disbelief emanating from him is really starting to rile Doyle.

'You're saying he orchestrated this?'

'Not a word I'd use, but yeah, that's exactly what I'm saying.'

'How'd he know Hamlyn would take the bait?'

'Because . . . I told him. I was giving him heat, and I let him know that Hamlyn would love to spend five minutes alone with him.'

'So wasn't he taking a pretty big risk? Suppose Hamlyn had turned up with a gun?'

Doyle shrugs. 'Like I already said, Proust doesn't think like we do.'

'And yet you claim you can read him like a book.'

'I know a killer when I see one. I don't always know what he's gonna do next, but I do know what he's already done. And just because I know that, it doesn't mean I beat the crap out of him. Why would I jeopardize a case like that?'

'Maybe there's another reason.'

'Such as?'

'Laura Marino.'

That name again. For a moment, Doyle is stunned into silence. Why does his ex-partner's name keep cropping up?

'What about her?'

'You saying you don't know? You were arguing with LeBlanc about her earlier.'

'He dropped her name on me just like you did. I never got an explanation. Now I'm asking you for one.'

Cesario leans forward and rests his forearms on the desk. He keeps his eyes locked on Doyle, watching for a reaction.

'Proust says he saw you and Marino, necking in the car outside his tattoo joint.'

Doyle's jaw drops open, but he can't find any words. Oh, Christ, he thinks. That is clever. What a smart fucking son-ofabitch you are, Stan. Give them a reason why I would hate you, and give them a reason to hate me. A reason that some cops have been looking for all along. People like Schneider have been dying to hear something like this. Something that confirms in their twisted minds that I really did have an affair with Laura, and so really did have a need to waste her when it turned sour. Real clever, Stan.

His reaction surprises even himself. He starts laughing.

Says Cesario, 'You find it funny?'

'Yeah,' says Doyle. 'Yeah, I do. I find it funny how Proust has got everybody in the Department thinking exactly what he wants them to think. He murders two people, maybe three if it goes bad for Hamlyn, and yet I'm the bad guy. He's the victim and I'm the criminal. He's got the whole fucking PD twisted around his little finger. I have to hand it to him, the man's a fucking genius.'

'So he's lying about Marino too?'

'It's a crock of shit, Lou, and you know it is.'

'Then where did he get this? How'd he even hear the rumors about you and Marino?'

'Who knows? It was never exactly confidential. Maybe Schneider told him. The point is, it's bullshit.'

Cesario falls silent and lowers his gaze. Doyle would like to believe his boss is mulling over what to do next, but he fears that what he's really doing is deciding how to break the bad news to him.

When Cesario finally lifts his eyes again he says, 'It doesn't look good, Cal.'

'Yeah, you told me that already.'

It's the wrong answer. Cesario slams his palm on the desk. 'Jesus Christ, man! Listen to yourself. When did you get to be so holier than thou? You fucked up, man. What's worse, you can't even see how badly you fucked up. Whether you laid a finger on Proust or not, it doesn't really matter. If Proust puts in a complaint, we're screwed. If the press gets hold of it, we're screwed. If we even go near Proust with anything less than a cast-iron case against him, we are so screwed. And all because of you, Cal. All because you refused to obey my direct order to stay away from him. From now on, we have to treat Proust with kid gloves.'

Doyle shakes his head. 'You can't back off from Proust. That's exactly what he wants you to do. You have to keep the pressure on him.'

'Oh yeah? What kind of pressure do you have in mind? Thumbscrews, maybe? Waterboarding?'

'That's not what I meant.'

'I'll bet it's what you'd like to do, though.'

'In my head, sure. I admit it, and I make no apology for it. Proust is scum. But I'm a cop, Lou. A good cop. I would never beat on a perp, and I would never jeopardize a case.'

'You already have jeopardized the case, Doyle. And that's why I'm reining you in.'

Doyle tenses. 'You're taking me off the case?'

Cesario pauses for a brief moment, adding weight to his next pronouncement. 'I'm taking you off the squad.'

'What? Off the . . . What are you talking about?'

'I'm sending you home for a while. Until the dust settles.'

'Why? That's ridiculous. Hit me with a Command Discipline if you want. You don't have to suspend me.'

'Yes I do, Doyle. I don't know what the truth is here, but there are a lot of people who have already made up their minds. Your own partner doesn't want to work with you. Others think you've totally lost it with regard to Proust. And now that Laura Marino's name is in the air again, well that's turned the clock back to a darker time for some.'

Doyle sits there in silence, shaking his head. But he knows he can't win this one.

Says Cesario, 'I have to consider the squad as a whole. I also have to protect the case you've been on. For both of those reasons I can't have you around here. Oh, and in case you're thinking of taking this out on any particular individuals, you should know that LeBlanc didn't bring this to me. In fact, when I questioned him he didn't want to say anything that might get you into trouble. I'm not sure you deserve it, but that's what he did for you. Now collect your things and go home, Doyle.'

Doyle rises slowly from his chair. 'You're making a mistake, Lou. I'm the only one who gives a damn about nailing Proust. He's gonna walk away from this.'

But Cesario doesn't give him an answer. He's done debating this.

At the door, Doyle turns to his boss one last time.

'He walked away once before, and now he's gonna do it again.'

And then he leaves.

Back in the squadroom, he's painfully aware of the silence. Word has got around. They know why he was called in, and they expected it to be bad. Some of them undoubtedly wanted it to be bad.

He doesn't talk to them. Doesn't try to explain or defend his actions. He's too tired for that. Tired of this place. Tired of all the shit that's come his way when all he's trying to do is put a vicious killer behind bars.

When he walks out of the squadroom, he's not sure he ever wants to come back.

Home sweet home.

It's a refuge. A haven. It seems to him that ton weights drop from him as he walks through the door. All he can think about is having a beer and vegging out in front of the TV. Watch a comedy or a drama. No news. Nothing about the shit that goes on outside these windows. He wants to forget all that. Pretend it doesn't even exist. No doubt it won't be as easy as that – too many thoughts and mixed emotions are bubbling in a cauldron at the back of his mind – but he's going to give it a damn good try.

But then he sees Rachel, and bang go his thoughts of escape.

She's sitting at the table, and it's clear she's been crying. As he walks in, she glares at him.

'Oh, shit,' he says. 'Amy again? What's she done this time?'

'No,' she says. 'Not Amy. You.'

'Me? What have I done?'

'You tell me. I bumped into a friend today at a deli. Well, at least I thought she was a friend. I wasn't so sure, the way she was pretending not to notice me. She's the wife of one of your colleagues on the squad.'

Doyle gears himself up for what's coming.

'Which colleague?'

'Does it matter? I don't thinks he's unique in what he knows. Seems like everyone's heard the news except me. So I get talking to this woman, and I can tell she's in a hurry to pay up and get out of there, so I ask her direct. I ask her what's on her mind. And she tells me. Do you know what she says?'

The tension comes flooding back into Doyle. It's like facing Cesario again. He's back on the defensive. No quarter given by the opposing forces.

'I can guess,' he answers.

But she tells him anyway. And after she tells him she asks him if any of it is true, even though they had this discussion a million times, back when his life was turning to shit. And after he denies it she tells him that she always believed they would never need to have a conversation about 'that woman' ever again. And after that, she asks why the fuck 'that woman' is even back on the fucking agenda. And then she brings in the old 'no smoke without fire' argument. And following that . . .

Well, Doyle begins to think that 'Home sweet home' is the stupidest fucking phrase ever invented.

TWENTY-FIVE

His plan is not to tell Rachel where he is right now. Somehow he doesn't think she will understand.

Their discussion seemed to take for ever, and even now he's not sure that anything was resolved. There was a lot of anger in there. Plenty of wailing. Copious amounts of tears. Doyle tried to explain, as patiently and as calmly as he could, that it was just a story, made up by some dirtbag who was trying to get him into trouble. But Rachel, bless her, had a battery of intelligent and incisive questions to put to him. She'd clearly done a lot of pondering about this before he got home. She wanted to know, for example, how this so-called dirtbag had even heard of the rumored relationship between Doyle and Laura Marino. She also wanted to know why, if this dirtbag was considered such a troublemaker with a penchant for making stuff up, the other cops of the Eighth Precinct were lending the story so much currency that it spread like wildfire. Wildfire that quickly burned the ears of Doyle's own wife.

He did his best to assuage her doubts and fears. But when Rachel left to pick up Amy from a party there was still confusion and sadness and anger on her face. And when she returned with Amy, the topic could not be raised in front of their daughter. Nor could it surface once Amy had been put to bed, because

Rachel also decided she wanted an early night. Not the 'Coming to bed, darling?' type of early night, but the 'I'm going to bed' type. The type that emphasizes the single-participant nature of the activity.

He didn't help matters at that point. He told her he had to go out again, which was true, but he didn't specify where. The response from Rachel consisted of a single word – 'Fine' – plus a door slam that seemed to say a whole lot more. Thinking about it now, Doyle realizes that it probably came across that he was simply being petulant. That he was trying to show her who was boss by storming out to seek solace elsewhere. Maybe in a bar.

Or a strip joint.

She wouldn't see the funny side. *Honey, I wasn't avoiding the issue, okay? I just needed to visit this strip club. Yes, it had to be tonight. And no, I'm not at all interested in the girls. Is it work? Well, not exactly . . .*

He hasn't told her that he's been taken off the job, and he prays that word doesn't leak back to her. If it does, then the pile of shit he's in right now will seem positively fragrant in comparison with the one that could get dumped on him tomorrow.

And it's all thanks to Proust.

He's good. Doyle knew that already from the Alyssa Palmer case. But what Proust has proved now is that he's far more dangerous than Doyle ever suspected.

Doyle can understand how others are taken in by Proust. He looks so normal, so innocent. He earns a meager living from doing a job he loves. He keeps himself to himself. He's harmless. And look what's happened to him, the poor guy. How could anybody who is a danger to others end up looking like he does? Surely he's the one who needs protecting?

Ah, but protecting from whom? We don't need to look far

for the answer to that one, do we? It's obviously the cop. You know, the one who got his partner killed. The one who cheats on his wife. The one who's been thrown off the squad. The one who's under investigation by Internal Affairs. The one who—

'You look like you could use some company.'

Before Doyle can answer, the voluptuous redhead is pulling out a chair and sitting next to him. He remembers her from a few minutes ago, when all she was wearing was a smile. The diaphanous robe she has put on since then makes her the most overdressed woman in this place.

'Actually, I prefer to be alone,' he says.

'Sure,' she says. 'There are no lonely guys in here. You got all the love you need. You come in here just for the cultural experience.'

He can't help but smile. She's one of those people who are instantly likeable.

'Beats the art gallery,' he says.

'What, even Rubens? You don't dig plus-sized women?'

He likes the fact that she's heard of Rubens, and he likes the fact that she can jolt preconceptions. Even people who take their clothes off for a living can be thoughtful, amusing human beings.

'Size ain't the issue,' he says. 'Personality does it for me every time.'

'Sure,' she says again. She gestures toward the central stage, where a blond girl who came on in a full sailor outfit is now down to a hat and a thong. 'Those double-D personalities really are something, aren't they?'

Doyle maintains his smile. He'd like to continue talking to this girl, especially since her presence at his table helps to bolster the illusion that he's just another customer. But she's also a distraction, and right now he needs to keep his mind on other things.

Like Ramone, for example, sitting just a few tables away. Doyle has waited for days to latch onto this guy, and he doesn't want to fuck it up now. Ramone is one step further along the trail of pond life that will lead him to Anton Ruger, and he's only got a few hours left to get to the end. If he loses Ramone then he's screwed: Bartok will keep his promise to mail a corpse to Police HQ, and Doyle can start saying his goodbyes.

Doyle reaches into his jacket for his wallet. He knows how these things work. He will be enticed into buying a couple rounds of drinks for him and the girl, at the astronomical prices they charge here. Then she'll invite him into one of the curtained-off areas they have for a private show, and his wallet will take a fatal wound.

'No offense,' he says, 'but do you mind hitting on somebody else? Here, buy some drinks for you and the bald guy at that table over there. He looks like he hasn't seen a naked woman since he got married.'

'Now you're being insulting.'

'I thought that was pretty mild. I could tell you what I really think, but I wouldn't want to put you off the guy. Underneath that sweat-covered, drooling exterior he's probably a real charmer.'

'I meant insulting to me. I didn't come over here for your money. I came because I thought you looked interesting. Just because I'm a stripper, it doesn't mean I can't occasionally take an interest in people.'

Doyle nods and puts his wallet away. 'My mistake,' he says. Another preconception shattered.

'What are you doing here?' she asks.

'Isn't it obvious?'

She studies him for a few seconds. 'Actually, no. You're not like the others.'

'I'm not?'

'No. I've been watching you. You're not here for the girls. You're more interested in that dark-haired guy at the table behind me.'

Doyle glances over the stripper's shoulder. The man he believes to be Ramone is still at his table, talking to a brunette in a black camisole. Doyle hopes he's not planning to spend most of the night here, and that when he leaves, it will be without the brunette.

Doyle raises his palms in mock-surrender. 'You got me. I'm confused about my sexuality. I come to places like this so I can tell myself it's the girls turning me on, when really—'

'Are you going to kill him?'

Doyle's eyes lock onto hers. He can tell she is not joking.

'No. I only kill people on Wednesdays.'

She doesn't smile. She believes she's on to something.

'You know what I think?'

'What do you think?'

'I think one of you is gonna end up dead tonight. I hope it's not you.'

He stares at her. She has made her prediction in the omniscient tone of a fortune teller. There's a certainty to her words that is chilling.

She reaches across to him, and he notices there is a card in her hand that he is sure wasn't there a moment ago. With what she's wearing, he wonders where she's been keeping it.

'Call me sometime,' she says. 'If you live.'

As soon as he takes the card from her, she gets up and swishes her hips over to the bar. Doyle slips the card into his pocket without even glancing at it. He knows he's not going to call her, but there's something about the girl that makes him think they'll meet again at some point.

If you live.

He wishes she hadn't said that. He wishes especially that she hadn't said it in the way she did. What started off as a simple surveillance suddenly seems so much more dangerous.

Forget it, he tells himself. You've done jobs like this lots of times. Don't let her spook you.

He takes a sip of his drink, then glances across the tables to where Ramone is seated. Ramone has his back to Doyle, and is leaning close to the brunette, whispering into her ear. But then he suddenly draws away from her and reaches into his pocket. He pulls out a cellphone and answers a call. It's brief, but it's something of apparent urgency, because he gives the girl a peck on the cheek, then gets up and heads for the door.

Here we go, thinks Doyle. He waits for Ramone to leave, then gets up himself. On the way out, he takes a last look at the redhead, now seated at the bar. She's watching him, and the look on her face can only be described as one of concern.

He nods at her, as if to say, *I'll be careful.* Then he leaves too.

Outside, it's raining. Big surprise. Doyle shelters under the green awning of the strip club while he scans the street for any sign of Ramone.

Don't tell me I've lost him already, he thinks. Some piss-poor detective that would make me.

But he sees Ramone then, walking quickly to the corner of the block, his shoulders hunched against the weather. Doyle abandons his dry spot beneath the awning and takes up pursuit.

The joint he's just been in is called the Arabesque Gentleman's Club, even though most of its clientele can hardly be classed as gentlemen. It's located on the eastern edge of Vinegar Hill in Brooklyn, close to the old Navy Yard. The buildings here are mostly warehouses. No bars, no stores. No reason to come here at night unless you want the strip club. It means that Ramone can't be swallowed up in a crowd, but it also means that he could easily spot a close tail if he turns around, and so Doyle has to keep his distance.

Ramone is heading north, toward the East River. Ahead are the huge humming transformers of the Con Ed substation. When a flash of lightning lights up the sky, Doyle is not so sure he wants to get much nearer to those devices. He doesn't know much about electricity, but he doesn't feel comfortable being surrounded by so much of it. He feels like he's in one of those old horror movies, with some mad scientist about to yell 'More power, Igor!'

When Ramone takes a left turn, Doyle picks up the pace. At the end of the block, he stops and peers around the corner. Ramone is still marching purposefully. Doyle waits for him to put a respectable distance between them, then follows again.

They are heading west now. Toward the neighborhood known as DUMBO, the comical acronym for Down Under the Manhattan Bridge Overpass. Straight ahead are the lights of the Manhattan Bridge, then the Brooklyn Bridge, then the city skyscrapers jutting up on the other side of the river, although it's difficult to see any of that through this driving rain.

Doyle walks quickly, feeling the slick Belgian cobbles beneath his feet. The warehouses to either side are shuttered and dark. Some have become construction sites, fronted by scaffolding, fenced-off machinery and building materials, while others lie empty and forlorn.

Ramone disappears. Another turn, toward the river again. We have to be near the destination now, thinks Doyle. He steps up the pace once more. There is another flash of lightning. The whole street lights up.

The electricity of which Doyle is so afraid probably saves his life.

Without that short-lived moment of illumination, he probably wouldn't have noticed the shape leaping out at him from behind the parked van. He probably wouldn't have had time to duck as the shape swung at him. He would probably have taken the full force of the blow to his head, getting his skull crushed rather than just being knocked senseless.

Doyle collapses onto the hard wet cobbles. He raises his hands to protect his head from another strike, but the next blow lands on his ribs instead.

Knowing that he's dead if he stays on the ground, Doyle pulls his feet under him and launches himself in the direction of his attacker. He hits something. Hears a grunt. Doyle takes hold of the man's clothing and drives him backwards. They crash into the side of the van, and the attacker issues another grunt.

I can win this, thinks Doyle. I've got this sonofabitch.

But that's before he takes the massive impact to the back of his head and goes down again.

Two of them, he thinks. But now it doesn't really matter how many, because he has lost the fight and will probably die here on this black, rain-soaked street. And even as he reaches for his gun – the Beretta he went to all that trouble to obtain for eventualities such as this – he suspects it's a futile gesture. He's right. The preventative blow feels like it breaks his arm, and then further blows rain down on him, and then there are hands all over him, stealing his gun and dragging him across the cobblestones, drag-

ging him to a door set in one of those dark, forbidding warehouses, dragging him into the black innards of the building and
down a set of hard stairs that punch and scrape his bones as he
passes over them.

If you live, the stripper had said. Her words echo in his head
as he lies on the floor and waits for death.

TWENTY-SIX

The darkness vanishes, and Doyle can see again. With him are two men – both white, both large. One of them trains a gun on Doyle. The other is standing next to a lamp he has just switched on. He is carrying a short baseball bat.

Doyle raises himself to a sitting position and surveys his surroundings. The lamp isn't powerful, but it casts enough of a glow to show Doyle that he's in a huge storage room. It's clear that the place is no longer in use, but there are enough empty boxes around to tell him that it once housed printer paper.

With his free hand, the gunman takes a cellphone from his pocket, stabs a button on it, then puts the phone to his ear.

'We got him,' is all he says into the phone before putting it back into his pocket. Then to Doyle: 'Better start saying your prayers, asshole.'

Doyle doesn't want to pray. What he wants to do is kick himself for being so stupid. He should have been prepared for a trap. He should have kept open the possibility that, despite being dangled out of a fifth-floor window, Cubo might not have been as scared of Doyle as he seemed, and might have contacted Ramone to let him know there was a guy looking for him – a guy who might turn up at the strip club this very night.

But he didn't do any of that. In his arrogance, he assumed that he was the one calling all the shots. It never crossed his mind that Ramone was leading him straight into the arms of his two buddies here. He never considered that the phone call that Ramone took in the club was from these goons, telling him they were lying in wait. He never imagined that one of the warehouses on his route might already have been broken into and assessed for its suitability as his final resting place.

And because of all this short-sightedness, he's going to pay the ultimate price.

The man with the bat advances toward Doyle. He has a scruffy ginger beard and mean little eyes, and looks wide enough to take up two seats on an airplane. He slaps the bat rhythmically into the palm of his left hand.

He says, 'How 'bout I play a tune on that ugly fucking head of yours?'

Doyle glares back at him and says, 'You know anything from *West Side Story*? You look like you dig musicals.'

The man tightens his lips and raises his bat as he accelerates toward Doyle.

'Zack!' the other man yells.

Zack stops in his tracks, staring down at Doyle through those piss-hole eyes as he snorts angrily.

'Wait for Ramone,' the gunman says. 'We got some questions for this motherfucker. After that you can have all the fun you want.'

Zack stares for a few seconds more, then he hawks up some phlegm and lets fly. Doyle twists his face away just in time, and the foul viscous fluid catches him on the side of his neck and trickles under his collar.

Zack backs away slowly, smacking the bat into his hand again, then half turns to his partner. 'Where the fuck is Ramone, anyhow?'

As if in answer to his question, there comes a rattling noise as the handle of the door is tried, immediately followed by a heavy pounding. Doyle looks up to see the silhouette of a head through the small glass panel in the door.

Ramone has returned.

'Let him in,' says the man with the gun. Zack doesn't question the command. He just sneers at Doyle before turning to trudge up the staircase.

Doyle takes the opportunity to consider his options. Which doesn't take long, as he doesn't have any. Even with Ramone outside and Zack where he is, there is still a third man with a cannon pointed squarely at Doyle's face. Doyle would need legs like a frog's to get from his position on the floor to the gunman before being shot, and even then he would still have to deal with Zack over there, who probably also has a gun and is just wielding the bat for its amusement value.

At the top of the stairs, Zack studies the face at the door panel. As if to help him, another flash of lightning gives him a clearer view of the visitor's features. Even from where he is sitting, Doyle can tell it's Ramone. He starts to wonder if the elements are conspiring against him. Revenge for abandoning his faith in higher forces all those years ago.

Zack fiddles with a lock. Pulls the door open to the accompaniment of thunder. Doyle feels the hairs rise on his neck. He knows this isn't going to be pleasant. It's going to be painful and it's going to last a long time and it's going to end in his death. And he sees no way out. These men will kill him and they will leave his body here to rot, and not even his wife will know what has happened to him. Doyle feels a pang of regret. He wishes he had not parted from his wife on such bad terms. For her sake.

Then Ramone enters the building.

Or, rather, he flies in.

Ramone's whole body jerks forward and he smashes into Zack, propelling him backwards into the metal balustrade of the staircase. Zack loses his footing and crashes onto the stairs, Ramone on top of him. The two men tumble noisily down the short staircase, a curious two-headed creature with flailing limbs.

As shocked and confused as Doyle, the man with the gun whirls round, seeking out something to aim at.

He is too slow. From the open doorway come two flashes of light in rapid succession. Not lightning this time, but gunfire from a silenced pistol. Doyle's assailant staggers backwards into a pillar, then slides down it to the floor, leaving a bloody trail above his head.

The man who threw Ramone's lifeless body at Zack comes into the room and pushes the door closed behind him. He descends the staircase slowly and steadily, his gun outstretched before him as though it is some kind of proboscis, sniffing out prey to be terminated.

At the bottom of the stairs, lying dazed and bleeding profusely from his head, Zack struggles to extricate himself from beneath the dead weight of Ramone that is pinning him down. He succeeds just as the uninvited assassin reaches the last stair, and when Zack makes the mistake of reaching under his jacket, the gun spits twice into his face, and he goes quiet and still.

The stranger steps over to Zack's colleague, who is still alive. He is making wheezing noises, and scarlet froth is bubbling from his mouth, but he is still alive.

The killer puts an end to that with a single shot that takes out the prone man's left eye and explodes the back of his head across the pillar.

Then the gun is turned toward Doyle.

Doyle takes his first good look at this man who has just wordlessly slaughtered three others. He is tall and dark-haired, with thick eyebrows and a pall of stubble that is so uniform and black it almost looks painted on. There is no emotion in his eyes. No trace of the after-effects of adrenalin or exertion. It is clear that he excels at his profession, and his profession is killing. The question in Doyle's mind is: has he just been saved, or is he about to become the fourth victim?

Doyle stays sitting on the concrete floor as the man slowly walks around him. When he is out of sight behind him, Doyle closes his eyes and waits for his brains to be evacuated. But then the man appears in front of him again, and Doyle lets out a long silent sigh.

The man crouches down, a few paces in front of Doyle.

'Who are you?' the man asks.

'I could ask you the same question,' says Doyle.

'Yeah, but I asked first. And I'm the one with the gun.'

'Fair point well made,' says Doyle. 'My name's O'Dowd. I'm a private investigator.'

'Who are you working for?'

'Can't tell you that. Client confidentiality is the cornerstone of my business.'

The killer raises his gun and points it at Doyle's face.

Says Doyle, 'But then my business is going down the tubes anyway. I'm working for a man named Lucas Bartok.'

The killer nods. He doesn't seem surprised. But then Doyle isn't sure that this man knows how to register surprise on those stony features of his.

'And you were following Ramone here because . . .?'

Doyle considers lying. Looks at the gun. Rejects lying.

'Because he works for – *worked* for – someone called Anton Ruger.'

'What business do you have with Ruger?'

'Me? None. I'm paid to find him, end of story.'

More nods. Nothing more on the emotion front, though. The man gestures vaguely behind him with the gun.

'They would have killed you. You know that, don't you?'

'Actually, I was hoping to get away with a wedgie or two. But now that you mention it, they did seem a tad annoyed about something.'

'These guys are what happens when you go looking for a man like Anton Ruger.'

'And you? When do you happen?'

'I happen when somebody is stupid enough to go around shooting his mouth off about how he works for Mr Ruger.'

'So . . . this was their punishment? You're not my knight in shining armour?'

'Uh-uh. Sorry to disappoint. I'm more like the plumber or the mechanic. Here to fix things. To put them right again.'

'Just so you know, I had a medical last week. I'm in perfect working order. No fixing required.'

The man considers this. 'I think you could still be useful. You could take a message back to Lucas Bartok. Let him know what happens to people who go against Mr Ruger.'

'I could do that. I delivered newspapers when I was a kid. Never messed up once.'

'The question is, would the message be stronger if I sent you back alive . . . or dead?'

'If there's a choice, I'd say alive. I can be a lot more persuasive when I have a pulse.'

The man stands up again. A sudden jump to his feet that startles Doyle. For all Doyle's facetiousness, he is filled with fear. The joking around is his way of trying to hide it.

Doyle's dread increases as the killer slowly starts to circle him again. He suspects that this time the man will not complete the circle.

He's right. The footsteps halt behind Doyle. He feels the hard tip of the silencer as it is pressed into the nape of his neck. He doesn't dare move – not even a fraction of an inch.

'Give me one good reason why I shouldn't kill you.'

Doyle's mind races. He thinks of his wife, his child, but decides that all the things that mean everything to him will not penetrate the cold heart of this killer.

'I can't think of one,' he says.

The man chuckles then. Something of which Doyle thought he was incapable. But the laugh carries no humor. It carries only the promise of evil.

'You're the first person who's ever given that answer,' the man says, and Doyle knows it is the case that he has done this many times before.

And then, in an instant, all that Doyle knows and feels is snatched away from him.

TWENTY-SEVEN

He's not sure how long he's been out. He stares at his watch and waits for the face to come back into focus. Figures it must have been only a couple of minutes.

Long enough for the killer to make his getaway.

Doyle sits up and puts tentative fingers to the back of his head. Winces at the stab of pain. That was one hell of a whack. And that's on top of the previous blows from Ramone's goons.

Speaking of which . . .

They're still here. It wasn't a dream. Three dead bodies, plus a cop who should be sound asleep in bed right now.

Jesus, how did I get into this mess?

Doyle gets to his feet slowly. His head swims, and it takes him a minute before he feels steady enough to walk. He meanders over to Zack's partner – the one who had the gun on him. He stares back at Doyle with his remaining eye. On the other side of his nose is just a glistening red hole. Doyle pulls the man's jacket open. Finds the Beretta tucked into his waistband. He takes it back, then searches the man's pockets. Nothing of interest.

He heads back toward the staircase. Toward the bodies lying at its foot. Zack's head is like a Swiss cheese. Doyle searches him too and comes up with zilch. Then he flips Ramone's body over. Sees that there are several bullet holes in his chest.

I think one of you is gonna end up dead tonight, the stripper had said. Bang on the money.

Once again, Doyle goes through the pockets. If he can't find anything, his mission will be at an end. He won't be able to meet Bartok's deadline, and then everything will depend on what Bartok decides to do. Will he throw Doyle to the wolves? Extend the deadline? Give him another task? There are too many possibilities, none of which Doyle finds attractive.

And then he finds Ramone's wallet. And in the wallet he finds a card from an Italian restaurant. And on the back of the card he finds a brief, hand-scrawled message:

> 347 Corbin Place
> A.R.

A.R. Anton Ruger.

It looks like Doyle's night isn't over just yet.

Corbin Place is in South Brooklyn. It runs down the eastern edge of Brighton Beach. Home to a large Jewish community, the neighborhood was once renowned for its connections with the Russian Mafia – not for nothing did it earn the nickname Little Odessa. Doyle hopes he doesn't encounter any Russian mafiosi tonight. Or any members of the criminal fraternity other than Ruger, for that matter. He especially doesn't want to meet up with Mr Stubble again – the guy who can dispatch three men in the space of several minutes without even stepping up his pulse rate. He's hoping that the killer will have reported back to

Ruger that the man searching for him is no longer a threat. He's hoping that Ruger will have relaxed at that news, and will now be sound asleep in bed, cuddling into his favorite teddy bear. He's also hoping that Ruger will have taken off Bartok's garish ring and placed it somewhere obvious, like next to the glass with his false teeth or something, and that Doyle can just sneak in, pick up the ring, and tippy-toe out again.

That's what he hopes. But he's also painfully aware – witness the lumps on the back of his head – that life often likes to challenge him a little more than that.

The street is pleasant enough, containing mostly tidy detached houses with tidy front yards. The south end is a cul-de-sac, cut off by the esplanade that stretches to the beach. There's no reason to drive down this street unless you live here. Or unless – like Doyle – you're up to no good.

Doyle parks where he can't be seen from Ruger's windows, turns his lights off, and waits for a few minutes. In this weather, and at this time of night, he thinks it unlikely that anyone will have noticed him arrive. Even less chance that someone will walk by. But he plays it safe.

He pulls on a pair of gloves and gets out of the car. Tries not to look suspicious as he leans against the wind to get to Ruger's house. He doesn't hesitate. Just walks straight up the driveway, past the SUV that's parked there, and down the side of the house. When he gets to the rear door, he slips the jimmy out from underneath his jacket. Seconds later, he's in the house.

He takes out his ski mask – the same one he used when he frightened the crap out of Lorenze Wheaton and Cubo – and pulls it over his head, then switches on his Mini-Maglite. He finds he's in a small kitchen, which he would have known anyway from the lingering aroma of fried fish. He waits and listens for a moment. There's a lot of noise, but it's all of the right kind. The hums and burbles of the refrigerator. The rain battering against the door and windows. The howling wind. A clap of thunder. It'll all help to keep his presence here undetected.

He steps out into the hallway, then starts up the stairs. Chooses the door most likely to lead to the master bedroom.

He turns off the Maglite and transfers it to his left hand, then pulls out his gun. He stands there for a few minutes, willing his breathing to calm down a little, while his eyes adjust to the darkness. He tries not to think about how absurd this situation is. Him, a cop, acting like the very burglars he's supposed to catch.

Then he opens the door.

Eases it open, as slowly and as quietly as he can. Praying that it doesn't squeak on its hinges.

He steps into the room. The noises from outside seem even louder in here. He blinks. The thin curtains admit a small amount of the street lighting from outside. Just enough to show him vague shapes. He maps out the room and its furniture. Peers down at the bed and makes out the outline of a head against a pillow. A sudden flash of lightning through the curtains, followed almost immediately by a window-rattling thunderclap, causes the bed's occupant to stir and mutter something in his sleep.

Doyle holds his breath and counts to twenty.

He moves closer to the nightstand, knowing that it won't be that easy. The ring won't be there. It'll be on the sonofabitch's hand. Or locked away somewhere else in the house. Things are never that easy. He'll have to wake this bastard up and he'll have to wave a gun in his face and . . .

There it is.

What, Doyle? Are you seeing things?

But it's there, all right. On the nightstand. In plain view. Practically begging to be taken. No false teeth, but hey, you can't predict everything, right?

Doyle wants to yell in triumph. He wants to jump up and click his heels together. For once, things are going his way.

And that's when all hell breaks loose.

The screaming begins just after the light goes on. A high-pitched shriek, like something out of *Psycho*.

Only, instead of Janet Leigh – instead of someone who could at least be pleasing on the eye at a pants-exploding moment such as this – Doyle gets a guy. A naked guy. A young streak of white skin and bone who has his hands pressed to his cheeks as he emits sonic waves that threaten to bust Doyle's eardrums.

Doyle whirls back to Ruger, who is already scrabbling out from under his covers. The man has a shaven head and a flat nose, and is wearing an expression that could kill most men at ten paces. He looks exactly like the mean son of a bitch he's reputed to be, happy to exterminate anyone who gets in his way, and so Doyle points the Beretta at Ruger's face to keep him where he is. The problem is, it doesn't keep the naked guy where *he* is.

The young man leaps onto Doyle's back, his fingers tearing at Doyle's mask, trying to rip through to the soft flesh beneath. Doyle pushes backwards, driving his attacker into a dresser. He hears a clatter and a cry of pain. Ruger seizes his chance and jumps out of bed, and now Doyle has two butt-naked guys attacking him. Doyle continues to lean back into the young guy, then raises his leg and kicks hard into Ruger's chest, sending him flying back onto the bed. He drives his elbow hard into the solar plexus of the kid. He hears a whoosh of breath, and the grip on him loosens. As Ruger comes at him again, Doyle reaches behind himself, grabs the kid, and throws him hard into Ruger. There is a clash of skulls and more cries of pain, but Doyle finally has both opponents in front of him. He raises his gun, alternating its aim between Ruger and his companion.

'Don't move,' he says.

Ruger bares his teeth and flexes his muscles. His nakedness takes the edge off it, however.

'Who the fuck are you?'

'Santa. I'm early this year.'

The young guy takes hold of Ruger's bicep with both hands. 'He hit me. I think I'm gonna be sick.'

Ruger yanks his arm away. 'Shut up.' Then to Doyle: 'You're a dead man. You know that, don't you?'

'Keep talking like that and you won't get any presents. Get on the bed, face down.'

'You picked the wrong house, asshole. You know who I am?'

'I see bald naked guys all the time. They all blur into one. Now you can get on the bed alive, or you can get on it dead. Your choice.'

Ruger pauses long enough to show he's not afraid, then does as he's been told. Doyle tosses two sets of Plasti-Cuffs over to the other guy.

'You. What's your name?'

The kid is shivering, and looks ready to pee himself. Doyle would feel sorry for him if he didn't think the kid would gouge his eyes out given half a chance.

'S–Samuel.'

'Okay, Samuel. I want you to tie your boyfriend up. One set of cuffs on his wrists, the other on his ankles.'

Samuel looks down at Ruger, then back at Doyle.

'C'mon,' says Doyle. 'I'm not asking you to do anything you haven't done before.'

Reluctantly, Samuel kneels on the bed and begins to bind Ruger's wrists behind him.

'I'm sorry, Anton,' he says, a tear rolling down his cheek.

Ruger continues to stare at Doyle. 'I'll find you. If it's the last thing I do, I'll hunt you down, you motherfucking piece of shit. And then I'm gonna make you realize what a big mistake you've made. You hear me, you cocksucker?'

'That's rich, coming from you,' says Doyle. He waits for Samuel to finish, then points the gun at him. 'All right, Samuel. Now it's your turn. On the bed, next to Mr Potty Mouth here.'

Samuel puts his hands over his shriveled genitals and shakes his head.

'It's all right,' says Doyle. 'I'm not gonna hurt you. I just wanna make sure you can't attack me again. Okay?'

Keeping his eyes on Doyle, Samuel slides himself onto the bed.

'Good,' says Doyle. 'Now, hands behind your back.'

Doyle takes two more sets of nylon Plasti-Cuffs from his pocket and ties up the kid. Then he checks that the cuffs on Ruger are tight. When he is finally satisfied that the pair no longer pose a threat, he puts his gun away.

'Now what?' Ruger asks.

'Good question. See, I lied about being Santa. I'm actually Anti-Santa. Instead of leaving presents, I take them away. But only from naughty boys like you, Anton.'

Doyle walks over to the nightstand and picks up the ring. 'I think I'll start with this.'

He expects a howl of anguish, and is surprised when he gets instead a vicious smile of insight.

'Oh, so that's it,' says Ruger. 'You're no burglar. Burglars boost TVs and hi-fi and shit. No burglar I know would take a risk like this and go straight for that ring. Did Bartok send you here? Is that it? Did that cock-eyed freak send you to do his dirty work?'

'Goodbye, Anton.'

Doyle drops the ring in his pocket and turns to leave.

'You're dead, you dumb fuck. You and that freak. And you can tell him that from me. Tell him . . .'

But Doyle is no longer listening. The rant continues behind him while he descends the staircase. He retraces his steps to the kitchen door and out into the night. Ruger and his boyfriend will release themselves from the cuffs eventually, but by that time Doyle will be long gone.

Stripping off his gloves and his ski mask, he returns to his car, never once looking back.

He drives for about five minutes, then pulls the car over and takes out his cellphone. He dials the number that Bartok's man gave him.

'Hello?'

It's Sven's voice, heavy with tiredness.

'It's Doyle. Tell your boss I got what he wanted.'

'Do you know what time it is, asshole?'

'Just tell him I'll be there at eight.'

Doyle hangs up without waiting for a reply. He looks at the clock on his dash. It's three-thirty in the morning. No point in going home and waking everyone up and putting Rachel in an even grouchier mood.

Instead, he finds a quiet Brooklyn street and sleeps for three hours in his car. After that, he finds a diner and wakes himself up with some strong coffee accompanied by some bacon and egg.

And then it's time to join the party.

TWENTY-EIGHT

It's not the happiest of parties. No balloons, no cake, not even any music. Bartok the clown could be funnier, although that trick with his eyes is pretty good. The dark-suited Sven and his partner are acting like they've just had a tiff because they're wearing matching outfits. And that guy over there? Sonny Rocca? He's a real barrel of laughs. Looks like he's had one over the eight, and then some.

Doyle takes his seat in front of Bartok's huge desk. Tries to stop his gaze wandering to the left, where Rocca is slumped on a chair. It looks to Doyle as though Rocca has been fully defrosted. He is all white and limp, and one of his arms is drooped over the back of the chair, keeping him from sliding to the floor. He stares at Doyle, his dramatic recline like one from a classical painting, only without the same spark of life.

'So,' says Bartok. 'You managed to find Anton Ruger. You mind telling me how?'

'I put an ad in the dating section. Wanted: Man with good sense of humor and a huge ring. It worked, although I did get a few weird calls from people who misunderstood.'

'To be honest, I wasn't sure you could do it. Looks like I underestimated you.'

'A lot of people do that. I think I must have some kind of

aura of ineffectiveness. At school I was always being told I would never amount to much. But now look at me. Sitting here with you three guys – four if you count the corpse. How wrong could they have been, huh?'

'Did Ruger put up much of a fight?'

'Nah. We wrestled a little, and then I tied him naked on the bed, and then . . . no, wait a minute: that's not coming out how I intended.'

'So where is my old friend Anton? For future reference.'

For the first time, there's a hint of a smile on Bartok's face. No doubt as he contemplates what horrors he might inflict on his betrayer.

'Funnily enough, as soon as I mentioned your name he said he was thinking of booking himself in for a long cruise.'

Bartok drops his smile, but doesn't pursue the matter.

'All right, let's get this business out of the way. Rocca here is starting to smell funny.'

'Are you sure it's not Snow White over there?'

Doyle notices the way in which Sven suddenly squares himself up. He's itching to go another round with Doyle, and Doyle feels likewise.

Says Bartok, 'You got the ring?'

Doyle pats his pockets. 'Shit, I knew there was something.'

'Don't fuck with me, Doyle. Show me the fucking ring.'

Doyle raises his eyebrows at him. 'Sheesh. Some priest you'd make at a wedding.'

He reaches into his inside pocket and takes out the lump of gaudiness. Holds it in the air like it's a plucked flower.

Bartok opens a drawer in his desk and takes out a black box. He gestures to Sven, who collects the box, opens it, and transports it to Doyle. Doyle sees that it's one of those jewelry presentation cases, with a velvet cushion inside. He wants to laugh at the absurdity of all this ceremony, but he places the ring on the cushion anyway.

'Is this Pass the Parcel?' he asks. 'Because we should have music for that. Can your buddy over there carry a tune?'

Sven gives him a stony glare before conveying the box back to his boss. He hands it to Bartok, who gazes lovingly at the prized possession that has finally been returned to him.

'Beautiful,' says Bartok. It's the most emotionally positive that Doyle has ever heard him get about anything. Except when he's killing someone.

'Okay, so you've got your Precious. Can we close the deal now?'

Bartok snaps the lid of the box shut. He puts it into his drawer, then opens another drawer and takes out a roll of cloth, tied with a ribbon around its center. He gets out of his chair and comes around his desk. He unties the ribbon and unrolls the cloth on his desk. Its contents clink together, metal on metal. Bartok turns to Doyle and sweeps a hand across his display, like he's fronting a shopping channel for the deranged.

'What d'ya wanna start with, Doyle? I got scalpels, scissors, saws . . .'

'Good job you don't have a lisp. You got one of those remote-control bullet-extraction tools in there?'

'I'm all out.' He reaches into his array of instruments and slides one out of its pocket, then holds it up for Doyle to see. 'I think a scalpel, don't you? Come on, you musta seen plenty autopsies. A slash here, a slash there. Hell, it's not like he's gonna complain about you being untidy or nothing.'

Doyle looks at Rocca's lifeless body, as if expecting it to put in an objection. It's true that Doyle has seen many autopsies, and many corpses in various states of destruction and decay. But now that he's faced with the task of burrowing into and exploring the body cavity of a man he quite liked, he finds himself repulsed by it. Swallowing hard against the bacon and egg that's threatening to reverse its way out of his stomach, he turns back to Bartok, who is now wearing a grin as menacing as the scalpel glinting in his hand.

When Bartok's smile is broken through by an explosion of manic laughter, the extent of the troubles in his mind is made all the more apparent.

'Ha!' he says. 'You should see your face! You think I'm gonna let you spill this wop's filthy organs all over my nice clean office? Fuck that.'

Doyle feels a surge of anger. 'We had a deal, Lucas. I hope you haven't forgotten that.'

Bartok chuckles. 'You dumb mick. How the hell did a peabrain like you get to be a detective anyhow?'

Doyle doesn't know what Bartok is talking about, but he doesn't like the sound of it. He suspects that what's about to come next will be pretty unpalatable.

And what does come next is Bartok raising his hand and throwing the scalpel. Doyle watches it fly through the air and straight into the chest of Rocca. It lands with an audible thud that makes Doyle wince. But Rocca doesn't budge an inch. Doesn't protest either.

Bartok marches toward the body. 'You're an asshole, Doyle. A witless, brainless fuck-up. How many times did you shoot this guinea? Four times, right? See the bullet holes here? One, two, three, four. Only what you ain't seen – what you never even thought to ask about – was this . . .'

Bartok grabs hold of Rocca's hair and drags him forward and down. Rocca's arms flop and sway like he's a ragdoll.

'Look, you dumb bastard. The exit wounds. One, two, three, four. Either you need to change that hollow-point ammo you've been using, Doyle, or else Rocca here was made of mush. All the slugs went straight through him. I never had the fucking bullets. Ever. Do you get what I'm saying, Doyle? You've been had. It was all a lie, and you fell for it. How's it feel, Doyle? Knowing you ain't so clever? Knowing that someone you consider unfit to shine your shoes can pull the wool over your eyes like that? Just how does that feel?'

As soon as Doyle jumps to his feet he hears the guns leave their holsters. His fists are clenched and he is bristling with anger, but he's also well aware that the smallest of steps closer to Bartok will mean his instant execution.

Says Bartok, 'Not so good, I take it. Don't feel bad. We all make mistakes. Although you have to admit, this was a pretty big one on your part. Oh, and in case you think I put those holes there myself, you're welcome to take Rocca with you and do your own digging around. Just say the word, and Sven here will load him into the trunk of your car.'

Doyle wants to hit someone. Preferably Bartok, but anyone will do. He was suckered into this one, all right.

'I'm going home now, Lucas. You got what you wanted. You got your jewelry and you got to put one over on me, and I hope both give you many hours of pleasure. We're quits now, and I don't ever want to see your ugly mug again. Not unless it's behind bars.'

'Never happen, Doyle. See, you need to re-think where you are on the scale. My brother was the smart one in the family.

Everyone knew that. Made me look stupid. Doesn't mean I am, though. Put me next to you and I'm a positive genius. It's all relative, Doyle.'

Doyle doesn't want to get into a debate. Right now, he's not feeling as though he occupies a superior position from which to argue the point.

Instead, he turns and walks over to the door. Waits for Bartok to signal his men to show him out.

Says Bartok, 'Bye-bye, Detective. See you around sometime.'

Sven and his pal escort Doyle downstairs, then push him out of the side door leading to the alley. Sven tosses Doyle's gun onto the sidewalk behind him. He says, 'Another time, hotshot,' then slams the door.

Doyle picks up his gun, puts it away, then trudges through the rain back to his car. He sits in his car for some time, just thinking. Bartok is right, he decides. I *am* stupid. I've lost the ability to make correct decisions. It's why I'm in this mess.

He tries telling himself he should be grateful. Bartok is finally off his back. Doyle has wondered for a long time if and when Bartok would come back at him over the Rocca threat. And now he has, and it's been cleared. Never mind that Doyle nearly lost his life and three people did lose theirs. What's important is that he can't be blackmailed anymore. Hear that? That's the weight dropping off my shoulders. Time for the big sigh of relief, right?

Somehow he finds himself unconvincing.

My wife thinks I cheated on her and won't talk to me. My daughter is upset with me because she thinks she has been unjustly accused. The squad detectives don't trust me. My own partner doesn't want to work with me. I'm under investigation by IAB. I can't go into work. The man I know to be a murderer is about to walk away from his crimes.

How much worse can things get?

Doyle doesn't want to know the answer to that question.

TWENTY-NINE

The apartment echoes with emptiness when he gets home. Rachel has presumably taken Amy shopping. Or to her parents' place. Or to the park. Or someplace else where Doyle is not.

He thinks about calling her on her cellphone. Decides not to. She needs her own space right now. Tonight they will talk. They will sort things out.

It seems to him that he's always having to tell himself this lately. Always having to reassure himself that he will have no difficulty in ironing out the consequences of his actions. And he wonders how many times he can get away with it. How often can he put a patch on something before it decays beyond repair?

He sighs and looks around the depressingly silent room, debating how best to kill time – the one thing he's not short of at the moment. He should make himself useful. Deal with some of the tasks that normal people with normal occupations do on their Sundays. Clean the bathroom. Wash the windows. Change the batteries in that mechanical bear Amy keeps asking him to fix. Screw that handle back onto the closet door. Life things.

He settles in front of the TV – all that thinking about chores has tired him out – and stares at an old episode of *Frasier*. Minutes later he's asleep.

It's his cellphone bursting into life that drags him back into the land of the living. He answers the call.

'Hello?'

'Cal? It's me. Tommy.'

Doyle is surprised, and then wary. This isn't going to be one of those calls where they discuss football or the next drunken night out with the boys. This is going to be one of those calls filled with awkwardness.

He drags a hand down his face, trying to wipe away the tiredness.

'Tommy? What's up?'

'I, uhm, I need to ask you something, Cal. It's connected with Proust.'

Here we go again, thinks Doyle. Tommy agonizing over what to believe. Trying to put things into neat little boxes in his head.

'I can't give you any more, Tommy. What I told you before is the truth. Proust is a murdering scumbag, and I didn't do any of the things people are saying I did. I don't know what else—'

'I'm not talking about that. I don't even want to discuss that with you now.'

Doyle can hear traffic in the background. He guesses that LeBlanc has left the squadroom to have this conversation in private.

'Okay. So then, what?'

'I went to see Proust first thing this morning. He—'

'That's great, Tommy. You have to keep the pressure on this guy. The only way you're gonna get—'

'Will you listen to me for one damn minute? For one thing, I don't need you to tell me how to work my case. And for another, this wasn't about hassling Proust. This was about damage limitation. This was about making sure Proust doesn't shoot the whole thing down in flames – the case and the squad.'

Doyle listens. It's LeBlanc speaking, but those are Cesario's words. LeBlanc was sent to Proust to suck ass. Doyle can imagine the apologizing and forelock tugging that went on in front of Proust, and it sickens him to the core. And there is also in those words the thinly disguised attack on Doyle's own way of doing things.

But worst of all is the way in which LeBlanc has just emphasized how he has taken ownership of the case. Could he have made it any clearer that Doyle's role is valueless?

Doyle suddenly feels very depressed.

'All right, so what do you want from me?'

'Something Proust said. He asked if you'd managed to verify his alibi yet.'

'What alibi?'

'That's what I said. He wouldn't tell me. He said he spoke with you about it the last time you went to see him.'

Doyle casts his mind back to that time. He doesn't recall anything remotely connected with an alibi.

'It's bullshit. He's fucking with us again. He never mentioned an alibi. And if he's got one, why doesn't he tell you?'

'He said it was private. Between him and you.'

'It's crap, Tommy. You got an alibi for a murder, you don't keep it private. I don't know what he's talking about.'

'You're sure?'

There's more than a hint of accusation tingeing the doubt in that question.

'Yes. I'm positive. You mind if I get back to my TV now? I'm watching a show called 'Famous Fish from History'. It's very educational. Did you know that Napoleon always kept a sardine in his coat pocket? I bet you didn't know that.'

'See you around, Cal.'

'Fine.'

Doyle stabs at the call-end button with a force he wishes could be transmitted into the ear of the man at the other end, then hurls his cellphone into a cushion on the sofa. He's angry, but he's also perplexed and intrigued.

An alibi? What the fuck is that all about?

He re-runs the last encounter with Proust through his mind once again. Nope. Nothing.

Which means it's a scam. Another of Proust's little games. What's he playing at this time? Where is this leading?

He knows what Proust wants. Proust is trying to entice him back into his lair. This is the tasty crumb, designed to lure Doyle into another trap. Proust, clever Proust, has a plan in mind for Doyle that is even more malicious and devious than his previous machinations.

But only if I go there, thinks Doyle. If I don't respond, there's nothing he can do to me. Let LeBlanc deal with this lunatic. I'm out of it.

So what if the guy walks? Haven't I done all I can? If the Department doesn't want to listen, that's their problem. Fuck 'em.

He drops onto the sofa again. Turns up the volume on the TV, hoping to drown out the voices nagging at him. Because although he's telling himself that Proust is no longer his concern, his own voice is just background noise. It's the other voices he can't help hearing. The insistent little bastards who keep telling him he can't shuck it off like this. *You need to know*, they say. *You need to find out what Proust is doing.*

His phone rings again. He retrieves it from the cushion and answers the call.

'Hello?'

'Good morning, Doyle. You not at work today?'

Doyle sighs. 'Paulson, how'd you get my cell number?'

'You called me on it, remember? Last Christmas, when you were in such desperate need of my assistance. I saved it on my phone. Just in case.'

'In case of what?'

'In case of moments like this.'

'Moments like what? What is this, Paulson?'

'I want to talk.'

'So talk.'

'Let's at least make it civilized, can't we? I'm outside your apartment.'

'You're not coming in, Paulson. My wife would go ape-shit.'

'Is what I thought you would say. Looks like you'll have to come to me. I'll wait.'

The line goes dead. Doyle thinks about calling him back, but figures he'd be wasting his breath. Might as well get this over with.

He grabs his coat and leaves the apartment. Outside, he spots Paulson's vehicle and jogs over to it. As soon as he gets in, Paulson fires up the engine and takes off.

'Where are we going?'

Paulson smiles at him. 'You'll see.'

They drive down to the East Village, hardly a word passing between them. When they turn onto Eighth Street, Doyle realizes where they're heading.

Paulson pulls the car into a space. 'Here we are. Kath's Koffees.'

'Paulson, what are we doing here?'

'This is where we had coffee and donuts together last Christmas. Remember?'

'Of course I remember. What I want to know is what we're doing here now.'

'I thought we'd do it again. My treat this time. Who knows, this could become an annual event.'

Before Doyle can protest, Paulson is out of the car and leading the way into the coffee shop. Doyle trails along sullenly, thinking that annual is far too frequent for him.

They take the same window booth they occupied last time. Paulson summons a waitress and orders two coffees and two donuts. Again, just like last time. Doyle is starting to feel like he's stuck in a time warp.

'So,' says Paulson. 'This is nice. Brings back memories, huh?'

'A lot of which I'd prefer to forget,' says Doyle.

'Our experiences make us what we are. All of the stuff you've been through, even the bad things, have helped to fashion the fine upstanding law-enforcement officer I see before me now.'

'Yeah, where would I be without you, Paulson?'

'Because you *are* a paragon of virtue, aren't you, Doyle? All these things I'm hearing about you and this Proust character, that's all a load of crap, right?'

'Actually, no. I beat the hell out of him. I tried to kill him. And when I couldn't do that, I sent someone else to kill him. That's how I solve all my cases.'

Paulson smiles. 'You've got a great sense of humor. It's one of the things I've always liked about you. Even under adversity, you can manage to make people smile. I bet you'd even crack a joke if a judge sent you to prison.'

'I'm not always like this. I think it's your sunny disposition brings out the happiness in me. You never notice how faces light up as you walk by?'

'That is true. I do tend to have that effect. So Proust doesn't worry you?'

'Why should he? I haven't done anything wrong.'

'You disobeyed a direct order to stay away from him. That's a Command Discipline at least.'

'So let them hit me with the CD. I've had worse thrown at me.'

The waitress arrives with the coffees and donuts. Paulson thanks her, then wastes no time in ripping open several packets of sugar to pour into his cup.

Doyle grimaces. 'How can you drink it like that?'

Paulson peers into the swirling gloom of his coffee. 'You're right,' he says. He tears open another sachet and adds its contents. 'That's better. Anyways, what was I saying? Oh, yeah. Our friend Proust. That's some leverage he's got, don't you think? One word from him and you're history.'

Doyle takes a sip of his own unsweetened beverage. 'Proust is too clever for that.'

'What do you mean?'

'It's a balancing act. Proust has got the whole fucking Department tiptoeing around him like he's an unexploded bomb. He's got them, and me, where he wants us. If he pushes, it all collapses. An overt attack on me is an attack on the whole PD. They will have to investigate his claims, and that means they will have to investigate him. They'll push back. Hard. And that's the last thing he wants.'

Paulson takes a bite of his donut, then wipes the crumbs from his mouth with a napkin.

'So what are you going to do about it?'

'What? Nothing. There's nothing I can do. I'm off the squad. I just have to hope the investigating detectives find something that clears me and implicates him.'

'And if they don't?'

Doyle shrugs. Sips his coffee again. Paulson takes a swallow from his own cup, then leans back in his seat, studying Doyle.

'That's it? That's all you're gonna do about this situation?'

Doyle searches Paulson's face for some clue as to where he's steering this. 'Paulson, what are you suggesting?'

Paulson pokes a finger into his mouth and digs a nail between his teeth. He takes his finger out again, examines whatever it is he's managed to extract, then flicks the suspect particle across the room.

'I'm not suggesting anything. Just asking questions. Here's another one for you. Suppose you do nothing. What do you think are the chances of Proust becoming a collar for murder?'

Doyle considers this. He'd like to believe that the solid detective work of his colleagues will eventually bear fruit. But wanting to believe is not the same as believing.

'I think those chances are slim.'

'That's what I thought you'd say. And for what it's worth, I don't think you're being arrogant when you say that. Next question: how do you feel about being where a perp wants you?'

'How d'you mean?'

'You said that Proust has your whole squad in the palm of his hand – you included. By doing nothing you maintain the status quo. You allow him to keep the ball. Is that what you want?'

'Of course it's not what I want. But I don't have a choice. Proust has already won.'

'Has he? Or does he just have the advantage? Is he just going to stand there with that ball, or is he going to take it into your end zone? I never met Proust, and the only things I know about this case are what I've been told. But if what you say is true, Doyle, then this guy is one smart sonofabitch who's out to get you. You know him better than anyone, so answer me this: is he finished with you?'

Doyle thinks about what LeBlanc told him this morning. About Proust having an alibi, and about his lie that he revealed it to Doyle. It doesn't make any sense. Unless, of course, Paulson is right. This is the start of Proust's next move. This is where he tries to destroy Doyle once and for all. If that's the case, then maybe Paulson is also correct that backing away like this is totally the wrong thing to do.

But then another question is formulated. And this time it's in Doyle's mind.

'What is this, Paulson?'

Paulson swallows down a barely chewed hunk of donut. 'What do you mean?'

'This. These questions you're asking me. Like you're trying to goad me into visiting Proust again. Why would you do that?'

'You think I got some kind of ulterior motive?'

'Do you? Could it be that you *want* me to fuck things up? I'm on the edge of losing my job as it is. Is this your way of giving me a little nudge to send me over?'

'Is that what you think?'

'I don't know. I think it could be. You couldn't get me before, and this is your way of fixing things. Finally putting a tick in that one blank box on your record sheet.'

Paulson stares for a while in silence. Then he throws the remains of his donut back onto the plate.

'Fuck you, Doyle.'

'What, you're going all sensitive on me now?'

'Something wrong with that? You think just because I'm with IAB that I don't have any emotions?'

'No, but I think you leave them at home when you're on the job. How else could you do what you do? You live for jamming up other cops. Am I supposed to forget that, just because it's your turn to buy the coffee?'

'The only reason you're here with me now is because of my job. It's because you know I'm investigating you. Suppose I left my shield at home one night and asked you to join me for a beer. What would you say?'

'I'd say no, you want the honest truth.'

'Exactly. You don't want to see the man behind the shield. You don't want to see that maybe, just maybe, I'm trying to help you. For which, by the way, precedent does exist in our relationship.'

Doyle throws his hands up. 'Here we go again with the life-saving bit.'

'Only because you conveniently keep forgetting about it. Could that be because it doesn't fit neatly into your world view?'

Doyle shakes his head. Takes another sip of his murky coffee and tries to fathom the even murkier connection with the man opposite.

'All right, suppose I accept that you're trying to help me. What I don't understand is why you would do that.'

Paulson taps the table as he chooses his words. 'I've learned a lot about you, Doyle. At first it was because I had to. It was my job. I was trying to find out if you were dirty. So I read everything I could about you. I talked to a lot of people about you. I looked into all the cases you'd worked.'

'Don't forget my wife. You talked to her too. Put a lot of doubts in her mind.'

Paulson looks down at the table. 'Yes,' he says simply, and it surprises Doyle that the man actually appears ashamed.

Says Paulson, 'Even when we dropped the investigation, I kept an interest in you. I still follow your cases now.'

'You waiting for me to slip up?'

'Actually, no. Although there are times when I think I need to step in and remind you of my existence. Times like this, for example.'

'Don't worry, Paulson. I'll never forget you. Your face and your voice and what you did to me are burned into my brain for eternity.'

Paulson's mouth twitches. 'I don't think you understand how easy it would be for me to bring your career to an end if I really wanted to. You're like a wind-up toy that goes off in random directions. Left alone, you'd knock things over, maybe even break something. What you need from time to time is somebody to guide you back where you belong, keep you out of harm's way.'

'And that's where you come in?'

Paulson nods. 'You're a fascinating creature, Doyle. A lot of shit gets thrown your way, and you keep on coming back for more. You could put an end to it by towing the line, but you don't. Or you could go the other way and become what everybody else thinks you are already. That must be tempting sometimes. But you don't do that either, far as I can tell. All that shit, and yet none of it sticks. That makes you a rarity in my book, Doyle.'

'So I'm an interesting specimen. There has to be more to it than that. I can't believe you want to help me just so you can add me to your butterfly collection. What's the real reason, Paulson?'

'The real reason?'

'Yeah. Where's the pay-off for you?'

'There's no pay-off. I'm doing it because you remind me of someone.'

'Who?'

'Me.'

Doyle almost chokes on his coffee.

'Jesus, Paulson! Couldn't you at least have said something complimentary? What kind of . . . You think I'm like you? Fuhgeddaboudit. I mean, seriously, man, that has to be one of the most out-there comments ever to leave your mouth.'

Paulson's lips harden. Like this wasn't the response he'd hoped for. 'You can deny it all you want, Doyle, but like it or not, we're not so different. We both do what we do because we think it's right, not because it's what other people expect of us. And sometimes that lands us in trouble.'

Doyle shakes his head. 'That's gotta be the dumbest comparison I ever heard.'

'Don't be so quick to dismiss it, Doyle. It's not so long ago that I was where you are right now.'

'So what happened?'

Paulson hesitates, and Doyle can tell there's a life-changing story in that pause.

'Let's just say I didn't stick to my guns. I forgot who I was and what was right. It was a momentary lapse, but it was enough. Enough for the bastards to nail me.'

'And you think that's what I'm doing? Forgetting who I am?'

Paulson drains his cup and sets it down. 'To be honest, maybe going after Proust is the worst thing you could do. Maybe it'll be the last thing you do as a cop. But if Proust is as clever as you say, then it sounds like he's gonna bring you down anyway. The question is, do you want to go out fighting, or do you want to take a beating while you're cowering in your apartment?'

Understanding hits Doyle. Paulson gave up the fight. He took the easy way out and ended up in IAB, hunting other cops, taking out his bitterness on the very people he used to call his brothers. And now he's trying to rewrite his life, with Doyle playing his role. He wants to see Doyle doing all the things he should have done himself. The outcome isn't important: Doyle could get destroyed in the process. The important thing is how he acts on the journey.

Paulson takes out his wallet. Throws a few bills on the table. Starts to slide out of the booth.

'We going?' Doyle asks.

'We?'

'You brought me here, remember? I don't have my car.'

Paulson stands and looks out of the window. 'Yeah, I could take you home, that's what you want. Is that what you want?'

So there it is. The challenge. Take control of your destiny or leave it to others.

He knew it would come to this. Even without Paulson he would have had to face this question. And he has always known what the answer would be.

He says, 'I could do with a walk. Think a few things over.'

Paulson lowers his gaze to Doyle. He nods, and in that minimal gesture he conveys respect and gratitude and admiration. It's the answer he hoped for. The answer that somehow helps to make things a bit more balanced in Paulson's mind.

And then he walks away and out of the coffee shop, leaving Doyle staring at two empty cups and his untouched donut.

It's a walk of only a few minutes, but he has no hat and no umbrella, and once again the rain refuses to show sympathy. He is soaked when he reaches the top of Avenue B.

He stands at the very edge of the sidewalk, staring at the shop across the street, debating his next move.

He doesn't know how long he stands there. He doesn't notice the vehicles that keep flashing past him, interrupting his view. He doesn't hear the traffic or the rain or the pedestrians behind him. He doesn't know why he's waiting. He knows only that he should.

His patience is eventually rewarded.

Movement. Behind the glass of the door. Then the door opening. Proust, standing there, staring straight back at Doyle. The two men stand like that for a full minute.

Then Proust turns. Disappears into his shop. Leaves the door yawning wide.

Come into my parlor, said the spider to the fly.

Doyle steps off the curb.

There's an oddness to Proust. He seems more upright. Less afraid. He has the air of a man with a trick up his sleeve. He doesn't even bother to hide himself behind his counter.

Doyle glances up at the new security camera.

Proust says, 'I switched them off. There's no record of you being here. You want, we can talk out back.'

'Let's do that,' says Doyle.

Proust smiles. Starts to turn. Before he follows, Doyle locks the front door and flips the sign to 'Closed'.

'Good idea,' says Proust. 'Wouldn't want anyone disturbing us.'

He walks through into the back room. Doyle finds himself hesitating. Why is Proust so confident? *What's he planning to spring on me?*

He wonders whether it was a good idea, coming here. *Never shoulda listened to Paulson. What was I thinking? Paulson is the enemy. He wants to see me taken down. This is a bad move.*

'You coming?' Proust's mocking voice from the dimness. *Are you scared, Doyle? Are you just a big fraidy-cat?*

Doyle follows. Through the storage room. Through the empty frame of a door. Into the tiny living area. Proust is already seated at his dining table. Facing Doyle. Waiting.

'Please,' says Proust. 'Take a seat. Would you like some tea? Coffee?'

'Cut the crap, Stan. I ain't your buddy. Just say what you gotta say.'

Big bad cop words. But Doyle doesn't feel it inside.

Proust raises his eyebrows. 'But it was you who came to see me, Detective. I couldn't leave you out in the rain, like a dog. Look at you. You're wet through. You want a towel or something? How about I get you—'

Doyle picks up the chair in front of him and slams it down again. 'No more games, Stan. It's over. You're going to prison. It's time for you to face facts.'

Proust puts a hand to his chest. 'Prison? No. That's not right. I got an alibi. I told you about it. You said you'd look into it.'

Doyle hears the conviction. Starts to wonder if one of them

is going crazy. Did he tell me something, and I've forgotten? No. That's ridiculous. He's playing you, Doyle. Don't fall for it.

'Stan, what the fuck are you talking about? You didn't tell me anything about an alibi.'

'Yes, yes, I did. I told you. The last time you were here. I told you what I was doing that night. The night when somebody killed that poor girl and put her in the trash.'

'No, Stan. Nice try, but no cigar. We asked you about an alibi, remember? When I came here the day after we found the body parts? When I was with Detective LeBlanc? You said you stayed here alone, watching a movie.'

Proust looks down at his hands. 'Yeah, yeah, I know. I lied. I couldn't tell you the truth then. I was too . . . I was ashamed. I only told you later because you were scaring me. I didn't want it to come out.'

Doyle isn't sure what to say. This whole situation is absurd. Proust is talking nonsense, but acting like he believes every word. Has he lost it? Is this some kind of a breakdown he's having?

'Stan, Stan, look at me. That's right. Now watch my lips. There is no alibi. And the stuff about me scaring you? You made it up. You're screwed, Stan, and it's fucking with your mind.'

'No. I told you. About the guy.'

'What guy?'

'The one I was with that night. I stayed with him all night. Jesus, I'm so ashamed. I didn't want this to get out. You gave me no choice. But you've looked into it now, haven't you? You checked out my story, right? You know I'm innocent?'

There's something building. Here, in this room. Doyle can feel it. A tension. An electricity. It's going to zap him. A hundred thousand volts are going to course through him and blast him apart.

'What guy, Stan? Who are we talking about here?'
'I told you. I gave you his name, his address. Everything.'
'Tell me again, Stan. What's his name?'
A smile plays across Proust's lips.
'His name is Anton Ruger.'

THIRTY

No, no, no, no, no.

This can't be right.

Who broke the universe? Who tore up the cosmic rulebook?

Proust and Ruger are in separate existences. Parallel, yes. But separate. Distinct. No overlap. Never the twain shall meet.

So what is Proust doing, uttering that name? Which deity gave him permission to disrupt all that is rational, all that is meaningful?

Doyle finds himself falling onto a chair. He had no intention of sitting. He was quite content to tower over his quarry, to overshadow him. But now Doyle's legs have been hacked away from him. His very breath seems to have been sucked from his lungs.

'Where . . . where did you hear that name?'

'Anton? I told you. It's the guy I stayed with that night. I told you all about him. You forced me to.'

Doyle lands a hammer-like fist on the table. 'DON'T . . . fuck with me. I am this close to ripping off your limbs. Now, once again, tell me where you heard about Anton Ruger.'

Proust purses his lips and sucks air noisily, as if deciding whether to grant the request. His way of letting Doyle know who holds the high card.

'Let me tell you a story, Detective. It's a story with two sides. Two explanations for the same facts.'

Doyle says nothing. His mind is too busy racing ahead. Trying to catch up with Proust. Struggling to figure out how this can possibly make any sense.

Says Proust, 'Here's the first interpretation. An innocent citizen, such as myself, is continually harassed by an obsessed cop, such as yourself. The cop is determined to pin a murder on this guy, even though he has no proof. In fact, he is so determined, so fucked up about the whole thing, that he becomes violent. He beats the guy up. He tosses him through a glass door. It's hard to believe that a cop could do anything like this, but then it comes out that the citizen knows about the cop's sordid affair with a former female partner – a partner who was killed in mysterious circumstances, no less – and suddenly it all makes sense. Everyone can see this cop for what he is – what many of them believed all along. They all see a dangerous lunatic with a gun and a badge.'

'You're starting to irritate me, Stan. You got five seconds to get to the bit about Ruger in this story of yours.'

'See, that's the tragedy of this little tale. Our helpless citizen, he *does* have an alibi. Only he's embarrassed about it. Ashamed. He's never done anything like that before. He couldn't admit it to himself, let alone the cops. And what's more, the guy he did it with threatened to kill him if he ever told anybody else. But what choice does our hero have? If he keeps quiet, the cop will probably kill him anyway. So he comes clean. He tells the cop about the guy he slept with. He gives up the name of Anton Ruger.'

Which is where we are now, thinks Doyle. Except it's not, because there's a lot more to this. And I ain't gonna like it.

'Skip to the last chapter, Stan.'

'You sure you won't have some tea? I got some great lapsang souchong.'

'Just finish the goddamn story.'

'Okay, so the crazy cop, he's all bent out of shape about this. How could he have gotten it so wrong? How could that little murdering prick possibly have an alibi? The cop gets real worked up. His world's falling apart at the seams. Everyone hates him. Nobody believes him. And now this – the final nail in his coffin. He's got to come up with a way to rescue this situation, no matter what it takes. Desperate measures are called for here. And believe me, this cop is desperate. So he tries to trick another guy into killing our citizen, only the plan backfires, and the cop looks even more suspicious. Things are going from bad to worse. He's sliding into hell. What else can he do? What choices does he have left?'

'You tell me.'

'Only one, right? If he wants this to come out right for him, he's gotta take the alibi out of the equation. So that's what he does. He goes to the house of the only man in the world who can save the citizen's ass. And he kills him.'

Silence. Doyle doesn't know what he's supposed to do with this. Doesn't know what Proust is trying to achieve. Still doesn't know where he got hold of Ruger's name.

Says Doyle, 'Nice story, Stan. I'll read it to my kid when she goes to bed. You got any more like that?'

'Did you hear what I said, Detective? The cop whacks Ruger.'

'Yeah, I heard you. But me, I prefer non-fiction. So how about you telling me how you—'

'He goes there at night, the cop. Jimmies open the rear door. Sneaks up the stairs to the guy's bedroom.'

Doyle's mouth dries up. This is guesswork. Has to be.

Proust presses on. 'Ruger's asleep, but he wakes up. There's a fight. The cop ties Ruger up on the bed. And then he puts a bullet in his brain.'

Extremely dry throat now. It's all too accurate to be guesswork. All except that last bit. The bit about—

'The kid too,' Proust adds.

'What?' Doyle croaks.

'The boyfriend. Ties him up too. Another slug in the head. I tell ya, this cop is off the rails. He's certifiable.'

He knows about the youth. The one called Samuel. How does he know that?

Act nonchalant, Doyle. Don't confirm anything. Don't damn yourself.

'I don't get the point of your story. The bad cop wins, doesn't he? If he removes the alibi like that, he wins.'

'You'd think so, huh? But to me that wouldn't be a very satisfying ending. I like stories where the good guy triumphs. So in my story he comes up with proof of what the cop did, the cop goes to jail, and all's right with the world. The end.'

Proof? What kind of proof could he have for something that didn't even happen?

'That's a neat ending, all right.'

'I think so.'

'Of course, if it went down the way you said it did, the citizen would have to know where these killings took place. If he slept with Ruger at his place, he must know where he lived. I mean, you even said he gave Ruger's address to the cop, right?'

There, you sneaky sonofabitch. Fit that into your damn story.

'Yeah, I did say that, didn't I?'

'Yeah, you did.'

'It's a detail. I can make something up.'

Gotcha, thinks Doyle. You don't know shit. It's all fantasy.

'An important detail, though. I mean, this whole story hinges on the believability of the citizen versus the cop. If the guy can't even say where his little soirée took place, can't tell the authorities where to find the bodies . . .'

'Okay, then, so I'll pick an address. All right? Let's make it at . . .'

Go on, you douchebag. Fuck it all up. You don't know the address. Nobody but me knows the address. Even Bartok couldn't find where Ruger lived.

'. . . 347 Corbin Place. That's in Brooklyn.'

Doyle stares. It's the only power he has left. His whole body has been stunned into numbness.

And then he's off his chair. Springing at Proust. Grabbing at him and yanking him upward and pinning him against the wall and closing his hand around Proust's throat and raising his other hand and bunching his fist.

'Where'd you get that address? Who told you about Ruger?'

Proust tries to speak, but all that comes out is a meaningless squawk. He'd probably turn purple too if he wasn't already covered in bruises.

A sense of déjà vu floods into Doyle. He remembers the last time he did this. With LeBlanc.

He relaxes his fingers. Lets the man breathe and speak.

'Go ahead, man. Hit me if you want. I can take it. Prove to everyone how true my story is. You can't win. Whatever you do now, you can't win.'

For a while, Doyle doesn't move. His fist trembles with the tension of holding it there, ready to strike. He so wants to mash Proust's face to a pulp. But he also wants answers. He's floundering at the moment, unable to find any logic to which he can cling.

He takes hold of Proust by the shirt. Manhandles him back into his chair.

'Talk to me, Stan.'

Proust rubs his neck. 'Like I told you, there's two sides to this story. I got the other one for you, if you're interested.'

Doyle sits down. 'I'm interested. Talk.'

'Okay, so it goes like this. Chapter one is the same – our hero getting a lot of heat from the cop. The cop's like a dog with a bone. He's not letting go. Our guy is afraid something is gonna get pinned on him whether he did it or not. He needs help. And then he gets it. Someone reaches out to him.'

'Who?'

'A man called Lucas Bartok.'

The name resounds around Doyle's brain. He tries to fix it in his mind, examine it for clues as to Bartok's role in all this.

'You know Bartok?'

'I know lots of people. You'd be surprised who I get coming through the doors of my shop.'

'Why would Bartok come to you?'

'Not to me. You're forgetting. This is a story. Bartok goes to see our hero. He's heard about the man's plight, and he wants to do a deal with him.'

'What kind of deal?'

'They both need something. What our citizen needs more than anything is an alibi, and what Bartok needs is something to get the cop into his pocket, to pull out as and when.'

'So Bartok doesn't already have something like that?'

A tester. Just how close are these two?

Proust smiles. 'He has something, but it's not enough. A

bluff, is what he has. And he's worried that the cop will call it, and then he'll have nothing.'

Okay, so pretty close then. And that also explains how Proust got to hear about the rumors of an affair between Doyle and his ex-partner, Laura Marino. Bartok told him.

'Why doesn't Bartok offer to provide the guy with an alibi? Why doesn't he just say he was with him on the night of the murder?'

'For one thing, that wouldn't give Bartok what he wants. Lucas Bartok is many things, but a charity worker he's not. And then you gotta ask yourself how credible he'd be. No offense to Mr Bartok, but asking him to speak up for you is like asking a fox to guard your chickens. It don't necessarily help the situation.'

'So what's Bartok's solution?'

'This doesn't come from Bartok. Again, no offense to the man, but Lucas Bartok ain't exactly a criminal mastermind, ya know? Nah, this comes from our hero, who is smarter than the average bear. See, setting up a fake alibi is not the easiest thing to accomplish. You can get someone to lie for you, but then you have to depend on them. They could break under police questioning. Or they might say something which can be proved false. Or they might turn on you and try to blackmail you. All sorts of shit can happen.

'But now suppose the guy providing the alibi gets whacked before he can say or do anything to upset the apple cart. In normal circumstances, you might say what a crap choice he turned out to be. But not in my story. In my story it looks like the cop has investigated the alibi and believes every word of it. Believes it so strongly, in fact, that he's the one who takes out Ruger, just to nail this guy he's been persecuting. And if *he* believed it, why should anyone else question it? Especially when it turns out that certain possessions and DNA of our citizen are to be found in Ruger's house.'

'You've been there?'

Proust doesn't answer. Just arches a knowing eyebrow.

Says Doyle, 'How? How did you get Ruger's address?'

Proust emits an exaggerated sigh. 'You still don't get it, do you? All right, listen up. Our hero needs to make it look like the cop nixed the alibi. That means he needs to get him to Ruger's house. How does he do that? He gives him a mission.'

Doyle feels his stomach drop like a stone. 'The ring.'

'Exactly. The ring. You ever hear of a MacGuffin, Detective?'

'A what?'

'A MacGuffin. Alfred Hitchcock used the word in reference to something that drives the plot of a movie. The thing itself isn't important to the story. It could be money or a diamond or even something like the key to a secret code. It don't matter. What is important, though, is that it exists, because that's what motivates the characters. In my story, Ruger's ring is the MacGuffin. Sure, Bartok wanted it back, but what he really wanted was to get you into Ruger's house.'

Tell me I'm not hearing this, thinks Doyle. Tell me this is all a dream. Tell me this isn't going where I think it's going.

'Why him? Why Ruger?'

Proust shrugs. He's enjoying this. 'Didn't have to be Ruger. Coulda been anyone. But it had to be someone who deserved to die. In Mr Bartok's eyes, that made Ruger a prime candidate.'

Realization seeps in. Oozes through the cracks forming in Doyle's previous picture of reality.

'Bartok knew where Ruger was all along.'

Another smile from Proust. 'Now you're getting it. 'Course,

Lucas couldn't tell you that, because then you'd wanna know why he didn't just go after the ring himself. Hence that little odyssey he sent you on. He had to let you find Ruger for yourself.'

Anger bubbles up in Doyle. 'That sonofabitch. I could have been killed going after Ruger.'

Proust shakes his head. 'Mr Bartok couldn't let that happen. You had protection.'

Doyle narrows his eyes. 'What do you mean?' But then it hits him. Another wake-up slap.

'The warehouse. The guy with the five o'clock shadow.'

Proust nods now. Huge, emphatic nods. 'Lucas sent him to look after you.'

Doyle could cry with embarrassment at how completely he has been taken in. Mr Stubble wasn't there to cut off Doyle's only lead to Ruger. He was doing the exact opposite: making sure that Doyle *did* get to Ruger. In fact . . .

'The address. Ruger's address. I found it in Ramone's wallet . . .'

'That's right. Precisely where Lucas's man left it. Didn't you think it was a little convenient, the way Ramone was just carrying it around with him like that?'

Fuck! Of course it was too fucking convenient. Why didn't I see that? Why didn't I question it?

Doyle sits there in silence for a while. Absorbing it all. Adjusting to this new slant on things. His whole world view has been turned upside down, and all he wants to do is smack himself around the head for not seeing it like that in the first place. He feels like he's the only person not to realize that the planet is round rather than flat.

He fixes his eyes on Proust. 'So what happens now, Stan? What do you do with this clever little story of yours?'

'I publish it, of course. Tomorrow morning, I go to the cops and I tell them what you did to poor Mr Ruger and his young friend just to make sure I got no lifeline.'

'Forget it, Stan. You really think they'll go for that? In your dreams, man.'

'Actually, yeah, I do think they'll believe me. Especially after everything that's happened between us. But like I said before, I can always make sure they see the proof.'

'A story is all you got, Stan. No proof. No fucking proof whatsoever.'

'Hmm,' says Stan. And Doyle prepares himself for the lead weight hidden in his opponent's glove. It's heading his way and it's too late to duck.

Says Proust, 'There's always the video.'

Blammo! Knockout punch to the jaw.

'What video, Stan?'

'The one that Lucas's men took last night when they were hiding in that parked van on Corbin Place. The one that clearly shows your car, with your license plates, turning up there. The one that clearly shows you getting out of your car and sneaking up Ruger's driveway. The one that clearly shows you coming out of Ruger's house some minutes later and hurrying back to your car. That's the video I'm talking about.'

Doyle is paralyzed. Never has he felt so beaten into the ground. In all the fights he had as a boxer in his youth, he was never so completely demolished as this. And all without a single physical blow being landed on him.

Says Proust, 'Ruger and his boy were killed directly after you left. Not long enough for the experts to say there was anything untoward about the time of death. And oh, yeah. I nearly forgot to mention. There's one other thing. The ring you took from Ruger. The ring everyone knew he'd been wearing. The ring that has now mysteriously disappeared from the deceased man's house, but which could easily turn up again. With your fingerprints on it.'

Flashback. Bartok's little ceremony. Getting Doyle to place the ring directly into its box. Nobody else touching it. Nobody else putting their prints on it.

Shit.

Doyle rolls his tongue around in his mouth. Tries to work up a little lubrication so that he can regain the power of speech.

'Why are you telling me all this, Stan? Why haven't you already gone to the cops with your story? What's holding you back?'

'I told you. This ain't just about me. I have a deal with Mr Bartok. I get off the hook, and he gets you. He knew that Rocca was never enough of a bargaining tool. Even if your bullets were still in the body, you probably could have found a way of explaining it somehow. And Lucas was sure that if he ever asked you to do something too much to your distaste, you woulda told him you'd take your chances. But a little task like finding a ring for him? Different matter. You'd probably go for a simple job like that if it meant clearing up the Rocca thing once and for all. Now, though, Bartok's got you by the balls. Unless, of course, I go to your bosses with my story. If I do that, you're finished. Which is fine by me, but not so good for Mr Bartok. He wants you back on the job, where you can be of some use to him.'

'So what are you saying?'

'What I'm saying, Detective Doyle, is that I'm giving you a chance. A chance to stay out of prison. A chance to keep your job. A chance to stay with your family and get on with your life.'

'But working for Lucas Bartok.'

Proust shrugs. 'A small price to pay.'

'And to take advantage of this generous offer, I'd have to do what exactly?'

'Find a way to take me off the radar. Clear my name.'

'How am I supposed to do that?'

'I don't care. You're a resourceful guy. Come up with something. Make up a new alibi for me. Plant some evidence. Whatever it is you cops do when you need to fake a story. But it's gotta be convincing. If it's good, then Ruger and his boy will disappear for ever. But if it's not good – if LeBlanc or any of his buddies start sniffing around me again – then the deal's off. Oh, and in case you're thinking of doing anything stupid like trying to move the bodies yourself – don't. Lucas has put a watch on Ruger's house.'

'What about Ruger's men? Ramone and the others in the warehouse? Sooner or later somebody's gonna find them and start asking questions.'

'What men?'

Doyle understands. He's saying that the bodies have already been disposed of. Proust has been meticulous in his planning of this little operation. Every last detail has been considered. All it required was for Doyle to play along. And boy, did he do that.

'What you're asking, it'll take some time.'

'Tomorrow morning. That's your deadline. Put something in place by ten o'clock, or I start making calls.'

Doyle looks across the table. Sees beyond the battered and bruised exterior of the man opposite. Sees into his soul. Sees the darkness there. The perfect combination of deviousness and malevolence that makes him so dangerous. Proust wasn't being arrogant when he said that Bartok played no part in concocting this scheme. This is all Proust. Doyle was right about him all along – the man is pure evil. But he was also wrong, because he thought he could defeat him.

Proust has won. He will step away from murder yet again. There is no escaping that outcome.

Says Doyle, 'You killed them.'

'Ruger and the kid? No. I had nothing to do with—'

'The girls. Alyssa Palmer and Megan Hamlyn. You killed them.'

That smile again. That grin of smug supremacy. He probably wore that smile when he was torturing those poor girls.

'I killed nobody, Detective. And you will make sure that nobody believes I did. Kinda ironic when you think about it. The only person who thinks I'm a murderer is the one who ends up proving my innocence.'

Yeah, ironic. Doyle could vomit at the irony.

Doyle stands up. It takes an effort, because his legs seem weak. His whole body seems feeble somehow.

'Yeah,' says Proust. 'You should go. I imagine you must have a lot to do today. Thanks for dropping by, though.'

Doyle tries to shape his features to reflect the contempt he feels, but even that seems pathetic. Insignificant. Like shining a flashlight back at the sun.

And when he leaves, it is not with head held high. It is the slow slinking away of a lowly creature from its almighty owner.

THIRTY-ONE

Doyle back in his apartment. Gazing unseeingly out of the window. No sign yet of Rachel or Amy. If they knew what he'd done, maybe they'd never come back.

How do you do it, Doyle? How do you get yourself into these messes? Do you even know what you're doing anymore?

Let's consider the evidence, shall we?

Exhibit one. You fucked up the case against Proust. I mean royally fucked that one up. He comes out of this cleaner than one of his sterilized needles. And you, Doyle, are the one who's going to make sure of that.

Exhibit two. Whereas Proust gets to keep his freedom, you have signed yours away. Marked on the dotted line that you wish to be in slavery to Lucas Bartok for the rest of your life. What a happy marriage that will be.

Exhibit three. Your family. It's a good thing you got hitched to Bartok, because your own family environment is a disaster zone. Rachel can't even bear your presence, and Amy is afraid of what you think of her. This apartment is like the *Mary Celeste* at the moment. Even when the two loves of your life are at home, it's as if they're ghosts with whom you can have no proper communication.

Exhibit four. The job, or what's left of it. LeBlanc wants

nothing to do with you, other people on the squad distrust or despise you, and you're not even allowed to work the most minor of cases at the moment, let alone a homicide. And when you do find a way to worm yourself back in, it will be with the ulterior motive of helping out Proust. And after that, your primary lord and master will be Lucas Bartok. So that'll be rewarding.

Exhibit five. Is there an exhibit five? Probably. And probably a six, seven and eight too. Might as well be a gazillion exhibits, because they couldn't make it any worse. How could it possibly get any worse?

Doyle's cellphone rings.

He checks the display before answering. A number he doesn't recognize.

'Hello?'

'Detective Doyle? It's Nicole Hamlyn here. I hope it's okay to call you like this.'

He remembers that he gave her a card with his number on it when he sat with her at the hospital.

'No. It's fine. How's your husband?'

'That's what I'm calling about. I thought you should know. Steve, he . . . he died this morning.'

Doyle closes his eyes. Lets out a long, slow breath. Feels her sadness.

'Oh, God, I'm so sorry.'

'I just . . . I just thought you'd want to know.'

The silence that follows is an awkward one. It demands to be filled, but Doyle isn't sure what will fit there.

He says, 'I'll come over to see you.'

'No, no. I don't want to put you to any trouble.'

Doyle hears her words, but senses her meaning. She wants

desperately to talk to him about this. It's why she's clinging on to this conversation.

'No trouble. I'll be there as soon as I can.'

When she doesn't protest further, he knows he is right.

'Thank you,' she says.

'No problem,' Doyle responds.

When he hangs up, he looks out of the window again, but this time up at the leaden sky.

How could it get any worse? There's your answer, Doyle. You had to ask, didn't you? And now you have your answer.

He feels the emptiness of the house as soon as he walks through the front door.

His own place was bad enough, but at least he still has a spouse and a daughter, emotionally distant as they might be right now. This woman has lost both. The content of this woman's life has been cruelly poured away before her eyes. She has nothing left to love, and probably no love left to give.

They sit in the same seats they occupied the first time Doyle came to visit. Her husband and LeBlanc were here on that occasion. Now there seem to be too many empty chairs.

'Thank you,' says Nicole. 'For coming all the way out here. I know how busy you must be.'

Funnily enough, no, thinks Doyle. Not busy at all. Not unless you count dreaming up ways to clear the man who slaughtered your family.

'You shouldn't be alone,' he says. 'Not at a time like this.'

'I've had people here all morning. To be honest, I'm sick of hearing the same old sentiments again and again. So if you're thinking of telling me how sorry you are for my loss, don't. That's not what I need right now.'

Doyle looks across at her, and she holds his gaze. Her eyes glisten, but she is not crying. He wonders whether she will ever cry again. Not because he thinks she is heartless, but because that heart must have been wrung dry by now. She seems devoid of emotion, absent of feeling. It's all gone. It's all been taken from her.

'So what do you need?'

'Answers. Explanations.'

It's a fair enough request. For natural disasters, it's reasonable to look to the heavens for answers. When they're man-made, it's logical to look to one's fellow human beings.

'I, uhm, I'm not sure I have any.'

Her scrutiny doesn't waver. 'Yes, you do. You know things. Things you haven't revealed to me.'

Got me there. I know everything. The who, the what, the why, the where. I know so much that I'm struggling to hold it all in. I'm screaming with the pressure of it.

'What makes you think that?'

'Cal – is it okay if I call you Cal? – we've got to know each other a little over the past few days. Now I haven't met many other cops, but I've met plenty people in positions of authority. I work at a hospital, and doctors and surgeons are the worst for keeping things under wraps. They tell you only what you need to know. But you, you're different.'

'You mean I'm a lousy cop because I can't keep my mouth shut.'

'No, I think it makes you a better cop. You've been open with me all along. Told me things that maybe could have gotten you into trouble. You put the victim above everything else. That makes you special.'

He smiles at her. 'Now I know who to come to for a reference.'

When she continues to wait patiently, it pains him to be blunt. 'Nicole, listen to me. I can only go so far. Yes, there are things I know. There are also things I don't know, and things I can't prove. In a job like mine, you have to be careful. What you said about doctors, I can understand that. We're not gods. We can't play with people's lives. We have to be sure.'

She doesn't show any sign of relenting. 'Then let me get more specific. If there are things you can't tell me, fine. But I'm guessing there are things you can't deny either.'

She wants to go fishing, thinks Doyle. I should advise her not to. The sensible thing here is for me to get up and leave.

But it's not the human thing, is it? And that's why I can't abandon her. She knows this.

'What's on your mind, Nicole?'

'You know who killed my daughter, don't you?'

'I have a strong suspect.'

'But no proof?'

What is proof? Tricking me into providing a false alibi? Is that proof enough?

'Nothing that would stand up in court.'

'But in your own mind? If you had to bet everything you own on it being this person? Would you do it?'

'Nicole, I . . .' He struggles to find words that will appease her.

'The tattoo guy. Proust – is that his name? It's him, isn't it? Steve thought it was. That's why he went there. Because he believed it was him. That's why they got into a fight. Steve was certain.'

'Steve believed it was him because somebody sent him a note saying it was Proust. That's all, Nicole.'

She shakes her head. 'No. No, that's not all. Proust must

have said something or done something for Steve to react like that.'

'Nicole, you saw how upset Steve was about Megan. You saw how crazy it made him. And I'm not criticizing him, because I think I'd be exactly the same way. But the thing you gotta understand is that Steve wasn't exactly in a rational frame of mind when he went to talk to Proust. Somebody had planted a seed that this was his guy, and that's what he wanted to believe. He saw how the police were getting nowhere, and here was the answer being handed to him. Right or wrong, here was the closure he needed.'

'So who's your suspect? If it's not Proust, then who is it? One of the last things Megan did before she was killed was to get a stupid tattoo on her butt. And the last thing Steve did was to go talk to a tattooist. Now I don't think that's a coincidence. But if you want to tell me I'm reading too much into this, then go ahead. Give me something on this other suspect of yours.'

'You know I can't tell you who—'

'All right. Not a name, okay? A piece of information. How about we start with something simple? Male or female?'

Doyle doesn't answer.

She says, 'You can't even tell me if this other suspect of yours is male or female? Uh-huh. I see.'

'Nicole, what good would it do to—'

'I think you should go now.'

Doyle looks into her eyes. 'What?'

'I was wrong about you. I thought you wanted to help me. You know what? Ever since Megan went missing, you're the only person who I really believed could help us. The only person who actually seemed to give a damn.'

'I do. I want to help. It's just that—'

'Imagine if it was you, Cal. You have a wife and daughter, right? I'm not wishing anything bad on you, but imagine if you lost both of them. They're both killed, within days of each other. Imagine how you'd feel. Can you even contemplate how terrible that would be? Now imagine that I know something. I know who killed them, or at least I have a pretty good idea. But I refuse to tell you. I won't even give you the slightest clue. What would you think of me, Cal?'

'It's a different situation, Nicole. I'm a cop. I have to follow procedures.'

'Fuck the procedures! And fuck you too if you're going to treat me like just another statistic, another faceless victim of violent crime.'

He was wrong about her lack of emotion. There is still some there. Anger, mostly. Fury at the unjustness of it all. Throughout this ordeal, she has never allowed her rage to surface. But now there is nothing left to keep it suppressed. It is finding its way out, and Doyle is in its path.

He says, 'I'm not doing that. I'm just trying to explain—'

'*I have nothing!*'

Her cry sends a current through his being. If true loss can be captured in three words, then she has just done it, and it shocks him to the core.

Her voice softens again, but there is a bitterness there. 'I have nothing left. I had a life. I had a family. It's all gone. But I don't even know why. I don't know who's responsible . . .'

Doyle feels something building, deep inside him.

'. . . And you dare to sit there, in my house, knowing all these things but refusing to tell me . . .'

It rises. It pushes up into his throat. He's finding it difficult to breathe.

'. . . You won't even tell me if it's a man or a woman who did these things . . .'

It's choking him as it tries to escape. I should get out of here, he thinks. Before it's too late.

'. . . I thought you were on my side. I thought you were—'

'ALL RIGHT!'

His voice reverberates around the room. And now it *is* too late. The firing pin has struck home. The blast cannot be contained.

Doyle is on his feet, but doesn't even know he has jumped up. His conscious thought is devoted solely to vomiting out the words he's needed to say to someone for so long.

'It was Proust! There. Happy now? Has that fixed everything for you? It was Stanley Francis Proust. He's the man who killed your daughter and your husband and another girl called Alyssa Palmer. Only nothing's gonna happen to Proust, and you know why? Because I fucked up. I fucked up the investigation. The cop you think so highly of because of his interpersonal skills is the one who's letting your family's killer off the hook. And maybe if I hadn't screwed up so badly, your husband would still be alive. That's what you get for relying on me. That's what I did for you. All right? Is that really what you wanted to hear?'

He realizes there are tears in his eyes, and he curses himself for it. Pull yourself together, Doyle. What kind of cop are you?

But he can't stop them welling up, and his lip starts to quiver as he battles against all the emotions flooding his system. Thoughts that had been pushed to the back of his mind are jumping out of their hidey-holes. Thoughts about what he's done to his family, his work colleagues, and himself. But also about what he's going to do to Nicole's chances of ever finding justice.

Nicole is staring at him, trying to comprehend the outburst. 'I don't understand. What do you mean, you messed up? If you know it's him, why can't you arrest him?'

It's a sensible question. Sensible is good. Gives him something to focus on. Something black and white rather than all this fuzzy gray stuff that just sends him into a tailspin.

He clears his throat. 'For one thing, there's no proof, okay? For another, I'm no longer on the case.'

'No longer on . . . You've given up? Already? How can you—'

'No, not given up. I've been taken off it. I've been suspended from duty.'

'Why? What did you do?'

'I did what you think is such a good thing. I got too involved. I didn't play by the rules.'

'Okay, but . . . There are other cops. They can go after Proust, can't they? They can question him. They can come up with the proof.'

Doyle looks down at her. She looks like a child, asking him to confirm that Santa is real.

'Sure. They can do all that.'

He hears the lack of conviction in his own voice, and knows that it won't escape Nicole's attention.

'You don't believe they'll get him, do you?'

By the time I've finished fixing him up with a cast-iron alibi? No, I don't.

'I . . . Maybe they will. I don't know. They're looking at all possibilities, so yeah, maybe.'

'Maybe isn't good enough, Cal. You said you were sure. Why aren't they as sure as you?'

'They think . . . They don't trust me, okay? Proust has made

331

up some crap about me, and they believe it. They think my beef with Proust is personal.'

'But it isn't? You know he did this?'

Doyle fills his lungs and lets it out slowly. 'I know it. But what I know ain't worth shit.'

Nicole stands up then. She walks right up to Doyle, then puts her arms around him and holds him close. He's not sure what to do. This is nice, but truth be told, he wishes this were Rachel hugging him like this. God, he thinks, I miss her.

Nicole pulls away. Says, 'Thank you.'

'What for?'

'For being honest with me. For doing what you thought was right. For sticking to your principles.'

Doyle thinks back to his conversation with Paulson. Same take-home message: *Do what you think is right.*

Yeah. Look where that got me. Principles I'm loaded with. Be nice to trade a few for some happy outcomes now and again.

'And for being a fuck-up?'

'Yes,' she says. 'That too.'

'All this stuff I just told you . . .'

'Don't worry,' she says. 'I won't tell anyone what you said to me.'

'Actually, I wasn't going to ask that. To be honest, the pit I already dug for myself couldn't get any deeper. Nah, I was gonna ask if it makes any difference.'

She nods. 'It makes a difference. I know something more about what happened to Megan. And I know that I'm not the only one who cares. And I'm not just talking about words. I'm talking about someone who cares enough to do something about it. That's going to help me through this.'

Doyle watches her for a while. She seems somehow more

content, if anyone can be content after what she's been through. He's not sure what magic he's worked here. Doesn't understand how his words could provide any comfort. But if that's the effect they've had, then his trip here has done some good. And it also seems to him that he has lightened his own load a little.

'I should, uhm, I should go now. If there's anything you need, just give me a call, okay?'

She nods again. 'You're a good man, Callum Doyle. I won't let anyone say otherwise.'

And now the load weighs heavy again. Because you're not good, are you, Doyle? She doesn't know the full story. Go on, tell her. Tell her how you're planning to keep Proust out of prison, just to save your own lousy neck. See what she thinks of you then.

And when it gets out that Proust has this unbreakable alibi, and she comes to you for an explanation, what are you going to tell her then? Say that you must've made a mistake? Say that you must've been wrong about Proust all along? Could you look this woman in the eye again and lie like that?

When Doyle leaves, he uses the rain as an excuse to jog back to the car, and then he wastes no time in driving away from that house.

For a while after he's gone, she does nothing. Time becomes immaterial again. She sits and she broods. She thinks on what Doyle has told her. She has some answers now. Not many, but some. She marvels at how it is possible for one man – Proust – to cause such devastation. To rip a family he doesn't even know into shreds. Astonishing.

From what Doyle said, it seems likely the police will be unable to do anything about Proust, but that no longer matters. He has done all the damage he can to this family.

She feels sorry for Doyle. She meant it when she said he was a good man. He tried and he failed. Things went badly for him, but at least he had the guts to go with his convictions. She knows she will never see him again. She hopes it works out for him.

When an eternity has passed, she gets up from the sofa and goes into the kitchen. She doesn't know what's drawing her there, but then her eyes lock immediately on the door leading to the garage, to the place where she had the huge argument with Steve. She hasn't been back there since then.

She opens the door. Slowly pushes it wide. Snaps on the light switch and enters.

It's a sight to behold.

Not all of the shelves are up, and so the work table and various tools still occupy the center of the garage floor. But that's not what grabs her attention.

She steps closer. It's directly opposite the door, so she can't miss it.

A whole section of shelving, filled with wondrous things. Megan's things. All taken out of the cardboard boxes and arranged neatly on display. Her old school notebooks. Certificates. Trophies. Photographs.

And there, right in the center of the middle shelf, a gift. Still wrapped. It was the present that Megan bought for Nicole's birthday. The one Nicole refused to let Steve give to her.

She picks it up. Strokes the paper. Megan wrapped this herself. Lovingly.

Nicole brings the gift to her nose and breathes deep. She convinces herself that the smell of Megan still lingers there.

She turns it over. Carefully peels the tape away. She doesn't want to rip the paper.

She opens it up. It contains a book:

Springboard and Platform Diving for Beginners.

Nicole smiles. Clutches the book to her chest.

I'll do it, she thinks. I'll do the best dive ever. Just for you. You'll see.

THIRTY-TWO

It's after five o'clock when he gets back to the apartment, and still no sign of Rachel and Amy. Now he's starting to worry. Starting to get the uncomfortable feeling he should check the bedroom closet for empty hangers.

He takes out his cellphone and speed-dials her number. It rings several times before being answered.

'Yes?'

A single word, but caked in a hard frost.

'Rachel, where are you? I haven't seen you all day.'

'And why would that be? I wonder. Could it be because you disappeared last night and didn't even bother to come home again until God knows when?'

'I've been home a coupla times.'

'You weren't there a half-hour ago when we called in.'

'No. I had to go out again.'

'I see. That's a busy schedule you've got there, Cal.'

'It gets like that sometimes. You know it does. We're still working the Hamlyn homicide and—'

'Don't, Cal. Don't even go there, okay?'

'Go where? What do you mean?'

'I'm talking about the lies. Don't compound it, all right? Isn't it bad enough as it is without you making it worse?'

'Rach—'

'No! I *know*, okay? I know you were suspended from duty. Something like that, word gets around. You're not working a homicide. You're not working anything right now. You had other reasons for disappearing last night. Reasons you don't want to tell me about. Well, fine. Now it's my turn. I'm not coming home tonight, Cal. In fact, I'm not sure when I'll be back. Maybe I'll consider it when we can start trusting each other again.'

'Rach—' he says again, but the line has already gone dead.

Crap!

Crap, crap, crap!

Doyle, if you were to make a list of the worst days of your life, this has to be someplace near the top, right?

How are you gonna fix this? Is it even possible to fix this? There are too many people wanting different things. Conflicting things. Proust, Bartok, Nicole, Rachel. How can you keep them all sweet without screwing up your own life? You've got one night to sort it all out. One night before Proust throws you to the lions. What are you gonna do?

The answer comes to him forty minutes later. After he has downed two beers and opened up a third. It comes to him in a phone call.

It's Rachel's number.

He jabs the call-answer button, and as he raises the phone to his ear he thinks, She's thought better of it. She wants to come home.

There's a smile of relief on his face as he speaks: 'Rachel?'

Silence for a second. Then some fumbling noises. And then: 'Hi, Daddy.'

Amy always sounds so different on the phone. Her voice more squeaky. She sounds so small and fragile.

'Hi, sweetie. Whatcha doin'?'

'I . . . I just wanted to talk to you. Mommy said I could.'

Not a total pariah, then. At least that's something.

'Cool. I'm real glad you called. It's not the same here without you.'

'It's not the same for me too. I want to be home, with you. I don't want to be here.'

'You mean at Grandma's?'

'Yes. No. I mean . . . I'm not supposed to say where I am. Mommy said—'

'That's okay, hon. I won't tell anyone.'

It was a shot in the dark, but it was always a pretty good bet that Rachel would go to her parents' place. And oh, how they'll love that. They'll be lapping it up. They've always despised Doyle, and now they've got their opportunity to congratulate themselves on being right about him all along, and to crow at Rachel about how they always knew he was a good-for-nothing scoundrel.

Calling Rachel's mother Grandma was Doyle's subtle way of taking a shot back at her. She detests being called Grandma. Says it makes her feel ancient. The decrepit old bat.

'Daddy, why is Mommy angry? She says she isn't, but I can tell. She keeps yelling about things. And she keeps crying too.'

Doyle feels an ache in his chest. 'Nothing for you to worry about, Amy. It's just some stuff we have to deal with at the moment.'

And then Amy says, 'It's cuz of me, isn't it? It's because you think I stole stuff.'

Doyle feels as though his heart has been clenched by steel fingers. 'Honey, no! Absolutely not. It has nothing to do with that. I promise you.'

'Are you sure?'

'Yes.'

'Cross your heart and hope to die?'

'Stick a needle in my eye.'

'Cuz I didn't do it, Daddy. I didn't take those things. I wouldn't do that. It's naughty. You do believe me, don't you?'

'I believe you one hundred percent, Amy.'

'A hunnerd cents? That's a lot of money.'

'Yes, it is. And that's how much I trust you. So stop worrying about it, okay? Me and your mom are gonna fix this problem we got, and then you can both come home again. All right? We cool?'

'We cool . . . Oh, Mommy says I have to come off the phone now.'

'Okay, sweetie. Do as Mommy says. I'll see you soon, all right?'

'Yeah. Bye, Daddy. I love you.'

'I love you too, Amy.'

And then she's gone, and the line goes dead, and Doyle's world is suddenly light years away. And all he can do now is sit and reflect.

But he knows. He has his answers. There are tears in his eyes as he recognizes them for what they are.

See, it's all about trust and belief and faith. It's about doing what's right. It's about going with the heart rather than the head.

I don't know much, he thinks, but I know this: Amy didn't steal that stationery. All the evidence says she did, but she says she didn't. And that's enough for me. I don't know what the explanation is, but I do know that my Amy didn't take those things.

That's faith. That's what keeps us together.

I believe Amy, but I didn't believe Proust. I followed my instincts in both cases, even though they took me in different directions. Proust proved me right. Amy will prove me right.

Like Paulson said and like Nicole said, I have to continue doing what I think is right. Otherwise, I have nothing. I am nothing.

So that's what I do about Proust . . .

Nothing.

Let him go to the cops, if he has the balls. Let him tell his story. Let him try to take me down. I can't create an alibi for him. I can't help him cheat justice.

Whatever that means for me, I can take it. And tomorrow, when Rachel comes home, I will tell her everything.

And in the meantime . . .

. . . I'll drink my beer and wait.

Stanley Proust has a huge stupid grin on his face as he works. It won't go away. Sometimes it turns into a little chuckle of amusement.

He's proud of himself, of what he's managed to achieve. It took some planning, but it's really paid off. Tomorrow morning, all suspicion will be removed from him. He will be free. Doyle, on the other hand, will be shackled. He will be under Lucas Bartok's control for the rest of his life.

What a stupid bastard Doyle is. Why didn't he leave well alone? Why didn't he just do his job properly, instead of getting all zealous like that? Where did that come from?

Who gives a shit? You met your match here, boy. You thought I was scum, but look who's crawling in the dirt now.

All's right in the world.

It's as if others have sensed it too. The customers are drifting back. Proust is working on his third one of the day. Number three, and on a Sunday too! He had that construction worker in here earlier, then the guy with the hairy back, and now this chick with the fishnet stockings who's heavily into S&M. He's thinking he might even hit on her a little when he's finished up. Find out just how much pain she can really endure.

Pain. It's all about pain. He has seen what pain does to others, and now he's explored it more fully himself. He's been on a true voyage of discovery in the past few days.

But pain isn't only physical. It can be mental too. The kind of pain that Doyle is going through now is worse than anything Proust has experienced. Physical pain is easily mastered, as Proust himself has proved. But your mental torture, Doyle – well, I don't envy you that one, my friend. You'll be lucky to come through this with all your marbles still present.

Ain't life a bitch?

One of his chuckles escapes as he thinks this, and the chick under his fingers flashes her false lashes at him and asks what the joke is.

'The joke? A guy I know, is all. He's the joke.'

He finishes the tattoo. It's high on her arm. No opportunity to stick needles in her snatch, but hey, maybe she'll be game for a little of that too.

He tidies her up. Tells her again how she should keep it clean. Too many people, they don't look after their tats properly and they get infected.

There's almost a swagger in his walk as he goes around the counter to the cash register. If his battered body would allow it, he'd be moonwalking now.

The chick picks up her heavy-looking gym bag from the floor and follows him over. She has glossy black hair and bright-red lipstick and fuck-me heels, and her own walk is like that of a gyroscope – a multitude of curves rotating hypnotically about a fixed point of reference.

He tells her how much she owes, and she lifts the bag onto the counter, unzips it, and starts rummaging around inside.

He folds his arms on the counter and leans forward, then chin-points at the ornate lettering he's just put on her arm. Three characters: 'S&M'. Intertwined and flowing into each other. Looks pretty good, if he says so himself.

'So. You're into that kinda thing, huh?'

She gives him a smile that could harden jello. 'Oh yeah. Next time I come in, I want one of those . . .'

She points to the photographs on the wall behind him. He turns.

The smack to his neck is a big surprise.

'Jesus!' he yells, jumping out of her reach. 'What the fuck?'

She's walking backwards. Why is she backing off? Why that look of fear in her eyes?

And then he feels the stab of pain in his neck. He reaches up his hand. Touches the hard object lodged there. He grabs it, yanks it out, looks at it.

A hypodermic needle. Its plunger has been depressed. It's empty now. Whatever it contained is now in his bloodstream.

He turns to her again. 'What did you do to me? What the hell did you . . .'

But then her edges soften. The room melts. Consciousness dissolves.

His chin strikes the edge of the counter on the way down.

THIRTY-THREE

She wastes no time.

She locks up the shop and draws the blinds. She kicks off the high-heeled shoes, then takes off the black wig and tosses it. The shoes, the wig, the fishnets, the make-up, the sexy walk – all part of the look. All designed to make her appear to be what she's not. Like a single woman who could be taken to be in her twenties and into kinky sex. Instead of what she really is. A woman who is not far short of forty. A loving wife. A devoted mother.

Proust had no idea.

And he has no idea of what's to come.

Nicole sets to work.

The cameras first. She got a good look around when she was lying on the chair. She saw the cameras, and then her eyes traced the wires to the point where they disappeared behind the counter. She continues to follow their route now. Finds they end up going through a hole in a small door at floor level. The door is locked, but the key is in it. She unlocks the door. There's a black box of tricks here, plugged into a socket in the wall. She yanks out the plug. The box's lights go out and its whirring dies. She goes back around the counter and checks the cameras. Their tiny red lights have gone out too.

She returns her attention to Proust.

She drags across a heavy floor-standing lamp. Switches it on and angles it directly over Proust. Then she finds the main light switches for the shop and turns them all out.

She grabs her gym bag and places it on the floor. Kneels down next to it and unties Proust's sneakers. Slips them off, then removes his malodorous socks. Then she reaches into her gym bag and takes out a pair of scissors. They're large and heavy. Dressmaking scissors. She lifts the bottom of Proust's red T-shirt and starts to cut. Slices it through from hem to neckline. When she parts the material she sees the tattoo on his chest. The self-portrait of the anguished Proust trying to escape his own body.

'There's no escape,' she tells the unconscious figure. 'Not this time.'

She continues cutting. Cutting and cutting until he is naked.

When she is done, she stands for a while, looking down at him. She sees how scrawny he is, how pathetic. She wonders how it is possible for such power over the lives of others to be contained in such insubstantial flesh and bone.

He has cuts and bruises all over his body, and she wonders why. Not from Steve, surely? From Doyle, then? Is this what he meant about getting too involved?

Not to worry. She'll find out soon enough.

Proust stirs. His mouth opens and closes, and a line of saliva escapes his lips and dribbles down his chin.

Not yet. There is still work to be done.

She takes another hypodermic syringe from her bag. Propofol is fast-acting, but its effects don't last very long. She finds a vein in his arm, jabs the needle in, squirts the milky-white liquid into his blood. His eyelids flicker and then go still.

She knew what they were all thinking in the hospital: *How can she come back to work so soon after the deaths of her loved ones?* She told them she needed to take her mind off things, and that she would go home again if she couldn't cope. She walked out an hour later, but only after stealing the drugs she needed.

She tidies away the scraps of Proust's clothing. Then she takes hold of one of his arms and drags him over to the wall. Despite his puny appearance, it takes some effort to position him where she wants him, with his head and shoulders propped up against the wall. So he can look down. So he can see.

She moves the lamp so that it is once again over his body. Then she brings her bag across and takes out what she needs.

The drill, plus its attachments.

The screws.

The strips of thick, tough leather, obtained by cutting up Steve's belts.

She practiced at home, in the garage, but it still takes her a while to get it right now. She has to administer another dose of anesthetic to keep him under. But finally she gets it done, and she stands and surveys her handiwork.

Four leather bonds, pulled tight over Proust's wrists and ankles, and screwed firmly into the floor.

You're not going anywhere, she thinks. You're mine.

She brings across a low stool and sits on it.

Then she waits.

His head moves first. He rolls it around, then mutters something incomprehensible. His eyelids flutter open. He blinks against the light. He's awake. Another good thing about propofol: the rapid recovery when it wears off.

He realizes she's sitting there watching him, and his eyes

register confusion. Then he looks at his nakedness, and his eyes register fear.

He tries to move an arm. Realizes he can't. He tries his other arm, his legs. He can do nothing. She can see how his fear is escalating.

Good.

'What the fuck is this?' he asks. 'Who are you?'

'You should know,' she says. 'You invited me here.'

'What are you talking about? Let me up. I don't know you.'

She leans forward into the cone of light from the lamp. Touches a finger to the tattoo on her upper arm.

'S&M,' she says. 'Steve and Megan. My husband and my daughter.'

Understanding crosses his features. He tries to mask it, but it's too late. He's betrayed himself.

'I don't know your family, and I don't know you either. This is crazy. You need to let me out of this now.'

He strains against his bindings. She can see his tendons flexing in his body as he struggles. But she has made too good a job of this.

'I'll let you go,' she says. 'But only after you've told me everything.'

'Everything about what? I don't know what you're talking about. You got the wrong guy.'

Nicole reaches into her bag and takes out a small box. She clicks a button on it, then places it on the floor between herself and Proust.

'What's that?' he asks.

'A voice recorder. You can start talking now.'

'Talking about what? What am I supposed to say? What the fuck do you want me to say?'

'Everything. Tell me everything. This is your chance to confess. Your chance to do something righteous for once in your miserable existence.' Her voice is flat, emotionless. She feels neither pity nor anger. She feels only a deep-rooted desire for truth. To know what happened. Doyle did what he could, but it wasn't enough. She needs more.

Proust's own voice heightens in both volume and tone: 'Confess to what? I got nothing to confess. Not to you, anyhow. I don't know nothing about you.'

'All right,' she says. 'I'll make it easy for you. I'll give you specifics. Start with Megan. Tell me how you met her. Tell me about how she came to you for that angel tattoo.'

He barks a forced laugh. 'Yeah, see, you definitely got the wrong guy. I really have no idea who you're talking about.'

'That's not what my husband thought.'

'I don't give a fuck what your husband thinks. He's as wrong as you are.'

'Past tense, Stanley. You need the past tense. My husband is dead. You killed him, remember? With a knife?'

Mock recognition on his face now. Sickening. 'Oh! Oh, that guy! He was your husband? Oh, I get it now. He's dead? I didn't know that. Listen, I'm sorry. I'm real sorry about that. But, see, he attacked me. Came in here yelling all kinds of crazy shit at me, and then he attacked me. With a hammer. I was just defending myself. Ask the cops. They'll tell you what happened. It was caught on the cameras. In fact – hey, yeah – why don't I show you? I can show you the video! You can see exactly what happened. We can clear this up right now.'

She says nothing for a while. She just stares at Proust. Wonders how long he intends to keep up this charade.

'I don't want to see the video. I know he came here, and I

know you got into a fight. What I want to know is why. But before all that, I want to know about Megan.'

Proust chews on his lip. She knows he's considering his options.

'This is Detective Doyle's doing, isn't it? He sent you here. He told you I had something to do with this. You don't believe him, do you? Do you know about him? Do you know how fucked-up he is? You see these bruises on me? Do you? Well, Doyle is responsible for those. He beat the crap out of me. He even threw me through my own door. Go ahead, take a look. Go back there to my apartment and take a look at my door. It's wrecked. The glass panel is shattered. And you know why? Because Doyle threw me into it. The man's a lunatic. He's not even allowed to work anymore. I bet you didn't know that, did you? He's off the force, because all the other cops know what a fuck-up he is. Are you listening to me? Are you listening?'

She's listening, but she's not getting what she came to hear. She lowers her head and closes her eyes. She thought it would come to this. It was always going to come to this. And she's ready.

'The letter,' says Proust. 'Do you know about the letter? Doyle sent your husband a note, telling him to come talk to me. That's why he thought the guy was me. It was all Doyle's fault. If anyone's to blame for your husband's death, it's Detective Doyle. He hates me. And you know why? Because of what I know about him and the partner he used to have. A female partner. You get my drift? They were getting it on, you know? And he was scared I was gonna tell someone. And then she got killed, in mysterious circumstances. Do you know this story? Have you heard about this before?'

He's talking too much now. Rambling in desperation. It's all garbage.

But she has to be sure.

She reaches behind her. Picks up another object. Brings it into view.

She sees his eyes widen. His verbal diarrhea has suddenly dried up. He chews on his lip again.

He says, 'What . . . What are you doing?'

She looks at the power drill in her hand. Slides a finger along the thin, shiny drill bit. She pulls the trigger briefly. Just enough to give it a nerve-grating whine of life.

'You haven't answered my questions. I asked you about my daughter.'

He seems suddenly full of uncertainty. 'I . . . I told you everything I know. Look, this is crazy. Why don't you just let me out of here so we can talk about this?'

She slides off the stool, onto her knees. She places the tip of the drill bit against the underside of Proust's left foot.

Proust tries to pull his foot away, but the leather binding is too secure.

'Lady . . . Lady, please . . . You got this all wrong. I swear to you, on my mother's life . . .'

'You have a mother? That's good. It's good that you have family. I had a family. I had a beautiful daughter and a wonderful caring husband. You took them from me. And all I want from you is to tell me why you did it and how it happened. Is that too much to ask?'

'But that's what I keep telling you. I didn't—'

The drill shrieks into life again. Proust shrieks too. His body tenses and trembles and he yells in pain and disbelief at the sight of the drill bit coming into view as it sears through his foot.

Nicole flicks the drill into reverse and withdraws it. She looks at the blood and the pink slivers of flesh on the drill bit, and then the blood flowing down Proust's foot and onto the floor.

Proust is screaming at her: 'Jesus Christ! You fucking bitch! Look what you did, you fucking stupid cunt! Jesus!'

She shuffles along the floor, getting closer to his face. She looks deep into his eyes, wondering what he sees. Puzzling over how their two views of the world can be so different.

'*What?*' he demands. 'What the fuck are you looking at?'

She blinks. What *am* I looking at? What is this thing in front of me? Not a man, no. Not a human being. A thing. A monster.

'Did that hurt, Stanley?'

He glares his malevolence at her, and then he shows her a smile of contempt. 'You can't hurt me, you dumb bitch. Look at me. Look at what I've been through. I know pain. You want to torture me, go ahead. You're wasting your fucking time. I ain't gonna say what you want me to say. I ain't gonna lie just to make you happy.'

She raises the drill. Pushes the bit up and into his right nostril.

'No,' she says. 'You don't know pain. I'm a midwife. I see pain every day. Real pain. You don't know anything about pain.'

'I know you're fucking mental, is what I know.'

She pulls on the trigger. Sees Proust's eyes cross and water as he watches the drill bit come up through the tip of his nose. A thin shaft of whirling steel, inches in front of those satanic eyes.

She says, 'My daughter felt pain, didn't she? Pain worse than any childbirth. Megan's birth was painful. So painful I can't have any more children. But her pain was much, much worse, I'm sure. Worse even than this . . .'

She yanks the drill away. Pulls it away so fast and hard that it tears through the soft flesh of Proust's nose. Rips right through it.

Proust lets out a roar. His whole body contracts as he throws his head back and releases a ferocious bellow.

When he has finished, he turns his eyes on Nicole again. Blood is spurting from the ragged gash in his nostril, and onto his heaving bony chest.

But still he smiles.

'Bring it on, bitch. You ain't getting nothing from me. NOTHING!'

She touches the drill point to his neck. Traces it down his sternum and across his tattoo. Onto his abdomen. Down to his groin. She brings it to rest on his scrotum, presses it into the soft, yielding flesh. She looks up at him again.

'Tell me about Megan. Tell me what you did to her.'

He stares back at her. Fixes her with his gaze. Shows her his blood-flecked teeth and gums.

'I don't know any Megan.'

Doyle was right, she thinks. He could see in Proust what nobody else could. This thing is evil. It is madness. It feeds on pain. But not its own pain. The pain of others. Megan's pain is locked up inside Proust. It needs to be released.

She pulls the trigger.

It takes over an hour.

When she's done, she puts down the power drill and stands over what's left of Stanley Francis Proust.

She is tired. Mentally and physically exhausted.

But still there is work to be done.

She goes over to a sink. Washes the bodily fluids and brain matter from her hands.

Then she goes back to the gym bag. Pulls out a small case containing her laptop.

This will take a while, she thinks. But I'm in no hurry. I have what I came for.

THIRTY-FOUR

The call comes at just after nine-thirty.

Doyle puts down his beer and finds his phone. Stares at the number. Doesn't recognize it. Wonders whether he should even bother answering it.

But he does. He answers it with the air of a man who no longer gives a shit. *Say what you wanna say, caller, because whatever it is, it's nothing compared with my problems.*

'Yeah,' he drawls. His eyes are still on the beer bottle. He suspects this may be the last one in the apartment. That's not good news. More alcohol is definitely required tonight.

'Cal? It's me. It's Nicole.'

Oh, yeah. Nicole. She has my number. I forgot. Well, I'm sorry, Nicole, but you're wasting your time. I can't do anything more for you. And to be honest, not having me meddling in your affairs is probably something you should be grateful for.

'Hey, Nicole. What's up?'

He doesn't really want to know what's up. She's not his problem anymore. Move on.

'You were right,' she says. 'About Proust.'

Which is a curious statement. One to grab the attention, all right. One that says, *Okay, sober up, Doyle. You need to listen to this.*

'What do you mean? How am I right?'

'He murdered Megan and he murdered Steve. He murdered that other girl too. Alyssa Palmer.'

Doyle shifts himself out of his slouch. Sits bolt upright.

'You know this for a fact? How do you know it?'

'He told me. Proust. He told me everything.'

'What . . . What do you mean, he told you? When did he tell you this?'

'A short while ago. I know it all now. I got my answers. I know exactly what he did to Megan. I know what he did with the pieces of her. And I know what he did to you, Cal.'

'To me? What do you mean?'

'His clever plan. With that other man. Lucas Bartok.'

And now Doyle is standing. Pacing, even. 'Nicole, where are you?'

'I understand now, Cal. They put you in an impossible position. You tried. You did what you could for me, when nobody else would. Answer me one thing, though, Cal.'

'I'm coming right over. Stay there, okay?'

'I'm not at home, Cal. Don't come looking for me. I just want to know something, all right?'

'Nicole . . . All right. What is it?'

'Were you planning to go through with it? The alibi for Proust? Were you going to set one up for him?'

Doyle is at the window. He touches his forehead to the cool glass. She knows so much. Too much. It can mean only one thing. And he's too late to do anything about it.

'No. I thought about it. But no. I couldn't live with myself. I decided to take my chances.'

'That's what I thought. Like I said, Cal, you're a good man. You do what's right. So I'm going to help you now.'

'Nicole, please. I really think—'

'Shh, Cal. Listen to me. I'm going to send you something. Do you have an email address?'

'Uh, yeah. I think. Hang on.'

He knows he has a private email address, but he never uses it. He has to go over to the computer in the corner of the room and sift through some papers to find it.

He says, 'Okay, I got it.' He tells her what it is.

'Thank you, Cal. I'm sending something to you right now. You need to open the attachment, okay?'

'Yeah. Yeah, sure. But—'

'There's something else I need to tell you, Cal. Something very important.'

'You can tell me in person. Just tell me where—'

'Hush, Cal. Listen to me now.'

The way she sounds those words reminds him of his mother. Reminds him of when he was young, his mother telling him stories as he sat cross-legged on the floor.

And so he goes small-boy quiet and attentive. He listens to a story that is filled with unimaginable horrors, but which, for Nicole at least, obviously brings some degree of comfort. Her voice remains level and peaceful, and when she ends her brief tale, it is with the finality of a narrator who wants to convey that all the loose ends have been neatly tied off. Doyle can almost hear, in his mother's lilt, those additional two words: *The End*.

Says Nicole, 'One final request, Cal, if I may.'

Doyle feels as though his throat has closed up. He has to clear it to allow his words to escape.

'Name it.'

'I know you'll have to make some calls when we're done here. I understand that. You're one of New York City's finest, so

I wouldn't expect anything less. All I ask is that you hang fire for a short while. Just a few minutes. Just to give me a little time.'

'Nicole, I . . .'

'Please, Cal. Will you do that small thing for me?'

'I . . . Of course I will. It's the least I can do.'

'Thank you. You know, I'm glad I met you, Callum Doyle.'

'I'm glad I met you too. Nicole, please. Tell me where you are right now.'

'Don't let them change you. Trust your heart. Goodbye, Cal.'

'Nicole . . .'

But she's gone. Out of his life. And Doyle, his head still pressed against the rain-spattered window pane, finds that he is crying.

He cries through the sheer relief of having an insoluble dilemma erased from his life. He cries because he knows definitively now that he was correct all along about Proust. He cries because his decision to stick to the path he believed to be right has been vindicated. But most of all he cries because of all the pain and the sadness in this case. For Alyssa. For Megan. For Steve. And for Nicole.

Sometimes there are no happy endings.

She inches her way to the edge, her toes feeling their way along. When they curl into free space she stops and gathers herself. She is looking straight ahead. Gradually she allows her eyes to roll down.

It's a hell of a long way. For a second she feels as though she will lose her balance and topple off, and she has to raise her eyes again.

She stands statue-still. Feet together. Arms at her sides.

'Go ahead, Mom. Don't be such a big wuss.'

She smiles. 'Easy for you to say. I've never done it from this height.'

'Always a first time for everyone, Mom. Come on, loser.'

'Hey! Who are you calling a loser?'

'Sorry, did I call you a loser? I meant chicken.'

Megan makes a chicken noise that causes Nicole to burst out laughing.

'Stop it! I need to focus here.'

'You're going to do it?'

'I'm going to do it. Now be quiet and let me concentrate.'

Megan clams up, but Nicole can picture her down there, a big smile on her face.

She's expecting me to back down, thinks Nicole. She knows I always back down. Well, not this time, buster. Watch this . . .

She waggles her fingers, flicking the water from them. She takes a deep breath. Another breath.

This is for you.

She goes. She enters space. And she knows.

She knows that this is a perfect dive. The best one ever. Megan will be mouthing a silent wow as she watches, so proud of her mother. Everyone will stop to watch. They will see this most sublime dive and they will talk about it for ever. But they don't matter. Only Megan matters. My Megan, whose heart is filled with pride and with love and who will always be a part of me, always be with me now. Megan, Megan, Megan . . .

This is for you.

They come eventually.

They come to a small tattoo shop on Avenue B. To the home of Stanley Francis Proust.

They will remember this scene for a long time. It's a new

one on most of them. What was done here is unusual, to say the least. I mean, drilling all those holes in a guy . . .

The other one, though. Not so uncommon, unfortunately. They get 'em all the time. Jumpers.

Looks like she tortured and killed the guy. Went up to the top floor. Drilled out the lock of the roof door. Jumped.

Funny thing, though.

That book on the ledge. About high-diving. Like she wanted to make sure this wasn't just any old jump. Like it really makes any difference how you get down there.

People.

The world is full of fucking crazy people.

THIRTY-FIVE

What it is, is an audio file.

Doyle surprises himself at how easily he manages to open and play the email attachment. But listening to it doesn't come so easy. It's not exactly Vivaldi or Bach. Not even Kenny Rogers.

It's stomach-churning stuff.

He never liked Proust. Thought he was the worst kind of scum. But what he's listening to now, he wouldn't wish that even on him.

It's all there, just as Nicole said. How Megan first called into Proust's shop to ask about getting a tattoo. How he told her to come back to him in secret. How he drugged her. The things he did with her then. How he disposed of the body.

There's also a confession about how he screwed Doyle. Paying a guy to beat him up. Jumping through the door. Telling LeBlanc he had seen Doyle sucking faces with Laura Marino when he hadn't. Sending a note to Megan's father. There's even a full admission of guilt concerning the murder of Alyssa Palmer.

This isn't one long monologue, of course. There are some intermissions. Some comfort breaks for the benefit of the audience. Interludes filled with screaming and yelling and pleading and some incoherent rambling, all set off nicely by the occasional nerve-grinding whirr of an electric drill and its change in tone as it burrows deep into flesh and bone.

What's interesting is what's missing, and it takes Doyle a while to realize the recording has been edited by Nicole. There's no mention of Lucas Bartok, even though Nicole must have got the whole story from Proust. And the reason there's no mention of Bartok is that Nicole was protecting Doyle. She found out about Bartok's role, all right, but leaving any mention of him on the audio would have exposed Doyle to investigation too.

Silently, he thanks her for that.

The calls start coming in eventually, as he knew they would. Earlier, he'd put in some calls of his own. Told the cops to check out both Nicole's house and Proust's place.

He hears what he expects to hear. That Proust is dead. That Nicole is dead. That the bosses want him to come into the station house right away so that he can tell them what the hell he knows about this mess.

He's sobered up since the call from Nicole, and so he drives across town. When he gets to the station house, the atmosphere is decidedly hostile. He gets the impression he's being blamed for everything. He almost expects to be frisked for a power drill.

They march him into the captain's office, where the commander and Lieutenant Cesario, both of whom have undoubtedly been dragged away from pressing social engagements, grill him about his involvement. How is it, they want to know, that everyone connected with this case – the case that was assigned to *you*, Detective – ends up dead? How is it that, even though you've been taken off the case, you still seem to be very much the focal point of all this mayhem and massacre?

He tells them. Says what he's already said before. That this is all the result of Proust's plan to discredit him backfiring. He listens to the patronizing hums and harrumphs of his superiors, sees their expressions of disbelief. And it's only when they seriously start to get in his face – only when their own faces become red with fury as they start tossing out hints about possible disciplinary action against him – that he produces his trump card.

A memory stick. Containing the audio file of Proust's confessions to Nicole. Confessions that fully confirm Doyle's version of events.

And suddenly, miraculously, the captain wants nothing more to do with this conversation. He's glaring hotly at Cesario. Cesario is looking sheepish. Doyle is feeling just a little bit triumphant, and in his mind there's a huge fat finger being flipped at these two men.

The captain ends the meeting and empties his office of visitors so that he can steam off his embarrassment in private. In the hallway, Cesario accosts Doyle.

'I'll need to listen to that recording,' he says.

Doyle tosses the memory stick to him. 'Knock yourself out.'

Cesario examines the stick as he mulls over his next words. Maybe building himself up to apologize, thinks Doyle.

Says Cesario, 'You know I did what I had to do, right? I had to take you off the case.'

So much for an apology.

'Did you? Or could you have just listened to me?'

'There are rules. Procedures. You disobeyed an order. My order. Maybe if you hadn't gone at Proust the way you did, none of this shit would've happened.'

'Maybe. Or maybe he would've beaten the rap. Just like he did last time.'

Cesario shakes his head. 'This is not a good outcome. Whether you were right or you were wrong about Proust, it doesn't make this a good outcome. A whole family dead. A man tortured to death.'

'I know it,' says Doyle. 'I know it.'

He turns and starts to walk away, but Cesario calls after him.

'You're back on duty tomorrow. Four o'clock. Don't be late.'

Doyle keeps on walking.

He sleeps well, despite the absence of his family. Mental exhaustion, probably. Doesn't get out of bed until almost nine in the morning.

He showers. Eats a large breakfast. At 9.45 there is still no sign of Rachel, and it's really starting to hurt. He needs to talk to her. Needs to clear the air.

As he picks up his cellphone, it rings in his hand. He stabs the answer button.

'Rachel?'

'Cal? It's me. Tommy.'

He tries to smother the disappointment. 'Hey, Tommy.'

'I, uhm, just a quick call, okay? We, uhm, we heard. About what happened, I mean. About the recording.'

'Tommy, it's okay.'

'No. No, it's not okay. I didn't believe you. I wanted to, but I didn't. The way it looked . . .'

'You weren't the only one, Tommy.'

'I know. But that doesn't make it any better. You were my partner. I should have trusted you.'

'Yeah, well, maybe I shoulda made it easier for you to trust me. Don't beat yourself up about it, all right?'

'Yeah. Okay. I just thought you should know. And if you ever want to work with me again, I'd be proud to.'

'Sure. I'd like that. Take it easy, Tommy.'

'You too, Cal.'

Doyle hangs up. He looks at his phone and smiles. Tommy's a good kid. He had the guts to call. Doyle imagines there are a few others in the squad who will be too embarrassed even to look at him when he clocks on again later.

He almost drops his cellphone as it bursts into life again.

'Hello?'

'Hello, Doyle. Remember me? It's Sven. Mr Bartok would like to meet with you.'

Whaddya know? It's actually stopped raining.

Doyle sits in his car in the alleyway, looking up at the sky. The clouds are still ominously gray, but at least they're not as incontinent.

The expectation here is that he will be pissed upon from a different source. And he'll have to lie there and soak it up. This moment had to come. Proust might be out of the picture, but no way is Bartok going to miss out on his chance to control a detective. This meeting is where he makes that clear. This meeting is where he tells Doyle that his life will never be his own again.

Doyle gets out of his car. Locks it up. Strolls over to the side door of the nightclub and thumbs the buzzer.

The square-shaped goon who opens the door wears an ugly grin of superiority. An expression that says he regards Doyle as his bitch now. He beckons Doyle inside with a twitch of his fingers, and it's clear that he will tolerate no demurral.

Doyle steps into the dimly lit utility room and pushes the door closed behind him. The thug scowls at Doyle, then moves closer to him. He raises a hand and slaps Doyle hard across the face. Then a second hit, a backhand to the other cheek. He moves back slightly, then raises his eyebrows as if to say, *Well? What are you waiting for? You know the score.*

Doyle reaches slowly under his jacket. He pulls out his nine-millimeter and presents it to the man, butt first. The guy will be expecting to frisk him too, of course. He will be expecting to do whatever he wants with this lowlife cop who has crossed the divide. What he won't be expecting is any trouble from this pathetic loser who has forsaken all rights to any respect.

Doyle decides it's time to give him trouble.

As the man reaches out for the gun, Doyle hands it over. He hands it over into the man's face. He hands it over so hard there is the crack of bone as the man's nose shatters. Only the man doesn't seem to have managed to accept the offering yet, so Doyle has to try handing it over again. Several times, in fact. Always into his face. Smashing bones and teeth and lips and flesh and cartilage. Until there is only raw glistening redness, and the man lies senseless on the floor.

Doyle moves quickly, taking the man's gun, then binding his wrists and ankles with Plasti-Cuffs. He moves to the end of the hallway, preparing to sneak in on whoever might be on the other side of the door. But he's too late. He hears noises of somebody approaching.

Doyle sees a mop sitting in an empty bucket. He takes the mop and moves to one side of the door.

The door opens.

'Hey! Eddie! What the fuck are you—'

There is a whipping of air as Doyle brings the handle of the mop down on to the outstretched gun hand, followed by a snap of bone, a scream of pain and the clatter of the gun as it hits the floor.

Doyle pulls the mop back, then swings the handle into the

man's face. It connects nicely, reshaping the target's nose to match his buddy's. The man reels backwards into a wall, then bounces off it, coming at Doyle like a truck with no brakes. Doyle gives him the handle again, end-on this time. There's a crunch as it punches through teeth, and the man crumples to the ground, trying to hold back the geyser of blood gushing from his broken mouth. Doyle gives him another whack across the cranium for good measure, then sets about trussing him up. To stop the man calling out, Doyle pushes a balled-up handkerchief into the bloody hole in the man's face, then binds it into place around his head with duct tape. As he does so, he realizes he could probably have got to this position by simply pointing a gun at the man after disarming him. But it wouldn't have been as satisfying. Right now, there is a boiling inside Doyle that he needs to release.

Doyle pulls his gun and moves to the door. He peeks around it, sees nothing. He steps cautiously into the interior of the huge nightclub, adopting a two-handed combat stance as he scans the area. There is no sign of anyone else down here.

He hurries across the dance floor, his ears alert for the slightest noise, his eyes straining to pick out the subtlest of movements in the dark corners and recesses. At the foot of the metal staircase he pauses only briefly, then ascends two steps at a time. When he gets to the top, he moves silently up to the oak door to Bartok's office. He halts for a few seconds, trying to calm his breathing. He puts his free hand on the doorknob.

A quick turn and he's in.

Two men in here. Bartok at his desk. A few feet to his left, Sven lounging in a wing-back chair.

Sven makes the first move. Jumps to his feet, yanking out his gun.

Doyle was expecting this. Hoping for it, if truth be told.

He shoots Sven. Low, in the gut.

Sven drops his gun and falls back into his chair, staring down at the hole in his abdomen.

Doyle turns the gun on Bartok, who is reaching for a drawer in his desk. Doyle fires again, deliberately wide this time. The bullet enters the shiny top of Bartok's oak desk, sending splinters of wood spitting into his face. Bartok has a sudden change of mind about the drawer.

Doyle strides over to Bartok. Spins him around in his chair, then grabs the back of the chair and wheels it out from behind the desk. Then he spins Bartok to face him again and puts the muzzle of his gun to Bartok's cheek.

'Don't fucking move.'

Doyle heads over to Sven. He kicks Sven's gun away, and it goes sliding across the wooden floor to the far side of the room.

Sven is still staring at his wound. The dark-red stain on his shirt is spreading rapidly.

'Look at what you did,' he says. 'You fucking shot me, you motherfucker.'

'Shut the fuck up, Snowball.'

Doyle moves back to Bartok, whose crossed eyes are beaming death rays all over the room.

Says Bartok, 'Big mistake, you dumb mick. You are so fucked now.'

'Yeah?' says Doyle. 'Yeah? *I'm* fucked? *I'm* the one who's fucked?'

Doyle slams the butt of his gun into Bartok's forehead, then he rakes the muzzle across his cheek, the gunsight gouging out a trench in his flesh.

'Come here, ass-wipe.'

Doyle grabs Bartok by the hair and yanks him out of his chair and onto the floor. He kneels down next to the spread-eagled figure and presses the gun to a point behind Bartok's ear.

'I'm pissed, Lucas. And I think you know why.'

'What, because your squeeze took a tumble off a building before you could shaft her?'

Doyle pistol-whips him again.

'Right person, wrong reason. Try again. Does your boy Sven over there know? Why don't you tell him, huh? Go ahead, tell Sven why it is I'm so pissed at you right now.'

'I don't know what the fuck you're talking about.'

'Yeah. Yeah, you do.'

Doyle produces a pocket knife. Opens up its shiny blade and holds it in front of Bartok's face.

'You see that, Lucas? Your crazy fucked-up eyes see that?'

'I see it. So what?'

'So what? So what? This is what. This is fucking what, you sick bastard.'

Doyle moves down to the other end of Bartok's body.

'See, before she killed herself, Nicole Hamlyn told me something. Something that Proust told her. About you, Lucas. It explained a lot. You didn't just reach out to Proust. You didn't just hear about what he was going through and offer to make a deal with a perfect stranger. You knew him already, didn't you, Lucas? He was a buddy of yours from way back. Someone who could give you what you wanted, you sick fuck.'

And then Doyle cuts.

He cuts right along the leg of Bartok's pants, from ankle to thigh. And then he rips the material apart.

And there it is. The proof. On the back of Bartok's calf.

A tattoo of a skull and crossbones held within an ace of spades.

Doyle looks across at Sven. 'You know what this means? It means your boss here tortures and rapes and kills young girls. A teenage girl called Alyssa Palmer. And my guess is a girl called Megan Hamlyn too.'

He doesn't know whether Sven has heard him. The man seems too engrossed in his own problems. He continues to watch the blood pouring out of himself, his head lolling to one side. But it occurs to Doyle that maybe Sven doesn't care. Maybe he did things to the girls too. Maybe everyone in this fucking building was given a turn with them.

Feeling sick with revulsion and hatred, Doyle stands up.

'Where's the video, Lucas?'

'What video?'

'The video of me going into Ruger's house in Brooklyn.'

'Fuck you, Doyle. You really think—'

The shot reverberates around the room. Bartok screams with the pain of the bullet that has just gone into the back of his leg and blasted out through his kneecap.

'The video, Lucas.'

'The drawer, you fucking lunatic. The desk drawer. It's still in the camera.'

Keeping his gun trained on Bartok, Doyle backs up to the desk. He opens the drawer. Glancing down, he sees a video camera and the box containing the ring with his fingerprints on. He takes both items and drops them into his pocket, then approaches Bartok again.

'This is the only copy?'

Bartok mutters something that Doyle doesn't catch. Doyle

puts his foot onto the site of Bartok's gunshot injury and presses down.

More screams from Bartok, and then: 'Yes. The only fucking copy. All right?'

Doyle takes his foot away. 'It better be, Lucas. I don't want to have to come back here.'

'You come back here and you're a fucking dead man, you Irish cocksucker. In fact, you're a dead man anyway. Nobody does this to Lucas Bartok. Nobody.'

'Enough of the threats already, Lucas. You're finished. I'm gonna make sure word gets around about what you do to little girls. Your reputation ain't worth shit from now on. Crawl back under whatever rock you came from and stay there. If I ever see you again, if I ever hear you're asking about me or anyone I know, I will kill you. I will make you experience the pain you dealt out to those girls, and then I will kill you. Do you understand me?'

Spittle flies from Bartok's mouth as he releases his venom. 'You don't scare me, you little fuck. I'm coming after you, Doyle. I will personally rip out your liver and make you eat it, you fucking piece of shit.'

Doyle sighs. 'Then I better make sure I can hear you coming.'

He blasts away Bartok's other kneecap.

When the screams die down he says, 'I'll be listening out for you on your sticks, Lucas. Come after me, that's what you want. I'll be waiting.'

And then he leaves.

She's there when he walks through the door. He doesn't expect her to be, but there she is. She's in the living room, just standing and waiting and staring. The rawness of her eyes tells him she has been crying.

'Rach—' he begins.

But she doesn't let him continue. She races across the room and she wraps her arms around him and she hugs the breath out of him.

'I heard,' she says. 'I know all about it. What that man said about you, it was all lies. I know that now. I'm sorry. I didn't believe you when you needed me to, and I'm so, so sorry.'

She starts sobbing then. Her body heaves against his as she lets out her remorse. He pulls her in close and absorbs her warmth and her love.

A minute later she pulls away and blinks her twinkling eyes at him.

'There's something else too,' she says. 'I had a call from the school. The kid who says he saw Amy take the stationery stuff? Turns out he made it up. He put the stuff in her bag to get her into trouble. The school has talked with his parents about it.' She sniffs. 'So you were right about that, too. How come you're always so right about things, Detective?'

'I'm not always,' he answers. 'There was this one time when I thought I was wrong, but it turned out I wasn't.'

She laughs, and pulls him to her again like she never intends to let go.

But while Doyle is trying to experience happiness and grati-tude and relief, he's also aware that a part of him is holding back.

So he was right. About Proust, and about his daughter. Paulson, Nicole, LeBlanc and Rachel – all telling him how he got it right. All telling him what a good guy he is.

But they don't know.

They don't know about the things he's done. They don't know about the havoc he's wreaked. They don't know about the violence he has unleashed – violence he never imagined he would be capable of perpetrating.

He has changed. Was a time, he was just a cop doing his job. But things have conspired against him. He has stepped across a line. Several lines.

With Proust, and then with Bartok, he played the parts of both judge and jury.

But there were a couple of times he came within a hair's breadth of putting a bullet in both of their skulls.

He wonders how long it will be before he becomes an executioner too.